ALMAYER'S FOLLY

THE ROVER

Almayer's Folly

The Rover

JOSEPH CONRAD

with Introduction and Notes by
JOHN LESTER

WORDSWORTH CLASSICS

For my husband
ANTHONY JOHN RANSON
with love from your wife, the publisher.
Eternally grateful for your unconditional love,
not just for me but for our children,
Simon, Andrew and Nichola Trayler

1

Readers who are interested in other titles from
Wordsworth Editions are invited to visit our website at
www.wordsworth-editions.com

For our latest list and a full mail-order service, contact
Bibliophile Books, 5 Datapoint, South Crescent, London E16 4TL
TEL: +44 (0)20 7474 2474 FAX: +44 (0)20 7474 8589
ORDERS: orders@bibliophilebooks.com
WEBSITE: www.bibliophilebooks.com

This edition first published in 2011 by
Wordsworth Editions Limited
8B East Street, Ware, Hertfordshire SG12 9HJ

ISBN 978 1 84022 664 5

Text © Wordsworth Editions Limited 2011
Introductions and Notes © John Lester 2011

Wordsworth® is a registered trademark of
Wordsworth Editions Limited,
the company founded by Michael Trayler in 1987

Typeset in Great Britain by Antony Gray
Printed and bound by Clays Ltd, St Ives plc

CONTENTS

GENERAL INTRODUCTION

Wordsworth Classics are inexpensive editions designed to appeal to the general reader and students. We commission teachers and specialists to write wide-ranging, jargon-free introductions and to provide notes that will assist the understanding of our readers rather than interpret the stories for them. In the same spirit, because the pleasures of reading are inseparable from the surprises, secrets and revelations that all narratives contain, we strongly advise you to enjoy the book before turning to the Introduction.

General Advisor
KEITH CARABINE
Rutherford College, University of Kent

INTRODUCTION

Almayer's Folly and *The Rover* are the first and last novels that Joseph Conrad completed. A 1928 edition of early and late novels included them both but they do not often keep company as they do here. Moving from one to another there is the sensation of coming out of the clammy gloom of a tropical rainforest into the bright sunshine and wide horizons of the Mediterranean coast. The warm sun of *The Rover*, however, beats down on the oppression of a bloody revolution and its traumatic aftermath, and there are more points of similarity between the novels than might first appear, as will be seen.

The greatest contrast, in fact, comes with the circumstances of composition. The writing of *Almayer's Folly* – as Conrad vividly reports in *A Personal Record* – took the best part of five years to complete. He began the novel in Bessborough Gardens, London, in September 1889 and finished it in nearby Gillingham Street (both a short stroll away from Victoria Station) in April 1894 at, Conrad claimed, '3 o'clock' in the morning.[1] At different times, however, the ever expanding

1 On 24 April 1894, at 11 a.m., Conrad reported to Marguerite Poradowska,

manuscript survived the vicissitudes of a voyage up the River Congo, was almost left behind at a German railway station and accompanied Conrad on a winter visit to his uncle through the snows of the Ukraine. Crucially, on its way to Australia in the *Torrens* (Conrad's final berth as a seaman), its early chapters were perused by a man called Jacques whose laconic approval encouraged Conrad to carry on (*A Personal Record*, pp. 16–18).

The composition of *The Rover* was far less dramatic. Conrad was having problems with what was planned as his great Napoleonic novel (the unfinished *Suspense*) and, as he had done earlier in his career with *The Rescue*, decided on a brief change of course, only to find it (as ever) extending further than he had intended. *The Rover*, begun in October 1921, was initially conceived as a tale of about thirty thousand words, planned to join with others to make up a volume of short stories. 'More of course it will not be,' he wrote misleadingly to his agent J. B. Pinker on 19 December 1921 (*CL* 7, pp. 396–7). In fact the novel was about ninety thousand words long by the time of its completion the following June but, by Conrad's standards, its composition was relatively straightforward. It has certainly been regarded as one of the more accessible of his works and became familiar to a succession of A Level students in England (myself included) some years later. In writing it Conrad hoped (he told Edward Garnett) 'to achieve a feat of artistic brevity' (*CL 8*, p. 239). In effect he fulfilled this ambition with both these novels.

I

'Kaspar! Makan!'

Two unfamiliar words greet the curious reader at the beginning of Conrad's first published work. Only with the second paragraph – 'The well-known shrill voice startled Almayer from his dream of splendid future into the unpleasant realities of the present hour' – are we on

---

a favourite relative with whom he had shared each stage of the novel's composition, 'It's finished! A scratching of the pen writing the final word, and suddenly this entire company of people who have spoken into my ear, gesticulated before my eyes, lived with me for so many years, becomes a band of phantoms who retreat, fade, and dissolve – are made pallid and indistinct by the sunlight of this brilliant and sombre day' (*The Collected Letters of Joseph Conrad*, Vol. 1, p. 153). There are nine volumes of Conrad's letters now and further references to them will be abbreviated to *CL* plus the volume number and page and appear in parentheses after the quotation.

home ground, so to speak, in our own language. If, though, we replace the Dutch name with an English one, a loose translation might be: 'Bill! Dinner's ready!' – which would seem a particularly banal way to start a story. As it is, the two alien words invoke the exotic, the repetition of vowel sounds making it seem almost like an incantation, and tell us immediately that we are nowhere that we know. It is, we soon discover, up a river on the east coast of Borneo. Conrad himself steamed that way in 1887 and his main character was inspired by a Charles Olmeijer whom he met there and subsequently wrote about at length in *A Personal Record*. Only inspired, though – this is not Olmeijer's Folly.

We also have to be aware of the time frame. By the second page a log drifting downstream has taken Almayer's thoughts to his past and the early chapters are much concerned with chronicling the events in his life that have brought him to his current state. A major figure in this past is Tom Lingard, the Rajah Laut (the King of the Sea), but Lingard appears only through the filter of Almayer's recollections or the haze of narrative retrospect; not till Conrad's second novel, *An Outcast of the Islands*, do we have the chance to see him directly. Charles Olmeijer had close links with a William Lingard, upon whom Tom is based, and Norman Sherry's invaluable book *Conrad's Eastern World* points out a number of parallels between Tom of the fiction and William the fact.[2]

The end of Chapter 5 reprises the end of Chapter 1, but whereas then we knew little more than Almayer knows, now we look on the scene with more enlightened eyes, aware of what has happened and is being planned around him, of which he is ignorant. This would become a common Conrad device, used with especial effect in stories such as *Nostromo* and *The Secret Agent*, where we regard a particular moment in a very different manner on the second occasion from the way we observed it earlier. It is repeated later when Chapter 7 reports the finding of a battered body, apparently that of the Malay prince, Dain Maroola – though there are hints that throw doubt on this identification – only for time to retreat once more in Chapter 8 and inform us, through the eyes of the slave girl Taminah, that this is not Dain.

Almayer is quickly established as a character possessed by obsessions destined to remain unachieved and illusory. This much becomes obvious as he gazes at the river:

---

2 Chapters 5–7 of Sherry's book are particularly relevant to *Almayer's Folly*. He identifies the river as being a branch of the River Berau and Sambir as the settlement Tandjong Redeb.

He liked to look at it about the time of sunset; perhaps because at that time the sinking sun would spread a glowing golden tinge on the waters of the Pantai, and Almayer's thoughts were often busy with gold; gold he had failed to secure; gold the others had secured – dishonestly, of course – or gold he meant to secure yet, through his own honest exertions, for himself and Nina. He absorbed himself in his dream of wealth and power away from this coast where he had dwelt for so many years, forgetting the bitterness of toil and strife in the vision of a great and splendid reward. [p. 7]

Gold is thus immediately seen as an illusion – a fleeting effect of the setting sun – destined to exist for Almayer only in his dreams, its reality forever out of sight, a mirage that he and Lingard futilely pursue. That these illusions are about to be destroyed is ominously portended by the fact that the river has 'no tinge on it this evening, for it had been swollen by the rains, and rolled an angry and muddy flood under his *inattentive* eyes' (italics mine). The long-awaited arrival of Dain, his new partner in this quest for riches, offers hope but Almayer is too blinded by his own plans and outlook to be aware of reality and Dain's return signals an end to his dreams, not a fulfilment.

Gold, indeed, could be said to symbolise illusion, not only in this book but elsewhere in the Conrad canon. Thus Almayer's memories of the moment when he agreed to marry Lingard's adopted Malay daughter include 'the smooth black surface of the sea with a great bar of gold laid on it by the rising moon' (p. 12). His dreams of acquiring gold, shaken by Lingard's disappearance in frenzied, feverish search for it and revived by Dain's expedition to the 'Gunong Mas – the mountain of gold' – are shattered by the sight of gold: Dain's gold ring on a drowned and mutilated man's finger. In fact this, too, is an illusion since the ring is Dain's but not the finger. Dain is engaged in destroying Almayer's fanciful future for his daughter, Nina, by planning to elope with her and, as Almayer (to save his pride) helps him to evade the Dutch, the gold illusion appears again as if mocking him, the yellow sands 'shining like an inlaid golden disc on the polished steel of the unwrinkled sea' (p. 131).

The illusion of gold may be responsible for Almayer's downfall but he is betrayed by way of silver, a stream of which is poured by Dain 'into Mrs Almayer's greedy lap'. Nina observes her mother revelling in her accumulating wealth and notes that the 'music of tinkling silver seemed to delight her, and her eyes sparkled with the reflected gleam of freshly-minted coins' (p. 50). Silver has been a symbol for betrayal since thirty pieces of it facilitated the capturing of Christ; Mrs Almayer's fee is much larger. It is tempting to extend the idea to embrace the 'silvery-grey tint' (p. 52) by which Taminah sees Dain and Nina together – this light betrays the lovers to one destined to become a jealous enemy – and when Taminah spies on Babalatchi and Mrs Almayer, the grass she disturbs is likened to 'a design of silver sprays embroidered on a sombre background' (p. 111).

One must be careful here, though, not to be carried away by symbolism. These last two examples also illustrate Conrad's care for precise colour, making us 'see' more clearly – the goal he would set himself later in his Preface to *The Nigger of the 'Narcissus'*. There are many examples of vivid imagery satisfying this goal. When the Dutch warship arrives, for instance, 'Above the trees lining the reach a slight puff of smoke appeared like a black stain on the brilliant blue of the cloudless sky' (p. 76). And here is a vital example, at a pivotal moment in the book, where the description itself seems to decide Dain to cross the raging river:

> Dain glanced doubtfully on the livid expanse of seething water bounded far away on the other side by the narrow black line of the forests. Suddenly, in a vivid white flash, the low point of land with the bending trees on it and Almayer's house leaped into view, flickered and disappeared. Dain pushed Babalatchi aside and ran down to the water-gate followed by his shivering boatmen.   [p. 63]

The other senses are not neglected either. At times our nostrils are positively assailed by the odours of the jungle, though these are not pleasant scents:

> In the space sheltered by the high palisades there lingered the smell of decaying blossoms from the surrounding forest, a taint of drying fish; with now and then a whiff of acrid smoke from the cooking fires when it eddied down from under the leafy boughs and clung lazily about the burnt-up grass.   [p. 94]

Victorian readers may have been ready to step into the exotic world of the Dutch East Indies for adventure but they must have been surprised by such unromantic descriptions and by the unprepossessing character of the main protagonist.[3] Obsessed by his unrealistic dreams

3 Some other writers, however, notably Robert Louis Stevenson in stories such as 'The Beach at Falesa', had already begun to depict European colonists in a less than desirable mould.

of gold and by his acute sense of racial superiority, probably made all the more acute by the fact that he is such a feeble representative of the Colonial Powers, Almayer never lives in a world of reality. Even when these dreams have perished, he retreats into opium so he can obliterate his memory. Conveying the state of someone completely self-centred, George Eliot writes that it is 'as when we look through the window from a lighted room, the objects we turn our backs on are still before us, instead of the grass and the trees'.[4] Almayer, similarly, sees only his own hopes and feelings and never acknowledges the reality before him.

Lingard is the kind of character one would expect to find in a story depicting Europeans in their colonies: he finds rivers, fights pirates, earns himself legendary status. The problem is he is in the wrong novel. The romantic era of colonial fiction and colonial fact (the days of Rajah Brooke in neighbouring Sarawak) is over; no longer does the European adventurer sweep all before him. The ship Conrad was serving in when he met Charles Olmeijer, the *Vidar*, was owned by an Arab, not a European, and the steamers that serve Sambir are brought in by Abdulla, not Lingard.[5] Lingard's exchanges with Hudig, the great trader, are regarded by Almayer as being 'like a quarrel of Titans – a battle of the gods', but the narrator likens them, almost contemptuously, to 'two mastiffs fighting over a marrowy bone' (p. 10). Indeed Lingard's decline is accelerated by Hudig's own failure. Lingard sees himself as a kind of classic hero, rescuing an innocent Malay maiden from ruthless pirates, when in fact, until the girl had been knocked unconscious, she was fighting as savagely as the rest. He too has been looking out of that lighted room and failing to see what is really before him. By the start of the novel he has been reduced to a fading name on a dusty unused door and when Almayer obliterates this in the course of burning down his old house he obliterates the final traces of Lingard as well.

In a way the future Mrs Almayer also has illusions. In her world she would be claimed as a wife by the victorious warrior and she looks forward to fulfilling this role for Lingard, never dreaming that her fate will be to marry his feeble follower. She becomes very rich with all the money she receives from Dain and, effectively, this makes her a more successful version of Almayer. He seeks gold: she acquires silver. There is, though, nothing much to spend Dutch guilders on in the Borneo jungle and she can do little more than simply revel in their existence – and bury them.

4 *Middlemarch*, p. 663
5 See Sherry, p. 107.

In fact the lovers alone (Nina and Dain) achieve contentment within the confines of the book. Taminah, the slave girl, almost mirrors Almayer. A kind word from Dain triggers her hopeless passion for him: her awareness of his love for Nina kindles a ruthless jealousy. She fails in both. Instead of the youthful, handsome Dain it is the ugly, aging Babalatchi who commandeers her, and her decline and death immediately precede that of Almayer and confound Babalatchi's expectations of 'a young face and the sound of a young voice' in his house (p. 144). Moreover, Almayer's death brings no comfort for his rivals, reminding Abdulla of his own impending departure and Babalatchi of his own age and decline. The overwhelming sensation of decay that pervades Almayer's life (and thus much of the book, including the vegetation) gives the novel a *fin-de-siècle* (end of the [nineteenth] century) feel; that sense of things running down that was a common component of literature at the time.

With Lingard's star patently set, Almayer ignores the two opportunities he has to restore his position. Were he to allow Reshid and Nina to marry, this would bring him into an alliance with Abdulla, now the successful trader in Sambir. Nina is not consulted and there are hints that she might not have been wholly averse to the match, which might assuage our European objections to an arranged marriage (even though Almayer's own is hardly an advertisement for the practice). Instead Almayer's outraged sense of racial superiority creates a cunning and persistent enemy for him. Were he to approve the Nina and Dain match, he would be related to a great Malay prince – he would retain the love of his daughter and the friendship of a powerful ruler. Again Almayer does everything he can to ensure his own failure and misery. To what extent this reflects the attitudes to interracial relationships in 1890s' Dutch East Indies society is open to question; it was certainly refuted by a forthright letter from 'G' to the *Straits Times* (17 January 1896), which labelled Conrad's depiction as 'ludicrous' and accused the author of knowing 'very little of Dutch Indian society'.[6] That assertion remains untested (it was clearly a European who wrote, not a Malay) but, as far as the Asian population was concerned, Conrad admitted later that he 'didn't know anything about Malays', in his Author's Note to *A Personal Record* (p. iv).

Religion appears in an uncertain light throughout the novel, as it did in the latter part of the century once Darwin's *The Origin of Species* had reduced the creation stories in Genesis from history to myth, albeit

6   quoted in *Almayer's Folly* (Cambridge University Press, 1994), p. xlvii

with allegorical significance. In a sense there is a new AD (After Darwin) about many works written at the end of the century. The confident Christianity, often a feature of the European adventurer bringing civilisation to the wild parts of the earth, is no more. Thus Almayer applies its terms to his own visions, where he sees gleaming 'like a fairy palace the big mansion in Amsterdam, that earthly paradise of his dreams' (p. 11), but the presence of fairy-tale imagery accompanies that of religion and underlines just how fanciful all these hopes really are. Towards the end of the book, Almayer's new home, to which he retreats to smoke himself into oblivion and die, is named by the Chinaman, Jim Eng, its new sharer, 'House of heavenly delight' (p. 144), an ironic fulfilment of that 'big mansion' and 'earthly paradise'. Folly, besides its usual meaning of foolishness, also means a lavish building that fulfils no purpose and is often just a façade – Almayer's new house is clearly such a structure; it is indeed named as such by visiting Dutch officers early in the book and adopted by the narrator – and there is no doubt about the depth of Almayer's foolishness; the word, derived from the French word *folie*, can indicate a kind of mania.

In its literal sense religion fares no better. All Mrs Almayer carries away from her convent education are the superstitious trappings of Roman Catholicism, her feelings towards the little brass cross around her neck being 'connected with some vague talismanic properties of the little bit of metal and the still more hazy but terrible notion of some bad Djinns and horrible torments invented, as she thought, for her especial punishment by the good Mother Superior in case of the loss of the above charm' (p. 33). Her daughter encounters the 'Protestant wing of the proper Mrs Vinck' (p. 33), who reacts vindictively when she realises that Nina is more attractive to a promising male visitor than her own, plainer daughters. Were Nina to be a beautiful Dutch girl she might suffer the same fate for such a reason but the racial motivation is manifest and confirmed by Captain Ford's report. The adjectives 'good' and 'proper' are clearly ironic here. Neither woman has encountered Christianity as it ought to be and, indeed, Nina is advised by her mother to forget the Europeans with 'their many gods' and their duplicity (p. 107).

Like Christianity, Islam is made use of rather than practised in the novel. The pious Abdulla, for example, is happy to accept 'the decrees of Fate, especially if they were propitious to the True Believers' (p. 79), and the novel ends with the Arab leaving the scene of Almayer's death, clicking his prayer beads, 'while in a solemn whisper he breathed out piously the name of Allah! The Merciful! The Compassionate!'

(p. 145). When *Almayer's Folly* was about to be translated into Polish, Conrad stressed that 'Abdulla recites the well-known formula mechanically'.[7] Earlier, the predecessor of Lakamba, the current Rajah, is said to have departed this life 'by a convenient decree of Providence' to which is added 'and the help of a little scientific manipulation' (p. 23). The second part of this was deleted from later editions, making it more equivocal and perhaps more ironic. It is nevertheless significant that Lakamba's bodyguard consists solely of 'friends or relations' (p. 56).

Religion is also used by its adherents (or proclaimed adherents) to bestow a sense of superiority and exclusiveness upon them. Christianity is pressed upon Mrs Almayer and Nina (albeit precepts rather than practice) with the clear assumption of this being the only correct religion and this is mirrored both by the Muslims – Abdulla considers Almayer to be an 'Infidel' and himself a 'True Believer' (p. 145), while Mahmat fears he may have been defiled by touching a non-Muslim before eating (p. 70) – and by Dain, who, as a Brahmin (high-caste Hindu), will not eat food prepared by those of other faiths.

For those in the lower stratum of society, in contradiction of its precepts, religion has no place. The slave girl, Taminah, in her despair, can find 'no words to pray for relief, she knew of no heaven to send her prayer to' (p. 65). Despite the fact that Nina and Dain are the only people in the village to treat her kindly, her jealousy drives her to try to undermine the progress of their relationship. *Almayer's Folly* is, in fact, a novel where most characters are willing to sacrifice anyone else on the altar of their own self-interest, which is likened to the frantic vegetation, its plants feeding off and smothering each other in their battle for life (p. 53). The Darwinian concept of survival of the fittest is very much at home in the Dutch East Indies among all the nationalities represented there.

The parallels between the behaviour exhibited by Malays and Europeans are quickly established through the wounded eyes of the two women Lingard tries to assimilate into Western society. During her time among Europeans, Nina observes 'only the same manifestations of love and hate and of sordid greed chasing the uncertain dollar in all its multifarious and vanishing shapes' as in the Malay culture, the only difference being the 'sleek hypocrisy' that cloaks the real motives of Europeans (p. 34). Mrs Almayer, whose lack of a given name illustrates that she has never been thought of affectionately by her husband but is,

7 'To Aniela Zagorska', 12 February 1923 (*CL* 8, p. 28)

nevertheless, his wife, cites 'lies' and 'contempt' during her indictment of the white race (p. 107). At one stage the narrator notes, ironically: 'There are some situations where the barbarian and the, so called, civilised man meet upon the same ground' (pp. 50–1).[8]

This factor denotes another difference between the exotic tales Victorians were accustomed to and *Almayer's Folly*. H. Rider Haggard's Allan Quatermain, for instance, in novels such as *King Solomon's Mines*, is the narrator of his own adventures – our viewpoint is solely a European one. The point of view in *Almayer's Folly* does not confine itself to the frequently exasperating Almayer. We are privy to the thoughts of Nina, of Dain, of Babalatchi and Taminah at various parts of the novel, aware of each as separate human beings, each with his or her own agenda. This multiple point of view prevents us from taking a solely European outlook of the proceedings – indeed the romantics among us must surely look with favour at the love match of beautiful maiden (Nina) and handsome prince (Dain). There is a love story here and a successful one, blessed with a son in the final pages. But our probable satisfaction at this event is tempered by a memory. Like any traditional English mother, Mrs Almayer gives her daughter advice on (effectively) the eve of her nuptials. Here, though, the 'facts of life' concern Dain's inevitable attraction to and for other women and an admonition to deal ruthlessly with any serious threat to her primacy in Dain's affections (p. 109). We cannot, then, with certainty, attach the 'happy ever after' sign to the relationship – only a 'happy at the end of the novel' one.

These multiple viewpoints give us varying degrees of sympathy and understanding for other characters, too. Babalatchi, the elder statesman of the Rajah, is a Malay Machiavelli, who would have been quite at home in the Italian Renaissance intrigues of the sixteenth century (partaking of refreshments could be a risky business there too). When he sets off to poison Almayer, there is nothing personal in the proposed act – it is a simple matter of political necessity. Fortunately (or perhaps unfortunately) for Almayer, events cause a change of policy before the deed is done. The task Babalatchi really detests is that of turning the handle of the hand organ (given by Lingard) that Lakamba delights in and that sends the strains of a Verdi opera incongruously into the

---

8 Conrad's Author's Note, which sympathised 'with common mortals, no matter where they live', was prompted by a lady's criticism of stories set in distant lands as being 'decivilised'. The 1994 Cambridge University Press edition of *Almayer's Folly* (p. xxxix) identifies the lady as Alice Meynell.

tropical night. Here is one form of European intrusion that threatens to endure; Lakamba's acceptance of it and Babalatchi's distaste may reflect the latter's uncompromising attitude towards Europeans that he voices to Captain Ford towards the end. Our prevailing impression of Lakamba, meanwhile, is that he is lazy and indolent, in some ways a *fin-de-siècle* Rajah. Unlike Mrs Almayer, who destroys signs of Western culture such as curtains and furniture in her eagerness to distance herself from it (though she has no such distaste for European money), there is much emphasis on the European curtains and European lamp (not to mention the rifles – also European) that Dain notes on his entry to the Rajah's residence (p. 56). Babalatchi's nostalgia for 'the old times' is thus no more than a wistful memory – there is no going back.

The self-centredness of most of the characters is frequently accompanied (or undercut) by the mocking irony of the narrator. When, for instance, Babalatchi assures Dain that his 'heart had hungered for the sight of Dain's face, and his ears were withering for the want of the refreshing sound of his voice', the narrator's apparent agreement – 'Everybody's hearts and ears were in the same sad predicament, according to Babalatchi' – underlines the hypocrisy of the old one-eyed statesman (p. 57). When he speaks of the apparently dead Dain as one who 'drank the white man's strong water' (an Islamic prohibition) his horror is 'affected' (p. 75), as becomes one who consumed large quantities of Jim Eng's gin earlier in the book (p. 45). Mrs Almayer's contempt at her husband's reluctance to kill people is apparently supported by the narrator's reference to 'Almayer's weak-minded aversion to sudden bloodshed' (p. 97) and apparent sympathy for a woman 'lamenting the lost possibilities of murder and mischief that could have fallen to her lot had she been mated with a congenial spirit' (p. 106). Consequently, for once we have sympathy with Almayer here. Not much, though, if we recall that when he married her he hoped that she might 'mercifully die' (p. 12) and 'even planned murder in an undecided and feeble sort of way' (p. 22), which doesn't make him much better than Babalatchi and co. But, then, that is what Conrad is saying all through the book.

As we have seen, *The Rover* was, effectively, a digression from that great Napoleonic story that would occupy Conrad till his death and languish unfinished (and at a frustratingly exciting moment) with the enigmatic title *Suspense*. *Suspense* is set towards the end of the Napoleonic Wars, with the vanquished emperor in Elba; *The Rover* begins in the atmosphere of the French Revolution, just two years after the Terror and the horrors of the guillotine that had finally claimed the life of its most fanatical exponent, Citizen Robespierre. Those turbulent years, beginning in 1789, had seen the execution of the king, Louis XVI, and his wife, Marie Antoinette, in 1793, and war with Britain and others in that same year, during which the Port of Toulon on the south coast, a Royalist stronghold, had gone over to the British under Admiral Lord Hood with much of the French Fleet – a crucial incident in terms of the book. When it was retaken by the French (whose artillery there was commanded by a young Napoleon Bonaparte), the atrocities that occurred in the city were very much in line with what is related in the novel.[9] The main part of the story takes place in the France of Napoleon, now First Consul, soon to be Emperor, and in this sense it is almost a prelude to that projected larger work which never reached its end.[10]

Perhaps aware that he had not written the 'great Napoleonic novel' first dreamt of many years before, Conrad spoke, somewhat disparagingly, of the book as 'a tale about an old rover and a half-crazed farm girl'.[11] This might suggest that *The Rover* is a lesser story but that would be an unfair conclusion. Many, in fact, consider it to be his most satisfying work since *The Shadow Line*, published in 1916. Indeed, the first three chapters, relating the return of Peyrol to a France very different from the one he had left many years before, convey vividly the sense of oppressive suspicion that pervaded the country in its revolutionary phase; the atmosphere of mistrust and thinly bridled fanaticism is overwhelming. In just under forty pages we are given a real

9 Nelson was serving under Lord Hood in the Mediterranean at this time but was mainly involved in operations around Corsica (Napoleon's birthplace), during which he lost his right eye.

10 As it is, *Suspense*, with a long way still to go, is only twelve pages shorter than *The Rover*.

11 to F. N. Doubleday, 29 November 1923 (*CL* 8, p. 232)

feeling of what it is to live under such trying conditions. Here he is on his arrival:

> Peyrol noted particularly a good many men in red caps and said to himself – 'Here they are.' Amongst the crews of ships that had brought the tricolour into the seas of the East, there were hundreds professing sans-culotte principles; boastful and declamatory beggars he had thought them. But now he was beholding the shore breed. Those who had made the revolution safe. The real thing. Peyrol, after taking a good long look, went below into his cabin to make himself ready to go ashore. [p. 151]

This passage is made especially sinister by its reticence. Peyrol's first sight of the red caps prompt his reminiscence of ship's crews he has known, but the shore breed of revolutionaries disturbs him, as the jolting, progressively shorter sentences chillingly reveal. There is something particularly ominous about the simple climactic phrase 'The real thing' and the feeling of duration dramatised by his 'good long look'. The revolution may be safe but Peyrol's return may well be fraught with danger.

When we come to Peyrol's history, there are echoes of Conrad's own life. Like Peyrol, Conrad lost his mother when he was young; like Peyrol he used the South of France (Marseilles) as the starting point for a career at sea. One of his early shipmates was not unlike Peyrol – Dominic Cervoni, a Corsican with whom the author made clandestine voyages carrying 'various unlawful goods' on behalf of Royalists in Spain (*The Mirror of the Sea*, p. 173). Like Arlette and Réal, he experienced the persecution of his parents by an oppressive regime that they opposed, suffering exile with them in Russia, and was an orphan under the care of an uncle at the age of twelve. At the time of publication, moreover (3 December 1923, exactly sixty-six years after his birth), Conrad was precisely the age of his protagonist and, like his eponymous hero, he too would not greet another birthday. He wrote, indeed (to John Galsworthy), 'I am glad you think well of *The Rover*. I have wanted for a long time to do a seaman's "return" (before my own departure) and this seemed a possible peg to hang it on' (*CL* 8, p. 318). Of Peyrol, Conrad wrote, 'Of course there are obvious things that could be said about it, but not by me. That in Peyrol I have a creation that resembles neither Lingard nor Dominique nor Nostromo and yet belongs to the same family . . . ' (*CL* 8, p. 192).

In a way Peyrol is the antithesis of Almayer. While Almayer longs for gold that will take him home, Peyrol returns from the East to France with a small fortune tied into a garment he wears close to his skin. Most of this fortune remains unspent – the major outlay is on the boat that will eventually serve as his coffin – and is discovered down a well after Peyrol is gone. One is reminded of Mrs Almayer burying hers in the ground. Almayer tries desperately to prevent the union of Nina and Dain; Peyrol sacrifices himself so that Arlette – young enough to be his granddaughter, though we are never quite sure what his feelings for her are – and Réal can marry. There is an echo of Charles Dickens's *A Tale of Two Cities* and Sidney Carton about Peyrol's final decision. Peyrol is mourned by those he leaves behind and prayers are requested for him by old Catherine (p. 337); Almayer is mourned by nobody and has only the sanctimonious Abdulla to end the novel with his pious incantations.

Our attitude to the events of the book is partly governed by our knowledge. We know that however successful the French scheme is to deceive the English Fleet that is blockading it – and the French Fleet did elude Nelson in the Mediterranean – all this will end on 21 October 1805 with the French defeat at Trafalgar, as the final pages confirm. In this sense Peyrol's sacrifice seems futile. Yet in ridding the Escampobar Farm of the murderous fanatic, Scevola, it succeeds in ensuring happiness for the orphans of the Revolution, Réal and Arlette. He also dies in triumph, having fulfilled his dream of outwitting the English captain and, maybe, Nelson himself.[12]

---

12 However fanciful the scheme may appear it had a real-life counterpart in World War II when at the end of April 1943 the body of a Royal Marine officer, Acting Major W. Martin, was discovered off the Spanish coast and found to be carrying secret documents that suggested that the Allies were preparing attacks on Sardinia and Greece instead of the more likely Sicily. Just as Nelson in *The Rover* is willing to accept news of an expedition to Egypt, despite a fleetingly expressed doubt, because it confirms his own expectations, so Hitler, also despite a momentary suspicion, diverted many thousands of German troops to protect those two areas, partly persuaded by his own fears of an attack on Greece. As a result, the Allies' invasion of Sicily was accomplished with far more ease and fewer casualties than would otherwise have been the case. The papers, false as in *The Rover*, were aimed at achieving just such a success. In fact the body was that of a homeless Welshman (Glyndwr Michael), his corpse made available to the intelligence services by the Coroner of St Pancras, Sir Bentley Purchase, and given a fictitious identity by the two intelligence officers masterminding the operation (Operation Mincemeat): Charles Cholmondeley (an RAF officer seconded to MI5) and Lieutenant Commander Ewen Montagu, head of Section 17M. Here is another coincidence since, like Michel in name as

The word 'sacrifice' has religious overtones, of course, and Conrad is at pains to reveal how the language of revolutionary terror borrows and transforms words that most of his readers would associate with Christianity. In an earlier work, *Under Western Eyes*, published six years before the Russian Revolution of 1917, Conrad made some perceptive predictions about how such an insurrection would progress. His characters there (both revolutionary and autocratic) attach religious terms and even biblical allusions to their conduct and ideals, however unchristian these may be. In *The Rover*, written after the Russian Revolution and looking back to the French, there is similar usage. The Revolution itself attracts terms such as 'sacrificed' and a 'sacred fire' from the bloodthirsty Scevola (p. 204), has a 'republican god' (p. 200) and 'sacred revolutionary principles' (289), and it is likened by Peyrol to 'the tale of an intelligent islander on the other side of the world talking of bloody rites and amazing hopes of some religion unknown to the rest of mankind' (p. 213). As in *Under Western Eyes*, there is scepticism for the role of the established church. When Peyrol arrives, Roman Catholicism, which like the Orthodox Church in Russia supported autocracy, is undercover. Having been told that he 'might be a priest' he is informed that 'Some of them skulk amongst the villages yet, for all the chasing they got from the patriots' (p. 162). Nevertheless, it is the newly restored abbé who rushes to prevent Scevola being lynched by vengeful villagers.[13] When Arlette goes to consult the priest, though, her view of the presbytery is unpromising:

She pushed open the little gate with the broken latch. The humble building of rough stones, from between which much mortar had crumbled out, looked as though it had been sinking slowly into the ground. The beds of the plot in front were choked with weeds, because the abbé had no taste for gardening.   [p. 248]

well as social status, Michael had no relatives or friends to be concerned at his loss. A film, *The Man Who Never Was* (1956), commemorated the story. One of those credited with the initial idea is Ian Fleming but one does wonder if anyone along the way had read *The Rover* and whether that had any influence in a significant moment in the war.

13 He is more successful than his real-life counterpart in *A Personal Record* (pp. 58–62), who tries in vain to prevent unruly peasants from sacking the residence of Conrad's grand-uncle Nicholas Bobrowski in the incident that probably inspired this passage.

The whole feeling here is one of decline, the words 'broken', 'crumbled', 'sinking', 'choked' conveying the sense of a place ill-fitted to current use. As such it seems symbolic of the doctrines and character of its incumbent, since the only advice the priest can give Arlette is to 'Repent!' and embrace 'a life of seclusion and prayer' (p. 254). Peyrol's opinion – 'All this only shows what an ass the curé is' (p. 303) – seems justified. As the exchange between Arlette and the abbé at the end of her visit suggests, the priest is unable to cope with her passionate love for Réal:

> 'Yes, Monsieur l'Abbé,' she said in her clear seductive voice. 'I have prayed and I feel answered. I entreated the merciful God to keep the heart of the man I love always true to me or else to let me die before I set my eyes on him again.'
> The abbé paled under his tan of a village priest and leaned his shoulders against the wall without a word.   [p. 255]

To the abbé this is the response of a 'heathen', her appearance suggesting 'a strain of Saracen blood' (p. 256). Arlette's prayer is answered, though, suggesting that Divine Providence favours her sentiments rather than those of the priest. She and Réal marry and end the book happily with no hints that this will not continue. Indeed, when Réal becomes mayor, Arlette, as his wife, attains a position of esteem in her community (just as Nina, by marrying Dain, becomes the daughter-in-law of a rajah). She has better luck than her aunt, Catherine, whose love for a priest in her youth has blighted her life. Catherine's regard for Peyrol, perhaps the second man she has felt some affection for (Peyrol's regular joke that they should marry indicates an ease of relationship between them), leads to her becoming reconciled with the church when she asks for prayers for the soul of the dead rover. Their final scene together shows elements of affection on both sides, ending with Peyrol's final words to her, which smack of mutual domesticity. 'It will be a good soup, I see, at noon today,' he says (p. 307) – but he will not be there to drink it. Ironically her pessimistic prediction that Arlette 'is for no man' (p. 299) aligns with the priest's view in this respect, though she is appalled to learn that 'He wanted to shut her up from everybody' (p. 303).

The main action of *The Rover*, like that of *Almayer's Folly*, takes place over a period of about two days, but, once again, the narrative does not proceed chronologically. After noting his arrival at the farmhouse and the circumstances that attend the inhabitants of that building, we next view Peyrol eight years later and we are soon to discover not only that something is about to happen but that much has already occurred. Mysteries relating to the night before, posed by Lieutenant Réal in Chapter 4, are gradually unveiled as the story proceeds. Again we return to an incident and view it with more knowing eyes, this time the minor mystery of Peyrol being startled by a leaping goat.

Conrad often spoke of entertaining his fictional creations as if they were real people. In *The Rover* there are actual historical figures present, notably Lord Nelson, who, Conrad informed an unnamed correspondent, 'has a speaking part of about 100 words in it' (*CL* 7, p. 491). The same letter promised 'a speaking part of about twenty-two words' for Napoleon Bonaparte in the major Napoleonic novel – but *Suspense* never reached that anticipated cameo.

The fictional characters are varied. Conrad might have spoken of Arlette as 'half-crazed' but at least she is able to resume full sanity with Réal. Scevola cannot move on and Conrad had much to say about him in a letter to Edward Garnett, defending the fact that 'he does look to me too like a bit of "a scarecrow of the Revolution"' (*CL* 8, p. 238). Conrad continues:

Postulating that Arlette had to remain untouched, the terrorist that brought her back could have been nothing else than what he is or the book would have had to be altogether different. To me S is not revolutionary; he is, to be frank about it, a pathological case more than anything else . . . The situation at Escampobar could not have lasted seven or eight years if S had been formidable. But he was never formidable except as a creature of mob psychology. Away from the mob he is just a weak-minded creature . . . I tried to give a hint of it in what Catherine says about him: 'the butt of all the girls', 'always mooning about', 'run away from his home to join the Revolution'. He is weak-minded in a way as much as my poor Michel, the man with the dog, whose resigned philosophy was that 'somebody must be last'. Even amongst terrorists S was considered a poor creature. But his half-witted soul received the impress of the Revolution which has missed the simple-minded Michel altogether. I never intended S to be a figure of the Revolution. As a matter of fact if there is a child of the Revolution there at all, it is Réal, with his austere and pedantic turn of mind and conscience.

Later in that letter Conrad comments:

What I regret now is the rejection of a half thought-out scene, four pages or so, between Catherine and Scevola. But when it came to me the development of the story was already marked and the person of Catherine established psychologically as she is now. The scene would have checked the movement and damaged the conception of Catherine.   [*CL* 8, p. 239]

Scevola is a particularly virulent case of one looking out of a lighted room and not seeing what is outside: a terrorist of his time. When he strides down to the church he discovers, to his panic, that he is no longer with the mob but against it and, but for the priest, would become a victim of the hysteria he himself was such a part of. Ironically, the 'patriot' dies serving France without actually having any conception of it and is treated (along with Peyrol and Michel) as a dead hero by Captain Vincent, who is the epitome of a noble, scrupulously just English captain. Vincent, indeed, is a forerunner of similar incarnations in twentieth-century Napoleonic War novels, such as C. S. Forester's Horatio Hornblower and his successors.

Vincent's good character is also an important ingredient of a story in which, for most of the time, the British Navy constitutes the enemy. Conrad was patently fascinated by his grand-uncle Nicholas Bobrowski, who had been part of the Polish contingent of Napoleon's Grand Armée. Some of his experiences are included in *A Personal Record*, including the time when, to a young Conrad's horror, he had eaten a dog during the notorious retreat from Moscow in 1812 (*A Personal Record*, p. 34). A novella, 'The Duel' (in *A Set of Six*), had concerned two French officers fighting for Napoleon and, having quarrelled, conducting a series of duels along the way; only the much slighter 'The Inn of the Two Witches' (in *Within the Tides*) had fought the war from a British perspective. It was important then to achieve some kind of balance and it is the fact that we have viewpoints from both the French and the British sides – and that the British are portrayed so positively – that brings this about. Symons' dogged resistance to Peyrol – whom he does not recognise as a fellow member of the lawless 'Brotherhood of the Coast' in days gone by – and his emphatic, 'I am an Englishman, I am' (p. 239), when he feels he is in a tight spot, are overt examples of this.

One feature of *The Rover* is the nobility bestowed upon the simple country folk Peyrol finds himself among and he is aware on more than one occasion that he might have been just like them had he stayed at home instead of roaming the world. At Escampobar he settles into a sort of family (at least with Catherine and the reviving Arlette) but has an attraction for those who are still alone. The cripple who helps him repair the tartane in a neighbouring village shows qualities beyond those of the able-bodied residents and is embarrassed at Peyrol's praise – clearly not something he has received much of during his difficult existence. Michel, the fisherman, once his dog has died, instinctively seeks Peyrol's presence and is a loyal companion to the end. Catherine, Arlette, Michel, the cripple – all feel the beneficent influence of the old rover. He is one of Conrad's most endearing characters and, like those he leaves behind, we mourn his passing

The prevailing memory of the book, though, is of the aftermath of revolution. The luckless Catherine is initially a victim of the attitudes of the old order before being forced to endure the horrors of the new, which will not go away while Scevola is still in residence. Even after the drama has passed, she finds it hard to escape from the conviction that her niece is 'a selected object of God's wrath' (p. 337). Arlette, traumatised by the atrocities she has been forced to witness and, eventually, to take part in, is revived first by Peyrol's presence and then by Réal, whose arrival awakens her to full life and love.

Effectively she does the same for him. The excesses of the Revolution have stifled his emotions, detaching him from close relationships with others. His self-imposed rigid sense of duty – Conrad described him as 'doctrinaire' in the letter to Garnett – inhibits him from reacting normally to the discovery that he can feel love for someone and causes him to contemplate suicide when he reveals his affection, regarding this act, not as natural but as deriving from 'a base impulse' (p. 289). He is almost as possessed by his fanatical idea of rectitude as Scevola is by the fever of revolution. Normality is forced upon him by Peyrol's sacrifice, just when it seems that the exigencies of war will destroy the romance and the two lovers. He can see clearly at last.

As in *Almayer's Folly*, therefore, hope resides in the young couple that will carry life forward. Unusually for Conrad, the story has moved from darkness to light, which makes it one of his most pleasing and popular works. But the main protagonist, who played such a key role in the process, is not forgotten. Peyrol is recalled with affection by young and old and in the final sentence of the story even the lone mulberry tree seems to regret the passing of 'the man of dark deeds, but of large heart, who often at noonday would lie down to sleep under its shade' (p. 339).

BIBLIOGRAPHY

1 Previous Editions

I have consulted and am indebted to the editions of *Almayer's Folly* edited by Jacques Berthoud for World's Classics (Oxford, 1992), by Owen Knowles for Everyman (Dent, 1995) and by Floyd Eugene Eddleman and David Leon Higdon (Introduction by Ian Watt) for Cambridge (1994), and of *The Rover* edited by Andrzej Busza and J. H. Stape (Introduction by Andrzej Busza) for World's Classics (Oxford, 1992). Both novels were published initially by Unwin and then by Dent. This current edition is based on the Unwin version of *Almayer's Folly* (which retains several passages deleted in the Dent) and the Dent version of *The Rover* (which corrects errors made in the Unwin).

2 Other Works

Henri F. Amiel, *Amiel's Journal: The Journal Intime of Henri-Frédéric Amiel*, trans. Mrs Humphry Ward, 2 vols, Macmillan, London, 1885

Joseph Conrad, *Collected Letters, Vol. 1*, Frederick R. Karl and Laurence Davies (eds), Cambridge University Press, Cambridge, 1983

Joseph Conrad, *Collected Letters, Vol. 7*, Laurence Davies and J. H. Stape (eds), Cambridge University Press, Cambridge, 2005

Joseph Conrad, *Collected Letters, Vol. 8*, Laurence Davies and Gene M. Moore (eds), Cambridge University Press, Cambridge, 2007

Joseph Conrad, *Suspense*, J. M. Dent, London, 1954

Joseph Conrad, 'The Duel', in *A Set of Six*, J. M. Dent, London, 1954, pp. 163–266

Joseph Conrad, 'The Inn of the Two Witches', in *Within the Tides*, Penguin, London, 1978, pp. 116–46

Joseph Conrad, *The Mirror of the Sea and A Personal Record*, J. M. Dent, London, 1946

Joseph Conrad, *Under Western Eyes*, Penguin, London, 1964

Laurence Davies, 'Conrad in the Operatic Mode', in *Joseph Conrad and the Performing Arts*, Katherine Isobel Baxter and Richard J. Hand (eds), Ashgate, Farnham, Surrey, 2009, pp. 127–45

Laurence Davies, 'Fin de siècle', in *Joseph Conrad in Context*, Allan H. Simmons (ed.), Cambridge University Press, Cambridge 2009, pp. 147–54

Linda Dryden, *Joseph Conrad and the Imperial Romance*, Macmillan, Basingstoke, 2000

George Eliot, *Middlemarch*, Penguin, London, 1965

H. Rider Haggard, *King Solomon's Mines*, Macdonald, London, 1956

Norman Hampson, *The First European Revolution 1776–1815*, Thames and Hudson, London, 1969

G. Jean Aubry (ed.), *Joseph Conrad: Life and Letters*, 2 vols., Heinemann, London, 1927

Heliéna Krenn, *Conrad's Lingard Trilogy: Empire, Race and Women in the Malay Novels*, Garland, London, 1990

Albert Lee, *Famous British Admirals*, Andrew Melrose, London, 1905

John Lester, *Conrad and Religion*, Macmillan, London, 1988

Norman Sherry, *Conrad's Eastern World*, Cambridge University Press, Cambridge, 1966

Allan H. Simmons, 'Nationalism and Empire', in *Joseph Conrad in Context*, Cambridge University Press, Cambridge, 2009

J. H. Stape, *The Several Lives of Joseph Conrad*, Heinemann, London, 2007

J. H. Stape, 'The Far East' in *Joseph Conrad in Context*, Allan H. Simmons (ed.), Cambridge University Press, Cambridge, 2009, pp. 139–46

Ian Watt, *Conrad in the Nineteenth Century*, Chatto & Windus, London, 1980

Cedric Watts, *The Deceptive Text: An Introduction to Covert Plots*, Harvester Press, Brighton, 1984

Andrea White, 'Conrad and Imperialism', in *The Cambridge Companion to Joseph Conrad*, J. H. Stape (ed.), Cambridge University Press, Cambridge, 1996, pp. 179–202

ALMAYER'S FOLLY

ALMAYER'S FOLLY

A Story of an Eastern River

━━━━━━━━━━━━ ◆ ━━━━━━━━━━━━

Joseph Conrad

Qui de nous n'a eu sa terre promise,
son jour d'extase et sa fin en exil?

AMIEL [1]

TO THE MEMORY OF

T. B.[2]

Author's Note

I am informed that, in criticising that literature which preys on strange people and prowls in far-off countries, under the shade of palms, in the unsheltered glare of sunbeaten beaches, amongst honest cannibals and the more sophisticated pioneers of our glorious virtues, a lady[3] – distinguished in the world of letters – summed up her disapproval of it by saying that the tales it produced were 'decivilised'. And in that sentence not only the tales but, I apprehend, the strange people and the far-off countries also are finally condemned in a verdict of contemptuous dislike.

A woman's judgement: intuitive, clever, expressed with felicitous charm – infallible. A judgement that has nothing to do with justice. The critic and the judge seems to think that in those distant lands all joy is a yell and a war dance, all pathos is a howl and a ghastly grin of filed teeth, and that the solution of all problems is found in the barrel of a revolver or on the point of an assegai. And yet it is not so. But the erring magistrate may plead in excuse the misleading nature of the evidence.

The picture of life, there as here, is drawn with the same elaboration of detail, coloured with the same tints. Only in the cruel serenity of the sky, under the merciless brilliance of the sun, the dazzled eye misses the delicate detail, sees only the strong outlines, while the colours, in the steady light, seem crude and without shadow. Nevertheless it is the same picture. And there is a bond between us and that humanity so far away. I am speaking here of men and women – not of the charming and graceful phantoms that move about in our mud and smoke and are softly luminous with the radiance of all our virtues; that are possessed of all refinements, of all sensibilities, of all wisdom – but, being only phantoms, possess no heart.

The sympathies of those are (probably) with the immortals: with the angels above or the devils below. I am content to sympathise with common mortals, no matter where they live: in houses or in tents, in the streets under a fog, or in the forests behind the dark line of dismal mangroves that fringe the vast solitude of the sea. For, their land – like ours – lies under the inscrutable eyes of the Most High. Their hearts – like ours – must endure the load of the gifts from Heaven: the curse of facts and the blessing of illusions, the bitterness of our wisdom and the deceptive consolation of our folly.

J. C.
1895

Chapter 1

'Kaspar! Makan!'

The well-known shrill voice startled Almayer from his dream of splendid future into the unpleasant realities of the present hour. An unpleasant voice too. He had heard it for many years, and with every year he liked it less. No matter; there would be an end to all this soon.

He shuffled uneasily, but took no further notice of the call. Leaning with both his elbows on the balustrade of the verandah, he went on looking fixedly at the great river that flowed – indifferent and hurried – before his eyes. He liked to look at it about the time of sunset; perhaps because at that time the sinking sun would spread a glowing gold tinge on the waters of the Pantai,[4] and Almayer's thoughts were often busy with gold; gold he had failed to secure; gold the others had secured – dishonestly, of course – or gold he meant to secure yet, through his own honest exertions, for himself and Nina. He absorbed himself in his dream of wealth and power away from this coast where he had dwelt for so many years, forgetting the bitterness of toil and strife in the vision of a great and splendid reward. They would live in Europe, he and his daughter. They would be rich and respected. Nobody would think of her mixed blood in the presence of her great beauty and of his immense wealth. Witnessing her triumphs he would grow young again, he would forget the twenty-five years of heartbreaking struggle on this coast where he felt like a prisoner. All this was nearly within his reach. Let only Dain return! And return soon he must – in his own interest, for his own share. He was now more than a week late! Perhaps he would return tonight. Such were Almayer's thoughts as, standing on the verandah of his new but already decaying house – that last failure of his life – he looked on the broad river. There was no tinge of gold on it this evening, for it had been swollen by the rains, and rolled an angry and muddy flood under his inattentive eyes, carrying small driftwood and big dead logs, and whole uprooted trees with branches and foliage, amongst which the water swirled and roared angrily.

One of those drifting trees grounded on the shelving shore, just by the house, and Almayer, neglecting his dream, watched it with languid interest. The tree swung slowly round, amid the hiss and foam of the water, and soon getting free of the obstruction began to move down stream again, rolling slowly over, raising upwards a long, denuded branch, like a hand lifted in mute appeal to heaven against the river's brutal and unnecessary violence. Almayer's interest in the fate of that tree increased rapidly. He leaned over to see if it would clear the low point below. It did; then he drew back, thinking that now its course was free down to the sea, and he envied the lot of that inanimate thing now growing small and indistinct in the deepening darkness. As he lost sight of it altogether he began to wonder how far out to sea it would drift. Would the current carry it north or south? South, probably, till it drifted in sight of Celebes,[5] as far as Macassar, perhaps!

Macassar! Almayer's quickened fancy distanced the tree on its imaginary voyage, but his memory lagging behind some twenty years or more in point of time saw a young and slim Almayer, clad all in white and modest-looking, landing from the Dutch mail-boat on the dusty jetty of Macassar, coming to woo fortune in the godowns[6] of old Hudig. It was an important epoch in his life, the beginning of a new existence for him. His father, a subordinate official employed in the Botanical Gardens of Buitenzorg,[7] was no doubt delighted to place his son in such a firm. The young man himself too was nothing loth to leave the poisonous shores of Java, and the meagre comforts of the parental bungalow, where the father grumbled all day at the stupidity of native gardeners, and the mother from the depths of her long easy-chair bewailed the lost glories of Amsterdam, where she had been brought up, and of her position as the daughter of a cigar dealer there.

Almayer had left his home with a light heart and a lighter pocket, speaking English well, and strong in arithmetic; ready to conquer the world, never doubting that he would.

After those twenty years, standing in the close and stifling heat of a Bornean evening, he recalled with pleasurable regret the image of Hudig's lofty and cool warehouses with their long and straight avenues of gin cases and bales of Manchester goods;[8] the big door swinging noiselessly; the dim light of the place, so delightful after the glare of the streets; the little railed-off spaces amongst piles of merchandise where the Chinese clerks, neat, cool and sad-eyed, wrote rapidly and in silence amidst the din of the working gangs rolling casks or shifting cases to a muttered song, ending with a desperate yell. At the upper end, facing the great door, there was a larger space railed off, well lighted; there the noise was subdued by distance, and above it rose the soft and continuous clink of silver guilders which other discreet Chinamen were counting and piling up under the supervision of Mr Vinck, the cashier, the genius presiding in the place – the right hand of the Master.

In that clear space Almayer worked at his table not far from a little green-painted door, by which always stood a Malay in a red sash and turban, and whose hand, holding a small string dangling from above, moved up and down with the regularity of a machine. The string worked a punkah[9] on the other side of the green door, where the so-called private office was, and where old Hudig – the Master – sat enthroned, holding noisy receptions. Sometimes the little door would fly open disclosing to the outer world, through the bluish haze of tobacco smoke, a long table loaded with bottles of various shapes and tall water-pitchers, rattan easy-chairs occupied by noisy men in sprawling attitudes, while the Master would put his head through and, holding it by the handle, would grunt confidentially to Vinck; perhaps send an order thundering down the warehouse, or spy a hesitating stranger and greet him with a friendly roar, 'Welcome, Gapitan! ver' you gome vrom? Bali, eh? Got bonies?[10] I vant bonies! Vant all you got; ha! ha! ha! Gome in!' Then the stranger was dragged in, in a tempest of yells, the door was shut, and the usual noises refilled the place: the song of the workmen, the rumble of barrels, the scratch of rapid pens; while above all rose the musical chink of broad silver pieces streaming ceaselessly through the yellow fingers of the attentive Chinamen.

At that time Macassar was teeming with life and commerce. It was the point in the islands where tended all those bold spirits who, fitting out schooners on the Australian coast, invaded the Malay Archipelago in search of money and adventure. Bold, reckless, keen in business, not disinclined for a brush with the pirates that were to be found on many a coast as yet, making money fast, they used to have a general 'rendezvous' in the bay for purposes of trade and dissipation. The Dutch merchants called those men English pedlars; some of them were undoubtedly gentlemen for whom that kind of life had a charm; most were seamen; the acknowledged king of them all was Tom Lingard, he whom the Malays, honest or dishonest, quiet fishermen or desperate cut-throats, recognised as 'the Rajah-Laut' – the King of the Sea.

Almayer had heard of him before he had been three days in Macassar, had heard the stories of his smart business transactions, his loves, and also of his desperate fights with the Sulu pirates,[11] together with the romantic tale of some child – a girl – found in a piratical prau[12] by the victorious Lingard, when, after a long contest, he boarded the craft, driving the crew overboard. This girl, it was generally known, Lingard had adopted, was having her educated in some convent in Java, and spoke of her as 'my daughter'. He had sworn a mighty oath to marry her to a white man before he went home and to leave her all his money.

'And Captain Lingard has lots of money,' would say Mr Vinck solemnly, with his head on one side, 'lots of money; more than Hudig!' And after a pause – just to let his hearers recover from their astonishment at such an incredible assertion – he would add in an explanatory whisper, 'You know, he has discovered a river.'

That was it! He had discovered a river! That was the fact placing old Lingard so much above the common crowd of seagoing adventurers who traded with Hudig in the daytime and drank champagne, gambled, sang noisy songs and made love to half-caste girls under the broad verandah of the Sunda Hotel at night. Into that river, whose entrances only he himself knew, Lingard used to take his assorted cargo of Manchester goods, brass gongs, rifles and gunpowder. His brig *Flash*, which he commanded himself, would on those occasions disappear quietly during the night from the roadstead while his companions were sleeping off the effects of the midnight carouse, Lingard seeing them drunk under the table before going on board, himself unaffected by any amount of liquor. Many tried to follow him and find that land of plenty for gutta-percha[13] and rattans, pearl shells and birds' nests, wax and gum-dammar, but the little *Flash* could outsail every craft in those seas. A few of them came to grief on hidden sandbanks and coral reefs, losing their all and barely escaping with life from the cruel grip of this sunny and smiling sea; others got discouraged; and for many years the green and peaceful-looking islands guarding the entrances to the promised land kept their secret with all the merciless serenity of tropical nature. And so Lingard came and went on his secret or open expeditions, becoming a hero in Almayer's eyes by the boldness and enormous profits of his ventures, seeming to Almayer a very great man indeed as he saw him marching up the warehouse, grunting a 'How are you?' to Vinck, or greeting Hudig, the Master, with a boisterous 'Hallo, old pirate! Alive yet?' as a preliminary to transacting business behind the little green door. Often of an evening, in the silence of the then deserted warehouse, Almayer putting away his papers before driving home with Mr Vinck, in whose household he lived, would pause listening to the noise of a hot discussion in the private office, would hear the deep and monotonous growl of the Master, and the roared-out interruptions of Lingard – two mastiffs fighting over a marrowy bone. But to Almayer's ears it sounded like a quarrel of Titans[14] – a battle of the gods.

After a year or so Lingard, having been brought often in contact with Almayer in the course of business, took a sudden and, to the onlookers, a rather inexplicable fancy to the young man. He sang his praises, late at night over a convivial glass, to his cronies in the Sunda Hotel, and one fine morning electrified Vinck by declaring that he must have 'that young fellow for a supercargo. Kind of captain's clerk. Do all my quill-driving for me.' Hudig consented. Almayer, with youth's natural craving for change, was nothing loth, and packing his few belongings, started in the *Flash* on one of those long cruises when the old seaman was wont to visit almost every island in the Archipelago. Months slipped by, and Lingard's friendship seemed to increase. Often pacing the deck with Almayer, when the faint night breeze, heavy with aromatic exhalations of the islands, shoved the brig gently along under the peaceful and sparkling sky, did the old seaman open his heart to his entranced listener. He spoke of his past life, of escaped dangers, of big profits in his trade, of new combinations that were in the future to bring profits bigger still. Often he had mentioned his daughter, the girl found in the pirate prau, speaking of her with a strange assumption of fatherly tenderness. 'She must be a big girl now,' he used to say. 'It's nigh unto four years since I have seen her! Damme, Almayer, if I don't think we will run into Sourabaya[15] this trip.' And after such a declaration he always dived into his cabin muttering to himself, 'Something must be done – must be done.' More than once he would astonish Almayer by walking up to him rapidly, clearing his throat with a powerful 'Hem!' as if he was going to say something, and then turning abruptly away to lean over the bulwarks in silence, and watch, motionless, for hours, the gleam and sparkle of the phosphorescent sea along the ship's side. It was the night before arriving in Sourabaya when one of those attempts at confidential communication succeeded. After clearing his throat he spoke. He spoke to some purpose. He wanted Almayer to marry his adopted daughter. 'And don't you kick because you're white!' he shouted, suddenly, not giving the surprised young man the time to say a word. 'None of that with me! Nobody will see the colour of your wife's skin. The dollars are too thick for that, I tell you! And mind you, they will be thicker yet before I die. There will be millions, Kaspar! Millions I say! And all for her – and for you, if you do what you are told.'

Startled by the unexpected proposal, Almayer hesitated, and remained silent for a minute. He was gifted with a strong and active imagination, and in that short space of time he saw, as in a flash of dazzling light, great piles of shining guilders, and realised all the possibilities of an opulent existence. The consideration, the indolent ease of life – for which he felt himself so well fitted – his ships, his warehouses, his merchandise (old Lingard would not live for ever), and, crowning all, in the far future gleamed above char, where, made king amongst men by old Lingard's money, he would pass the evening of his days in inexpressible splendour. As to the other side of the picture – the companionship for life of a Malay girl, that legacy of a boatful of pirates – there was only within him a confused consciousness of shame that he a white man – Still, a convent education of four years! – and then she may mercifully die. He was always lucky, and money is powerful! Go through with it. Why not? He had a vague idea of shutting her up somewhere, anywhere, out of his gorgeous future. Easy enough to dispose of a Malay woman, a slave, after all, to his Eastern mind, convent or no convent, ceremony or no ceremony.

He lifted his head and confronted the anxious yet irate seaman.

'I – of course – anything you wish, Captain Lingard.'

'Call me father, my boy. She does,' said the mollified old adventurer. 'Damme, though, if I didn't think you were going to refuse. Mind you, Kaspar, I always get my way, so it would have been no use. But you are no fool.'

He remembered well that time – the look, the accent, the words, the effect they produced on him, his very surroundings. He remembered the narrow slanting deck of the brig, the silent sleeping coast, the smooth black surface of the sea with a great bar of gold laid on it by the rising moon. He remembered it all, and he remembered his feelings of mad exultation at the thought of that fortune thrown into his hands. He was no fool then, and he was no fool now. Circumstances had been against him; the fortune was gone, but hope remained.

He shivered in the night air, and suddenly became aware of the intense darkness which, on the sun's departure, had closed in upon the river, blotting out the outlines of the opposite shore. Only the fire of dry branches lit outside the stockade of the Rajah's compound called fitfully into view the ragged trunks of the surrounding trees, putting a stain of glowing red halfway across the river where the drifting logs were hurrying towards the sea through the impenetrable gloom. He had a hazy recollection of having been called some time during the evening by his wife. To his dinner probably. But a man busy contemplating the wreckage of his past in the dawn of new hopes cannot be hungry whenever his rice is ready. Time he went home, though; it was getting late.

He stepped cautiously on the loose planks towards the ladder. A lizard, disturbed by the noise, emitted a plaintive note and scurried through the long grass growing on the bank. Almayer descended the ladder carefully, now thoroughly recalled to the realities of life by the care necessary to prevent a fall on the uneven ground where the stones, decaying planks, and half-sawn beams were piled up in inextricable confusion. As he turned towards the house where he lived – 'my old house' he called it – his ear detected the splash of paddles away in the darkness of the river. He stood still in the path, attentive and surprised at anybody being on the river at this late hour during such a heavy freshet. Now he could hear the paddles distinctly, and even a rapidly exchanged word in low tones, the heavy breathing of men fighting with the current, and hugging the bank on which he stood. Quite close, too, but it was too dark to distinguish anything under the overhanging bushes.

'Arabs, no doubt,' muttered Almayer to himself, peering into the solid blackness. 'What are they up to now? Some of Abdulla's business; curse him!'

The boat was very close now.

'Oh, ya! Man!' hailed Almayer.

The sound of voices ceased, but the paddles worked as furiously as before. Then the bush in front of Almayer shook, and the sharp sound of the paddles falling into the canoe rang in the quiet night. They were holding on to the bush now; but Almayer could hardly make out an indistinct dark shape of a man's head and shoulders above the bank.

'You Abdulla?' said Almayer, doubtfully.

A grave voice answered –

'Tuan Almayer is speaking to a friend. There is no Arab here.'

Almayer's heart gave a great leap.

'Dain!' he exclaimed. 'At last! at last! I have been waiting for you every day and every night. I had nearly given you up.'

'Nothing could have stopped me from coming back here,' said the other, almost violently. 'Not even death,' he whispered to himself.

'This is a friend's talk, and is very good,' said Almayer, heartily. 'But you are too far here. Drop down to the jetty and let your men cook their rice in my campong while we talk in the house.'

There was no answer to that invitation.

'What is it?' asked Almayer, uneasily. 'There is nothing wrong with the brig, I hope?'

'The brig is where no Orang Blanda[16] can lay his hands on her,' said Dain, with a gloomy tone in his voice, which Almayer, in his elation, failed to notice.

'Right,' he said. 'But where are all your men? There are only two with you.'

'Listen, Tuan Almayer,' said Dain. 'Tomorrow's sun shall see me in your house, and then we will talk. Now I must go to the Rajah.'

'To the Rajah! Why? What do you want with Lakamba?'

'Tuan, tomorrow we talk like friends. I must see Lakamba tonight.'

'Dain, you are not going to abandon me now, when all is ready?' asked Almayer, in a pleading voice.

'Have I not returned? But I must see Lakamba first for your good and mine.'

The shadowy head disappeared abruptly. The bush, released from the grasp of the bowman, sprung back with a swish, scattering a shower of muddy water over Almayer, as he bent forward, trying to see.

In a little while the canoe shot into the streak of light that streamed on the river from the big fire on the opposite shore, disclosing the outline of two men bending to their work, and a third figure in the stern flourishing the steering paddle, his head covered with an enormous round hat, like a fantastically exaggerated mushroom.

Almayer watched the canoe till it passed out of the line of light. Shortly after the murmur of many voices reached him across the water. He could see the torches being snatched out of the burning pile, and rendering visible for a moment the gate in the stockade round which they crowded. Then they went in apparently. The torches disappeared, and the scattered fire sent out only a dim and fitful glare.

Almayer stepped homewards with long strides and mind uneasy. Surely Dain was not thinking of playing him false. It was absurd. Dain and Lakamba were both too much interested in the success of his scheme. Trusting to Malays was poor work; but then even Malays have some sense and understand their own interest. All would be well – must be well. At this point in his meditation he found himself at the foot of the steps leading to the verandah of his home. From the low point of land where he stood he could see both branches of the river. The main branch of the Pantai was lost in complete darkness, for the fire at the Rajah's had gone out altogether; but up the Sambir reach his eye could follow the long line of Malay houses crowding the bank, with here and there a dim light twinkling through bamboo walls, or a smoky torch burning on the platforms built out over the river. Farther away, where the island ended in a low cliff, rose a dark mass of buildings towering above the Malay structures. Founded solidly on firm ground with plenty of space, starred by many lights burning strong and white, with a suggestion of paraffin and lamp-glasses, stood the house and the godowns of Abdulla bin Selim, the great trader of Sambir. To Almayer the sight was very distasteful, and he shook his fist towards the buildings that in their evident prosperity looked to him cold and insolent, and contemptuous of his own fallen fortunes.

He mounted the steps of his house slowly.

In the middle of the verandah there was a round table. On it a paraffin lamp without a globe shed a hard glare on the three inner sides. The fourth side was open, and faced the river. Between the rough supports of the high-pitched roof hung torn rattan screens. There was no ceiling, and the harsh brilliance of the lamp was toned above into a soft half-light that lost itself in the obscurity amongst the rafters. The front wall was cut in two by the doorway of a central passage closed by a red curtain. The women's room opened into that passage, which led to the back courtyard and to the cooking shed. In one of the side walls there was a doorway. Half obliterated words – 'Office: Lingard and Co.' – were still legible on the dusty door, which looked as if it had not been opened for a very long time. Close to the other side wall stood a bentwood rocking-chair, and by the table and about the verandah four wooden armchairs straggled forlornly, as if ashamed of their shabby surroundings. A heap of common mats lay in one corner, with an old hammock slung diagonally above. In the other corner, his head wrapped in a piece of red calico, huddled into a shapeless heap, slept a Malay, one of Almayer's domestic slaves – 'my own people', he used to call them. A numerous and representative assembly of moths was holding high revels round the lamp to the spirited music of swarming mosquitoes. Under the palm-leaf thatch lizards raced on the beams calling softly. A monkey, chained to one of the verandah supports – retired for the night under the eaves – peered and grinned at Almayer, as it swung to one of the bamboo roof sticks and caused a shower of dust and bits of dried leaves to settle on the shabby table. The floor was uneven, with many withered plants and dried earth scattered about. A general air of squalid neglect pervaded the place. Great red stains on the floor and walls testified to frequent and indiscriminate betel-nut chewing. The light breeze from the river swayed gently the tattered blinds, sending from the woods opposite a faint and sickly perfume as of decaying flowers.

Under Almayer's heavy tread the boards of the verandah creaked loudly. The sleeper in the corner moved uneasily, muttering indistinct words. There was a slight rustle behind the curtained doorway, and a soft voice asked in Malay, 'Is it you, father?'

'Yes, Nina. I am hungry. Is everybody asleep in this house?'

Almayer spoke jovially and dropped with a contented sigh into the armchair nearest to the table. Nina Almayer came through the curtained doorway followed by an old Malay woman, who busied herself in setting upon the table a plateful of rice and fish, a jar of water, and a bottle half full of geneva.[17] After carefully placing before her master a cracked glass tumbler and a tin spoon she went away noiselessly. Nina stood by the table, one hand lightly resting on its edge, the other hanging listlessly by her side. Her face turned towards the outer darkness, through which her dreamy eyes seemed to see some entrancing picture, wore a look of impatient expectancy. She was tall for a half-caste, with the correct profile of the father, modified and strengthened by the squareness of the lower part of the face inherited from her maternal ancestors – the Sulu pirates. Her firm mouth, with the lips slightly parted and disclosing a gleam of white teeth, put a vague suggestion of ferocity into the impatient expression of her features. And yet her dark and perfect eyes had all the tender softness of expression common to Malay women, but with a gleam of superior intelligence; they looked gravely, wide open and steady, as if facing something invisible to all other eyes, while she stood there all in white, straight, flexible, graceful, unconscious of herself, her low but broad forehead crowned with a shining mass of long black hair that fell in heavy tresses over her shoulders, and made her pale olive complexion look paler still by the contrast of its coal-black hue.

Almayer attacked his rice greedily, but after a few mouthfuls he paused, spoon in hand, and looked at his daughter curiously.

'Did you hear a boat pass about half an hour ago, Nina?' he asked.

The girl gave him a quick glance, and moving away from the light stood with her back to the table.

'No,' she said, slowly.

'There was a boat. At last! Dain himself; and he went on to Lakamba. I know it, for he told me so. I spoke to him, but he would not come here tonight. Will come tomorrow, he said.'

He swallowed another spoonful, then said – 'I am almost happy tonight, Nina. I can see the end of a long road, and it leads us away from this miserable swamp. We shall soon get away from here, I and you, my dear little girl, and then – '

He rose from the table and stood looking fixedly before him as if contemplating some enchanting vision.

'And then,' he went on, 'we shall be happy, you and I. Live rich and respected far from here, and forget this life, and all this struggle, and all this misery!'

He approached his daughter and passed his hand caressingly over her hair.

'It is bad to have to trust a Malay,' he said, 'but I must own that this Dain is a perfect gentleman – a perfect gentleman,' he repeated.

'Did you ask him to come here, father?' enquired Nina, not looking at him.

'Well, of course. We shall start on the day after tomorrow,' said Almayer, joyously. 'We must not lose any time. Are you glad, little girl?'

She was nearly as tall as himself, but he liked to recall the time when she was little and they were all in all to each other.

'I am glad,' she said, very low.

'Of course,' said Almayer, vivaciously, 'you cannot imagine what is before you. I myself have not been to Europe, but I have heard my mother talk so often that I seem to know all about it. We shall live a – a glorious life. You shall see.'

Again he stood silent by his daughter's side looking at that enchanting vision. After a while he shook his clenched hand towards the sleeping settlement.

'Ah! my friend Abdulla,' he cried, 'we shall see who will have the best of it after all these years!'

He looked up the river and remarked calmly, 'Another thunderstorm. Well! No thunder will keep me awake tonight, I know! Goodnight, little girl,' he whispered, tenderly kissing her cheek. 'You do not seem to be very happy tonight, but tomorrow you will show a brighter face. Eh?'

Nina had listened to her father with her face unmoved, with her half-closed eyes still gazing into the night now made more intense by a heavy thunder-cloud that had crept down from the hills blotting out the stars, merging sky, forest and river into one mass of almost palpable blackness. The faint breeze had died out, but the distant rumble of thunder and pale flashes of lightning gave warning of the approaching storm. With a sigh the girl turned towards the table.

Almayer was in his hammock now, already half asleep.

'Take the lamp, Nina,' he muttered, drowsily. 'This place is full of mosquitoes. Go to sleep, daughter.'

But Nina put the lamp out and turned back again towards the balustrade of the verandah, standing with her arm round the wooden support and looking eagerly towards the Pantai reach. And motionless there in the oppressive calm of the tropical night she could see at each flash of lightning the forest lining both banks up the river, bending before the furious blast of the coming tempest, the upper reach of the river whipped into white foam by the wind, and the black clouds torn into fantastic shapes trailing low over the swaying trees. Round her all was as yet stillness and peace, but she could hear afar off the roar of the wind, the hiss of heavy rain, the wash of the waves on the tormented river. It came nearer and nearer, with loud thunder-claps and long flashes of vivid lightning, followed by short periods of appalling blackness. When the storm reached the low point dividing the river, the house shook in the wind, and the rain pattered loudly on the palm-leaf roof, the thunder spoke in one prolonged roll, and the incessant lightning disclosed a turmoil of leaping waters, driving logs and the big trees bending before a brutal and merciless force.

Undisturbed by the nightly event of the rainy monsoon, the father slept quietly, oblivious alike of his hopes, his misfortunes, his friends and his enemies; and the daughter stood motionless, at each flash of lightning eagerly scanning the broad river with a steady and anxious gaze.

Chapter 2

When, in compliance with Lingard's abrupt demand, Almayer consented to wed the Malay girl, no one knew that on the day when the interesting young convert had lost all her natural relations and found a white father, she had been fighting desperately like the rest of them on board the prau, and was only prevented from leaping overboard, like the few other survivors, by a severe wound in the leg. There, on the foredeck of the prau, old Lingard found her under a heap of dead and dying pirates, and had her carried on the poop of the *Flash* before the Malay craft was set on fire and sent adrift. She was conscious, and in the great peace and stillness of the tropical evening succeeding the turmoil of the battle, she watched all she held dear on earth after her own savage manner, drift away into the gloom in a great roar of flame and smoke. She lay there unheeding the careful hands attending to her wound, silent and absorbed in gazing at the funeral pile of those brave men she had so much admired and so well helped in their contest with the redoubtable 'Rajah-Laut'.

The light night breeze fanned the brig gently to the southward, and the great blaze of light got smaller and smaller till it twinkled only on the horizon like a setting star. It set: the heavy canopy of smoke reflected the glare of hidden flames for a short time and then disappeared also.

She realised that with this vanishing gleam her old life departed too. Thenceforth there was slavery in the far countries, amongst strangers, in unknown and perhaps terrible surroundings. Being fourteen years old, she realised her position and came to that conclusion, the only one possible to a Malay girl, soon ripened under a tropical sun, and not unaware of her personal charms, of which she heard many a young brave warrior of her father's crew express an appreciative admiration. There was in her the dread of the unknown; otherwise she accepted her position calmly, after the manner of her people, and even considered it quite natural; for was she not a daughter of warriors conquered in battle, and did she not belong rightfully to the victorious Rajah? Even the evident kindness of the terrible old man must spring, she thought, from admiration for his captive, and the flattered vanity eased for her the pangs of sorrow after such an awful calamity. Perhaps had she known of the high walls, the quiet gardens, and the silent nuns of the Samarang convent, where her destiny was leading her, she would have sought death in her dread and hate of such a restraint. But in imagination she pictured to herself the usual life of a Malay girl – the usual succession of heavy work and fierce love, of intrigues, gold ornaments, of domestic drudgery, and of that great but occult influence which is one of the few rights of half-savage womankind. But her destiny in the rough hands of the old sea-dog, acting under unreasoning impulses of the heart, took a strange and to her a terrible shape. She bore it all – the restraint and the teaching and the new faith – with calm submission, concealing her hate and contempt for all that new life. She learned the language very easily, yet understood but little of the new faith the good sisters taught her, assimilating quickly only the superstitious elements of the religion. She called Lingard father, gently and caressingly, at each of his short and noisy visits, under the clear impression that he was a great and dangerous power it was good to propitiate. Was he not now her master? And during those long four years she nourished a hope of finding favour in his eyes and ultimately becoming his wife, counsellor and guide.

Those dreams of the future were dispelled by the Rajah Laut's 'fiat', which made Almayer's fortune, as that young man fondly hoped. And dressed in the hateful finery of Europe, the centre of an interested circle of Batavian society, the young convert stood before the altar with an unknown and sulky-looking white man. For Almayer was uneasy, a little disgusted, and greatly inclined to run away. A judicious fear of the adopted father-in-law and a just regard for his own material welfare prevented him from making a scandal; yet, while swearing fidelity, he was concocting plans for getting rid of the pretty Malay girl in a more or less distant future. She, however, had retained enough of conventual teaching to understand well that according to white men's laws she was going to be Almayer's companion and not his slave, and promised to herself to act accordingly.

So when the *Flash* freighted with materials for building a new house left the harbour of Batavia,[18] taking away the young couple into the unknown Borneo, she did not carry on her deck so much love and happiness as old Lingard was wont to boast of before his casual friends in the verandahs of various hotels. The old seaman himself was perfectly happy. Now he had done his duty by the girl. 'You know I made her an orphan,' he often concluded solemnly, when talking about his own affairs to a scratch audience of shore loafers – as it was his habit to do. And the approbative shouts of his half-intoxicated auditors filled his simple soul with delight and pride. 'I carry everything right through,' was another of his sayings, and in pursuance of that principle he pushed the building of house and godowns on the Pantai River with feverish haste. The house for the young couple; the godowns for the big trade Almayer was going to develop while he (Lingard) would be able to give himself up to some mysterious work which was only spoken of in hints, but was understood to relate to gold and diamonds in the interior of the island. Almayer was impatient too. Had he known what was before him he might not have been so eager and full of hope as he stood watching the last canoe of the Lingard expedition disappear in the bend up the river. When, turning round, he beheld the pretty little house, the big godowns built neatly by an army of Chinese carpenters, the new jetty round which were clustered the trading canoes, he felt a sudden elation in the thought that the world was his.

But the world had to be conquered first, and its conquest was not so easy as he thought. He was very soon made to understand that he was not wanted in that corner of it where old Lingard and his own weak will placed him, in the midst of unscrupulous intrigues and of a fierce trade competition. The Arabs had found out the river, had established a trading post in Sambir, and where they traded they would be masters and suffer no rival. Lingard returned unsuccessful from his first expedition, and departed again spending all the profits of the legitimate trade on his mysterious journeys. Almayer struggled with the difficulties of his position, friendless and unaided, save for the protection given to him for Lingard's sake by the old Rajah, the predecessor of Lakamba. Lakamba himself, then living as a private individual on a rice clearing, seven miles down the river, exercised all his influence towards the help of the white man's enemies, plotting against the old Rajah and Almayer with a certainty of combination, pointing clearly to a profound knowledge of their most secret affairs. Outwardly friendly, his portly form was often to be seen on Almayer's verandah; his green turban and gold-embroidered jacket shone in the front rank of the decorous throng of Malays coming to greet Lingard on his returns from the interior; his salaams were of the lowest, and his hand-shakings of the heartiest, when welcoming the old trader. But his small eyes took in the signs of the times, and he departed from those interviews with a satisfied and furtive smile to hold long consultations with his friend and ally, Syed Abdulla,[19] the chief of the Arab trading post, a man of great wealth and of great influence in the islands.

It was currently believed at that time in the settlement that Lakamba's visits to Almayer's house were not limited to those official interviews. Often on moonlight nights the belated fishermen of Sambir saw a small canoe shooting out from the narrow creek at the back of the white man's house, and the solitary occupant paddle cautiously down the river in the deep shadows of the bank; and those events, duly reported, were discussed round the evening fires far into the night with the cynicism of expression common to aristocratic Malays, and with a malicious pleasure in the domestic misfortunes of the Orang Blanda – the hated Dutchman. Almayer went on struggling desperately, but with a feebleness of purpose depriving him of all chance of success against men so unscrupulous and resolute as his rivals the Arabs. The trade fell away from the large godowns, and the godowns themselves rotted piecemeal. The old man's banker, Hudig of Macassar, failed, and with this went the whole available capital. The profits of past years had been swallowed up in Lingard's exploring craze. Lingard was in the interior – perhaps dead – at all events giving no sign of life. Almayer stood alone in the midst of those adverse circumstances, deriving only a little comfort from the companionship of his little daughter, born two years after the marriage, and at the time some six years old. His wife had soon commenced to treat him with a savage contempt expressed by sulky silence, only occasionally varied by a flood of savage invective. He felt she hated him, and saw her jealous eyes watching himself and the child with almost an expression of hate. She was jealous of the little girl's evident preference for the father, and Almayer felt he was not safe with that woman in the house. While she was burning the furniture, and tearing down the pretty curtains in her unreasoning hate of those signs of civilisation, Almayer, cowed by these outbursts of savage nature, meditated in silence on the best way of getting rid of her. He thought of everything; even planned murder in an undecided and feeble sort of way, but dared do nothing – expecting every day the return of Lingard with news of some immense good fortune. He returned indeed, but aged, ill, a ghost of his former self, with the fire of fever burning in his sunken eyes, almost the only survivor of the numerous expedition. But he was successful at last! Untold riches were in his grasp; he wanted more money – only a little more to realise a dream of fabulous fortune. And Hudig had failed! Almayer scraped all he could together, but the old man wanted more. If Almayer could not get it he would go to Singapore – to Europe even, but before all to Singapore; and he would take the little Nina with him. The child must be brought up decently. He had good friends in Singapore who would take care of her and have her taught properly. All would be well, and that girl, upon whom the old seaman seemed to have transferred all his former affection for the mother, would be the richest woman in the East – in the world even. So old Lingard shouted, pacing the verandah with his heavy quarterdeck step, gesticulating with a smouldering cheroot; ragged, dishevelled, enthusiastic; and Almayer, sitting huddled up on a pile of mats, thought with dread of the separation from the only human being he loved – with greater dread still, perhaps, of the scene with his wife, the savage tigress deprived of her young. She will poison me, thought the poor wretch, well aware of that easy and final manner of solving the social, political or family problems in Malay life.

To his great surprise she took the news very quietly, giving only him and Lingard a furtive glance, and saying not a word. This, however, did not prevent her the next day from jumping into the river and swimming after the boat in which Lingard was carrying away the nurse with the screaming child. Almayer had to give chase with his whale-boat and drag her in by the hair in the midst of cries and curses enough to make heaven fall. Yet after two days spent in wailing, she returned to her former mode of life, chewing betel-nut, and sitting all day amongst her women in stupefied idleness. She aged very rapidly after that, and only roused herself from her apathy to acknowledge by a scathing remark or an insulting exclamation the accidental presence of her husband. He had built for her a riverside hut in the compound where she dwelt in perfect seclusion. Lakamba's visits had ceased when, by a convenient decree of Providence and the help of a little scientific manipulation, the old ruler of Sambir departed this life. Lakamba reigned in his stead now, having been well served by his Arab friends with the Dutch authorities. Syed Abdulla was the great man and trader of the Pantai. Almayer lay ruined and helpless under the close-meshed net of their intrigues, owing his life only to his supposed knowledge of Lingard's valuable secret. Lingard had disappeared. He wrote once from Singapore saying the child was well, and under the care of a Mrs Vinck, and that he himself was going to Europe to raise money for the great enterprise. 'He was coming back soon. There would be no difficulties,' he wrote; 'people would rush in with their money.' Evidently they did not, for there was only one letter more from him saying he was ill, had found no relation living, but little else besides. Then came a complete silence. Europe had swallowed up the Rajah Laut apparently, and Almayer looked vainly westward for a ray of light out of the gloom of his shattered hopes. Years passed, and the rare letters from Mrs Vinck, later on from the girl herself, were the only thing to be looked to to make life bearable amongst the triumphant savagery of the river. Almayer lived now alone, having even ceased to visit his debtors who would not pay, sure of Lakamba's protection. The faithful Sumatrese[20] Ali cooked his rice and made his coffee, for he dared not trust anyone else, and least of all his wife. He killed time wandering sadly in the overgrown paths round the house, visiting the ruined godowns where a few brass guns covered with verdigris and only a few broken cases of mouldering Manchester goods reminded him of the good early times when all this was full of life and merchandise, and he overlooked a busy scene on the river bank, his little daughter by his side. Now the up-country canoes glided past the little rotten wharf of Lingard and Co., to paddle up the Pantai branch, and cluster round the new jetty belonging to Abdulla. Not that they loved Abdulla, but they dared not trade with the man whose star had set. Had they done so they knew there was no mercy to be expected from Arab or Rajah; no rice to be got on credit in the times of scarcity from either; and Almayer could not help them, having at times hardly enough for himself. Almayer, in his isolation and despair, often envied his near neighbour the Chinaman, Jim-Eng, whom he could see stretched on a pile of cool mats, a wooden pillow under his head, an opium pipe in his nerveless fingers. He did not seek, however, consolation in opium – perhaps it was too expensive – perhaps his white man's pride saved him from that degradation; but most likely it was the thought of his little daughter in the far-off Straits Settlements. He heard from her oftener since Abdulla bought a steamer, which ran now between Singapore and the Pantai settlement every three months or so. Almayer felt himself nearer his daughter. He longed to see her, and planned a voyage to Singapore, but put off his departure from year to year, always expecting some favourable turn of fortune. He did not want to meet her with empty hands and with no words of hope on his lips. He could not take her back into that savage life to which he was condemned himself. He was also a little afraid of her. What would she think of him? He reckoned the years. A grown woman. A civilised woman, young and hopeful; while he felt old and hopeless, and very much like those savages round him. He asked himself what was going to be her future. He could not answer that question yet, and he dared not face her. And yet he longed after her. He hesitated for years.

His hesitation was put an end to by Nina's unexpected appearance in Sambir. She arrived in the steamer under the captain's care. Almayer beheld her with surprise not unmixed with wonder. During those ten years the child had changed into a woman, black-haired, olive-skinned, tall and beautiful, with great sad eyes, where the startled expression common to Malay womankind was modified by a thoughtful tinge inherited from her European ancestry. Almayer thought with dismay of the meeting of his wife and daughter, of what this grave girl in European clothes would think of her betel-nut-chewing mother, squatting in a dark hut, disorderly, half naked, and sulky. He also feared an outbreak of temper on the part of that pest of a woman he had hitherto managed to keep tolerably quiet, thereby saving the remnants of his dilapidated furniture. And he stood there before the closed door of the hut in the blazing sunshine listening to the murmur of voices, wondering what went on inside, wherefrom all the servant-maids had been expelled at the beginning of the interview, and now stood clustered by the palings with half-covered faces in a chatter of curious speculation. He forgot himself there trying to catch a stray word through the bamboo walls, till the captain of the steamer, who had walked up with the girl, fearing a sunstroke, took him under the arm and led him into the shade of his own verandah, where Nina's trunk stood already, having been landed by the steamer's men. As soon as Captain Ford had his glass before him and his cheroot lighted, Almayer asked for the explanation of his daughter's unexpected arrival. Ford said little beyond generalising in vague but violent terms upon the foolishness of women in general, and of Mrs Vinck in particular.

'You know, Kaspar,' said he, in conclusion, to the excited Almayer, 'it is deucedly awkward to have a half-caste girl in the house. There's such a lot of fools about. There was that young fellow from the bank who used to ride to the Vinck bungalow early and late. That old woman thought it was for that Emma of hers. When she found out what he wanted exactly, there was a row, I can tell you. She would not have Nina – not an hour longer – in the house. Fact is, I heard of this affair and took the girl to my wife. My wife is a pretty good woman – as women go – and upon my word we would have kept the girl for you, only she would not stay. Now, then! Don't flare up, Kaspar. Sit still. What can you do? It is better so. Let her stay with you. She was never happy over there. Those two Vinck girls are no better than dressed-up monkeys. They slighted her. You can't make her white. It's no use you swearing at me. You can't. She is a good girl for all that, but she would not tell my wife anything. If you want to know, ask her yourself; but if I was you, I would leave her alone. You are welcome to her passage money, old fellow, if you are short now.' And the skipper, throwing away his cigar, walked off to 'wake them up on board', as he expressed it.

Almayer vainly expected to hear of the cause of his daughter's return from his daughter's lips. Not that day, not on any other day did she ever allude to her Singapore life. He did not care to ask, awed by the calm impassiveness of her face, by those solemn eyes looking past him on the great, still forests sleeping in majestic repose to the murmur of the broad river. He accepted the situation, happy in the gentle and protecting affection the girl showed him, fitfully enough, for she had – as he called it – her bad days when she used to visit her mother and remain long hours in the riverside hut, coming out as inscrutable as ever, but with a contemptuous look and a short word ready to answer any of his speeches. He got used even to that, and on those days kept quiet, although greatly alarmed by his wife's influence upon the girl. Otherwise Nina adapted herself wonderfully to the circumstances of a half-savage and miserable life. She accepted without question or apparent disgust the neglect, the decay, the poverty of the household, the absence of furniture, and the preponderance of rice diet on the family table. She lived with Almayer in the little house (now sadly decaying) built originally by Lingard for the young couple. The Malays eagerly discussed her arrival. There were at the beginning crowded levées of Malay women with their children, seeking eagerly after 'Ubat'[21] for all the ills of the flesh from the young Mem Putih. In the cool of the evening grave Arabs in long white shirts and yellow sleeveless jackets walked slowly on the dusty path by the riverside towards Almayer's gate, and made solemn calls upon that Unbeliever under shallow pretences of business, only to get a glimpse of the young girl in a highly decorous manner. Even Lakamba came out of his stockade in a great pomp of war canoes and red umbrellas, and landed on the rotten little jetty of Lingard and Co. He came, he said, to buy a couple of brass guns as a present to his friend the chief of the Sambir Dyaks;[22] and while Almayer, suspicious but polite, busied himself in unearthing the old popguns in the godowns, the Rajah sat on an armchair in the verandah, surrounded by his respectful retinue, waiting in vain for Nina's appearance. She was in one of her bad days, and remained in her mother's hut watching with her the ceremonious proceedings on the verandah. The Rajah departed, baffled but courteous, and soon Almayer began to reap the benefit of improved relations with the ruler in the shape of the recovery of some debts, paid to him with many apologies and many a low salaam by debtors till then considered hopelessly insolvent. Under these improving circumstances Almayer brightened up a little. All was not lost perhaps. Those Arabs and Malays saw at last that he was a man of some ability, he thought. And he began, after his manner, to plan great things, to dream of great fortunes for himself and Nina. Especially for Nina! Under these vivifying impulses he asked Captain Ford to write to his friends in England making enquiries after Lingard. Was he alive or dead? If dead, had he left any papers, documents; any indications or hints as to his great enterprise? Meantime he had found amongst the rubbish in one of the empty rooms a notebook belonging to the old adventurer. He studied the crabbed handwriting of its pages and often grew meditative over it. Other things also woke him up from his apathy. The stir made in the whole of the island by the establishment of the British Borneo Company affected even the sluggish flow of the Pantai life. Great changes were expected; annexation was talked of; the Arabs grew civil. Almayer began building his new house for the use of the future engineers, agents or settlers of the new company. He spent every available guilder on it with a confiding heart. One thing only disturbed his happiness: his wife came out of her seclusion, importing her green jacket, scant sarongs, shrill voice and witch-like appearance into his quiet life in the small bungalow. And his daughter seemed to accept that savage intrusion into their daily existence with wonderful equanimity. He did not like it, but dared say nothing.

Chapter 3

The deliberations conducted in London have a far-reaching importance, and so the decision issued from the fog-veiled offices of the Borneo Company darkened for Almayer the brilliant sunshine of the Tropics, and added another drop of bitterness to the cup of his disenchantments. The claim to that part of the east coast was abandoned, leaving the Pantai River under the nominal power of Holland. In Sambir there was joy and excitement. The slaves were hurried out of sight into the forest and jungle, and the flags were run up tall poles in the Rajah's compound in expectation of a visit from Dutch man-of-war boats.

The frigate remained anchored outside the mouth of the river, and the boats came up in tow of the steam launch, threading their way cautiously amongst a crowd of canoes filled with gaily dressed Malays. The officer in command listened gravely to the loyal speeches of Lakamba, returned the salaams of Abdulla, and assured those gentlemen in choice Malay of the great Rajah's – down in Batavia – friendship and goodwill towards the ruler and inhabitants of this model state of Sambir.

Almayer from his verandah watched across the river the festive proceedings, heard the report of brass guns saluting the new flag presented to Lakamba, and the deep murmur of the crowd of spectators surging round the stockade. The smoke of the firing rose in white clouds on the green background of the forests, and he could not help comparing his own fleeting hopes to the rapidly disappearing vapour. He was by no means patriotically elated by the event, yet he had to force himself into a gracious behaviour when, the official reception being over, the naval officers of the Commission crossed the river to pay a visit to the solitary white man of whom they had heard, no doubt wishing also to catch a glimpse of his daughter. In that they were disappointed, Nina refusing to show herself; but they seemed easily consoled by the gin and cheroots set before them by the hospitable Almayer; and sprawling comfortably on the lame armchairs under the shade of the verandah, while the blazing sunshine outside seemed to set the great river simmering in the heat, they filled the little bungalow with the unusual sounds of European languages, with noise and laughter produced by naval witticisms at the expense of the fat Lakamba whom they had been complimenting so much that very morning. The younger men in an access of good fellowship made their host talk, and Almayer, excited by the sight of

European faces, by the sound of European voices, opened his heart before the sympathising strangers, unaware of the amusement the recital of his many misfortunes caused to those future admirals. They drank his health, wished him many big diamonds and a mountain of gold, expressed even an envy of the high destinies awaiting him yet. Encouraged by so much friendliness, the grey-headed and foolish dreamer invited his guests to visit his new house. They went there through the long grass in a straggling procession while their boats were got ready for the return down the river in the cool of the evening. And in the great empty rooms where the tepid wind entering through the sashless windows whirled gently the dried leaves and the dust of many days of neglect, Almayer in his white jacket and flowered sarong, surrounded by a circle of glittering uniforms, stamped his foot to show the solidity of the neatly-fitting floors and expatiated upon the beauties and convenience of the building. They listened and assented, amazed by the wonderful simplicity and the foolish hopefulness of the man, till Almayer, carried away by his excitement, disclosed his regret at the non-arrival of the English, 'who knew how to develop a rich country', as he expressed it. There was a general laugh amongst the Dutch officers at that unsophisticated statement, and a move was made towards the boats; but when Almayer, stepping cautiously on the rotten boards of the Lingard jetty, tried to approach the chief of the Commission with some timid hints anent the protection required by the Dutch subject against the wily Arabs, that salt-water diplomat told him significantly that the Arabs were better subjects than Hollanders who dealt illegally in gunpowder with the Malays. The innocent Almayer recognised there at once the oily tongue of Abdulla and the solemn persuasiveness of Lakamba, but ere he had time to frame an indignant protest the steam launch and the string of boats moved rapidly down the river leaving him on the jetty, standing open-mouthed in his surprise and anger. There are thirty miles of river from Sambir to the gemlike islands of the estuary where the frigate was awaiting the return of the boats. The moon rose long before the boats had traversed half that distance, and the black forest sleeping peacefully under her cold rays woke up that night to the ringing laughter in the small flotilla provoked by some reminiscence of Almayer's lamentable narrative. Salt-water jests at the poor man's expense were passed from boat to boat, the non-appearance of his daughter was commented upon with severe displeasure, and the half-finished house built for the reception of Englishmen received on that joyous night the name of 'Almayer's Folly' by the unanimous vote of the light-hearted seamen.

For many weeks after this visit life in Sambir resumed its even and uneventful flow. Each day's sun shooting its morning rays above the tree tops lit up the usual scene of daily activity. Nina walking on the path that formed the only street in the settlement saw the accustomed sight of men lolling on the shady side of the houses, on the high platforms; of women busily engaged in husking the daily rice; of naked brown children racing along the shady and narrow paths leading to the clearings. Jim-Eng, strolling before his house, greeted her with a friendly nod before climbing up indoors to seek his beloved opium pipe. The elder children clustered round her, daring from long acquaintance, pulling the skirts of her white robe with their dark fingers, and showing their brilliant teeth in expectation of a shower of glass beads. She greeted them with a quiet smile, but always had a few friendly words for a Siamese girl, a slave owned by Bulangi, whose numerous wives were said to be of a violent temper. Well-founded rumour said also that the domestic squabbles of that industrious cultivator ended generally in a combined assault by all his wives upon the Siamese slave. The girl herself never complained – perhaps from dictates of prudence, but more likely through the strange, resigned apathy of half-savage womankind. From early morning she was to be seen on the paths amongst the houses – by the riverside or on the jetties, the tray of pastry, it was her mission to sell, skilfully balanced on her head. During the great heat of the day she usually sought refuge in Almayer's campong, often finding shelter in a shady corner of the verandah, where she squatted with her tray before her, when invited by Nina. For 'Mem Putih' she had always a smile, but the presence of Mrs Almayer, the very sound of her shrill voice, was the signal for a hurried departure.

To this girl Nina often spoke; the other inhabitants of Sambir seldom or never heard the sound of her voice. They got used to the silent figure moving in their midst calm and white-robed, a being from another world and incomprehensible to them. Yet Nina's life for all her outward composure, for all the seeming detachment from the things and people surrounding her, was far from quiet, in consequence of Mrs Almayer being much too active for the happiness and even safety of the household. She had resumed some intercourse with Lakamba, not personally, it is true (for the dignity of that potentate kept him inside his stockade), but through the agency of that potentate's prime minister, harbour master, financial adviser and general factotum. That gentleman – of Sulu origin – was certainly endowed with statesmanlike qualities, although he was totally devoid of personal charms. In truth he was perfectly repulsive, possessing only one eye and a pockmarked face, with nose and lips horribly disfigured by the smallpox. This unengaging individual often strolled in unofficial costume, composed of a piece of pink calico round his waist, into Almayer's garden. There at the back of the house, squatting on his heels on scattered embers, in close proximity to the great iron boiler, where the family daily rice was being cooked by the women under Mrs Almayer's superintendence, did that astute negotiator carry on long conversations in Sulu language with Almayer's wife. What the subject of their discourses was might have been guessed from the subsequent domestic scenes by Almayer's hearthstone.

Of late Almayer had taken to excursions up the river. In a small canoe with two paddlers and the faithful Ali for a steersman he would disappear for a few days at a time. All his movements were no doubt closely watched by Lakamba and Abdulla, for the man once in the confidence of Rajah Laut was supposed to be in possession of valuable secrets. The coast population of Borneo believes implicitly in diamonds of fabulous value, in gold mines of enormous richness in the interior. And all those imaginings are heightened by the difficulty of penetrating far inland, especially on the north-east coast, where the Malays and the river tribes of Dyaks or head-hunters are eternally quarrelling. It is true enough that some gold reaches the coast in the hands of those Dyaks when, during short periods of truce in the desultory warfare, they visit the coast settlements of Malays. And so the wildest exaggerations are built up and added to on the slight basis of that fact.

Almayer in his quality of white man – as Lingard before him – had somewhat better relations with the up-river tribes. Yet even his excursions were not without danger, and his returns were eagerly looked for by the impatient Lakamba. But every time the Rajah was disappointed. Vain were the conferences by the rice-pot of his factotum Babalatchi with the white man's wife. The white man himself was impenetrable – impenetrable to persuasion, coaxing, abuse; to soft words and shrill revilings; to desperate beseechings or murderous threats; for Mrs Almayer, in her extreme desire to persuade her husband into an alliance with Lakamba, played upon the whole gamut of passion. With her soiled robe wound tightly under the armpits across her lean bosom, her scant greyish hair tumbled in disorder over her projecting cheek-bones, in suppliant attitude, she depicted with shrill volubility the advantages of close union with a man so good and so fair dealing.

'Why don't you go to the Rajah?' she screamed. 'Why do you go back to those Dyaks in the great forest? They should be killed. You cannot kill them, you cannot; but our Rajah's men are brave! You tell the Rajah where the old white man's treasure is. Our Rajah is good! He is our very grandfather, Datu Besar![23] He will kill those wretched Dyaks, and you shall have half the treasure. Oh, Kaspar, tell where the treasure is! Tell me! Tell me out of the old man's surat[24] where you read so often at night.'

On those occasions Almayer sat with rounded shoulders bending to the blast of this domestic tempest, accentuating only each pause in the torrent of his wife's eloquence by an angry growl, 'There is no treasure! Go away, woman!' Exasperated by the sight of his patiently bent back, she would at last walk round so as to face him across the table, and clasping her robe with one hand she stretched the other lean arm and claw-like hand to emphasise, in a passion of anger and contempt, the rapid rush of scathing remarks and bitter cursings heaped on the head of the man unworthy to associate with brave Malay chiefs. It ended generally by Almayer rising slowly, his long pipe in hand, his face set into a look of inward pain, and walking away in silence. He descended the steps and plunged into the long grass on his way to the solitude of his new house, dragging his feet in a state of physical collapse from disgust and fear before that fury. She followed to the head of the steps, and sent the shafts of indiscriminate abuse after the retreating form. And each of those scenes was concluded by a piercing shriek, reaching him far away. 'You know, Kaspar, I am your wife! your own Christian wife after your own Blanda law!' For she knew that this was the bitterest thing of all; the greatest regret of that man's life.

All these scenes Nina witnessed unmoved. She might have been deaf, dumb, without any feeling as far as any expression of opinion went. Yet oft when her father had sought the refuge of the great dusty rooms of Almayer's Folly, and her mother, exhausted by rhetorical efforts, squatted wearily on her heels with her back against the leg of the table, Nina would approach her curiously, guarding her skirts from betel juice besprinkling the floor, and gaze down upon her as one might look into the quiescent crater of a volcano after a destructive eruption. Mrs Almayer's thoughts, after these scenes, were usually turned into a channel of childhood reminiscences, and she gave them utterance in a kind of monotonous recitative – slightly disconnected, but generally describing the glories of the Sultan of Sulu, his great splendour, his power, his great prowess; the fear which benumbed the hearts of white men at the sight of his swift piratical praus. And these muttered statements of her grandfather's might were mixed up with bits of later recollections, where the great fight with the 'White Devil's' brig and the convent life in Samarang[25] occupied the principal place. At that point she usually dropped the thread of her narrative, and pulling out the little brass cross, always suspended round her neck, she contemplated it with superstitious awe. That superstitious feeling connected with some vague talismanic properties of the little bit of metal, and the still more hazy but terrible notion of some bad Djinns and horrible torments invented, as she thought, for her especial punishment by the good Mother Superior in case of the loss of the above charm, were Mrs Almayer's only theological luggage for the stormy road of life. Mrs Almayer had at least something tangible to cling to, but Nina, brought up under the Protestant wing of the proper Mrs Vinck, had not even a little piece of brass to remind her of past teaching. And listening to the recital of those savage glories, those barbarous fights and savage feasting, to the story of deeds valorous, albeit somewhat bloodthirsty, where men of her mother's race shone far above the Orang Blanda, she felt herself irresistibly fascinated, and saw with vague surprise the narrow mantle of civilised morality, in which good-meaning people had wrapped her young soul, fall away and leave her shivering and helpless as if on the edge of some deep and unknown abyss. Strangest of all, this abyss did not frighten her when she was under the influence of the witch-like being she called her mother. She seemed to have forgotten in civilised surroundings her life before the time when Lingard had, so to speak, kidnapped her from Brow.[26] Since then she had had Christian teaching, social education, and a good glimpse of civilised life. Unfortunately her teachers did not understand her nature, and the education ended in a scene of humiliation, in an outburst of contempt from white people for her mixed blood. She had tasted the whole bitterness of it and remembered distinctly that the virtuous Mrs Vinck's indignation was not so much directed against the young man from the bank as against the innocent cause of that young man's infatuation. And there was also no doubt in her mind that the principal cause of Mrs Vinck's indignation was the thought that such a thing should happen in a white nest, where her snow-white doves, the two Misses Vinck, had just returned from Europe, to find shelter under the maternal wing, and there await the coming of irreproachable men of their destiny. Not even the thought of the money so painfully scraped together by Almayer, and so punctually sent for Nina's expenses, could dissuade Mrs Vinck from her virtuous resolve. Nina was sent away, and in truth the girl herself wanted to go, although a little frightened by the impending change. And now she had lived on the river for three years with a savage mother and a father walking about amongst pitfalls, with his head in the clouds, weak, irresolute and unhappy. She had lived a life devoid of all the decencies of civilisation, in miserable domestic conditions; she had breathed in the atmosphere of sordid plottings for gain, of the no less disgusting intrigues and crimes for lust or money; and those things, together with the domestic quarrels, were the only events of her three years' existence. She did not die from despair and disgust the first month, as she expected and almost hoped for. On the contrary, at the end of half a year it had seemed to her that she had known no other life. Her young mind having been unskilfully permitted to glance at better things, and then thrown back again into the hopeless quagmire of barbarism, full of strong and uncontrolled passions, had lost the power to discriminate. It seemed to Nina that there was no change and no difference. Whether they traded in brick godowns or on the muddy river bank; whether they reached after much or little; whether they made love under the shadows of the great trees or in the shadow of the cathedral on the Singapore promenade; whether they plotted for their own ends under the protection of laws and according to the rules of Christian conduct, or whether they sought the gratification of their desires with the savage cunning and the unrestrained fierceness of natures as innocent of culture as their own immense and gloomy forests, Nina saw only the same manifestations of love and hate and of sordid greed chasing the uncertain dollar in all its multifarious and vanishing shapes. To her resolute nature, however, after all these years, the savage and uncompromising sincerity of purpose shown by her Malay kinsmen seemed at last preferable to the sleek hypocrisy, to the polite disguises, to the virtuous pretences of such white people as she had had the misfortune to come in contact with. After all it was her life; it was going to be her life, and so thinking she fell more and more under the influence of her mother. Seeking, in her ignorance, a better side to that life, she listened with avidity to the old woman's tales of the departed glories of the Rajahs, from whose race she had sprung, and she became gradually more indifferent, more contemptuous of the white side of her descent represented by a feeble and traditionless father.

Almayer's difficulties were by no means diminished by the girl's presence in Sambir. The stir caused by her arrival had died out, it is true, and Lakamba had not renewed his visits; but about a year after the departure of the man-of-war boats the nephew of Abdulla, Syed Reshid, returned from his pilgrimage to Mecca, rejoicing in a green jacket and the proud title of Hadji.[27] There was a great letting off of rockets on board the steamer which brought him in, and a great beating of drums all night in Abdulla's compound, while the feast of welcome was prolonged far into the small hours of the morning. Reshid was the favourite nephew and heir of Abdulla, and that loving uncle, meeting Almayer one day by the riverside, stopped politely to exchange civilities and to ask solemnly for an interview. Almayer suspected some attempt at a swindle, or at any rate something unpleasant, but of course consented with a great show of rejoicing. Accordingly the next evening, after sunset, Abdulla came, accompanied by several other grey-beards and by his nephew. That young man – of a very rakish and dissipated appearance – affected the greatest indifference as to the whole of the proceedings. When the torch-bearers had grouped themselves below the steps, and the visitors had seated themselves on various lame chairs, Reshid stood apart in the shadow, examining his aristocratically small hands with great attention. Almayer, surprised by the great solemnity of his visitors, perched himself on the corner of the table with a characteristic want of dignity quickly noted by the Arabs with grave disapproval. But Abdulla spoke now, looking straight past Almayer at the red curtain hanging in the doorway, where a slight tremor disclosed the presence of women on the other side. He began by neatly complimenting Almayer upon the long years they had dwelt together in cordial neighbourhood, and called upon Allah to give him many more years to gladden the eyes of his friends by his welcome presence. He made a polite allusion to the great consideration shown him (Almayer) by the Dutch 'Commissie',[28] and drew thence the flattering inference of Almayer's great importance amongst his own people. He – Abdulla – was also important amongst all the Arabs, and his nephew Reshid would be heir of that social position and of great riches. Now Reshid was a Hadji. He was possessor of several Malay women, went on Abdulla, but it was time he had a favourite wife, the first of the four allowed by the Prophet.[29] And, speaking with well-bred politeness, he explained further to the dumbfounded Almayer that, if he would consent to the alliance of his offspring with that true believer and virtuous man Reshid, she would be the mistress of all the splendours of Reshid's house, and first wife of the first Arab in the Islands, when he – Abdulla – was called to the joys of Paradise by Allah the All-merciful. 'You know, Tuan,' he said, in conclusion, 'the other women would be her slaves, and Reshid's house is great. From Bombay he has brought great divans, and costly carpets, and European furniture. There is also a great looking-glass in a frame shining like gold. What could a girl want more?' And while Almayer looked upon him in silent dismay Abdulla spoke in a more confidential tone, waving his attendants away, and finished his speech by pointing out the material advantages of such an alliance, and offering to settle upon Almayer three thousand dollars as a sign of his sincere friendship and the price of the girl.

Poor Almayer was nearly having a fit. Burning with the desire of taking Abdulla by the throat, he had but to think of his helpless position in the midst of lawless men to comprehend the necessity of diplomatic conciliation. He mastered his impulses, and spoke politely and coldly, saying the girl was young and was the apple of his eye. Tuan Reshid, a Faithful and a Hadji, would not want an infidel woman in his harem; and, seeing Abdulla smile sceptically at that last objection, he remained silent, not trusting himself to speak more, not daring to refuse point-blank, nor yet to say anything compromising. Abdulla understood the meaning of that silence, and rose to take leave with a grave salaam.[30] He wished his friend Almayer 'a thousand years', and moved down the steps, helped dutifully by Reshid. The torch-bearers shook their torches, scattering a shower of sparks into the river, and the cortège moved off, leaving Almayer agitated but greatly relieved by their departure. He dropped into a chair and watched the glimmer of the lights amongst the tree trunks till they disappeared and complete silence succeeded the tramp of feet and the murmur of voices. He did not move till the curtain rustled and Nina came out on the verandah and sat in the rocking-chair, where she used to spend many hours every day. She gave a slight rocking motion to her seat, leaning back with half-closed eyes, her long hair shading her face from the smoky light of the lamp on the table. Almayer looked at her furtively, but the face was as impassible as ever. She turned her head slightly towards her father, and speaking, to his great surprise, in English, asked, 'Was that Abdulla here?'

'Yes,' said Almayer – 'just gone.'

'And what did he want, father?'

'He wanted to buy you for Reshid,' answered Almayer, brutally, his anger getting the better of him, and looking at the girl as if in expectation of some outbreak of feeling. But Nina remained apparently unmoved, gazing dreamily into the black night outside.

'Be careful, Nina,' said Almayer, after a short silence and rising from his chair, 'when you go paddling alone into the creeks in your canoe. That Reshid is a violent scoundrel, and there is no saying what he may do. Do you hear me?'

She was standing now, ready to go in, one hand grasping the curtain in the doorway. She turned round, throwing her heavy tresses back by a sudden gesture.

'Do you think he would dare?' she asked, quickly, and then turned again to go in, adding in a lower tone, 'He would not dare. Arabs are all cowards.'

Almayer looked after her, astonished. He did not seek the repose of his hammock. He walked the floor absently, sometimes stopping by the balustrade to think. The lamp went out. The first streak of dawn broke over the forest; Almayer shivered in the damp air. 'I give it up,' he muttered to himself, lying down wearily. 'Damn those women! Well! If the girl did not look as if she wanted to be kidnapped!'

And he felt a nameless fear creep into his heart, making him shiver again.

Chapter 4

That year, towards the breaking up of the south-west monsoon, disquieting rumours reached Sambir. Captain Ford, coming up to Almayer's house for an evening's chat, brought late numbers of the *Straits Times* giving news of the Acheen War[31] and of the unsuccessful Dutch expedition. The Nakhodas[32] of the rare trading praus ascending the river paid visits to Lakamba, discussing with that potentate the unsettled state of affairs, and wagged their heads gravely over the recital of Orang Blanda exaction, severity and general tyranny, as exemplified in the total stoppage of gunpowder trade and the rigorous visiting of all suspicious craft trading in the straits of Macassar. Even the loyal soul of Lakamba was stirred into a state of inward discontent by the withdrawal of his licence for powder and by the abrupt confiscation of one hundred and fifty barrels of that commodity by the gunboat *Princess Amelia*, when, after a hazardous voyage, it had almost reached the mouth of the river. The unpleasant news was given him by Reshid, who, after the unsuccessful issue of his matrimonial projects, had made a long voyage amongst the islands for trading purposes; had bought the powder for his friend, and was overhauled and deprived of it on his return when actually congratulating himself on his acuteness in avoiding detection. Reshid's wrath was principally directed against Almayer, whom he suspected of having notified the Dutch authorities of the desultory warfare carried on by the Arabs and the Rajah with the up-river Dyak tribes.

To Reshid's great surprise the Rajah received his complaints very coldly, and showed no signs of vengeful disposition towards the white man. In truth, Lakamba knew very well that Almayer was perfectly innocent of any meddling in state affairs; and besides, his attitude towards that much persecuted individual was wholly changed in consequence of a reconciliation effected between him and his old enemy by Almayer's newly-found friend, Dain Maroola.

Almayer had now a friend. Shortly after Reshid's departure on his commercial journey, Nina, drifting slowly with the tide in the canoe on her return home after one of her solitary excursions, heard in one of the small creeks a splashing, as if of heavy ropes dropping in the water, and the prolonged song of Malay seamen when some heavy pulling is to be done. Through the thick fringe of bushes hiding the mouth of the creek

she saw the tall spars of some European-rigged sailing vessel over-
topping the summits of the nipa palms.[33] A brig was being hauled out of
the small creek into the main stream. The sun had set, and during the
short moments of twilight Nina saw the brig, aided by the evening
breeze and the flowing tide, head towards Sambir under her set foresail.
The girl turned her canoe out of the main river into one of the many
narrow channels amongst the wooded islets, and paddled vigorously
over the black and sleepy backwaters towards Sambir. Her canoe
brushed the water-palms, skirted the short spaces of muddy bank where
sedate alligators looked at her with lazy unconcern, and, just as darkness
was setting in, shot out into the broad junction of the two main branches
of the river, where the brig was already at anchor with sails furled, yards
squared, and decks seemingly untenanted by any human being. Nina
had to cross the river and pass pretty close to the brig in order to reach
home on the low promontory between the two branches of the Pantai.
Up both branches, in the houses built on the banks and over the water,
the lights twinkled already, reflected in the still waters below. The hum
of voices, the occasional cry of a child, the rapid and abruptly interrupted
roll of a wooden drum, together with some distant hailing in the
darkness by the returning fishermen, reached her over the broad
expanse of the river. She hesitated a little before crossing, the sight of
such an unusual object as an European-rigged vessel causing her some
uneasiness, but the river in its wide expansion was dark enough to
render a small canoe invisible. She urged her small craft with swift
strokes of her paddle, kneeling in the bottom and bending forward to
catch any suspicious sound while she steered towards the little jetty of
Lingard and Co., to which the strong light of the paraffin lamp shining
on the whitewashed verandah of Almayer's bungalow served as a
convenient guide. The jetty itself, under the shadow of the bank
overgrown by drooping bushes, was hidden in darkness. Before even
she could see it she heard the hollow bumping of a large boat against its
rotten posts, and heard also the murmur of whispered conversation in
that boat whose white paint and great dimensions, faintly visible on
nearer approach, made her rightly guess that it belonged to the brig just
anchored. Stopping her course by a rapid motion of her paddle, with
another swift stroke she sent it whirling away from the wharf and
steered for a little rivulet which gave access to the back courtyard of the
house. She landed at the muddy head of the creek and made her way
towards the house over the trodden grass of the courtyard. To the left,
from the cooking shed, shone a red glare through the banana plantation
she skirted, and the noise of feminine laughter reached her from there

in the silent evening. She rightly judged her mother was not near, laughter and Mrs Almayer not being close neighbours. She must be in the house, thought Nina, as she ran lightly up the inclined plane of shaky planks leading to the back door of the narrow passage dividing the house in two. Outside the doorway, in the black shadow, stood the faithful Ali.

'Who is there?' asked Nina.

'A great Malay man has come,' answered Ali, in a tone of suppressed excitement. 'He is a rich man. There are six men with lances. Real Soldat, you understand. And his dress is very brave. I have seen his dress. It shines! What jewels! Don't go there, Mem Nina. Tuan said not; but the old Mem is gone. Tuan will be angry. Merciful Allah! what jewels that man has got!'

Nina slipped past the outstretched hand of the slave into the dark passage where, in the crimson glow of the hanging curtain, close by its other end, she could see a small dark form crouching near the wall. Her mother was feasting her eyes and ears with what was taking place on the front verandah, and Nina approached to take her share in the rare pleasure of some novelty. She was met by her mother's extended arm and by a low murmured warning not to make a noise.

'Have you seen them, mother?' asked Nina, in a breathless whisper.

Mrs Almayer turned her face towards the girl, and her sunken eyes shone strangely in the red half-light of the passage.

'I saw him,' she said, in an almost inaudible tone, pressing her daughter's hand with her bony fingers. 'A great Rajah has come to Sambir – a Son of Heaven,' muttered the old woman to herself. 'Go away, girl!'

The two women stood close to the curtain, Nina wishing to approach the rent in the stuff, and her mother defending the position with angry obstinacy. On the other side there was a lull in the conversation, but the breathing of several men, the occasional light tinkling of some ornaments, the clink of metal scabbards, or of brass siri vessels[34] passed from hand to hand, was audible during the short pause. The women struggled silently, when there was a shuffling noise and the shadow of Almayer's burly form fell on the curtain.

The women ceased struggling and remained motionless. Almayer had stood up to answer his guest, turning his back to the doorway, unaware of what was going on on the other side. He spoke in a tone of regretful irritation.

'You have come to the wrong house, Tuan Maroola, if you want to trade as you say. I was a trader once, not now, whatever you may have heard about me in Macassar. And if you want anything, you will not find it here; I have nothing to give, and want nothing myself. You should go to the Rajah here; you can see in the daytime his houses across the river, there, where those fires are burning on the shore. He will help you and trade with you. Or, better still, go to the Arabs over there,' he went on bitterly, pointing with his hand towards the houses of Sambir. 'Abdulla is the man you want. There is nothing he would not buy, and there is nothing he would not sell; believe me, I know him well.'

He waited for an answer a short time, then added, 'All that I have said is true, and there is nothing more.'

Nina, held back by her mother, heard a soft voice reply with a calm evenness of intonation peculiar to the better-class Malays, 'Who would doubt a white Tuan's words? A man seeks his friends where his heart tells him. Is this not true also? I have come, although so late, for I have something to say which you may be glad to hear. Tomorrow I will go to the Sultan; a trader wants the friendship of great men. Then I shall return here to speak serious words, if Tuan permits. I shall not go to the Arabs; their lies are very great! What are they? Chelakka!'[35]

Almayer's voice sounded a little more pleasantly in reply.

'Well, as you like. I can hear you tomorrow at any time if you have anything to say. Bah! After you have seen the Sultan Lakamba you will not want to return here, Inchi Dain.[36] You will see. Only mind, I will have nothing to do with Lakamba. You may tell him so. What is your business with me, after all?'

'Tomorrow we talk, Tuan, now I know you,' answered the Malay. 'I speak English a little, so we can talk and nobody will understand, and then – ' He interrupted himself suddenly, asking surprised, 'What's that noise, Tuan?'

Almayer had also heard the increasing noise of the scuffle recommenced on the women's side of the curtain. Evidently Nina's strong curiosity was on the point of overcoming Mrs Almayer's exalted sense of social proprieties. Hard breathing was distinctly audible, and the curtain shook during the contest, which was mainly physical, although Mrs Almayer's voice was heard in angry remonstrance with its usual want of strictly logical reasoning, but with the well-known richness of invective.

'You shameless woman! Are you a slave?' shouted shrilly the irate matron. 'Veil your face, abandoned wretch! You white snake, I will not let you!'

Almayer's face expressed annoyance and also doubt as to the

advisability of interfering between mother and daughter. He glanced at his Malay visitor, who was waiting silently for the end of the uproar in an attitude of amused expectation, and waving his hand contemptuously he murmured, 'It is nothing. Some women.'

The Malay nodded his head gravely, and his face assumed an expression of serene indifference, as etiquette demanded after such an explanation. The contest was ended behind the curtain, and evidently the younger will had its way, for the rapid shuffle and click of Mrs Almayer's high-heeled sandals died away in the distance. The tranquillised master of the house was going to resume the conversation when, struck by an unexpected change in the expression of his guest's countenance, he turned his head and saw Nina standing in the doorway.

After Mrs Almayer's retreat from the field of battle, Nina, with a contemptuous exclamation, 'It's only a trader,' had lifted the conquered curtain and now stood in full light, framed in the dark background of the passage, her lips slightly parted, her hair in disorder after the exertion, the angry gleam not yet faded out of her glorious and sparkling eyes. She took in at a glance the group of white-clad lancemen standing motionless in the shadow of the far-off end of the verandah, and her gaze rested curiously on the chief of that imposing cortège. He stood, almost facing her, a little to one side, and struck by the beauty of the unexpected apparition had bent low, elevating his joint hands above his head in a sign of respect accorded by Malays only to the great of this earth. The crude light of the lamp shone on the gold embroidery of his black silk jacket, broke in a thousand sparkling rays on the jewelled hilt of his kriss protruding from under the many folds of the red sarong gathered into a sash round his waist, and played on the precious stones of the many rings on his dark fingers. He straightened himself up quickly after the low bow, putting his hand with a graceful ease on the hilt of his heavy short sword ornamented with brilliantly dyed fringes of horsehair. Nina, hesitating on the threshold, saw an erect lithe figure of medium height with a breadth of shoulder suggesting great power. Under the folds of a blue turban, whose fringed ends hung gracefully over the left shoulder, was a face full of determination and expressing a reckless good-humour, not devoid, however, of some dignity. The squareness of the lower jaw, the full red lips, the mobile nostrils, and the proud carriage of the head gave the impression of a being half-savage, untamed, perhaps cruel, and corrected the liquid softness of the almost feminine eye, that general characteristic of the race. Now, the first surprise over, Nina saw those eyes fixed upon her with such an uncontrolled expression of admiration and desire that she felt a hitherto unknown feeling of shyness, mixed with alarm and some delight, enter and penetrate her whole being.

Confused by those unusual sensations she stopped in the doorway and instinctively drew the lower part of the curtain across her face, leaving exposed only half a rounded cheek, a stray tress and one eye, wherewith to contemplate the gorgeous and bold being so unlike in appearance to the rare specimens of traders she had seen before on that same verandah.

Dain Maroola, dazzled by the unexpected vision, forgot the confused Almayer, forgot his brig, his escort staring in open-mouthed admiration, the object of his visit and all things else, in his overpowering desire to prolong the contemplation of so much loveliness met so suddenly in such an unlikely place – as he thought.

'It is my daughter,' said Almayer, in an embarrassed manner. 'It is of no consequence. White women have their customs, as you know, Tuan, having travelled much, as you say. However, it is late; we will finish our talk tomorrow.'

Dain bent low trying to convey in a last glance towards the girl the bold expression of his overwhelming admiration. The next minute he was shaking Almayer's hand with grave courtesy, his face wearing a look of stolid unconcern as to any feminine presence. His men filed off, and he followed them quickly, closely attended by a thickset, savage-looking Sumatrese he had introduced before as the commander of his brig. Nina walked to the balustrade of the verandah and saw the sheen of moonlight on the steel spear-heads and heard the rhythmic jingle of brass anklets as the men moved in single file towards the jetty. The boat shoved off after a little while, looming large in the full light of the moon, a black shapeless mass in the slight haze hanging over the water. Nina fancied she could distinguish the graceful figure of the trader standing erect in the stern sheets, but in a little while all the outlines got blurred, confused, and soon disappeared in the folds of white vapour shrouding the middle of the river.

Almayer had approached his daughter, and, leaning with both arms over the rail, was looking moodily down on the heap of rubbish and broken bottles at the foot of the verandah.

'What was all that noise just now?' he growled peevishly, without looking up. 'Confound you and your mother! What did she want? What did you come out for?'

'She did not want to let me come out,' said Nina. 'She is angry. She says the man just gone is some Rajah. I think she is right now.'

'I believe all you women are crazy,' snarled Almayer. 'What's that to you, to her, to anybody? The man wants to collect trepang[37] and birds' nests on the islands. He told me so, that Rajah of yours. He will come tomorrow. I want you both to keep away from the house, and let me attend to my business in peace.'

Dain Maroola came the next day and had a long conversation with Almayer. This was the beginning of a close and friendly intercourse which, at first, was much remarked in Sambir, till the population got used to the frequent sight of many fires burning in Almayer's campong, where Maroola's men were warming themselves during the cold nights of the north-east monsoon, while their master had long conferences with the Tuan[38] Putih – as they styled Almayer amongst themselves. Great was the curiosity in Sambir on the subject of the new trader. Had he seen the Sultan? What did the Sultan say? Had he given any presents? What would he sell? What would he buy? Those were the questions broached eagerly by the inhabitants of bamboo houses built over the river. Even in more substantial buildings, in Abdulla's house, in the residences of principal traders, Arab, Chinese and Bugis,[39] the excitement ran high, and lasted many days. With inborn suspicion they would not believe the simple account of himself the young trader was always ready to give. Yet it had all the appearance of truth. He said he was a trader, and sold rice. He did not want to buy gutta-percha or beeswax, because he intended to employ his numerous crew in collecting trepang on the coral reefs outside the river, and also in seeking for birds' nests on the mainland. Those two articles he professed himself ready to buy if there were any to be obtained in that way. He said he was from Bali, and a Brahmin,[40] which last statement he made good by refusing all food during his often repeated visits to Lakamba's and Almayer's houses. To Lakamba he went generally at night and had long audiences. Babalatchi, who was always a third party at those meetings of potentate and trader, knew how to resist all attempts on the part of the curious to ascertain the subject of so many long talks. When questioned with languid courtesy by the grave Abdulla he sought refuge in a vacant stare of his one eye, and in the affectation of extreme simplicity.

'I am only my master's slave,' murmured Babalatchi, in a hesitating manner. Then as if making up his mind suddenly for a reckless confidence he would inform Abdulla of some transaction in rice, repeating the words, 'A hundred big bags the Sultan bought; a hundred, Tuan!' in a tone of mysterious solemnity. Abdulla, firmly persuaded of the existence of some more important dealings, received, however, the information with all the signs of respectful astonishment. And the two would separate, the Arab cursing inwardly the wily dog, while Babalatchi went on his way walking on the dusty path, his body swaying, his chin with its few grey hairs pushed forward, resembling an inquisitive goat bent on some unlawful expedition. Attentive eyes watched his movements. Jim-Eng, descrying Babalatchi far away, would shake off the stupor of an habitual opium smoker and, tottering on to the middle of the road, would await the approach of that important person, ready with his hospitable invitation. But Babalatchi's discretion was proof even against the combined assaults of good fellowship and of strong gin generously administered by the open-hearted Chinaman. Jim-Eng, owning himself beaten, was left uninformed with the empty bottle, and gazed sadly after the departing form of the statesman of Sambir pursuing his devious and unsteady way, which, as usual, led him to Almayer's compound. Ever since a reconciliation had been effected by Dain Maroola between his white friend and the Rajah, the one-eyed diplomatist had again become a frequent guest in the Dutchman's house. To Almayer's great disgust he was to be seen there at all times, strolling about in an abstracted kind of way on the verandah, skulking in the passages, or else popping round unexpected corners, always willing to engage Mrs Almayer in confidential conversation. He was very shy of the master himself, as if suspicious that the pent-up feelings of the white man towards his person might find vent in a sudden kick. But the cooking shed was his favourite place, and he became an habitual guest there, squatting for hours amongst the busy women, with his chin resting on his knees, his lean arms clasped round his legs, and his one eye roving uneasily – the very picture of watchful ugliness. Almayer wanted more than once to complain to Lakamba of his Prime Minister's intrusion, but Dain dissuaded him. 'We cannot say a word here that he does not hear,' growled Almayer.

'Then come and talk on board the brig,' retorted Dain, with a quiet smile. 'It is good to let the man come here. Lakamba thinks he knows much. Perhaps the Sultan thinks I want to run away. Better let the one-eyed crocodile sun himself in your campong, Tuan.'

And Almayer assented unwillingly muttering vague threats of personal violence, while he eyed malevolently the aged statesman sitting with quiet obstinacy by his domestic rice-pot.

Chapter 5

At last the excitement had died out in Sambir. The inhabitants got used to the sight of comings and goings between Almayer's house and the vessel, now moored to the opposite bank, and speculation as to the feverish activity displayed by Almayer's boatmen in repairing old canoes ceased to interfere with the due discharge of domestic duties by the women of the settlement. Even the baffled Jim-Eng left off troubling his muddled brain with secrets of trade, and relapsed by the aid of his opium pipe into a state of stupefied bliss, letting Babalatchi pursue his way past his house uninvited and seemingly unnoticed.

So on that warm afternoon, when the deserted river sparkled under the vertical sun, the statesman of Sambir could, without any hindrance from friendly enquirers, shove off his little canoe from under the bushes, where it was usually hidden during his visits to Almayer's compound. Slowly and languidly Babalatchi paddled, crouching low in the boat, making himself small under his enormous sun hat to escape the scorching heat reflected from the water. He was not in a hurry; his master, Lakamba, was surely reposing at this time of the day. He would have ample time to cross over and greet him on his waking with important news. Will he be displeased? Will he strike his ebony wood staff angrily on the floor, frightening him by the incoherent violence of his exclamations; or will he squat down with a good-humoured smile, and, rubbing his hands gently over his stomach with a familiar gesture, expectorate copiously into the brass siri-vessel, giving vent to a low, approbative murmur? Such were Babalatchi's thoughts as he skilfully handled his paddle, crossing the river on his way to the Rajah's campong, whose stockades showed from behind the dense foliage of the bank just opposite to Almayer's bungalow.

Indeed, he had a report to make. Something certain at last to confirm the daily tale of suspicions, the daily hints of familiarity, of stolen glances he had seen, of short and burning words he had overheard exchanged between Dain Maroola and Almayer's daughter.

Lakamba had, till then, listened to it all, calmly and with evident distrust; now he was going to be convinced, for Babalatchi had the proof; had it this very morning, when fishing at break of day in the creek over which stood Bulangi's house. There from his skiff he saw Nina's long canoe drift past, the girl sitting in the stern bending over

Dain, who was stretched in the bottom with his head resting on the girl's knees. He saw it. He followed them, but in a short time they took to the paddles and got away from under his observant eye. A few minutes afterwards he saw Bulangi's slave-girl paddling in a small dug-out to the town with her cakes for sale. She also had seen them in the grey dawn. And Babalatchi grinned confidentially to himself at the recollection of the slave-girl's discomposed face, of the hard look in her eyes, of the tremble in her voice, when answering his questions. That little Taminah evidently admired Dain Maroola. That was good! And Babalatchi laughed aloud at the notion; then becoming suddenly serious, he began by some strange association of ideas to speculate upon the price for which Bulangi would, possibly, sell the girl. He shook his head sadly at the thought that Bulangi was a hard man, and had refused one hundred dollars for that same Taminah only a few weeks ago; then he became suddenly aware that the canoe had drifted too far down during his meditation. He shook off the despondency caused by the certitude of Bulangi's mercenary disposition, and, taking up his paddle, in a few strokes sheered alongside the water-gate of the Rajah's house.

That afternoon Almayer, as was his wont lately, moved about on the waterside, overlooking the repairs to his boats. He had decided at last. Guided by the scraps of information contained in old Lingard's pocketbook, he was going to seek for the rich gold-mine, for that place where he had only to stoop to gather up an immense fortune and realise the dream of his young days. To obtain the necessary help he had shared his knowledge with Dain Maroola, he had consented to be reconciled with Lakamba, who gave his support to the enterprise on condition of sharing the profits; he had sacrificed his pride, his honour and his loyalty in the face of the enormous risk of his undertaking, dazzled by the greatness of the results to be achieved by this alliance so distasteful yet so necessary. The dangers were great, but Maroola was brave; his men seemed as reckless as their chief, and with Lakamba's aid success seemed assured.

For the last fortnight Almayer was absorbed in the preparations, walking amongst his workmen and slaves in a kind of waking trance, where practical details as to the fitting out of the boats were mixed up with vivid dreams of untold wealth, where the present misery of the burning sun, of the muddy and malodorous riverbank disappeared in a gorgeous vision of a splendid future existence for himself and Nina. He hardly saw Nina during these last days, although the beloved daughter was ever present in his thoughts. He hardly took notice of Dain, whose constant presence in his house had become a matter of course to him now they were connected by a community of interests. When meeting the young chief he gave him an absent greeting and passed on, seemingly wishing to avoid him, bent upon forgetting the hated reality of the present by absorbing himself in his work, or else by letting his imagination soar far above the tree tops into the great white clouds away to the westward, where the paradise of Europe was awaiting the future Eastern millionaire. And Maroola, now the bargain was struck and there was no more business to be talked over, evidently did not care for the white man's company. Yet Dain was always about the house, but he seldom stayed long by the riverside. On his daily visits to the white man the Malay chief preferred to make his way quietly through the central passage of the house, and would come out into the garden at the back, where the fire was burning in the cooking shed, with the rice kettle swinging over it, under the watchful supervision of Mrs Almayer. Avoiding that shed, with its black smoke and the warbling of soft, feminine voices, Dain would turn to the left. There, on the edge of a banana plantation, a clump of palms and mango trees formed a shady spot, a few scattered bushes giving it a certain seclusion into which only the serving women's chatter or an occasional burst of laughter could penetrate. Once in, he was invisible; and hidden there, leaning against the smooth trunk of a tall palm, he waited with gleaming eyes and an assured smile to hear the faint rustle of dried grass under the light footsteps of Nina.

From the very first moment when his eyes beheld this – to him – perfection of loveliness he felt in his inmost heart the conviction that she would be his; he felt the subtle breath of mutual understanding passing between their two savage natures, and he did not want Mrs Almayer's encouraging smiles to take every opportunity of approaching the girl; and every time he spoke to her, every time he looked into her eyes, Nina, although averting her face, felt as if this bold-looking being who spoke burning words into her willing ear was the embodiment of her fate, the creature of her dreams – reckless, ferocious, ready with flashing kriss for his enemies, and with passionate embrace for his beloved – the ideal Malay chief of her mother's tradition.

She recognised with a thrill of delicious fear the mysterious consciousness of her identity with that being. Listening to his words, it seemed to her she was born only then to a knowledge of a new existence, that her life was complete only when near him, and she abandoned herself to a feeling of dreamy happiness, while with half-veiled face and in silence – as became a Malay girl – she listened to Dain's words giving up to her the whole treasure of love and passion his nature was capable of with all the unrestrained enthusiasm of a man totally untrammelled by any influence of civilised self-discipline.

And they used to pass many a delicious and fast-fleeting hour under the mango trees behind the friendly curtain of bushes till Mrs Almayer's shrill voice gave the signal of unwilling separation. Mrs Almayer had undertaken the easy task of watching her husband lest he should interrupt the smooth course of her daughter's love affair, in which she took a great and benignant interest. She was happy and proud to see Dain's infatuation, believing him to be a great and powerful chief, and she found also a gratification of her mercenary instincts in Dain's open-handed generosity.

On the eve of the day when Babalatchi's suspicions were confirmed by ocular demonstration, Dain and Nina had remained longer than usual in their shady retreat. Only Almayer's heavy step on the verandah and his querulous clamour for food decided Mrs Almayer to lift a warning cry. Maroola leaped lightly over the low bamboo fence, and made his way stealthily through the banana plantation down to the muddy shore of the back creek, while Nina walked slowly towards the house to minister to her father's wants, as was her wont every evening. Almayer felt happy enough that evening; the preparations were nearly completed; tomorrow he would launch his boats. In his mind's eye he saw the rich prize in his grasp; and, with tin spoon in his hand, he was forgetting the plateful of rice before him in the fanciful arrangement of some splendid banquet to take place on his arrival in Amsterdam. Nina, reclining in the long chair, listened absently to the few disconnected words escaping from her father's lips. Expedition! Gold! What did she care for all that? But at the name of Maroola mentioned by her father she was all attention. Dain was going down the river with his brig tomorrow to remain away for a few days, said Almayer. It was very annoying, this delay. As soon as Dain returned they would have to start without loss of time, for the river was rising. He would not be surprised if a great flood was coming. And he pushed away his plate with an impatient gesture on rising from the table. But now Nina heard him not. Dain going away! That's why he had ordered her, with that quiet masterfulness it was her delight to obey, to meet him at break of day in Bulangi's creek. Was there a paddle in her canoe? she thought. Was it ready? She would have to start early – at four in the morning, in a very few hours.

She rose from her chair, thinking she would require rest before the long pull in the early morning. The lamp was burning dimly, and her father, tired with the day's labour, was already in his hammock. Nina put the lamp out and passed into a large room she shared with her mother on the left of the central passage. Entering, she saw that Mrs Almayer had deserted the pile of mats serving her as bed in one corner of the room, and was now bending over the opened lid of her large wooden chest. Half a shell of coconut filled with oil, where a cotton rag floated for a wick, stood on the floor, surrounding her with a ruddy halo of light shining through the black and odorous smoke. Mrs Almayer's back was bent, and her head and shoulders hidden in the deep box. Her hands rummaged in the interior, where a soft clink as of silver money could be heard. She did not notice at first her daughter's approach, and Nina, standing silently by her, looked down on many little canvas bags ranged in the bottom of the chest, wherefrom her mother extracted handfuls of shining guilders and Mexican dollars, letting them stream slowly back again through her claw-like fingers. The music of tinkling silver seemed to delight her, and her eyes sparkled with the reflected gleam of freshly-minted coins. She was muttering to herself: 'And this, and this, and yet this! Soon he will give more – as much more as I ask. He is a great Rajah – a Son of Heaven! And she will be a Ranee – he gave all this for her! Who ever gave anything for me? I am a slave! Am I? I am the mother of a great Ranee!' She became aware suddenly of her daughter's presence, and ceased her droning, shutting the lid down violently; then, without rising from her crouching position, she looked up at the girl standing by with a vague smile on her dreamy face.

'You have seen? Have you?' she shouted, shrilly. 'That is all mine, and for you. It is not enough! He will have to give more before he takes you away to the southern island where his father is king. You hear me? You are worth more, granddaughter of Rajahs! More! More!'

The sleepy voice of Almayer was heard on the verandah recommending silence. Mrs Almayer extinguished the light and crept into her corner of the room. Nina lay down on her back on a pile of soft mats, her hands entwined under her head, gazing through the shutterless hole serving as a window at the stars twinkling on the black sky; she was awaiting the time to start for her appointed meeting-place. With quiet happiness she thought of that meeting in the great forest, far from all human eyes and sounds. Her soul, lapsing again into the savage mood, which the genius of civilisation working by the hand of Mrs Vinck could never destroy, experienced a feeling of pride and of some slight trouble at the high value her worldly-wise mother had put upon her person; but she remembered the expressive glances and words of Dain, and, tranquillised, she closed her eyes in a shiver of pleasant anticipation.

There are some situations where the barbarian and the, so-called,

civilised man meet upon the same ground. It may be supposed that
Dain Maroola was not exceptionally delighted with his prospective
mother-in-law, nor that he actually approved of that worthy woman's
appetite for shining dollars. Yet on that foggy morning when Babalatchi,
laying aside the cares of state, went to visit his fish-baskets in the Bulangi
creek, Maroola had no misgivings, experienced no feelings but those of
impatience and longing, when paddling to the east side of the island
forming the backwater in question. He hid his canoe in the bushes and
strode rapidly across the islet, pushing with impatience through the
twigs of heavy undergrowth intercrossed over his path. From motives
of prudence he would not take his canoe to the meeting-place, as Nina
had done. He had left it in the main stream till his return from the other
side of the island. The heavy warm fog was closing rapidly round him,
but he managed to catch a fleeting glimpse of a light away to the left,
proceeding from Bulangi's house. Then he could see nothing in the
thickening vapour, and kept to the path only by a sort of instinct, which
also led him to the very point on the opposite shore he wished to reach.
A great log had stranded there, at right angles to the bank, forming a
kind of jetty against which the swiftly flowing stream broke with a loud
ripple. He stepped on it with a quick but steady motion, and in two
strides found himself at the outer end, with the rush and swirl of the
foaming water at his feet.

Standing there alone, as if separated from the world; the heavens,
earth, the very water roaring under him swallowed up in the thick veil
of the morning fog, he breathed out the name of Nina before him into
the apparently limitless space, sure of being heard, instinctively sure of
the nearness of the delightful creature; certain of her being aware of his
near presence as he was aware of hers.

The bow of Nina's canoe loomed up close to the log, canted high out
of the water by the weight of the sitter in the stern. Maroola laid his
hand on the stem and leaped lightly in, giving it a vigorous shove off.
The light craft, obeying the new impulse, cleared the log by a hair's
breadth, and the river, with obedient complicity, swung it broadside to
the current, and bore it off silently and rapidly between the invisible
banks. And once more Dain, at the feet of Nina, forgot the world, felt
himself carried away helpless by a great wave of supreme emotion, by a
rush of joy, pride and desire; understood once more with overpowering
certitude that there was no life possible without that being he held
clasped in his arms with passionate strength in a prolonged embrace.

Nina disengaged herself gently with a low laugh.

'You will overturn the boat, Dain,' she whispered.

He looked into her eyes eagerly for a minute and let her go with a sigh, then lying down in the canoe he put his head on her knees, gazing upwards and stretching his arms backwards till his hands met round the girl's waist. She bent over him, and, shaking her head, framed both their faces in the falling locks of her long black hair.

And so they drifted on, he speaking with all the rude eloquence of a savage nature giving itself up without restraint to an over-mastering passion, she bending low to catch the murmur of words sweeter to her than life itself. To those two nothing existed then outside the gunwales of the narrow and fragile craft. It was their world, filled with their intense and all-absorbing love. They took no heed of thickening mist, or of the breeze dying away before sunrise; they forgot the existence of the great forests surrounding them, of all the tropical nature awaiting the advent of the sun in a solemn and impressive silence.

Over the low river-mist hiding the boat with its freight of young passionate life and all-forgetful happiness, the stars paled, and a silvery-grey tint crept over the sky from the eastward. There was not a breath of wind, not a rustle of stirring leaf, not a splash of leaping fish to disturb the serene repose of all living things on the banks of the great river. Earth, river and sky were wrapped up in a deep sleep, from which it seemed there would be no waking. All the seething life and movement of tropical nature seemed concentrated in the ardent eyes, in the tumultuously beating hearts of the two beings drifting in the canoe, under the white canopy of mist, over the smooth surface of the river.

Suddenly a great sheaf of yellow rays shot upwards from behind the black curtain of trees lining the banks of the Pantai. The stars went out; the little black clouds at the zenith glowed for a moment with crimson tints, and the thick mist, stirred by the gentle breeze, the sigh of waking nature, whirled round and broke into fantastically torn pieces, disclosing the wrinkled surface of the river sparkling in the broad light of day. Great flocks of white birds wheeled screaming above the swaying tree tops. The sun had risen on the east coast.

Dain was the first to return to the cares of everyday life. He rose and glanced rapidly up and down the river. His eye detected Babalatchi's boat astern, and another small black speck on the glittering water, which was Taminah's canoe. He moved cautiously forward, and, kneeling, took up a paddle; Nina at the stern took hers. They bent their bodies to the work, throwing up the water at every stroke, and the small craft went swiftly ahead, leaving a narrow wake fringed with a lace-like border of white and gleaming foam.

Without turning his head, Dain spoke. 'Somebody behind us, Nina. We must not let him gain. I think he is too far to recognise us.'

'Somebody before us also,' panted out Nina, without ceasing to paddle.

'I think I know,' rejoined Dain. 'The sun shines over there, but I fancy it is the girl Taminah. She comes down every morning to my brig to sell cakes – stays often all day. It does not matter; steer more into the bank; we must get under the bushes. My canoe is hidden not far from here.'

As he spoke his eyes watched the broad-leaved nipas which they were brushing in their swift and silent course.

'Look out, Nina,' he said at last; 'there, where the water palms end and the twigs hang down under the leaning tree. Steer for the big green branch.'

He stood up attentive, and the boat drifted slowly inshore, Nina guiding it by a gentle and skilful movement of her paddle. When near enough Dain laid hold of the big branch, and leaning back shot the canoe under a low green archway of thickly matted creepers giving access to a miniature bay formed by the caving in of the bank during the last great flood. His own boat was there anchored by a stone, and he stepped into it, keeping his hand on the gunwale of Nina's canoe. In a moment the two little nutshells with their occupants floated quietly side by side, reflected by the black water in the dim light struggling through a high canopy of dense foliage; while above, away up in the broad day, flamed immense red blossoms sending down on their heads a shower of great dew-sparkling petals that descended rotating slowly in a continuous and perfumed stream; and over them, under them, in the sleeping water, all around them in a ring of luxuriant vegetation bathed in the warm air charged with strong and harsh perfumes, the intense work of tropical nature went on: plants shooting upward, entwined, interlaced in inextricable confusion, climbing madly and brutally over each other in the terrible silence of a desperate struggle towards the life-giving sunshine above – as if struck with sudden horror at the seething mass of corruption below, at the death and decay from which they sprang.

'We must part now,' said Dain, after a long silence. 'You must return at once, Nina. I will wait till the brig drifts down here, and shall get on board then.'

'And will you be long away, Dain?' asked Nina, in a low voice.

'Long!' exclaimed Dain. 'Would a man willingly remain long in a dark place? When I am not near you, Nina, I am like a man that is blind. What is life to me without light?'

Nina leaned over, and with a proud and happy smile took Dain's face between her hands, looking into his eyes with a fond yet questioning gaze. Apparently she found there the confirmation of the words just said, for a feeling of grateful security lightened for her the weight of sorrow at the hour of parting. She believed that he, the descendant of many great Rajahs, the son of a great chief, the master of life and death, knew the sunshine of life only in her presence. An immense wave of gratitude and love welled forth out of her heart towards him. How could she make an outward and visible sign of all she felt for the man who had filled her heart with so much joy and so much pride? And in the great tumult of passion, like a flash of lightning came to her the reminiscence of that despised and almost forgotten civilisation she had only glanced at in her days of restraint, of sorrow and of anger. In the cold ashes of that hateful and miserable past she would find the sign of love, the fitting expression of the boundless felicity of the present, the pledge of a bright and splendid future. She threw her arms around Dain's neck and pressed her lips to his in a long and burning kiss. He closed his eyes, surprised and frightened at the storm raised in his breast by the strange and to him hitherto unknown contact, and long after Nina had pushed her canoe into the river he remained motionless, without daring to open his eyes, afraid to lose the sensation of intoxicating delight he had tasted for the first time.

Now he wanted but immortality, he thought, to be the equal of gods, and the creature that could open so the gates of paradise must be his – soon would be his for ever!

He opened his eyes in time to see through the archway of creepers the bows of his brig come slowly into view, as the vessel drifted past on its way down the river. He must go on board now, he thought; yet he was loth to leave the place where he had learned to know what happiness meant. 'Time yet. Let them go,' he muttered to himself; and he closed his eyes again under the red shower of scented petals, trying to recall the scene with all its delight and all its fear.

He must have been able to join his brig in time, after all, and found much occupation outside, for it was in vain that Almayer looked for his friend's speedy return. The lower reach of the river where he so often and so impatiently directed his eyes remained deserted, save for the rapid flitting of some fishing canoe; but down the upper reaches came black clouds and heavy showers heralding the final setting in of the rainy season with its thunderstorms and great floods making the river almost impossible of ascent for native canoes.

Almayer, strolling along the muddy beach between his houses, watched uneasily the river rising inch by inch, creeping slowly nearer to the boats, now ready and hauled up in a row under the cover of dripping kajang-mats.[41] Fortune seemed to elude his grasp, and in his weary tramp backwards and forwards under the steady rain falling from the lowering sky, a sort of despairing indifference took possession of him. What did it matter? It was just his luck! Those two infernal savages, Lakamba and Dain, induced him, with their promises of help, to spend his last dollar in the fitting out of boats, and now one of them was gone somewhere, and the other shut up in his stockade would give no sign of life. No, not even the scoundrelly Babalatchi, thought Almayer, would show his face near him, now they had sold him all the rice, brass gongs and cloth necessary for his expedition. They had his very last coin, and did not care whether he went or stayed. And with a gesture of abandoned discouragement Almayer would climb up slowly to the verandah of his new house to get out of the rain, and leaning on the front rail with his head sunk between his shoulders he would abandon himself to the current of bitter thoughts, oblivious of the flight of time and the pangs of hunger, deaf to the shrill cries of his wife calling him to the evening meal. When, roused from his sad meditations by the first roll of the evening thunderstorm, he stumbled slowly towards the glimmering light of his old house, his half-dead hope made his ears preternaturally acute to any sound on the river. Several nights in succession he had heard the splash of paddles and had seen the indistinct form of a boat, but when hailing the shadowy apparition, his heart bounding with sudden hope of hearing Dain's voice, he was disappointed each time by the sulky answer conveying to him the intelligence that the Arabs were on the river, bound on a visit to the home-staying Lakamba. This caused him many sleepless nights, spent in speculating upon the kind of villainy those estimable personages were hatching now. At last, when all hope seemed dead, he was overjoyed on hearing Dain's voice; but Dain also appeared very anxious to see Lakamba, and Almayer felt uneasy owing to a deep and ineradicable distrust as to that ruler's disposition towards himself. Still, Dain had returned at last. Evidently he meant to keep to his bargain. Hope revived, and that night Almayer slept soundly, while Nina watched the angry river under the lash of the thunderstorm sweeping onward towards the sea.

Chapter 6

Dain was not long in crossing the river after leaving Almayer. He landed at the water-gate of the stockade enclosing the group of houses which composed the residence of the Rajah of Sambir. Evidently somebody was expected there, for the gate was open, and men with torches were ready to precede the visitor up the inclined plane of planks leading to the largest house where Lakamba actually resided, and where all the business of state was invariably transacted. The other buildings within the enclosure served only to accommodate the numerous household and the wives of the ruler.

Lakamba's own house was a strong structure of solid planks, raised on high piles, with a verandah of split bamboos surrounding it on all sides; the whole was covered in by an immensely high-pitched roof of palm-leaves, resting on beams blackened by the smoke of many torches.

The building stood parallel to the river, one of its long sides facing the water-gate of the stockade. There was a door in the short side looking up the river, and the inclined plank-way led straight from the gate to that door. By the uncertain light of smoky torches, Dain noticed the vague outlines of a group of armed men in the dark shadows to his right. From that group Babalatchi stepped forward to open the door, and Dain entered the audience chamber of the Rajah's residence. About one-third of the house was curtained off, by heavy stuff of European manufacture, for that purpose; close to the curtain there was a big armchair of some black wood, much carved, and before it a rough deal table. Otherwise the room was only furnished with mats in great profusion. To the left of the entrance stood a rude arm-rack, with three rifles with fixed bayonets in it. By the wall, in the shadow, the bodyguard of Lakamba – all friends or relations – slept in a confused heap of brown arms, legs and multicoloured garments, from whence issued an occasional snore or a subdued groan of some uneasy sleeper. An European lamp with a green shade standing on the table made all this indistinctly visible to Dain.

'You are welcome to your rest here,' said Babalatchi, looking at Dain interrogatively.

'I must speak to the Rajah at once,' answered Dain.

Babalatchi made a gesture of assent, and, turning to the brass gong suspended under the arm-rack, struck two sharp blows.

The ear-splitting din woke up the guard. The snores ceased; outstretched legs were drawn in; the whole heap moved, and slowly resolved itself into individual forms, with much yawning and rubbing of sleepy eyes; behind the curtains there was a burst of feminine chatter; then the bass voice of Lakamba was heard.

'Is that the Arab trader?'

'No, Tuan,' answered Babalatchi; 'Dain has returned at last. He is here for an important talk – bitcharra[42] – if you mercifully consent.'

Evidently Lakamba's mercy went so far – for in a short while he came out from behind the curtain – but it did not go to the length of inducing him to make an extensive toilet. A short red sarong tightened hastily round his hips was his only garment. The merciful ruler of Sambir looked sleepy and rather sulky. He sat in the armchair, his knees well apart, his elbows on the arm rests, his chin on his breast, breathing heavily and waiting malevolently for Dain to open the important talk.

But Dain did not seem anxious to begin. He directed his gaze towards Babalatchi, squatting comfortably at the feet of his master, and remained silent with a slightly bent head as if in attentive expectation of coming words of wisdom.

Babalatchi coughed discreetly, and, leaning forward, pushed over a few mats for Dain to sit upon, then lifting up his squeaky voice he assured him with eager volubility of everybody's delight at this long-looked-for return. His heart had hungered for the sight of Dain's face, and his ears were withering for the want of the refreshing sound of his voice. Everybody's hearts and ears were in the same sad predicament, according to Babalatchi, as he indicated with a sweeping gesture the other bank of the river where the settlement slumbered peacefully, unconscious of the great joy awaiting it on the morrow when Dain's presence amongst them would be disclosed. 'For' – went on Babalatchi – 'what is the joy of a poor man if not the open hand of a generous trader or of a great – '

Here he checked himself abruptly with a calculated embarrassment of manner, and his roving eye sought the floor, while an apologetic smile dwelt for a moment on his misshapen lips. Once or twice during this opening speech an amused expression flitted across Dain's face, soon to give way, however, to an appearance of grave concern. On Lakamba's brow a heavy frown had settled, and his lips moved angrily as he listened to his Prime Minister's oratory. In the silence that fell upon the room when Babalatchi ceased speaking arose a chorus of varied snores from the corner where the bodyguard had resumed their interrupted slumbers, but the distant rumble of thunder filling then

Nina's heart with apprehension for the safety of her lover passed unheeded by those three men intent each on their own purposes, for life or death.

After a short silence, Babalatchi, discarding now the flowers of polite eloquence, spoke again, but in short and hurried sentences and in a low voice. They had been very uneasy. Why did Dain remain so long absent? The men dwelling on the lower reaches of the river heard the reports of big guns and saw a fire-ship[43] of the Dutch among the islands of the estuary. So they were anxious. Rumours of a disaster had reached Abdulla a few days ago, and since then they had been waiting for Dain's return under the apprehension of some misfortune. For days they had closed their eyes in fear, and woke up alarmed, and walked abroad trembling, like men before an enemy. And all on account of Dain. Would he not allay their fears for his safety, not for themselves? They were quiet and faithful, and devoted to the great Rajah in Batavia – may his fate lead him ever to victory for the joy and profit of his servants! 'And here,' went on Babalatchi, 'Lakamba my master was getting thin in his anxiety for the trader he had taken under his protection; and so was Abdulla, for what would wicked men not say if perchance – '

'Be silent, fool!' growled Lakamba, angrily.

Babalatchi subsided into silence with a satisfied smile, while Dain, who had been watching him as if fascinated, turned with a sigh of relief towards the ruler of Sambir. Lakamba did not move, and, without raising his head, looked at Dain from under his eyebrows, breathing audibly, with pouted lips, in an air of general discontent.

'Speak! O Dain!' he said at last. 'We have heard many rumours. Many nights in succession has my friend Reshid come here with bad tidings. News travels fast along the coast. But they may be untrue; there are more lies in men's mouths in these days than when I was young, but I am not easier to deceive now.'

'All my words are true,' said Dain, carelessly. 'If you want to know what befell my brig, then learn that it is in the hands of the Dutch. Believe me, Rajah,' he went on, with sudden energy, 'the Orang Blanda have good friends in Sambir, or else how did they know I was coming thence?'

Lakamba gave Dain a short and hostile glance. Babalatchi rose quietly, and, going to the arm-rack, struck the gong violently.

Outside the door there was a shuffle of bare feet; inside, the guard woke up and sat staring in sleepy surprise.

'Yes, you faithful friend of the white Rajah,' went on Dain, scornfully, turning to Babalatchi, who had returned to his place, 'I have escaped, and I am here to gladden your heart. When I saw the Dutch ship I ran the brig inside the reefs and put her ashore. They did not dare to follow with the ship, so they sent the boats. We took to ours and tried to get away, but the ship dropped fireballs at us, and killed many of my men. But I am left, O Babalatchi! The Dutch are coming here. They are seeking for me. They are coming to ask their faithful friend Lakamba and his slave Babalatchi. Rejoice!'

But neither of his hearers appeared to be in a joyful mood. Lakamba had put one leg over his knee, and went on gently scratching it with a meditative air, while Babalatchi, sitting cross-legged, seemed suddenly to become smaller and very limp, staring straight before him vacantly. The guard evinced some interest in the proceedings, stretching themselves full length on the mats to be nearer the speaker. One of them got up and now stood leaning against the arm-rack, playing absently with the fringes of his sword-hilt.

Dain waited till the crash of thunder had died away in distant mutterings before he spoke again.

'Are you dumb, O ruler of Sambir, or is the son of a great Rajah unworthy of your notice? I am come here to seek refuge and to warn you, and want to know what you intend doing.'

'You came here because of the white man's daughter,' retorted Lakamba, quickly. 'Your refuge was with your father, the Rajah of Bali, the Son of Heaven, the "Anak Agong"[44] himself. What am I to protect great princes? Only yesterday I planted rice in a burnt clearing; today you say I hold your life in my hand.'

Babalatchi glanced at his master. 'No man can escape his fate,' he murmured piously. 'When love enters a man's heart he is like a child – without any understanding. Be merciful, Lakamba,' he added, twitching the corner of the Rajah's sarong warningly.

Lakamba snatched away the skirt of the sarong angrily. Under the dawning comprehension of intolerable embarrassments caused by Dain's return to Sambir he began to lose such composure as he had been, till then, able to maintain; and now he raised his voice loudly above the whistling of the wind and the patter of rain on the roof in the hard squall passing over the house.

'You came here first as a trader with sweet words and great promises, asking me to look the other way while you worked your will on the white man there. And I did. What do you want now? When I was young I fought. Now I am old, and want peace. It is easier for me to have you killed than to fight the Dutch. It is better for me.'

The squall had now passed, and, in the short stillness of the lull in the storm, Lakamba repeated softly, as if to himself, 'Much easier. Much better.'

Dain did not seem greatly discomposed by the Rajah's threatening words. While Lakamba was speaking he had glanced once rapidly over his shoulder, just to make sure that there was nobody behind him, and, tranquillised in that respect, he had extracted a siri-box out of the folds of his waist-cloth, and was wrapping carefully the little bit of betel-nut and a small pinch of lime in the green leaf tendered him politely by the watchful Babalatchi. He accepted this as a peace-offering from the silent statesman – a kind of mute protest against his master's undiplomatic violence, and as an omen of a possible understanding to be arrived at yet. Otherwise Dain was not uneasy. Although recognising the justice of Lakamba's surmise that he had come back to Sambir only for the sake of the white man's daughter, yet he was not conscious of any childish lack of understanding, as suggested by Babalatchi. In fact, Dain knew very well that Lakamba was too deeply implicated in the gunpowder smuggling to care for an investigation by the Dutch authorities into that matter. When sent off by his father, the independent Rajah of Bali, at the time when the hostilities between Dutch and Malays threatened to spread from Sumatra over the whole archipelago, Dain had found all the big traders deaf to his guarded proposals, and above the temptation of the great prices he was ready to give for gunpowder. He went to Sambir as a last and almost hopeless resort, having heard in Macassar of the white man there, and of the regular steamer trading from Singapore – allured also by the fact that there was no Dutch resident on the river, which would make things easier, no doubt. His hopes got nearly wrecked against the stubborn loyalty of Lakamba arising from well-understood self-interest; but at last the young man's generosity, his persuasive enthusiasm, the prestige of his father's great name, overpowered the prudent hesitation of the ruler of Sambir. Lakamba would have nothing to do himself with any illegal traffic. He also objected to the Arabs being made use of in that matter; but he suggested Almayer, saying that he was a weak man easily persuaded, and that his friend, the English captain of the steamer, could be made very useful – very likely even would join in the business, smuggling the powder in the steamer without Abdulla's knowledge. There again Dain met in Almayer with unexpected resistance; Lakamba had to send Babalatchi over with the solemn promise that his eyes would be shut in friendship for the white man, Dain paying for the promise and the friendship in good silver guilders of the hated Orang Blanda. Almayer, at last consenting, said the powder would be obtained, but Dain must trust him with dollars to send to Singapore in payment for it. He would induce Ford to buy and smuggle it in the steamer on board the brig. He did not want any money for himself out of the transaction, but Dain must help him in his great enterprise after sending off the brig. Almayer had explained to Dain that he could not trust Lakamba alone in that matter; he would be afraid of losing his treasure and his life through the cupidity of the Rajah; yet the Rajah had to be told, and insisted on taking a share in that operation, or else his eyes would remain shut no longer. To this Almayer had to submit. Had Dain not seen Nina he would have probably refused to engage himself and his men in the projected expedition to Gunong Mas – the mountain of gold. As it was he intended to return with half of his men as soon as the brig was clear of the reefs, but the persistent chase given him by the Dutch frigate had forced him to run south and ultimately to wreck and destroy his vessel in order to preserve his liberty or perhaps even his life. Yes, he had come back to Sambir for Nina, although aware that the Dutch would look for him there, but he had also calculated his chances of safety in Lakamba's hands. For all his ferocious talk, the merciful ruler would not kill him, for he had long ago been impressed with the notion that Dain possessed the secret of the white man's treasure; neither would he give him up to the Dutch, for fear of some fatal disclosure of complicity in the treasonable trade. So Dain felt tolerably secure as he sat meditating quietly his answer to the Rajah's bloodthirsty speech. Yes, he would point out to him the aspect of his position should he – Dain – fall into the hands of the Dutch and should he speak the truth. He would have nothing more to lose then, and he would speak the truth. And if he did return to Sambir, disturbing thereby Lakamba's peace of mind, what then? He came to look after his property. Did he not pour a stream of silver into Mrs Almayer's greedy lap? He had paid, for the girl, a price worthy of a great prince, although unworthy of that delightfully maddening creature for whom his untamed soul longed in an intensity of desire far more tormenting than the sharpest pain. He wanted his happiness. He had the right to be in Sambir.

He rose, and, approaching the table, leaned both his elbows on it; Lakamba responsively edged his seat a little closer, while Babalatchi scrambled to his feet and thrust his inquisitive head between his master's and Dain's. They interchanged their ideas rapidly, speaking in whispers into each other's faces, very close now, Dain suggesting, Lakamba contradicting, Babalatchi conciliating and anxious in his vivid apprehension of coming difficulties. He spoke most, whispering earnestly, turning his head slowly from side to side so as to bring his solitary eye to bear upon each of his interlocutors in turn. Why should there be strife? said he. Let Tuan Dain, whom he loved only less than his master, go trustfully into hiding. There were many places for that. Bulangi's house away in the clearing was best.

Bulangi was a safe man. In the network of crooked channels no white man could find his way. White men were strong, but very foolish. It was undesirable to fight them, but deception was easy. They were like silly women – they did not know the use of reason, and he was a match for any of them – went on Babalatchi, with all the confidence of deficient experience. Probably the Dutch would seek Almayer. Maybe they would take away their countryman if they were suspicious of him. That would be good. After the Dutch went away Lakamba and Dain would get the treasure without any trouble, and there would be one person less to share it. Did he not speak wisdom? Will Tuan Dain go to Bulangi's house till the danger is over, go at once?

Dain accepted this suggestion of going into hiding with a certain sense of conferring a favour upon Lakamba and the anxious statesman, but he met the proposal of going at once with a decided no, looking Babalatchi meaningly in the eye. The statesman sighed as a man accepting the inevitable would do, and pointed silently towards the other bank of the river. Dain bent his head slowly.

'Yes, I am going there,' he said.

'Before the day comes?' asked Babalatchi.

'I am going there now,' answered Dain, decisively. 'The Orang Blanda will not be here before tomorrow night, perhaps, and I must tell Almayer of our arrangements.'

'No, Tuan. No; say nothing,' protested Babalatchi. 'I will go over myself at sunrise and let him know.'

'I will see,' said Dain, preparing to go.

The thunderstorm was recommencing outside, the heavy clouds hanging low overhead now.

There was a constant rumble of distant thunder punctuated by the nearer sharp crashes, and in the continuous play of blue lightning the woods and the river showed fitfully, with all the elusive distinctness of detail characteristic of such a scene. Outside the door of the Rajah's house Dain and Babalatchi stood on the shaking verandah as if dazed and stunned by the violence of the storm. They stood there among the cowering forms of the Rajah's slaves and retainers seeking shelter from the rain, and Dain called aloud to his boatmen, who responded with a unanimous 'Ada, Tuan!'[45] while they looked uneasily at the river.

'This is a great flood!' shouted Babalatchi into Dain's ear. 'The river is very angry. Look! Look at the drifting logs! Can you go?'

Dain glanced doubtfully on the livid expanse of seething water bounded far away on the other side by the narrow black line of the forests. Suddenly, in a vivid white flash, the low point of land with the bending trees on it and Almayer's house leaped into view, flickered and disappeared. Dain pushed Babalatchi aside and ran down to the water-gate followed by his shivering boatmen.

Babalatchi backed slowly in and closed the door, then turned round and looked silently upon Lakamba. The Rajah sat still, glaring stonily upon the table, and Babalatchi gazed curiously at the perplexed mood of the man he had served so many years through good and evil fortune. No doubt the one-eyed statesman felt within his savage and much sophisticated breast the unwonted feelings of sympathy with, and perhaps even pity for, the man he called his master. From the safe position of a confidential adviser, he could, in the dim vista of past years, see himself – a casual cut-throat – finding shelter under that man's roof in the modest rice-clearing of early beginnings. Then came a long period of unbroken success, of wise counsels, and deep plottings resolutely carried out by the fearless Lakamba, till the whole east coast from Poulo Laut to Tanjong Batu[46] listened to Babalatchi's wisdom speaking through the mouth of the ruler of Sambir. In those long years how many dangers escaped, how many enemies bravely faced, how many white men successfully circumvented! And now he looked upon the result of so many years of patient toil: the fearless Lakamba cowed by the shadow of an impending trouble. The ruler was growing old, and Babalatchi, aware of an uneasy feeling at the pit of his stomach, put both his hands there with a suddenly vivid and sad perception of the fact that he himself was growing old too; that the time of reckless daring was past for both of them, and that they had to seek refuge in prudent cunning. They wanted peace; they were disposed to reform; they were ready even to retrench, so as to have the wherewithal to bribe the evil days away, if bribed away they could be. Babalatchi sighed for the second time that night as he squatted again at his master's feet and tendered him his betel-nut box in mute sympathy. And they sat there in close yet silent communion of betel-nut chewers, moving their jaws slowly, expectorating decorously into the wide-mouthed brass vessel they passed to one another, and listening to the awful din of the battling elements outside.

'There is a very great flood,' remarked Babalatchi, sadly.

'Yes,' said Lakamba. 'Did Dain go?'

'He went, Tuan. He ran down to the river like a man possessed of the Sheitan[47] himself.'

There was another long pause.

'He may get drowned,' suggested Lakamba at last, with some show of interest.

'The floating logs are many,' answered Babalatchi, 'but he is a good swimmer,' he added languidly.

'He ought to live,' said Lakamba; 'he knows where the treasure is.'

Babalatchi assented with an ill-humoured grunt. His want of success in penetrating the white man's secret as to the locality where the gold was to be found was a sore point with the statesman of Sambir, as the only conspicuous failure in an otherwise brilliant career.

A great peace had now succeeded the turmoil of the storm. Only the little belated clouds, which hurried past overhead to catch up the main body flashing silently in the distance, sent down short showers that pattered softly with a soothing hiss over the palm-leaf roof.

Lakamba roused himself from his apathy with an appearance of having grasped the situation at last.

'Babalatchi,' he called briskly, giving him a slight kick.

'Ada, Tuan! I am listening.'

'If the Orang Blanda come here, Babalatchi, and take Almayer to Batavia to punish him for smuggling gunpowder, what will he do, you think?'

'I do not know, Tuan.'

'You are a fool,' commented Lakamba, exultingly. 'He will tell them where the treasure is, so as to find mercy. He will.'

Babalatchi looked up at his master and nodded his head with by no means a joyful surprise. He had not thought of this; there was a new complication.

'Almayer must die,' said Lakamba, decisively, 'to make our secret safe. He must die quietly, Babalatchi. You must do it.'

Babalatchi assented, and rose wearily to his feet. 'Tomorrow?' he asked.

'Yes; before the Dutch come. He drinks much coffee,' answered Lakamba, with seeming irrelevancy.

Babalatchi stretched himself yawning, but Lakamba, in the flattering consciousness of a knotty problem solved by his own unaided intellectual efforts, grew suddenly very wakeful.

'Babalatchi,' he said to the exhausted statesman, 'fetch the box of music the white captain gave me. I cannot sleep.'

At this order a deep shade of melancholy settled upon Babalatchi's features. He went reluctantly behind the curtain and soon reappeared carrying in his arms a small hand-organ, which he put down on the table with an air of deep dejection. Lakamba settled himself comfortably in his armchair.

'Turn, Babalatchi, turn,' he murmured, with closed eyes.

Babalatchi's hand grasped the handle with the energy of despair, and as he turned, the deep gloom on his countenance changed into an expression of hopeless resignation. Through the open shutter the notes of Verdi's [48] music floated out on the great silence over the river and forest. Lakamba listened with closed eyes and a delighted smile; Babalatchi turned, at times dozing off and swaying over, then catching himself up in a great fright with a few quick turns of the handle. Nature slept in an exhausted repose after the fierce turmoil, while under the unsteady hand of the statesman of Sambir the Trovatore fitfully wept, wailed and bade goodbye to his Leonore again and again in a mournful round of tearful and endless iteration.

Chapter 7

The bright sunshine of the clear mistless morning, after the stormy night, flooded the main path of the settlement leading from the low shore of the Pantai branch of the river to the gate of Abdulla's compound. The path was deserted this morning; it stretched its dark yellow surface, hard beaten by the tramp of many bare feet, between the clusters of palm trees, whose tall trunks barred it with strong black lines at irregular intervals, while the newly risen sun threw the shadows of their leafy heads far away over the roofs of the buildings lining the river, even over the river itself as it flowed swiftly and silently past the deserted houses. For the houses were deserted too. On the narrow strip of trodden grass intervening between their open doors and the road, the morning fires smouldered untended, sending thin fluted columns of smoke into the cool air, and spreading the thinnest veil of mysterious blue haze over the sunlit solitude of the settlement. Almayer, just out of his hammock, gazed sleepily at the unwonted appearance of Sambir, wondering vaguely at the absence of life. His own house was very quiet; he could not hear his wife's voice, nor the sound of Nina's footsteps in the big room, opening on the verandah, which he called his sitting-room, whenever, in the company of white men, he wished to assert his claims to the commonplace decencies of civilisation. Nobody ever sat there; there was nothing there to sit upon, for Mrs Almayer in her savage moods, when excited by the reminiscences of the piratical period of her life, had torn off the curtains to make sarongs for the slave-girls, and had burnt the showy furniture piecemeal to cook the family rice. But Almayer was not thinking of his furniture now. He was thinking of Dain's return, of Dain's nocturnal interview with Lakamba, of its possible influence on his long-matured plans, now nearing the period of their execution. He was also uneasy at the non-appearance of Dain who had promised him an early visit. 'The fellow had plenty of time to cross the river,' he mused, 'and there was so much to be done today. The settling of details for the early start on the morrow; the launching of the boats; the thousand and one finishing touches. For the expedition must start complete, nothing should be forgotten, nothing should – '

The sense of the unwonted solitude grew upon him suddenly, and in the unusual silence he caught himself longing even for the usually unwelcome sound of his wife's voice to break the oppressive stillness which seemed, to his frightened fancy, to portend the advent of some new misfortune. 'What has happened?' he muttered half aloud, as he shuffled in his imperfectly adjusted slippers towards the balustrade of the verandah. 'Is everybody asleep or dead?'

The settlement was alive and very much awake. It was awake ever since the early break of day, when Mahmat Banjer, in a fit of unheard-of energy, arose and, taking up his hatchet, stepped over the sleeping forms of his two wives and walked shivering to the water's edge to make sure that the new house he was building had not floated away during the night.

The house was being built by the enterprising Mahmat on a large raft, and he had securely moored it just inside the muddy point of land at the junction of the two branches of the Pantai so as to be out of the way of drifting logs that would no doubt strand on the point during the freshet. Mahmat walked through the wet grass saying bourrough,[49] and cursing softly to himself the hard necessities of active life that drove him from his warm couch into the cold of the morning. A glance showed him that his house was still there, and he congratulated himself on his foresight in hauling it out of harm's way, for the increasing light showed him a confused wrack of drift-logs, half-stranded on the muddy flat, interlocked into a shapeless raft by their branches, tossing to and fro and grinding together in the eddy caused by the meeting currents of the two branches of the river. Mahmat walked down to the water's edge to examine the rattan moorings of his house just as the sun cleared the trees of the forest on the opposite shore. As he bent over the fastenings he glanced again carelessly at the unquiet jumble of logs and saw there something that caused him to drop his hatchet and stand up, shading his eyes with his hand from the rays of the rising sun. It was something red, and the logs rolled over it, at times closing round it, sometimes hiding it. It looked to him at first like a strip of red cloth. The next moment Mahmat had made it out and raised a great shout.

'Ah ya! There!' yelled Mahmat. 'There's a man among the logs.' He put the palms of his hands to his lips and shouted, enunciating distinctly, his face turned towards the settlement: 'There's a body of a man in the river! Come and see! A dead – stranger!'

The women of the nearest house were already outside kindling the fires and husking the morning rice. They took up the cry shrilly, and it travelled so from house to house, dying away in the distance. The men rushed out excited but silent, and ran towards the muddy point where the unconscious logs tossed and ground and bumped and rolled over the dead stranger with the stupid persistency of inanimate things. The women followed, neglecting their domestic duties and disregarding the possibilities of domestic discontent, while groups of children brought up the rear, warbling joyously in the delight of unexpected excitement.

Almayer called aloud for his wife and daughter, but receiving no response, stood listening intently. The murmur of the crowd reached him faintly, bringing with it the assurance of some unusual event. He glanced at the river just as he was going to leave the verandah and checked himself at the sight of a small canoe crossing over from the Rajah's landing-place. The solitary occupant (in whom Almayer soon recognised Babalatchi) effected the crossing a little below the house and paddled up to the Lingard jetty in the dead water under the bank. Babalatchi clambered out slowly and went on fastening his canoe with fastidious care, as if not in a hurry to meet Almayer, whom he saw looking at him from the verandah. This delay gave Almayer time to notice and greatly wonder at Babalatchi's official get-up. The statesman of Sambir was clad in a costume befitting his high rank. A loudly checkered sarong encircled his waist, and from its many folds peeped out the silver hilt of the kriss that saw the light only on great festivals or during official receptions. Over the left shoulder and across the otherwise unclad breast of the aged diplomatist glistened a patent-leather belt bearing a brass plate with the arms of the Netherlands under the inscription 'Sultan of Sambir'. Babalatchi's head was covered by a red turban, whose fringed ends falling over the left cheek and shoulder gave to his aged face a ludicrous expression of joyous reck-lessness. When the canoe was at last fastened to his satisfaction he straightened himself up, shaking down the folds of his sarong, and moved with long strides towards Almayer's house, swinging regularly his long ebony staff, whose gold head ornamented with precious stones flashed in the morning sun. Almayer waved his hand to the right towards the point of land, to him invisible, but in full view from the jetty.

'Oh, Babalatchi! Oh!' he called out; 'what is the matter there? Can you see?'

Babalatchi stopped and gazed intently at the crowd on the river bank, and after a little while the astonished Almayer saw him leave the path, gather up his sarong in one hand, and break into a trot through the grass towards the muddy point. Almayer, now greatly interested, ran down the steps of the verandah. The murmur of men's voices and the shrill cries of women reached him quite distinctly now, and as soon as he turned the corner of his house he could see the crowd on the low promontory swaying and pushing round some object of interest. He could indistinctly hear Babalatchi's voice, then the crowd opened before the aged statesman and closed after him with an excited hum, ending in a loud shout.

As Almayer approached the throng a man ran out and rushed past him towards the settlement, unheeding his call to stop and explain the cause of this excitement. On the very outskirts of the crowd Almayer found himself arrested by an unyielding mass of humanity, regardless of his entreaties for a passage, insensible to his gentle pushes as he tried to work his way through it towards the riverside.

In the midst of his gentle and slow progress he fancied suddenly he had heard his wife's voice in the thickest of the throng. He could not mistake very well Mrs Almayer's high-pitched tones, yet the words were too indistinct for him to understand their purport. He paused in his endeavours to make a passage for himself, intending to get some intelligence from those around him, when a long and piercing shriek rent the air, silencing the murmurs of the crowd and the voices of his informants. For a moment Almayer remained as if turned into stone with astonishment and horror, for he was certain now that he had heard his wife wailing for the dead. He remembered Nina's unusual absence, and maddened by his apprehensions as to her safety, he pushed blindly and violently forward, the crowd falling back with cries of surprise and pain before his frantic advance.

On the point of land in a little clear space lay the body of the stranger just hauled out from amongst the logs. On one side stood Babalatchi, his chin resting on the head of his staff and his one eye gazing steadily at the shapeless mass of broken limbs, torn flesh and bloodstained rags. As Almayer burst through the ring of horrified spectators, Mrs Almayer threw her own head-veil over the upturned face of the drowned man, and, squatting by it, with another mournful howl, sent a shiver through the now silent crowd. Mahmat, dripping wet, turned to Almayer, eager to tell his tale.

In the first moment of reaction from the anguish of his fear the sunshine seemed to waver before Almayer's eyes, and he listened to words spoken around him without comprehending their meaning. When, by a strong effort of will, he regained the possession of his senses, Mahmat was saying –

'That is the way, Tuan. His sarong was caught in the broken branch, and he hung with his head under water. When I saw what it was I did not want it here. I wanted it to get clear and drift away. Why should we bury a stranger in the midst of our houses for his ghost to frighten our women and children? Have we not enough ghosts about this place?'

A murmur of approval interrupted him here. Mahmat looked reproachfully at Babalatchi. 'But the Tuan Babalatchi ordered me to drag the body ashore' – he went on looking round at his audience, but addressing himself only to Almayer – 'and I dragged him by the feet; in through the mud I have dragged him, although my heart longed to see him float down the river to strand perchance on Bulangi's clearing – may his father's grave be defiled!'

There was subdued laughter at this, for the enmity of Mahmat and Bulangi was a matter of common notoriety and of undying interest to the inhabitants of Sambir. In the midst of that mirth Mrs Almayer wailed suddenly again.

'Allah! What ails the woman!' exclaimed Mahmat, angrily. 'Here, I have touched this carcass which came from nobody knows where, and have most likely defiled myself before eating rice. By orders of Tuan Babalatchi I did this thing to please the white man. Are you pleased, O Tuan Almayer? And what will be my recompense? Tuan Babalatchi said a recompense there will be, and from you. Now consider. I have been defiled, and if not defiled I may be under the spell. Look at his anklet! Who ever heard of a corpse appearing during the night amongst the logs with a gold anklet on its leg? There is witchcraft there. However,' added Mahmat, after a reflective pause, 'I will have the anklet if there is permission, for I have a charm against the ghosts and am not afraid. God is great!'

A fresh outburst of noisy grief from Mrs Almayer checked the flow of Mahmat's eloquence. Almayer, bewildered, looked in turn at his wife, at Mahmat, at Babalatchi, and at last arrested his fascinated gaze on the body lying on the mud with covered face in a grotesquely unnatural contortion of mangled and broken limbs, one twisted and lacerated arm, with white bones protruding in many places through the torn flesh, stretched out; the hand with outspread fingers nearly touching his foot.

'Do you know who this is?' he asked of Babalatchi, in a low voice.

Babalatchi, staring straight before him, hardly moved his lips, while Mrs Almayer's persistent lamentations drowned the whisper of his murmured reply intended only for Almayer's ear.

'It was fate. Look at your feet, white man. I can see a ring on those torn fingers which I know well.'

Saying this, Babalatchi stepped carelessly forward, putting his foot as if accidentally on the hand of the corpse and pressing it into the soft mud. He swung his staff menacingly towards the crowd, which fell back a little.

'Go away,' he said sternly, 'and send your women to their cooking fires, which they ought not to have left to run after a dead stranger. This is men's work here. I take him now in the name of the Rajah. Let no man remain here but Tuan Almayer's slaves. Now go!'

The crowd reluctantly began to disperse. The women went first, dragging away the children that hung back with all their weight on the maternal hand. The men strolled slowly after them in ever forming and changing groups that gradually dissolved as they neared the settlement and every man regained his own house with steps quickened by the hungry anticipation of the morning rice. Only on the slight elevation where the land sloped down towards the muddy point a few men, either friends or enemies of Mahmat, remained gazing curiously for some time longer at the small group standing around the body on the river bank.

'I do not understand what you mean, Babalatchi,' said Almayer. 'What is the ring you are talking about? Whoever he is, you have trodden the poor fellow's hand right into the mud. Uncover his face,' he went on, addressing Mrs Almayer, who, squatting by the head of the corpse, rocked herself to and fro, shaking from time to time her dishevelled grey locks, and muttering mournfully.

'Hai!' exclaimed Mahmat, who had lingered close by. 'Look, Tuan; the logs came together so,' and here he pressed the palms of his hands together, 'and his head must have been between them, and now there is no face for you to look at. There are his flesh and his bones, the nose and the lips, and maybe his eyes, but nobody could tell the one from the other. It was written the day he was born that no man could look at him in death and be able to say, "This is my friend's face." '

'Silence, Mahmat; enough!' said Babalatchi, 'and take thy eyes off his anklet, thou eater of pigs' flesh.[50] Tuan Almayer,' he went on, lowering his voice, 'have you seen Dain this morning?'

Almayer opened his eyes wide and looked alarmed. 'No,' he said quickly; 'haven't you seen him? Is he not with the Rajah? I am waiting; why does he not come?'

Babalatchi nodded his head sadly.

'He is come, Tuan. He left last night when the storm was great and the river spoke angrily. The night was very black, but he had within him a light that showed the way to your house as smooth as a narrow backwater, and the many logs no bigger than wisps of dried grass. Therefore he went; and now he lies here.' And Babalatchi nodded his head towards the body.

'How can you tell?' said Almayer, excitedly, pushing his wife aside.

He snatched the cover off and looked at the formless mass of flesh, hair and drying mud, where the face of the drowned man should have been. 'Nobody can tell,' he added, turning away with a shudder.

Babalatchi was on his knees wiping the mud from the stiffened fingers of the outstretched hand. He rose to his feet and flashed before Almayer's eyes a gold ring set with a large green stone.

'You know this well,' he said. 'This never left Dain's hand. I had to tear the flesh now to get it off. Do you believe now?'

Almayer raised his hands to his head and let them fall listlessly by his sides in the utter abandonment of despair. Babalatchi, looking at him curiously, was astonished to see him smile. A strange fancy had taken possession of Almayer's brain, distracted by this new misfortune. It seemed to him that for many years he had been falling down a deep precipice. Day after day, month after month, year after year, he had been falling, falling, falling; it was a smooth, round, black thing, and the black walls had been rushing upwards with wearisome rapidity. A great rush, the noise of which he fancied he could hear yet; and now, with an awful shock, he had reached the bottom, and behold! he was alive and whole, and Dain was dead with all his bones broken. It struck him as funny. A dead Malay; he had seen many dead Malays without any emotion; and now he felt inclined to weep, but it was over the fate of a white man he knew; a man that fell over a deep precipice and did not die. He seemed somehow to himself to be standing on one side, a little way off, looking at a certain Almayer who was in great trouble. Poor, poor fellow! Why doesn't he cut his throat? He wished to encourage him; he was very anxious to see him lying dead over that other corpse. Why does he not die and end this suffering? He groaned aloud unconsciously and started with affright at the sound of his own voice. Was he going mad? Terrified by the thought he turned away and ran towards his house repeating to himself, I am not going mad; of course not, no, no, no! He tried to keep a firm hold of the idea.

Not mad, not mad. He stumbled as he ran blindly up the steps repeating fast and ever faster those words wherein seemed to lie his salvation. He saw Nina standing there, and wished to say something to her, but could not remember what, in his extreme anxiety not to forget that he was not going mad, which he still kept repeating mentally as he ran round the table till he stumbled against one of the armchairs and dropped into it exhausted. He sat staring wildly at Nina, still assuring himself mentally of his own sanity and wondering why the girl shrank from him in open-eyed alarm. What was the matter with her? This was foolish. He struck the table violently with his clenched fist and shouted hoarsely, 'Give me some gin! Run!' Then, while Nina ran off, he remained in the chair, very still and quiet, astonished at the noise he had made.

Nina returned with a tumbler half filled with gin, and found her father staring absently before him. Almayer felt very tired now, as if he had come from a long journey. He felt as if he had walked miles and miles that morning and now wanted to rest very much. He took the tumbler with a shaking hand, and as he drank his teeth chattered against the glass which he drained and set down heavily on the table. He turned his eyes slowly towards Nina standing beside him, and said steadily, 'Now all is over, Nina. He is dead, and I may as well burn all my boats.'

He felt very proud of being able to speak so calmly. Decidedly he was not going mad. This certitude was very comforting, and he went on talking about the finding of the body, listening to his own voice complacently. Nina stood quietly, her hand resting lightly on her father's shoulder, her face unmoved, but every line of her features, the attitude of her whole body expressing the most keen and anxious attention.

'And so Dain is dead,' she said coldly, when her father ceased speaking.

Almayer's elaborately calm demeanour gave way in a moment to an outburst of violent indignation.

'You stand there as if you were only half alive, and talk to me,' he exclaimed angrily, 'as if it was a matter of no importance. Yes, he is dead! Do you understand? Dead! What do you care? You never cared; you saw me struggle, and work, and strive, unmoved; and my suffering you could never see. No, never. You have no heart, and you have no mind, or you would have understood that it was for you, for your happiness I was working. I wanted to be rich; I wanted to get away from here. I wanted to see white men bowing low before the power of your beauty and your wealth. Old as I am I wished to seek a strange land, a civilisation to which I am a stranger, so as to find a new life in the contemplation of your high fortunes, of your triumphs, of your happiness. For that I bore patiently the burden of work, of disappointment, of humiliation amongst these savages here, and I had it all nearly in my grasp.'

He looked at his daughter's attentive face and jumped to his feet upsetting the chair.

'Do you hear? I had it all there; so; within reach of my hand.'

He paused, trying to keep down his rising anger, and failed.

'Have you no feeling?' he went on. 'Have you lived without hope?'

Nina's silence exasperated him; his voice rose, although he tried to master his feelings.

'Are you content to live in this misery and die in this wretched hole? Say something, Nina; have you no sympathy? Have you no word of comfort for me? I that loved you so.'

He waited for a while for an answer, and receiving none shook his fist in his daughter's face.

'I believe you are an idiot!' he yelled.

He looked round for the chair, picked it up and sat down stiffly. His anger was dead within him, and he felt ashamed of his outburst, yet relieved to think that now he had laid clear before his daughter the inner meaning of his life. He thought so in perfect good faith, deceived by the emotional estimate of his motives, unable to see the crookedness of his ways, the unreality of his aims, the futility of his regrets. And now his heart was filled only with a great tenderness and love for his daughter. He wanted to see her miserable, and to share with her his despair; but he wanted it only as all weak natures long for a companionship in misfortune with beings innocent of its cause. If she suffered herself she would understand and pity him; but now she would not, or could not, find one word of comfort or love for him in his dire extremity. The sense of his absolute loneliness came home to his heart with a force that made him shudder. He swayed and fell forward with his face on the table, his arms stretched straight out, extended and rigid. Nina made a quick movement towards her father and stood looking at the grey head, on the broad shoulders shaken convulsively by the violence of feelings that found relief at last in sobs and tears.

Nina sighed deeply and moved away from the table. Her features lost the appearance of stony indifference that had exasperated her father into his outburst of anger and sorrow. The expression of her face, now unseen by her father, underwent a rapid change. She had listened to Almayer's appeal for sympathy, for one word of comfort, apparently indifferent, yet with her breast torn by conflicting impulses raised unexpectedly by events she had not foreseen, or at least did not expect to happen so soon. With her heart deeply moved by the sight of Almayer's misery, knowing it in her power to end it with a word, longing to bring peace to that troubled heart, she heard with terror the voice of her overpowering love commanding her to be silent. And she submitted after a short and fierce struggle of her old self against the new principle of her life. She wrapped herself up in absolute silence, the only safeguard against some fatal admission. She could not trust herself to make a sign, to murmur a word for fear of saying too much; and the very violence of the feelings that stirred the innermost recesses of her soul seemed to turn her person into a stone. The dilated nostrils and the flashing eyes were the only signs of the storm raging within, and those signs of his daughter's emotion Almayer did not see, for his sight was dimmed by self-pity, by anger and by despair.

Had Almayer looked at his daughter as she leant over the front rail of the verandah he could have seen the expression of indifference give way to a look of pain, and that again pass away, leaving the glorious beauty of her face marred by deep-drawn lines of watchful anxiety. The long grass in the neglected courtyard stood very straight before her eyes in the noonday heat. From the riverbank there were voices and a shuffle of bare feet approaching the house; Babalatchi could be heard giving directions to Almayer's men, and Mrs Almayer's subdued wailing became audible as the small procession bearing the body of the drowned man and headed by that sorrowful matron turned the corner of the house. Babalatchi had taken the broken anklet off the man's leg, and now held it in his hand as he moved by the side of the bearers, while Mahmat lingered behind timidly, in the hopes of the promised reward.

'Lay him there,' said Babalatchi to Almayer's men, pointing to a pile of drying planks in front of the verandah. 'Lay him there. He was a Kaffir[51] and the son of a dog, and he was the white man's friend. He drank the white man's strong water,'[52] he added, with affected horror. 'That I have seen myself.'

The men stretched out the broken limbs on two planks they had laid level, while Mrs Almayer covered the body with a piece of white cotton cloth, and after whispering for some time with Babalatchi departed to her domestic duties. Almayer's men, after laying down their burden, dispersed themselves in quest of shady spots wherein to idle the day away. Babalatchi was left alone by the corpse that lay rigid under the white cloth in the bright sunshine.

Nina came down the steps and joined Babalatchi, who put his hand to his forehead, and squatted down with great deference.

'You have a bangle there,' said Nina, looking down on Babalatchi's upturned face and into his solitary eye.

'I have, Mem Putih,' returned the polite statesman. Then turning towards Mahmat he beckoned him closer, calling out, 'Come here!'

Mahmat approached with some hesitation. He avoided looking at Nina, but fixed his eyes on Babalatchi.

'Now, listen,' said Babalatchi, sharply. 'The ring and the anklet you have seen, and you know they belonged to Dain the trader, and to no other. Dain returned last night in a canoe. He spoke with the Rajah, and in the middle of the night left to cross over to the white man's house. There was a great flood, and this morning you found him in the river.'

'By his feet I dragged him out,' muttered Mahmat under his breath. 'Tuan Babalatchi, there will be a recompense!' he exclaimed aloud.

Babalatchi held up the gold bangle before Mahmat's eyes. 'What I have told you, Mahmat, is for all ears. What I give you now is for your eyes only. Take.'

Mahmat took the bangle eagerly and hid it in the folds of his waist-cloth. 'Am I a fool to show this thing in a house with three women in it?' he growled. 'But I shall tell them about Dain the trader, and there will be talk enough.'

He turned and went away, increasing his pace as soon as he was outside Almayer's compound.

Babalatchi looked after him till he disappeared behind the bushes. 'Have I done well, Mem Putih?' he asked, humbly addressing Nina.

'You have,' answered Nina. 'The ring you may keep yourself.'

Babalatchi touched his lips and forehead, and scrambled to his feet. He looked at Nina, as if expecting her to say something more, but Nina turned towards the house and went up the steps, motioning him away with her hand.

Babalatchi picked up his staff and prepared to go. It was very warm, and he did not care for the long pull to the Rajah's house. Yet he must go and tell the Rajah – tell of the event; of the change in his plans; of all his suspicions. He walked to the jetty and began casting off the rattan painter of his canoe.

The broad expanse of the lower reach, with its shimmering surface dotted by the black specks of the fishing canoes, lay before his eyes. The fishermen seemed to be racing. Babalatchi paused in his work, and looked on with sudden interest. The man in the foremost canoe, now within hail of the first houses of Sambir, laid in his paddle and stood up shouting –

'The boats! the boats! The man-of-war's boats are coming! They are here!'

In a moment the settlement was again alive with people rushing to the riverside. The men began to unfasten their boats, the women stood in groups looking towards the bend down the river. Above the trees lining the reach a slight puff of smoke appeared like a black stain on the brilliant blue of the cloudless sky.

Babalatchi stood perplexed, the painter in his hand. He looked down the reach, then up towards Almayer's house, and back again at the river as if undecided what to do. At last he made the canoe fast again hastily, and ran towards the house and up the steps of the verandah.

'Tuan! Tuan!' he called, eagerly. 'The boats are coming. The man-of-war's boats. You had better get ready. The officers will come here, I know.'

Almayer lifted his head slowly from the table, and looked at him stupidly.

'Mem Putih!' exclaimed Babalatchi to Nina, 'look at him. He does not hear. You must take care,' he added meaningly.

Nina nodded to him with an uncertain smile, and was going to speak, when a sharp report from the gun mounted in the bow of the steam launch that was just then coming into view arrested the words on her parted lips. The smile died out, and was replaced by the old look of anxious attention. From the hills far away the echo came back like a long-drawn and mournful sigh, as if the land had sent it in answer to the voice of its masters.

Chapter 8

The news as to the identity of the body lying now in Almayer's compound spread rapidly over the settlement. During the forenoon most of the inhabitants remained in the long street discussing the mysterious return and the unexpected death of the man who had become known to them as 'the trader'. His arrival during the north-east monsoon, his long sojourn in their midst, his sudden departure with his brig, and, above all, the mysterious appearance of the body, said to be his, amongst the logs, were subjects to wonder at and to talk over and over again with undiminished interest. Mahmat moved from house to house and from group to group, always ready to repeat his tale: how he saw the body caught by the sarong in a forked log; how Mrs Almayer coming, one of the first, at his cries, recognised it, even before he had it hauled on shore; how Babalatchi ordered him to bring it out of the water. 'By the feet I dragged him in, and there was no head,' explained Mahmat, 'and how could the white man's wife know who it was? She was a witch, it was well known. And did you see how the white man himself ran away at the sight of the body? Like a deer he ran!' And here Mahmat imitated Almayer's long strides, to the great joy of the beholders. And for all his trouble he had nothing. The ring with the green stone Tuan Babalatchi kept. 'Nothing! Nothing!' He spat down at his feet in sign of disgust, and left that group to seek further for a fresh audience.

The news spreading to the furthermost parts of the settlement found out Abdulla in the cool recess of his godown, where he sat overlooking his Arab clerks and the men loading and unloading the up-country canoes. Reshid, who was busy on the jetty, was summoned into his uncle's presence and found him, as usual, very calm and even cheerful, but very much surprised. The rumour of the capture or destruction of Dain's brig had reached the Arab's ears three days before from the sea-fishermen and through the dwellers on the lower reaches of the river. It had been passed up-stream from neighbour to neighbour till Bulangi, whose clearing was nearest to the settlement, had brought that news himself to Abdulla whose favour he courted. But rumour also spoke of a fight and of Dain's death on board his own vessel. And now all the settlement talked of Dain's visit to the Rajah and of his death when crossing the river in the dark to see Almayer.

They could not understand this. Reshid thought that it was very strange. He felt uneasy and doubtful. But Abdulla, after the first shock of surprise, with the old age's dislike for solving riddles, showed a becoming resignation. He remarked that the man was dead now at all events, and consequently dangerous no more. Where was the use to wonder at the decrees of Fate, especially if they were propitious to the True Believers? And with a pious ejaculation to Allah the Merciful, the Compassionate,[53] Abdulla seemed to regard the incident as closed for the present.

Not so Reshid. He lingered by his uncle, pulling thoughtfully his neatly trimmed beard.

'There are many lies,' he murmured. 'He has been dead once before, and came to life to die again now. The Dutch will be here before many days and clamour for the man. Shall I not believe my eyes sooner than the tongues of women and idle men?'

'They say that the body is being taken to Almayer's compound,' said Abdulla. 'If you want to go there you must go before the Dutch arrive here. Go late. It should not be said that we have been seen inside that man's enclosure lately.'

Reshid assented to the truth of this last remark and left his uncle's side. He leaned against the lintel of the big doorway and looked idly across the courtyard through the open gate on to the main road of the settlement. It lay empty, straight and yellow under the flood of light. In the hot noontide the smooth trunks of palm trees, the outlines of the houses, and away there at the other end of the road the roof of Almayer's house visible over the bushes on the dark background of forest, seemed to quiver in the heat radiating from the steaming earth. Swarms of yellow butterflies rose, and settled to rise again in short flights before Reshid's half-closed eyes. From under his feet arose the dull hum of insects in the long grass of the courtyard. He looked on sleepily.

From one of the side paths amongst the houses a woman stepped out on the road, a slight girlish figure walking under the shade of a large tray balanced on her head. The consciousness of something moving stirred Reshid's half-sleeping senses into a comparative wakefulness. He recognised Taminah, Bulangi's slave-girl, with her tray of cakes for sale – an apparition of daily recurrence and of no importance whatever. She was going towards Almayer's house. She could be made useful. He roused himself up and ran towards the gate calling out, 'Taminah O!' The girl stopped, hesitated, and came back slowly.

Reshid waited, signing to her impatiently to come nearer.

When near Reshid, Taminah stood with downcast eyes.

Reshid looked at her a while before he asked, 'Are you going to Almayer's house? They say in the settlement that Dain the trader, he that was found drowned this morning, is lying in the white man's campong.'[54]

'I have heard this talk,' whispered Taminah; 'and this morning by the riverside I saw the body. Where it is now I do not know.'

'So you have seen it?' asked Reshid, eagerly. 'Is it Dain? You have seen him many times. You would know him.'

The girl's lips quivered and she remained silent for a while, breathing quickly.

'I have seen him, not a long time ago,' she said at last. 'The talk is true; he is dead. What do you want from me, Tuan? I must go.'

Just then the report of the gun fired on board the steam launch was heard, interrupting Reshid's reply. Leaving the girl he ran to the house, and met in the courtyard Abdulla coming towards the gate.

'The Orang Blanda are come,' said Reshid, 'and now we shall have our reward.'

Abdulla shook his head doubtfully. 'The white men's rewards are long in coming,' he said. 'White men are quick in anger and slow in gratitude. We shall see.'

He stood at the gate stroking his grey beard and listening to the distant cries of greeting at the other end of the settlement. As Taminah was turning to go he called her back.

'Listen, girl,' he said: 'there will be many white men in Almayer's house. You shall be there selling your cakes to the men of the sea. What you see and what you hear you may tell me. Come here before the sun sets and I will give you a blue handkerchief with red spots. Now go, and forget not to return.'

He gave her a push with the end of his long staff as she was going away and made her stumble.

'This slave is very slow,' he remarked to his nephew, looking after the girl with great disfavour.

Taminah walked on, her tray on her head, her eyes fixed on the ground. From the open doors of the houses were heard, as she passed, friendly calls inviting her within for business purposes, but she never heeded them, neglecting her sales in the preoccupation of intense thinking. Since the very early morning she had heard much, she had also seen much that filled her heart with a joy mingled with great suffering and fear. Before the dawn, before she left Bulangi's house to paddle up to Sambir she had heard voices outside the house when all in it but herself were asleep. And now, with her knowledge of the words spoken in the darkness, she held in her hand a life and carried in her breast a great sorrow. Yet from her springy step, erect figure, and face veiled over by the everyday look of apathetic indifference, nobody could have guessed at the double load she carried under the visible burden of the tray piled up high with cakes manufactured by the thrifty hands of Bulangi's wives. In that supple figure straight as an arrow, so graceful and free in its walk, behind those soft eyes that spoke of nothing but of unconscious resignation, there slept all feelings and all passions, all hopes and all fears, the curse of life and the consolation of death. And she knew nothing of it all. She lived like the tall palms amongst which she was passing now, seeking the light, desiring the sunshine, fearing the storm, unconscious of either. The slave had no hope, and knew of no change. She knew of no other sky, no other water, no other forest, no other world, no other life. She had no wish, no hope, no love, no fear except of a blow, and no vivid feeling but that of occasional hunger, which was seldom, for Bulangi was rich and rice was plentiful in the solitary house in his clearing. The absence of pain and hunger was her happiness, and when she felt unhappy she was simply tired, more than usual, after the day's labour. Then in the hot nights of the south-west monsoon she slept dreamlessly under the bright stars on the platform built outside the house and over the river. Inside they slept too: Bulangi by the door; his wives further in; the children with their mothers. She could hear their breathing; Bulangi's sleepy voice; the sharp cry of a child soon hushed with tender words. And she closed her eyes to the murmur of the water below her, to the whisper of the warm wind above, ignorant of the never-ceasing life of that tropical nature that spoke to her in vain with the thousand faint voices of the near forest, with the breath of tepid wind; in the heavy scents that lingered around her head; in the white wraiths of morning mist that hung over her in the solemn hush of all creation before the dawn.

Such had been her existence before the coming of the brig with the strangers. She remembered well that time: the uproar in the settlement, the never-ending wonder, the days and nights of talk and excitement. She remembered her own timidity with the strange men, till the brig moored to the bank became in a manner part of the settlement, and the fear wore off in the familiarity of constant intercourse. The call on board then became part of her daily round. She walked hesitatingly up the slanting planks of the gangway amid the encouraging shouts and more or less decent jokes of the men idling over the bulwarks. There she sold her wares to those men that spoke so loud and carried themselves so free. There was a throng, a constant coming and going; calls inter-changed, orders given and executed with shouts; the rattle of blocks, the flinging about of coils of rope. She sat out of the way under the shade of the awning, with her tray before her, the veil drawn well over her face, feeling shy amongst so many men. She smiled at all buyers, but spoke to none, letting their jests pass with stolid unconcern. She heard many tales told around her of far-off countries, of strange customs, of events stranger still. Those men were brave; but the most fearless of them spoke of their chief with fear. Often the man they called their master passed before her, walking erect and indifferent, in the pride of youth, in the flash of rich dress, with a tinkle of gold ornaments, while everybody stood aside watching anxiously for a movement of his lips, ready to do his bidding. Then all her life seemed to rush into her eyes, and from under her veil she gazed at him, charmed, yet fearful to attract attention. One day he noticed her and asked, 'Who is that girl?' 'A slave, Tuan! A girl that sells cakes,' a dozen voices replied together. She rose in terror to run on shore, when he called her back; and as she stood trembling with head hung down before him, he spoke kind words, lifting her chin with his hand and looking into her eyes with a smile. 'Do not be afraid,' he said. He never spoke to her any more. Somebody called out from the riverbank; he turned away and forgot her existence. Taminah saw Almayer standing on the shore with Nina on his arm. She heard Nina's voice calling out gaily, and saw Dain's face brighten with joy as he leaped on shore. She hated the sound of that voice ever since.

After that day she left off visiting Almayer's compound, and passed the noon hours under the shade of the brig awning. She watched for his coming, with heart beating quicker and quicker as he approached into a wild tumult of newly-aroused feelings of joy and hope and fear that died away with Dain's retreating figure, leaving her tired out, as if after a struggle, sitting still for a long time in dreamy languor. Then she paddled home slowly in the afternoon, often letting her canoe float with the lazy stream in the quiet backwater of the river. The paddle hung idle in the water as she sat in the stern, one hand supporting her chin, her eyes wide open, listening intently to the whispering of her heart that seemed to swell at last into a song of extreme sweetness. Listening to that song she husked the rice at home; it dulled her ears to the shrill bickerings of Bulangi's wives, to the sound of angry reproaches addressed to herself. And when the sun was near its setting she walked to the bathing-place and heard it as she stood on the tender grass of the low bank, her robe at her feet, and looked at the reflection of her figure on the glass-like surface of the creek. Listening to it she walked slowly back, her wet hair hanging over her shoulders; lying down to rest under the bright stars, she closed her eyes to the murmur of the water below, of the warm wind above; to the voice of nature speaking through the faint noises of the great forest, and to the song of her own heart.

She heard, but did not understand, and drank in the dreamy joy of her new existence without troubling about its meaning or its end, till the full consciousness of life came to her through pain and anger. And she suffered horribly the first time she saw Nina's long canoe drift silently past the sleeping house of Bulangi, bearing the two lovers into the white mist of the great river. Her jealousy and rage culminated in a paroxysm of physical pain that left her lying panting on the river bank, in the dumb agony of a wounded animal. But she went on moving patiently in the enchanted circle of slavery, going through her task day after day with all the pathos of the grief she could not express, even to herself, locked within her breast. She shrank from Nina as she would have shrunk from the sharp blade of a knife cutting into her flesh, but she kept on visiting the brig to feed her dumb, ignorant soul on her own despair. She saw Dain many times. He never spoke, he never looked. Could his eyes see only one woman's image? Could his ears hear only one woman's voice? He never noticed her; not once.

And then he went away. She saw him and Nina for the last time on that morning when Babalatchi, while visiting his fish baskets, had his suspicions of the white man's daughter's love affair with Dain confirmed beyond the shadow of doubt. Dain disappeared, and Taminah's heart, where lay useless and barren the seeds of all love and of all hate, the possibilities of all passions and of all sacrifices, forgot its joys and its sufferings when deprived of the help of the senses. Her half-formed, savage mind, the slave of her body – as her body was the slave of another's will – forgot the faint and vague image of the ideal that had found its beginning in the physical promptings of her savage nature. She dropped back into the torpor of her former life and found consolation – even a certain kind of happiness – in the thought that now Nina and Dain were separated, probably for ever. He would forget. This thought soothed the last pangs of dying jealousy that had nothing now to feed upon, and Taminah found peace. It was like the dreary tranquillity of a desert, where there is peace only because there is no life.

And now he had returned. She had recognised his voice calling aloud in the night for Bulangi. She had crept out after her master to listen

closer to the intoxicating sound. Dain was there, in a boat, talking to
Bulangi. Taminah, listening with arrested breath, heard another voice.
The maddening joy, that only a second before she thought herself
incapable of containing within her fast-beating heart, died out, and left
her shivering in the old anguish of physical pain that she had suffered
once before at the sight of Dain and Nina. Nina spoke now, ordering
and entreating in turns, and Bulangi was refusing, expostulating, at last
consenting. He went in to take a paddle from the heap lying behind the
door. Outside the murmur of two voices went on, and she caught a
word here and there. She understood that he was fleeing from white
men, that he was seeking a hiding-place, that he was in some danger.
But she heard also words which woke the rage of jealousy that had
been asleep for so many days in her bosom. Crouching low on the mud
in the black darkness amongst the piles, she heard the whisper in the
boat that made light of toil, of privation, of danger, of life itself, if in
exchange there could be but a short moment of close embrace, a look
from the eyes, the feel of light breath, the touch of soft lips. So spoke
Dain as he sat in the canoe holding Nina's hands while waiting for
Bulangi's return; and Taminah, supporting herself by the slimy pile,
felt as if a heavy weight was crushing her down, down into the black
oily water at her feet. She wanted to cry out; to rush at them and tear
their vague shadows apart; to throw Nina into the smooth water, cling
to her close, hold her to the bottom where that man could not find her.
She could not cry, she could not move. Then footsteps were heard on
the bamboo platform above her head; she saw Bulangi get into his
smallest canoe and take the lead, the other boat following, paddled by
Dain and Nina. With a slight splash of the paddles dipped stealthily
into the water, their indistinct forms passed before her aching eyes and
vanished in the darkness of the creek.

She remained there in the cold and wet, powerless to move, breathing
painfully under the crushing weight that the mysterious hand of Fate
had laid so suddenly upon her slender shoulders, and shivering, she felt
within a burning fire that seemed to feed upon her very life. When the
breaking day had spread a pale golden ribbon over the black outline of
the forests, she took up her tray and departed towards the settlement,
going about her task purely from the force of habit. As she approached
Sambir she could see the excitement and she heard with momentary
surprise of the finding of Dain's body. It was not true, of course. She
knew it well. She regretted that he was not dead. She should have liked
Dain to be dead, so as to be parted from that woman – from all women.
She felt a strong desire to see Nina, but without any clear object. She

hated her, and feared her, and she felt an irresistible impulse pushing her towards Almayer's house to see the white woman's face, to look close at those eyes, to hear again that voice, for the sound of which Dain was ready to risk his liberty, his life even. She had seen her many times; she had heard her voice daily for many months past. What was there in her? What was there in that being to make a man speak as Dain had spoken, to make him blind to all other faces, deaf to all other voices?

She left the crowd by the riverside, and wandered aimlessly among the empty houses, resisting the impulse that pushed her towards Almayer's campong to seek there in Nina's eyes the secret of her own misery. The sun mounting higher, shortened the shadows and poured down upon her a flood of light and of stifling heat as she passed on from shadow to light, from light to shadow, amongst the houses, the bushes, the tall trees, in her unconscious flight from the pain in her own heart. In the extremity of her distress she could find no words to pray for relief, she knew of no heaven to send her prayer to, and she wandered on with tired feet in the dumb surprise and terror at the injustice of the suffering inflicted upon her without cause and without redress.

The short talk with Reshid, the proposal of Abdulla steadied her a little and turned her thoughts into another channel. Dain was in some danger. He was hiding from white men. So much she had overheard last night. They all thought him dead. She knew he was alive, and she knew of his hiding-place. What did the Arabs want to know about the white men? The white men want with Dain? Did they wish to kill him? She could tell them all – no, she would say nothing, and in the night she would go to him and sell him his life for a word, for a smile, for a gesture even, and be his slave in far-off countries, away from Nina. But there were dangers. The one-eyed Babalatchi who knew everything; the white man's wife – she was a witch. Perhaps they would tell. And then there was Nina. She must hurry on and see.

In her impatience she left the path and ran towards Almayer's dwelling through the undergrowth between the palm trees. She came out at the back of the house, where a narrow ditch, full of stagnant water that overflowed from the river, separated Almayer's campong from the rest of the settlement. The thick bushes growing on the bank were hiding from her sight the large courtyard with its cooking shed. Above them rose several thin columns of smoke, and from behind the sound of strange voices informed Taminah that the men of the sea belonging to the warship had already landed and were camped between the ditch and the house. To the left one of Almayer's slave-girls came down to the ditch and bent over the shiny water, washing a kettle. To the right the tops of the banana plantation, visible above the bushes, swayed and shook under the touch of invisible hands gathering the fruit. On the calm water several canoes moored to a heavy stake were crowded together, nearly bridging the ditch just at the place where Taminah stood. The voices in the courtyard rose at times into an outburst of calls, replies and laughter, and then died away into a silence that soon was broken again by a fresh clamour. Now and again the thin blue smoke rushed out thicker and blacker, and drove in odorous masses over the creek, wrapping her for a moment in a suffocating veil; then, as the fresh wood caught well alight, the smoke vanished in the bright sunlight, and only the scent of aromatic wood drifted afar, to leeward of the crackling fires.

Taminah rested her tray on the stump of a tree, and remained standing with her eyes turned towards Almayer's house, whose roof and part of a whitewashed wall were visible over the bushes. The slave-girl finished her work, and after looking for a while curiously at Taminah, pushed her way through the dense thicket back to the courtyard. Round Taminah there was now a complete solitude. She threw herself down on the ground, and hid her face in her hands. Now when so close she had no courage to see Nina. At every burst of louder voices from the courtyard she shivered in the fear of hearing Nina's voice. She came to the resolution of waiting where she was till dark, and then going straight to Dain's hiding-place. From where she was she could watch the movements of white men, of Nina, of all Dain's friends, and of all his enemies. Both were hateful alike to her, for both would take him away beyond her reach. She hid herself in the long grass to wait anxiously for the sunset that seemed so slow to come.

On the other side of the ditch, behind the bushes, by the clear fires, the seamen of the frigate had encamped on the hospitable invitation of Almayer. Almayer, roused out of his apathy by the prayers and importunity of Nina, had managed to get down in time to the jetty so as to receive the officers at their landing. The lieutenant in command accepted his invitation to his house with the remark that in any case their business was with Almayer – and perhaps not very pleasant, he added. Almayer hardly heard him. He shook hands with them absently and led the way towards the house. He was scarcely conscious of the polite words of welcome he greeted the strangers with, and afterwards repeated several times over again in his efforts to appear at ease. The agitation of their host did not escape the officer's eyes, and the chief confided to his subordinate, in a low voice, his doubts as to Almayer's sobriety. The young sub-lieutenant laughed and expressed in a whisper the hope that the white man was not intoxicated enough to neglect the offer of some refreshments. 'He does not seem very dangerous,' he added, as they followed Almayer up the steps of the verandah.

'No, he seems more of a fool than a knave; I have heard of him,' returned the senior.

They sat around the table. Almayer with shaking hands made gin cocktails, offered them all round, and drank himself, with every gulp feeling stronger, steadier and better able to face all the difficulties of his position. Ignorant of the fate of the brig he did not suspect the real object of the officer's visit. He had a general notion that something must have leaked out about the gunpowder trade, but apprehended nothing beyond some temporary inconveniences. After emptying his glass he began to chat easily, lying back in his chair with one of his legs thrown negligently over the arm. The lieutenant astride on his chair, a glowing cheroot in the corner of his mouth, listened with a sly smile from behind the thick volumes of smoke that escaped from his compressed lips. The young sub-lieutenant, leaning with both elbows on the table, his head between his hands, looked on sleepily in the torpor induced by fatigue and the gin.

Almayer talked on: 'It is a great pleasure to see white faces here. I have lived here many years in great solitude. The Malays, you understand, are not company for a white man; moreover they are not friendly; they do not understand our ways. Great rascals they are. I believe I am the only white man on the east coast that is a settled resident. We get visitors from Macassar or Singapore sometimes – traders, agents or explorers, but they are rare. There was a scientific explorer here a year or more ago. He lived in my house: drank from morning to night. He lived joyously for a few months, and when the liquor he brought with him was gone he returned to Batavia with a report on the mineral wealth of the interior. Ha, ha, ha! Good, is it not?'

He ceased abruptly and looked at his guests with a meaningless stare. While they laughed he was reciting to himself the old story: 'Dain dead, all my plans destroyed. This is the end of all hope and of all things.' His heart sank within him. He felt a kind of deadly sickness.

'Very good. Capital!' exclaimed both officers. Almayer came out of his despondency with another burst of talk.

'Eh! what about the dinner? You have got a cook with you. That's all right. There is a cooking shed in the other courtyard. I can give you a goose. Look at my geese – the only geese on the east coast – perhaps on the whole island. Is that your cook? Very good. Here, Ali, show this Chinaman the cooking place and tell Mem Almayer to let him have room there. My wife, gentlemen, does not come out; my daughter may. Meantime have some more drink. It is a hot day.'

The lieutenant took the cigar out of his mouth, looked at the ash critically, shook it off and turned towards Almayer.

'We have rather unpleasant business with you,' he said.

'I am sorry,' returned Almayer. 'It can be nothing very serious, surely.'

'If you think an attempt to blow up forty men at least, not a serious matter you will not find many people of your opinion,' retorted the officer sharply.

'Blow up! What? I know nothing about it,' exclaimed Almayer. 'Who did that, or tried to do it?'

'A man with whom you had some dealings,' answered the lieutenant. 'He passed here under the name of Dain Maroola. You sold him the gunpowder he had in that brig we captured.'

'How did you hear about the brig?' asked Almayer. 'I know nothing about the powder he may have had.'

'An Arab trader of this place has sent the information about your goings on here to Batavia, a couple of months ago,' said the officer. 'We were waiting for the brig outside, but he slipped past us at the mouth of the river, and we had to chase the fellow to the southward. When he sighted us he ran inside the reefs and put the brig ashore. The crew escaped in boats before we could take possession. As our boats neared the craft it blew up with a tremendous explosion; one of the boats being too near got swamped. Two men drowned – that is the result of your speculation, Mr Almayer. Now we want this Dain. We have good grounds to suppose he is hiding in Sambir. Do you know where he is? You had better put yourself right with the authorities as much as possible by being perfectly frank with me. Where is this Dain?'

Almayer got up and walked towards the balustrade of the verandah. He seemed not to be thinking of the officer's question. He looked at the body lying straight and rigid under its white cover on which the sun, declining amongst the clouds to the westward, threw a pale tinge of red. The lieutenant waited for the answer, taking quick pulls at his half-extinguished cigar. Behind them Ali moved noiselessly laying the table, ranging solemnly the ill-assorted and shabby crockery, the tin spoons, the forks with broken prongs and the knives with saw-like blades and loose handles. He had almost forgotten how to prepare the table for white men. He felt aggrieved; Mem Nina would not help him. He stepped back to look at his work admiringly, feeling very proud.

This must be right; and if the master afterwards is angry and swears, then so much the worse for Mem Nina. Why did she not help? He left the verandah to fetch the dinner.

'Well, Mr Almayer, will you answer my question as frankly as it is put to you?' asked the lieutenant, after a long silence.

Almayer turned round and looked at his interlocutor steadily. 'If you catch this Dain what will you do with him?' he asked.

The officer's face flushed. 'This is not an answer,' he said, annoyed.

'And what will you do with me?' went on Almayer, not heeding the interruption.

'Are you inclined to bargain?' growled the other. 'It would be bad policy, I assure you. At present I have no orders about your person, but we expected your assistance in catching this Malay.'

'Ah!' interrupted Almayer, 'just so: you can do nothing without me, and I, knowing the man well, am to help you in finding him.'

'This is exactly what we expect,' assented the officer. 'You have broken the law, Mr Almayer, and you ought to make amends.'

'And save myself?'

'Well, in a sense yes. Your head is not in any danger,' said the lieutenant, with a short laugh.

'Very well,' said Almayer, with decision, 'I shall deliver the man up to you.'

Both officers rose to their feet quickly, and looked for their side-arms which they had unbuckled.

Almayer laughed harshly. 'Steady, gentlemen!' he exclaimed. 'In my own time and in my own way. After dinner, gentlemen, you shall have him.'

'This is preposterous,' urged the lieutenant. 'Mr Almayer, this is no joking matter. The man is a criminal. He deserves to hang. While we dine he may escape; the rumour of our arrival – '

Almayer walked towards the table. 'I give you my word of honour, gentlemen, that he shall not escape; I have him safe enough.'

'The arrest should be effected before dark,' remarked the young sub.

'I shall hold you responsible for any failure. We are ready, but can do nothing just now without you,' added the senior, with evident annoyance.

Almayer made a gesture of assent. 'On my word of honour,' he repeated vaguely. 'And now let us dine,' he added briskly.

Nina came through the doorway and stood for a moment holding the curtain aside for Ali and the old Malay woman bearing the dishes; then she moved towards the three men by the table.

'Allow me,' said Almayer, pompously. 'This is my daughter. Nina, these gentlemen, officers of the frigate outside, have done me the honour to accept my hospitality.'

Nina answered the low bows of the two officers by a slow inclination of the head and took her place at the table opposite her father. All sat down. The coxswain of the steam launch came up carrying some bottles of wine.

'You will allow me to have this put upon the table?' said the lieutenant to Almayer.

'What! Wine! You are very kind. Certainly, I have none myself. Times are very hard.'

The last words of his reply were spoken by Almayer in a faltering voice. The thought that Dain was dead recurred to him vividly again, and he felt as if an invisible hand was gripping his throat. He reached for the gin bottle while they were uncorking the wine and swallowed a big gulp. The lieutenant, who was speaking to Nina, gave him a quick glance. The young sub began to recover from the astonishment and confusion caused by Nina's unexpected appearance and great beauty. 'She is very beautiful and imposing,' he reflected, 'but after all a half-caste girl.' This thought caused him to pluck up heart and look at Nina sideways. Nina, with composed face, was answering in a low, even voice the elder officer's polite questions as to the country and her mode of life. Almayer pushed his plate away and drank his guest's wine in gloomy silence.

'Can I believe what you tell me? It is like a tale for men that listen only half awake by the camp fire, and it seems to have run off a woman's tongue.'

'Who is there here for me to deceive, O Rajah?' answered Babalatchi. 'Without you I am nothing. All I have told you I believe to be true. I have been safe for many years in the hollow of your hand. This is no time to harbour suspicions. The danger is very great. We should advise and act at once, before the sun sets.'

'Right. Right,' muttered Lakamba, pensively.

They had been sitting for the last hour together in the audience chamber of the Rajah's house, for Babalatchi, as soon as he had witnessed the landing of the Dutch officers, had crossed the river to report to his master the events of the morning, and to confer with him upon the line of conduct to pursue in the face of altered circumstances. They were both puzzled and frightened by the unexpected turn the events had taken. The Rajah, sitting cross-legged on his chair, looked fixedly at the floor; Babalatchi was squatting close by in an attitude of deep dejection.

'And where did you say he is hiding now?' asked Lakamba, breaking at last the silence full of gloomy forebodings in which they both had been lost for a long while.

'In Bulangi's clearing – the farthest one away from the house. They went there that very night. The white man's daughter took him there. She told me so herself, speaking to me openly, for she is half white and has no decency. She said she was waiting for him while he was here; then, after a long time, he came out of the darkness and fell at her feet exhausted. He lay like one dead, but she brought him back to life in her arms, and made him breathe again with her own breath. That is what she said, speaking to my face, as I am speaking now to you, Rajah. She is like a white woman and knows no shame.'

He paused, deeply shocked. Lakamba nodded his head. 'Well, and then?' he asked.

'They called the old woman,' went on Babalatchi, 'and he told them all – about the brig, and how he tried to kill many men. He knew the Orang Blanda were very near, although he had said nothing to us about that; he knew his great danger. He thought he had killed many, but there were only two dead, as I have heard from the men of the sea that came in the warship's boats.'

'And the other man, he that was found in the river?' interrupted Lakamba.

'That was one of his boatmen. When his canoe was overturned by the logs those two swam together, but the other man must have been hurt. Dain swam, holding him up. He left him in the bushes when he went up to the house. When they all came down his heart had ceased to beat; then the old woman spoke; Dain thought it was good. He took off his anklet and broke it, twisting it round the man's foot. His ring he put on that slave's hand. He took off his sarong and clothed that thing that wanted no clothes, the two women holding it up meanwhile, their intent being to deceive all eyes and to mislead the minds in the settlement, so that they could swear to the thing that was not, and that there could be no treachery when the white men came. Then Dain and the white woman departed to call up Bulangi and find a hiding-place. The old woman remained by the body.'

'Hai!' exclaimed Lakamba. 'She has wisdom.'

'Yes, she has a devil of her own to whisper counsel in her ear,' assented Babalatchi. 'She dragged the body with great toil to the point where many logs were stranded. All these things were done in the darkness after the storm had passed away. Then she waited. At the first sign of daylight she battered the face of the dead with a heavy stone, and she pushed him amongst the logs. She remained near, watching. At sunrise Mahmat Banjer came and found him. They all believed; I myself was deceived, but not for long. The white man believed, and, grieving, fled to his house. When we were alone I, having doubts, spoke to the woman, and she, fearing my anger and your might, told me all, asking for help in saving Dain.'

'He must not fall into the hands of the Orang Blanda,' said Lakamba; 'but let him die, if the thing can be done quietly.'

'It cannot, Tuan! Remember there is that woman who, being half white, is ungovernable, and would raise a great outcry. Also the officers are here. They are angry enough already. Dain must escape; he must go. We must help him now for our own safety.'

'Are the officers very angry?' enquired Lakamba, with interest.

'They are. The principal chief used strong words when speaking to me – to me when I salaamed in your name. I do not think,' added Babalatchi, after a short pause and looking very worried, 'I do not think I saw a white chief so angry before. He said we were careless or even worse. He told me he would speak to the Rajah, and that I was of no account.'

'Speak to the Rajah!' repeated Lakamba, thoughtfully. 'Listen, Babalatchi: I am sick, and shall withdraw; you cross over and tell the white men.'

'Yes,' said Babalatchi, 'I am going over at once; and as to Dain?'

'You get him away as you can best. This is a great trouble in my heart,' sighed Lakamba.

Babalatchi got up, and, going close to his master, spoke earnestly.

'There is one of our praus at the southern mouth of the river. The Dutch warship is to the northward watching the main entrance. I shall send Dain off tonight in a canoe, by the hidden channels, to board the prau. His father is a great prince, and shall hear of our generosity. Let the prau take him to Ampanam.[55] Your glory shall be great, and your reward in powerful friendship. Almayer will no doubt deliver the dead body as Dain's to the officers, and the foolish white men shall say, "This is very good; let there be peace." And the trouble shall be removed from your heart, Rajah.'

'True! true!' said Lakamba.

'And this, being accomplished by me who am your slave, you shall reward with a generous hand. That I know! The white man is grieving for the lost treasure, in the manner of white men who thirst after dollars. Now, when all other things are in order, we shall perhaps obtain the treasure from the white man. Dain must escape, and Almayer must live.'

'Now go, Babalatchi, go!' said Lakamba, getting off his chair. 'I am very sick, and want medicine. Tell the white chief so.'

But Babalatchi was not to be got rid of in this summary manner. He knew that his master, after the manner of the great, liked to shift the burden of toil and danger on to his servants' shoulders, but in the difficult straits in which they were now the Rajah must play his part. He may be very sick for the white men, for all the world if he liked, as long as he would take upon himself the execution of part at least of Babalatchi's carefully thought-out plan. Babalatchi wanted a big canoe manned by twelve men to be sent out after dark towards Bulangi's clearing. Dain may have to be overpowered. A man in love cannot be expected to see clearly the path of safety if it leads him away from the object of his affections, argued Babalatchi, and in that case they would have to use force in order to make him go. Would the Rajah see that trusty men manned the canoe? The thing must be done secretly. Perhaps the Rajah would come himself, so as to bring all the weight of his authority to bear upon Dain if he should prove obstinate and refuse to leave his hiding-place. The Rajah would not commit himself to a definite promise, and anxiously pressed Babalatchi to go, being afraid

of the white men paying him an unexpected visit. The aged statesman
reluctantly took his leave and went into the courtyard.

Before going down to his boat Babalatchi stopped for a while in the
big open space where the thick-leaved trees put black patches of shadow
which seemed to float on a flood of smooth, intense light that rolled up
to the houses and down to the stockade and over the river, where it
broke and sparkled in thousands of glittering wavelets, like a band
woven of azure and gold edged with the brilliant green of the forests
guarding both banks of the Pantai. In the perfect calm before the
coming of the afternoon breeze the irregularly jagged line of tree tops
stood unchanging, as if traced by an unsteady hand on the clear blue of
the hot sky. In the space sheltered by the high palisades there lingered
the smell of decaying blossoms from the surrounding forest, a taint of
drying fish; with now and then a whiff of acrid smoke from the cooking
fires when it eddied down from under the leafy boughs and clung lazily
about the burnt-up grass.

As Babalatchi looked up at the flagstaff over-topping a group of
low trees in the middle of the courtyard, the tricolour flag of the
Netherlands stirred slightly for the first time since it had been hoisted
that morning on the arrival of the man-of-war boats. With a faint rustle
of trees the breeze came down in light puffs, playing capriciously for a
time with this emblem of Lakamba's power, that was also the mark of
his servitude; then the breeze freshened in a sharp gust of wind, and the
flag flew out straight and steady above the trees. A dark shadow ran
along the river, rolling over and covering up the sparkle of declining
sunlight. A big white cloud sailed slowly across the darkening sky, and
hung to the westward as if waiting for the sun to join it there. Men and
things shook off the torpor of the hot afternoon and stirred into life
under the first breath of the sea breeze.

Babalatchi hurried down to the water-gate; yet before he passed
through it he paused to look round the courtyard, with its light and
shade, with its cheery fires, with the groups of Lakamba's soldiers and
retainers scattered about. His own house stood amongst the other
buildings in that enclosure, and the statesman of Sambir asked himself
with a sinking heart when and how would it be given him to return to
that house. He had to deal with a man more dangerous than any wild
beast of his experience: a proud man, a man wilful after the manner of
princes, a man in love. And he was going forth to speak to that man
words of cold and worldly wisdom. Could anything be more appalling?
What if that man should take umbrage at some fancied slight to his
honour or disregard of his affections and suddenly run amok?[56] The

wise adviser would be the first victim, no doubt, and death would be his reward. And underlying the horror of this situation there was the danger of those meddlesome fools, the white men. A vision of comfortless exile in far-off Madura[57] rose up before Babalatchi. Wouldn't that be worse than death itself? And there was that half-white woman with threatening eyes. How could he tell what an incomprehensible creature of that sort would or would not do? She knew so much that she made the killing of Dain an impossibility. That much was certain. And yet the sharp, rough-edged kriss is a good and discreet friend, thought Babalatchi, as he examined his own lovingly, and put it back in the sheath, with a sigh of regret, before unfastening his canoe. As he cast off the painter, pushed out into the stream and took up his paddle, he realised vividly how unsatisfactory it was to have women mixed up in state affairs. Young women, of course. For Mrs Almayer's mature wisdom, and for the easy aptitude in intrigue that comes with years to the feminine mind, he felt the most sincere respect.

He paddled leisurely, letting the canoe drift down as he crossed towards the point. The sun was high yet, and nothing pressed. His work would commence only with the coming of darkness. Avoiding the Lingard jetty, he rounded the point, and paddled up the creek at the back of Almayer's house. There were many canoes lying there, their noses all drawn together, fastened all to the same stake. Babalatchi pushed his little craft in amongst them and stepped on shore. On the other side of the ditch something moved in the grass.

'Who's that hiding?' hailed Babalatchi. 'Come out and speak to me.'

Nobody answered. Babalatchi crossed over, passing from boat to boat, and poked his staff viciously in the suspicious place. Taminah jumped up with a cry.

'What are you doing here?' he asked, surprised. 'I have nearly stepped on your tray. Am I a Dyak that you should hide at my sight?'

'I was weary, and – I slept,' whispered Taminah, confusedly.

'You slept! You have not sold anything today, and you will be beaten when you return home,' said Babalatchi.

Taminah stood before him abashed and silent. Babalatchi looked her over carefully with great satisfaction. Decidedly he would offer fifty dollars more to that thief Bulangi. The girl pleased him.

'Now you go home. It is late,' he said sharply. 'Tell Bulangi that I shall be near his house before the night is half over, and that I want him to make all things ready for a long journey. You understand? A long journey to the southward. Tell him that before sunset, and do not forget my words.'

Taminah made a gesture of assent, and watched Babalatchi recross the ditch and disappear through the bushes bordering Almayer's compound. She moved a little farther off the creek and sank in the grass again, lying down on her face, shivering in dry-eyed misery.

Babalatchi walked straight towards the cooking-shed looking for Mrs Almayer. The courtyard was in a great uproar. A strange Chinaman had possession of the kitchen fire and was noisily demanding another saucepan. He hurled objurgations, in the Canton dialect and bad Malay, against the group of slave-girls standing a little way off, half frightened, half amused, at his violence. From the camping fires round which the seamen of the frigate were sitting came words of encouragement, mingled with laughter and jeering. In the midst of this noise and confusion Babalatchi met Ali, an empty dish in his hand.

'Where are the white men?' asked Babalatchi.

'They are eating in the front verandah,' answered Ali. 'Do not stop me, Tuan. I am giving the white men their food and am busy.'

'Where's Mem Almayer?'

'Inside in the passage. She is listening to the talk.'

Ali grinned and passed on; Babalatchi ascended the plankway to the rear verandah, and beckoning out Mrs Almayer, engaged her in earnest conversation. Through the long passage, closed at the farther end by the red curtain, they could hear from time to time Almayer's voice mingling in conversation with an abrupt loudness that made Mrs Almayer look significantly at Babalatchi.

'Listen,' she said. 'He has drunk much.'

'He has,' whispered Babalatchi. 'He will sleep heavily tonight.'

Mrs Almayer looked doubtful.

'Sometimes the devil of strong gin makes him keep awake, and he walks up and down the verandah all night, cursing; then we stand afar off,' explained Mrs Almayer, with the fuller knowledge born of twenty odd years of married life.

'But then he does not hear, nor understand, and his hand, of course, has no strength. We do not want him to hear tonight.'

'No,' assented Mrs Almayer, energetically, but in a cautiously subdued voice. 'If he hears he will kill.'

Babalatchi looked incredulous.

'Hai, Tuan, you may believe me. Have I not lived many years with that man? Have I not seen death in that man's eyes more than once when I was younger and he guessed at many things. Had he been a man of my own people I would not have seen such a look twice; but he – '

With a contemptuous gesture she seemed to fling unutterable scorn on Almayer's weak-minded aversion to sudden bloodshed.

'If he has the wish but not the strength, then what do we fear?' asked Babalatchi, after a short silence during which they both listened to Almayer's loud talk till it subsided into the murmur of general conversation. 'What do we fear?' repeated Babalatchi again.

'To keep the daughter whom he loves he would strike into your heart and mine without hesitation,' said Mrs Almayer. 'When the girl is gone he will be like the devil unchained. Then you and I had better beware.'

'I am an old man and fear not death,' answered Babalatchi, with a mendacious assumption of indifference. 'But what will you do?'

'I am an old woman, and wish to live,' retorted Mrs Almayer. 'She is my daughter also. I shall seek safety at the feet of our Rajah, speaking in the name of the past when we both were young, and he – '

Babalatchi raised his hand.

'Enough. You shall be protected,' he said soothingly.

Again the sound of Almayer's voice was heard, and again interrupting their talk, they listened to the confused but loud utterance coming in bursts of unequal strength, with unexpected pauses and noisy repetitions that made some words and sentences fall clear and distinct on their ears out of the meaningless jumble of excited shoutings emphasised by the thumping of Almayer's fist upon the table. On the short intervals of silence, the high complaining note of tumblers, standing close together and vibrating to the shock, lingered, growing fainter, till it leapt up again into tumultuous ringing when a new idea started a new rush of words and brought down the heavy hand again. At last the quarrelsome shouting ceased, and the thin plaint of disturbed glass died away into reluctant quietude.

Babalatchi and Mrs Almayer had listened curiously, their bodies bent and their ears turned towards the passage. At every louder shout they nodded at each other with a ridiculous affectation of scandalised propriety, and they remained in the same attitude for some time after the noise had ceased.

'This is the devil of gin,' whispered Mrs Almayer. 'Yes; he talks like that sometimes when there is nobody to hear him.'

'What does he say?' enquired Babalatchi, eagerly. 'You ought to understand.'

'I have forgotten their talk. A little I understood. He spoke without any respect of the white ruler in Batavia, and of protection, and said he had been wronged; he said that several times. More I did not understand. Listen! Again he speaks!'

'Tse! tse! tse!' clicked Babalatchi, trying to appear shocked, but with a joyous twinkle of his solitary eye. 'There will be great trouble between those white men. I will go round now and see. You tell your daughter that there is a sudden and a long journey before her, with much glory and splendour at the end. And tell her that Dain must go, or he must die, and that he will not go alone.'

'No, he will not go alone,' slowly repeated Mrs Almayer, with a thoughtful air, as she crept into the passage after seeing Babalatchi disappear round the corner of the house.

The statesman of Sambir, under the impulse of vivid curiosity, made his way quickly to the front of the house, but once there he moved slowly and cautiously as he crept step by step up the stairs of the verandah. On the highest step he sat down quietly, his feet on the steps below, ready for flight should his presence prove unwelcome. He felt pretty safe so. The table stood nearly endways to him, and he saw Almayer's back; at Nina he looked full face, and had a side view of both officers; but of the four persons sitting at the table only Nina and the younger officer noticed his noiseless arrival. The momentary dropping of Nina's eyelids acknowledged Babalatchi's presence; she then spoke at once to the young sub, who turned towards her with attentive alacrity, but her gaze was fastened steadily on her father's face while Almayer was speaking uproariously.

' . . . disloyalty and unscrupulousness! What have you ever done to make me loyal? You have no grip on this country. I had to take care of myself, and when I asked for protection I was met with threats and contempt, and had Arab slander thrown in my face. I! a white man!'

'Don't be violent, Almayer,' remonstrated the lieutenant; 'I have heard all this already.'

'Then why do you talk to me about scruples? I wanted money, and I gave powder in exchange. How could I know that some of your wretched men were going to be blown up? Scruples! Pah!'

He groped unsteadily amongst the bottles, trying one after another, grumbling to himself the while.

'No more wine,' he muttered discontentedly.

'You have had enough, Almayer,' said the lieutenant, as he lighted a cigar. 'Is it not time to deliver to us your prisoner? I take it you have that Dain Maroola stowed away safely somewhere. Still we had better get that business over, and then we shall have more drink. Come! don't look at me like this.'

Almayer was staring with stony eyes, his trembling fingers fumbling about his throat.

'Gold,' he said with difficulty. 'Hem! A hand on the windpipe, you know. Sure you will excuse. I wanted to say – a little gold for a little powder. What's that?'

'I know, I know,' said the lieutenant soothingly.

'No! You don't know. Not one of you knows!' shouted Almayer. 'The government is a fool, I tell you. Heaps of gold. I am the man that knows; I and another one. But he won't speak. He is – '

He checked himself with a feeble smile, and, making an unsuccessful attempt to pat the officer on the shoulder, knocked over a couple of empty bottles.

'Personally you are a fine fellow,' he said very distinctly, in a patronising manner. His head nodded drowsily as he sat muttering to himself.

The two officers looked at each other helplessly.

'This won't do,' said the lieutenant, addressing his junior. 'Have the men mustered in the compound here. I must get some sense out of him. Hi! Almayer! Wake up, man. Redeem your word. You gave your word. You gave your word of honour, you know.'

Almayer shook off the officer's hand with impatience, but his ill-humour vanished at once, and he looked up, putting his forefinger to the side of his nose.

'You are very young; there is time for all things,' he said, with an air of great sagacity.

The lieutenant turned towards Nina, who, leaning back in her chair, watched her father steadily.

'Really I am very much distressed by all this for your sake,' he exclaimed. 'I do not know;' he went on, speaking with some embarrassment, 'whether I have any right to ask you anything, unless, perhaps, to withdraw from this painful scene, but I feel that I must – for your father's good – suggest that you should – I mean if you have any influence over him you ought to exert it now to make him keep the promise he gave me before he – before he got into this state.'

He observed with discouragement that she seemed not to take any notice of what he said, sitting still with half-closed eyes.

'I trust – ' he began again.

'What is the promise you speak of?' abruptly asked Nina, leaving her seat and moving towards her father.

'Nothing that is not just and proper. He promised to deliver to us a man who in time of profound peace took the lives of innocent men to escape the punishment he deserved for breaking the law. He planned his mischief on a large scale. It is not his fault if it failed, partially. Of

course you have heard of Dain Maroola. Your father secured him, I
understand. We know he escaped up this river. Perhaps you – '

'And he killed white men!' interrupted Nina.

'I regret to say they were white. Yes, two white men lost their lives
through that scoundrel's freak.'

'Two only!' exclaimed Nina.

The officer looked at her in amazement.

'Why! why! You – ' he stammered, confused.

'There might have been more,' interrupted Nina. 'And when you get
this – this scoundrel will you go?'

The lieutenant, still speechless, bowed his assent.

'Then I would get him for you if I had to seek him in a burning fire,'
she burst out with intense energy. 'I hate the sight of your white faces. I
hate the sound of your gentle voices. That is the way you speak to
women, dropping sweet words before any pretty face. I have heard your
voices before. I hoped to live here without seeing any other white face
but this,' she added in a gentler tone, touching lightly her father's
cheek.

Almayer ceased his mumbling and opened his eyes. He caught hold
of his daughter's hand and pressed it to his face, while Nina with the
other hand smoothed his rumpled grey hair, looking defiantly over her
father's head at the officer, who had now regained his composure and
returned her look with a cool, steady stare. Below, in front of the
verandah, they could hear the tramp of seamen mustering there
according to orders. The sub-lieutenant came up the steps, while
Babalatchi stood up uneasily and, with finger on lip, tried to catch
Nina's eye.

'You are a good girl,' whispered Almayer, absently, dropping his
daughter's hand.

'Father! father!' she cried, bending over him with passionate entreaty.
'See those two men looking at us. Send them away. I cannot bear it any
more. Send them away. Do what they want and let them go.'

She caught sight of Babalatchi and ceased speaking suddenly, but her
foot tapped the floor with rapid beats in a paroxysm of nervous restlessness. The two officers stood close together looking on curiously.

'What has happened? What is the matter?' whispered the younger
man.

'Don't know,' answered the other, under his breath. 'One is furious,
and the other is drunk. Not so drunk, either. Queer, this. Look!'

Almayer had risen, holding on to his daughter's arm. He hesitated
a moment, then he let go his hold and lurched halfway across the

verandah. There he pulled himself together, and stood very straight, breathing hard and glaring round angrily.

'Are the men ready?' asked the lieutenant.

'All ready, sir.'

'Now, Mr Almayer, lead the way,' said the lieutenant

Almayer rested his eyes on him as if he saw him for the first time.

'Two men,' he said thickly. The effort of speaking seemed to interfere with his equilibrium. He took a quick step to save himself from a fall, and remained swaying backwards and forwards. 'Two men,' he began again, speaking with difficulty. 'Two white men – men in uniform – honourable men. I want to say – men of honour. Are you?'

'Come! None of that,' said the officer impatiently. 'Let us have that friend of yours.'

'What do you think I am?' asked Almayer, fiercely.

'You are drunk, but not so drunk as not to know what you are doing. Enough of this tomfoolery,' said the officer sternly, 'or I will have you put under arrest in your own house.'

'Arrest!' laughed Almayer, discordantly. 'Ha! ha! ha! Arrest! Why, I have been trying to get out of this infernal place for twenty years, and I can't. You hear, man! I can't, and never shall! Never!'

He ended his words with a sob, and walked unsteadily down the stairs. When in the courtyard the lieutenant approached him, and took him by the arm. The sub-lieutenant and Babalatchi followed close.

'That's better, Almayer,' said the officer encouragingly. 'Where are you going to? There are only planks there. Here,' he went on, shaking him slightly, 'do we want the boats?'

'No,' answered Almayer, viciously. 'You want a grave.'

'What? Wild again! Try to talk sense.'

'Grave!' roared Almayer, struggling to get himself free. 'A hole in the ground. Don't you understand? You must be drunk. Let me go! Let go, I tell you!'

He tore away from the officer's grasp, and reeled towards the planks where the body lay under its white cover; then he turned round quickly, and faced the semicircle of interested faces. The sun was sinking rapidly, throwing long shadows of house and trees over the courtyard, but the light lingered yet on the river, where the logs went drifting past in midstream, looking very distinct and black in the pale red glow. The trunks of the trees in the forest on the east bank were lost in gloom while their highest branches swayed gently in the departing sunlight. The air felt heavy and cold in the breeze, expiring in slight puffs that came over the water.

Almayer shivered as he made an effort to speak, and again with an uncertain gesture he seemed to free his throat from the grip of an invisible hand. His bloodshot eyes wandered aimlessly from face to face.

'There!' he said at last. 'Are you all there? He is a dangerous man.'

He dragged at the cover with hasty violence, and the body rolled stiffly off the planks and fell at his feet in rigid helplessness.

'Cold, perfectly cold,' said Almayer, looking round with a mirthless smile. 'Sorry can do no better. And you can't hang him, either. As you observe, gentlemen,' he added gravely, 'there is no head, and hardly any neck.'

The last ray of light was snatched away from the tree tops, the river grew suddenly dark, and in the great stillness the murmur of the flowing water seemed to fill the vast expanse of grey shadow that descended upon the land.

'This is Dain,' went on Almayer to the silent group that surrounded him. 'And I have kept my word. First one hope, then another, and this is my last. Nothing is left now. You think there is one dead man here? Mistake, I 'sure you. I am much more dead. Why don't you hang me?' he suggested suddenly, in a friendly tone, addressing the lieutenant. 'I assure, assure you it would be a mat – matter of form altog – altogether.'

These last words he muttered to himself, and walked zigzaging towards his house. 'Get out!' he thundered at Ali, who was approaching timidly with offers of assistance. From afar, scared groups of men and women watched his devious progress. He dragged himself up the stairs by the banister, and managed to reach a chair into which he fell heavily. He sat for awhile panting with exertion and anger, and looking round vaguely for Nina; then, making a threatening gesture towards the compound, where he had heard Babalatchi's voice, he overturned the table with his foot in a great crash of smashed crockery. He muttered yet menacingly to himself, then his head fell on his breast, his eyes closed and with a deep sigh he fell asleep.

That night – for the first time in its history – the peaceful and flourishing settlement of Sambir saw the lights shining about Almayer's Folly. These were the lanterns of the boats hung up by the seamen under the verandah where the two officers were holding a court of enquiry into the truth of the story related to them by Babalatchi. Babalatchi had regained all his importance. He was eloquent and persuasive, calling Heaven and Earth to witness the truth of his statements. There were also other witnesses. Mahmat Banjer and a good many others underwent a close examination that dragged its weary length far into the evening. A messenger was sent for Abdulla, who excused himself from coming on the score of his venerable age, but sent Reshid. Mahmat had to produce the bangle, and saw with rage and mortification the lieutenant put it in his pocket, as one of the proofs of Dain's death, to be sent in with the official report of the mission. Babalatchi's ring was also impounded for the same purpose, but the experienced statesman was resigned to that loss from the very beginning. He did not mind as long as he was sure that the white men believed. He put that question to himself earnestly as he left, one of the last, when the proceedings came to a close. He was not certain. Still, if they believed only for a night, he would put Dain beyond their reach and feel safe himself. He walked away fast, looking from time to time over his shoulder in the fear of being followed, but he saw and heard nothing.

'Ten o'clock,' said the lieutenant, looking at his watch and yawning. 'I shall hear some of the captain's complimentary remarks when we get back. Miserable business, this.'

'Do you think all this is true?' asked the younger man.

'True! It is just possible. But if it isn't true what can we do? If we had a dozen boats we could patrol the creeks; and that wouldn't be much good. That drunken madman was right; we haven't enough hold on this coast. They do what they like. Are our hammocks slung?'

'Yes, I told the coxswain. Strange couple over there,' said the sub, with a wave of his hand towards Almayer's house.

'Hem! Queer, certainly. What have you been telling her? I was attending to the father most of the time.'

'I assure you I have been perfectly civil,' protested the other warmly.

'All right. Don't get excited. She objects to civility, then, from what I understand. I thought you might have been tender. You know we are on service.'

'Well, of course. Never forget that. Coldly civil. That's all.'

They both laughed a little, and not feeling sleepy began to pace the verandah side by side. The moon rose stealthily above the trees, and suddenly changed the river into a stream of scintillating silver. The forest came out of the black void and stood sombre and pensive over the sparkling water. The breeze died away into a breathless calm.

Seamanlike, the two officers tramped measuredly up and down without exchanging a word. The loose planks rattled rhythmically under their steps with obstrusive dry sound in the perfect silence of the night. As they were wheeling round again the younger man stood attentive.

'Did you hear that?' he asked.

'No!' said the other. 'Hear what?'

'I thought I heard a cry. Ever so faint. Seemed a woman's voice. In that other house. Ah! Again! Hear it?'

'No,' said the lieutenant, after listening awhile. 'You young fellows always hear women's voices. If you are going to dream you had better get into your hammock. Good-night.'

The moon mounted higher, and the warm shadows grew smaller and crept away as if hiding before the cold and cruel light.

Chapter 10

'It has set at last,' said Nina to her mother pointing towards the hills behind which the sun had sunk. 'Listen, mother, I am going now to Bulangi's creek, and if I should never return – '

She interrupted herself, and something like doubt dimmed for a moment the fire of suppressed exaltation that had glowed in her eyes and had illuminated the serene impassiveness of her features with a ray of eager life during all that long day of excitement – the day of joy and anxiety, of hope and terror, of vague grief and indistinct delight. While the sun shone with that dazzling light in which her love was born and grew till it possessed her whole being, she was kept firm in her unwavering resolve by the mysterious whisperings of desire which filled her heart with impatient longing for the darkness that would mean the end of danger and strife, the beginning of happiness, the fulfilling of love, the completeness of life. It had set at last! The short tropical twilight went out before she could draw the long breath of relief; and now the sudden darkness seemed to be full of menacing voices calling upon her to rush headlong into the unknown; to be true to her own impulses, to give herself up to the passion she had evoked and shared. He was waiting! In the solitude of the secluded clearing, in the vast silence of the forest he was waiting alone, a fugitive in fear of his life. Indifferent to his danger he was waiting for her. It was for her only that he had come; and now as the time approached when he should have his reward, she asked herself with dismay what meant that chilling doubt of her own will and of her own desire? With an effort she shook off the fear of the passing weakness. He should have his reward. Her woman's love and her woman's honour overcame the faltering distrust of that unknown future waiting for her in the darkness of the river.

'No, you will not return,' muttered Mrs Almayer, prophetically. 'Without you he will not go, and if he remains here – ' She waved her hand towards the lights of Almayer's Folly, and the unfinished sentence died out in a threatening murmur.

The two women had met behind the house, and now were walking slowly together towards the creek where all the canoes were moored. Arrived at the fringe of bushes they stopped by a common impulse, and Mrs Almayer, laying her hand on her daughter's arm, tried in vain to look close into the girl's averted face. When she attempted to speak her first words were lost in a stifled sob that sounded strangely coming from that woman who, of all human passions, seemed to know only those of anger and hate.

'You are going away to be a great Ranee,' she said at last, in a voice that was steady enough now, 'and if you be wise you shall have much power that will endure many days, and even last into your old age. What have I been? A slave all my life, and I have cooked rice for a man who had no courage and no wisdom. Hai! I – even I! – was given in gift by a chief and a warrior to a man that was neither. Hai! Hai!'

She wailed to herself softly, lamenting the lost possibilities of murder and mischief that could have fallen to her lot had she been mated with a congenial spirit. Nina bent down over Mrs Almayer's slight form and scanned attentively, under the stars that had rushed out on the black sky and now hung breathless over that strange parting, her mother's shrivelled features, and looked close into the sunken eyes that could see into her own dark future by the light of a long and a painful experience. Again she felt herself fascinated, as of old, by her mother's exalted mood and by the oracular certainty of expression which, together with her fits of violence, had contributed not a little to the reputation for witchcraft she enjoyed in the settlement.

'I was a slave, and you shall be a queen,' went on Mrs Almayer, looking straight before her; 'but remember men's strength and their weakness. Tremble before his anger, so that he may see your fear in the light of day; but in your heart you may laugh, for after sunset he is your slave.'

'A slave! He! The master of life! You do not know him, mother.'

Mrs Almayer condescended to laugh contemptuously.

'You speak like a fool of a white woman,' she exclaimed. 'What do you know of men's anger and of men's love? Have you watched the sleep of men weary of dealing death? Have you felt about you the strong arm that could drive a kriss deep into a beating heart? Yah! you are a white woman, and ought to pray to a woman-god!'

'Why do you say this? I have listened to your words so long that I have forgotten my old life. If I was white would I stand here, ready to go? Mother, I shall return to the house and look once more at my father's face.'

'No!' said Mrs Almayer, violently. 'No, he sleeps now the sleep of gin; and if you went back he might awake and see you. No, he shall never see you. When the terrible old man took you away from me when you were little, you remember – '

'It was such a long time ago,' murmured Nina.

'I remember,' went on Mrs Almayer, fiercely. 'I wanted to look at your face again. He said no! I heard you cry and jumped into the river. You were his daughter then; you are my daughter now. Never shall you go back to that house; you shall never cross this courtyard again. No! no!'

Her voice rose almost to a shout. On the other side of the creek there was a rustle in the long grass. The two women heard it, and listened for a while in startled silence. 'I shall go,' said Nina, in a cautious but intense whisper. 'What is your hate or your revenge to me?'

She moved towards the house, Mrs Almayer clinging to her and trying to pull her back.

'Stop, you shall not go!' she gasped.

Nina pushed away her mother impatiently and gathered up her skirts for a quick run, but Mrs Almayer ran forward and turned round, facing her daughter with outstretched arms.

'If you move another step,' she exclaimed, breathing quickly, 'I shall cry out. Do you see those lights in the big house? There sit two white men, angry because they cannot have the blood of the man you love. And in those dark houses,' she continued, more calmly as she pointed towards the settlement, 'my voice could wake up men that would lead the Orang Blanda soldiers to him who is waiting – for you.'

She could not see her daughter's face, but the white figure before her stood silent and irresolute in the darkness. Mrs Almayer pursued her advantage.

'Give up your old life! Forget!' she said in entreating tones. 'Forget that you ever looked at a white face; forget their words; forget their thoughts. They speak lies. And they think lies because they despise us that are better than they are, but not so strong. Forget their friendship and their contempt; forget their many gods. Girl, why do you want to remember the past when there is a warrior and a chief ready to give many lives – his own life – for one of your smiles?'

While she spoke she gently pushed her daughter towards the canoes, hiding her own fear, anxiety and doubt under the flood of passionate words that left Nina no time to think and no opportunity to protest, even if she had wished it. But she did not wish it now. At the bottom of that passing desire to look again at her father's face there was no strong affection. She felt no scruples and no remorse at leaving suddenly that man whose sentiment towards herself she could not understand, she could not even see. There was only an instinctive clinging to old life, to old habits, to old faces; that fear of finality which lurks in every human breast and prevents so many heroisms and so many crimes. For years she had stood between her mother and her father, the one so strong in her weakness, the other so weak where he could have been strong.

Between those two beings so dissimilar, so antagonistic, she stood with mute heart wondering and angry at the fact of her own existence. It seemed so unreasonable, so humiliating to be flung there in that settlement and to see the days rush by into the past, without a hope, a desire or an aim that would justify the life she had to endure in ever-growing weariness. She had little belief in and no sympathy for her father's dreams; but the savage ravings of her mother chanced to strike a responsive chord, deep down somewhere in her despairing heart; and she dreamed dreams of her own with the persistent absorption of a captive thinking of liberty within the walls of his prison cell. With the coming of Dain she found the road to freedom by obeying the voice of the new-born impulses, and with surprised joy she thought she could read in his eyes the answer to all the questionings of her heart. She understood now the reason and the aim of life; and in the triumphant unveiling of that mystery she threw away disdainfully her past with its sad thoughts, its bitter feelings and its faint affections, now withered and dead in contact with her fierce passion.

Mrs Almayer unmoored Nina's own canoe and, straightening herself painfully, stood, painter in hand, looking at her daughter.

'Quick,' she said; 'get away before the moon rises, while the river is dark. I am afraid of Abdulla's slaves. The wretches prowl in the night often, and might see and follow you. There are two paddles in the canoe.'

Nina approached her mother and hesitatingly touched lightly with her lips the wrinkled forehead. Mrs Almayer snorted contemptuously in protest against that tenderness which she, nevertheless, feared could be contagious.

'Shall I ever see you again, mother?' murmured Nina.

'No,' said Mrs Almayer, after a short silence. 'Why should you return here where it is my fate to die? You will live far away in splendour and might. When I hear of white men driven from the islands, then I shall know that you are alive, and that you remember my words.'

'I shall always remember,' returned Nina, earnestly; 'but where is my power, and what can I do?'

'Do not let him look too long in your eyes, nor lay his head on your knees without reminding him that men should fight before they rest. And if he lingers, give him his kriss yourself and bid him go, as the wife of a mighty prince should do when the enemies are near. Let him slay the white men that come to us to trade, with prayers on their lips and loaded guns in their hands. Ah!' – she ended with a sigh – 'they are on every sea, and on every shore; and they are very many!'

She swung the bow of the canoe towards the river, but did not let go the gunwale, keeping her hand on it in irresolute thoughtfulness.

Nina put the point of the paddle against the bank, ready to shove off into the stream.

'What is it, mother?' she asked, in a low voice. 'Do you hear anything?'

'No,' said Mrs Almayer, absently. 'Listen, Nina,' she continued, abruptly, after a slight pause, 'in after years there will be other women – '

A stifled cry in the boat interrupted her, and the paddle rattled in the canoe as it slipped from Nina's hands, which she put out in a protesting gesture. Mrs Almayer fell on her knees on the bank and leaned over the gunwale so as to bring her own face close to her daughter's.

'There will be other women,' she repeated firmly; 'I tell you that, because you are half white, and may forget that he is a great chief, and that such things must be. Hide your anger, and do not let him see on your face the pain that will eat your heart. Meet him with joy in your eyes and wisdom on your lips, for to you he will turn in sadness or in doubt. As long as he looks upon many women your power will last, but should there be one, one only with whom he seems to forget you, then – '

'I could not live,' exclaimed Nina, covering her face with both her hands. 'Do not speak so, mother; it could not be.'

'Then,' went on Mrs Almayer, steadily, 'to that woman, Nina, show no mercy.'

She moved the canoe down towards the stream by the gunwale, and gripped it with both her hands, the bow pointing into the river.

'Are you crying?' she asked sternly of her daughter, who sat still with covered face. 'Arise, and take your paddle, for he has waited long enough. And remember, Nina, no mercy; and if you must strike, strike with a steady hand.'

She put out all her strength, and swinging her body over the water, shot the light craft far into the stream. When she recovered herself from the effort she tried vainly to catch a glimpse of the canoe that seemed to have dissolved suddenly into the white mist trailing over the heated waters of the Pantai. After listening for a while intently on her knees, Mrs Almayer rose with a deep sigh, while two tears wandered slowly down her withered cheeks. She wiped them off quickly with a wisp of her grey hair as if ashamed of herself, but could not stifle another loud sigh, for her heart was heavy and she suffered much, being unused to tender emotions. This time she fancied she had heard a faint noise, like the echo of her own sigh, and she stopped, straining her ears to catch the slightest sound, and peering apprehensively towards the bushes near her.

'Who is there?' she asked, in an unsteady voice, while her imagination peopled the solitude of the riverside with ghost-like forms. 'Who is there?' she repeated faintly.

There was no answer: only the voice of the river murmuring in sad monotone behind the white veil seemed to swell louder for a moment, to die away again in a soft whisper of eddies washing against the bank.

Mrs Almayer shook her head as if in answer to her own thoughts, and walked quickly away from the bushes, looking to the right and left watchfully. She went straight towards the cooking-shed, observing that the embers of the fire there glowed more brightly than usual, as if somebody had been adding fresh fuel to the fires during the evening. As she approached, Babalatchi, who had been squatting in the warm glow, rose and met her in the shadow outside.

'Is she gone?' asked the anxious statesman, hastily.

'Yes,' answered Mrs Almayer. 'What are the white men doing? When did you leave them?'

'They are sleeping now, I think. May they never wake!' exclaimed Babalatchi, fervently. 'Oh! but they are devils, and made much talk and trouble over that carcass. The chief threatened me twice with his hand, and said he would have me tied up to a tree. Tie me up to a tree! Me!' he repeated, striking his breast violently.

Mrs Almayer laughed tauntingly.

'And you salaamed and asked for mercy. Men with arms by their side acted otherwise when I was young.'

'And where are they, the men of your youth? You mad woman!' retorted Babalatchi, angrily. 'Killed by the Dutch. Aha! But I shall live to deceive them. A man knows when to fight and when to tell peaceful lies. You would know that if you were not a woman.'

But Mrs Almayer did not seem to hear him. With bent body and outstretched arm she appeared to be listening to some noise behind the shed.

'There are strange sounds,' she whispered, with evident alarm. 'I have heard in the air the sounds of grief, as of a sigh and weeping. That was by the riverside. And now again I heard – '

'Where?' asked Babalatchi, in an altered voice. 'What did you hear?'

'Close here. It was like a breath long drawn. I wish I had burnt the paper over the body before it was buried.'

'Yes,' assented Babalatchi. 'But the white men had him thrown into a hole at once. You know he found his death on the river,' he added cheerfully, 'and his ghost may hail the canoes, but would leave the land alone.'

Mrs Almayer, who had been craning her neck to look round the corner of the shed, drew back her head.

'There is nobody there,' she said, reassured. 'Is it not time for the Rajah war-canoe[58] to go to the clearing?'

'I have been waiting for it here, for I myself must go,' explained Babalatchi. 'I think I will go over and see what makes them late. When will you come? The Rajah gives you refuge.'

'I shall paddle over before the break of day. I cannot leave my dollars behind,' muttered Mrs Almayer.

They separated. Babalatchi crossed the courtyard towards the creek to get his canoe, and Mrs Almayer walked slowly to the house, ascended the plankway, and passing through the back verandah entered the passage leading to the front of the house; but before going in she turned in the doorway and looked back at the empty and silent courtyard, now lit up by the rays of the rising moon. No sooner had she disappeared, however, than a vague shape flitted out from among the stalks of the banana plantation, darted over the moonlit space, and fell in the darkness at the foot of the verandah. It might have been the shadow of a driving cloud, so noiseless and rapid was its passage, but for the trail of disturbed grass, whose feathery heads trembled and swayed for a long time in the moonlight before they rested motionless and gleaming, like a design of silver sprays embroidered on a sombre background.

Mrs Almayer lighted the coconut lamp, and lifting cautiously the red curtain, gazed upon her husband, shading the light with her hand. Almayer, huddled up in the chair, one of his arms hanging down, the other thrown across the lower part of his face as if to ward off an invisible enemy, his legs stretched straight out, slept heavily, unconscious of the unfriendly eyes that looked upon him in disparaging criticism. At his feet lay the overturned table, among a wreck of crockery and broken bottles. The appearance as of traces left by a desperate struggle was accentuated by the chairs, which seemed to have been scattered violently all over the place, and now lay about the verandah with a lamentable aspect of inebriety in their helpless attitudes. Only Nina's big rocking-chair, standing black and motionless on its high runners, towered above the chaos of demoralised furniture, unflinchingly dignified and patient, waiting for its burden.

With a last scornful look towards the sleeper, Mrs Almayer passed behind the curtain into her own room. A couple of bats, encouraged by the darkness and the peaceful state of affairs, resumed their silent and oblique gambols above Almayer's head, and for a long time the profound quiet of the house was unbroken, save for the deep breathing of the sleeping man and the faint tinkle of silver in the hands of the woman preparing for flight. In the increasing light of the moon that had risen now above the night mist, the objects on the verandah came out strongly outlined in black splashes of shadow with all the uncompromising ugliness of their disorder, and a caricature of the sleeping Almayer appeared on the dirty whitewash of the wall behind him in a grotesquely exaggerated detail of attitude and feature enlarged to a heroic size. The discontented bats departed in quest of darker places, and a lizard came out in short, nervous rushes, and, pleased with the white tablecloth, stopped on it in breathless immobility that would have suggested sudden death had it not been for the melodious call he exchanged with a less adventurous friend hiding among the lumber in the courtyard. Then the boards in the passage creaked, the lizard vanished, and Almayer stirred uneasily with a sigh: slowly, out of the senseless annihilation of drunken sleep, he was returning, through the land of dreams, to waking consciousness. Almayer's head rolled from shoulder to shoulder in the oppression of his dream; the heavens had descended upon him like a heavy mantle, and trailed in starred folds far under him. Stars above, stars all round him; and from the stars under his feet rose a whisper full of entreaties and tears, and sorrowful faces flitted among the clusters of light filling the infinite space below. How escape from the importunity of lamentable cries and from the look of staring, sad eyes in the faces which pressed round him till he gasped for breath under the crushing weight of worlds that hung over his aching shoulders? Get away! But how? If he attempted to move he would step off into nothing, and perish in the crashing fall of that universe of which he was the only support. And what were the voices saying? Urging him to move! Why? Move to destruction! Not likely! The absurdity of the thing filled him with indignation. He got a firmer foothold and stiffened his muscles in heroic resolve to carry his burden to all eternity. And ages passed in the superhuman labour, amid the rush of circling worlds; in the plaintive murmur of sorrowful voices urging him to desist before it was too late – till the mysterious power that had laid upon him the giant task seemed at last to seek his destruction. With terror he felt an irresistible hand shaking him by the shoulder, while the chorus of voices swelled louder into an agonised prayer to go, go before it is too late. He felt himself slipping, losing his balance, as something dragged at his legs, and he fell. With a faint cry he glided out of the anguish of perishing creation into an imperfect waking that seemed to be still under the spell of his dream.

'What? What?' he murmured sleepily, without moving or opening his eyes. His head still felt heavy, and he had not the courage to raise his eyelids. In his ears there still lingered the sound of entreating whispers. 'Am I awake? – Why do I hear the voices?' he argued to himself, hazily. 'I cannot get rid of the horrible nightmare yet. – I have been very drunk. – What is that shaking me? I am dreaming yet – I must open my eyes and be done with it. I am only half awake, it is evident.'

He made an effort to shake off his stupor and saw a face close to his, glaring at him with staring eyeballs. He closed his eyes again in amazed horror and sat up straight in the chair, trembling in every limb. What was this apparition? – His own fancy, no doubt. – His nerves had been much tried the day before – and then the drink! He would not see it again if he had the courage to look. – He would look directly. – Get a little steadier first. – So. – Now.

He looked. The figure of a woman standing in the steely light, her hands stretched forth in a suppliant gesture, confronted him from the far-off end of the verandah; and in the space between him and the obstinate phantom floated the murmur of words that fell on his ears in a jumble of torturing sentences, the meaning of which escaped the utmost efforts of his brain. Who spoke the Malay words? Who ran away? Why too late – and too late for what? What meant those words of hate and love mixed so strangely together, the ever-recurring names falling on his ears again and again – Nina, Dain; Dain, Nina? Dain was dead, and Nina was sleeping, unaware of the terrible experience through which he was now passing. Was he going to be tormented for ever, sleeping or waking, and have no peace either night or day? What was the meaning of this?

He shouted the last words aloud. The shadowy woman seemed to shrink and recede a little from him towards the doorway, and there was a shriek. Exasperated by the incomprehensible nature of his torment, Almayer made a rush upon the apparition, which eluded his grasp, and he brought up heavily against the wall. Quick as lightning he turned round and pursued fiercely the mysterious figure fleeing from him with piercing shrieks that were like fuel to the flames of his anger. Over the furniture, round the overturned table, and now he had it cornered behind Nina's chair. To the left, to the right they dodged, the chair rocking madly between them, she sending out shriek after shriek at every feint, and he growling meaningless curses through his hard-set teeth. 'Oh! the fiendish noise that split his head and seemed to choke his breath. – It would kill him. – It must be stopped!' An insane desire to crush that yelling thing induced him to cast himself recklessly over the chair with a desperate grab, and they came down together in a cloud of dust among the splintered wood. The last shriek died out under him in a faint gurgle, and he had secured the relief of absolute silence.

He looked at the woman's face under him. A real woman! He knew her. By all that is wonderful! Taminah! He jumped up ashamed of his fury and stood perplexed, wiping his forehead. The girl struggled to a kneeling posture and embraced his legs in a frenzied prayer for mercy.

'Don't be afraid,' he said, raising her. 'I shall not hurt you. Why do you come to my house in the night? And if you had to come, why not go behind the curtain where the women sleep?'

'The place behind the curtain is empty,' gasped Taminah, catching her breath between the words. 'There are no women in your house any more, Tuan. I saw the old Mem go away before I tried to wake you. I did not want your women, I wanted you.'

'Old Mem!' repeated Almayer. 'Do you mean my wife?'

She nodded her head.

'But of my daughter you are not afraid?' said Almayer.

'Have you not heard me?' she exclaimed. 'Have I not spoken for a long time when you lay there with eyes half open? She is gone too.'

'I was asleep. Can you not tell when a man is sleeping and when awake?'

'Sometimes,' answered Taminah in a low voice; 'sometimes the spirit lingers close to a sleeping body and may hear. I spoke a long time before I touched you, and I spoke softly for fear it would depart at a sudden noise and leave you sleeping for ever. I took you by the shoulder only when you began to mutter words I could not understand. Have you not heard, then, and do you know nothing?'

'Nothing of what you said. What is it? Tell again if you want me to know.'

He took her by the shoulder and led her unresisting to the front of the verandah into a stronger light. She wrung her hands with such an appearance of grief that he began to be alarmed.

'Speak,' he said. 'You made noise enough to wake even dead men. And yet nobody living came,' he added to himself in an uneasy whisper. 'Are you mute? Speak!' he repeated.

In a rush of words which broke out after a short struggle from her trembling lips she told him the tale of Nina's love and her own jealousy.

Several times he looked angrily into her face and told her to be silent; but he could not stop the sounds that seemed to him to run out in a hot stream, swirl about his feet, and rise in scalding waves about him, higher, higher, drowning his heart, touching his lips with a feel of molten lead, blotting out his sight in scorching vapour, closing over his head, merciless and deadly. When she spoke of the deception as to Dain's death of which he had been the victim only that day, he glanced again at her with terrible eyes, and made her falter for a second, but he turned away directly, and his face suddenly lost all expression in a stony stare far away over the river. Ah! the river! His old friend and his old enemy, speaking always with the same voice as he runs from year to year bringing fortune or disappointment, happiness or pain, upon the same varying but unchanged surface of glancing currents and swirling eddies. For many years he had listened to the passionless and soothing murmur that sometimes was the song of hope, at times the song of triumph, of encouragement; more often the whisper of consolation that spoke of better days to come. For so many years! So many years! And now to the accompaniment of that murmur he listened to the slow and painful beating of his heart. He listened attentively, wondering at the regularity of its beats. He began to count mechanically. One, two. Why count? At the next beat it must stop. No heart could suffer so and beat so steadily for long. Those regular strokes as of a muffled hammer that rang in his ears must stop soon. Still beating unceasing and cruel. No man can bear this; and is this the last, or will the next one be the last? – How much longer? O God! how much longer? His hand weighed heavier unconsciously on the girl's shoulder, and she spoke the last words of her story crouching at his feet with tears of pain and shame and anger. Was her revenge to fail her? This white man was like a senseless stone. Too late! Too late!

'And you saw her go?' Almayer's voice sounded harshly above her head.

'Did I not tell you?' she sobbed, trying to wriggle gently out from under his grip. 'Did I not tell you that I saw the witchwoman push the canoe? I lay hidden in the grass and heard all the words. She that we used to call the White Mem wanted to return to look at your face, but the witchwoman forbade her, and – '

She sank lower yet on her elbow, turning half round under the downward push of the heavy hand, her face lifted up to him with spiteful eyes. 'And she obeyed,' she shouted out in a half-laugh, half-cry of pain. 'Let me go, Tuan. Why are you angry with me? Hasten, or you will be too late to show your anger to the deceitful woman.'

Almayer dragged her up to her feet and looked close into her face while she struggled, turning her head away from his wild stare.

'Who sent you here to torment me?' he asked, violently. 'I do not believe you. You lie.'

He straightened his arm suddenly and flung her across the verandah towards the doorway, where she lay immobile and silent, as if she had left her life in his grasp, a dark heap, without a sound or a stir.

'Oh! Nina!' whispered Almayer, in a voice in which reproach and love spoke together in pained tenderness. 'Oh! Nina! I do not believe.'

A light draught from the river ran over the courtyard in a wave of bowing grass and, entering the verandah, touched Almayer's forehead with its cool breath, in a caress of infinite pity. The curtain in the women's doorway blew out and instantly collapsed with startling helplessness. He stared at the fluttering stuff.

'Nina!' cried Almayer. 'Where are you, Nina?'

The wind passed out of the empty house in a tremulous sigh, and all was still.

Almayer hid his face in his hands as if to shut out a loathsome sight. When, hearing a slight rustle, he uncovered his eyes, the dark heap by the door was gone.

In the middle of a shadowless square of moonlight, shining on a smooth and level expanse of young rice-shoots, a little shelter-hut perched on high posts, the pile of brushwood near by and the glowing embers of a fire with a man stretched before it, seemed very small and as if lost in the pale green iridescence reflected from the ground. On three sides of the clearing, appearing very far away in the deceptive light, the big trees of the forest, lashed together with manifold bonds by a mass of tangled creepers, looked down at the growing young life at their feet with the sombre resignation of giants that had lost faith in their strength. And in the midst of them the merciless creepers clung to the big trunks in cable-like coils, leaped from tree to tree, hung in thorny festoons from the lower boughs, and, sending slender tendrils on high to seek out the smallest branches, carried death to their victims in an exulting riot of silent destruction.

On the fourth side, following the curve of the bank of that branch of the Pantai that formed the only access to the clearing, ran a black line of young trees, bushes and thick second growth, unbroken save for a small gap chopped out in one place. At that gap began the narrow footpath leading from the water's edge to the grass-built shelter used by the night watchers when the ripening crop had to be protected from the wild pigs. The pathway ended at the foot of the piles on which the hut was built, in a circular space covered with ashes and bits of burnt wood. In the middle of that space, by the dim fire, lay Dain.

He turned over on his side with an impatient sigh, and, pillowing his head on his bent arm, lay quietly with his face to the dying fire. The glowing embers shone redly in a small circle, throwing a gleam into his wide-open eyes, and at every deep breath the fine white ash of bygone fires rose in a light cloud before his parted lips, and danced away from the warm glow into the moonbeams pouring down upon Bulangi's clearing. His body was weary with the exertion of the past few days, his mind more weary still with the strain of solitary waiting for his fate. Never before had he felt so helpless. He had heard the report of the gun fired on board the launch, and he knew that his life was in untrustworthy hands, and that his enemies were very near. During the slow hours of the afternoon he roamed about on the edge of the forest, or, hiding in the bushes, watched the creek with unquiet eyes for some sign of danger.

He feared not death, yet he desired ardently to live, for life to him was Nina. She had promised to come, to follow him, to share his danger and his splendour. But with her by his side he cared not for danger, and without her there could be no splendour and no joy in existence.

Crouching in his shady hiding-place, he closed his eyes, trying to evoke the gracious and charming image of the white figure that for him was the beginning and the end of life. With eyes shut tight, his teeth hard set, he tried in a great effort of passionate will to keep his hold on that vision of supreme delight. In vain! His heart grew heavy as the figure of Nina faded away to be replaced by another vision this time – a vision of armed men, of angry faces, of glittering arms – and he seemed to hear the hum of excited and triumphant voices as they discovered him in his hiding-place. Startled by the vividness of his fancy, he would open his eyes, and, leaping out into the sunlight, resume his aimless wanderings around the clearing. As he skirted in his weary march the edge of the forest he glanced now and then into its dark shade, so enticing in its deceptive appearance of coolness, so repellent with its unrelieved gloom, where lay, entombed and rotting, countless generations of trees, and where their successors stood as if mourning, in dark green foliage, immense and helpless, awaiting their turn. Only the parasites seemed to live there in a sinuous rush upwards into the air and sunshine, feeding on the dead and the dying alike, and crowning their victims with pink and blue flowers that gleamed amongst the boughs, incongruous and cruel, like a strident and mocking note in the solemn harmony of the doomed trees.

A man could hide there, thought Dain, as he approached a place where the creepers had been torn and hacked into an archway that might have been the beginning of a path. As he bent down to look through he heard angry grunting, and a sounder of wild pigs crashed away in the undergrowth. An acrid smell of damp earth and of decaying leaves took him by the throat, and he drew back with a scared face, as if he had been touched by the breath of Death itself. The very air seemed dead in there – heavy and stagnating, poisoned with the corruption of countless ages. He went on, staggering on his way, urged by the nervous restlessness that made him feel tired yet caused him to loathe the very idea of immobility and repose. Was he a wild man to hide in the woods and perhaps be killed there – in the darkness – where there was no room to breathe? He would wait for his enemies in the sunlight, where he could see the sky and feel the breeze. He knew how a Malay chief should die. The sombre and desperate fury, that peculiar inheritance of his race, took possession of him, and he glared savagely across the clearing towards the gap in the bushes by the riverside. They would come from there. In imagination he saw them now. He saw the bearded faces and the white jackets of the officers, the light on the levelled barrels of the rifles. What is the bravery of the greatest warrior before the firearms in the hand of a slave? He would walk towards them with a smiling face, with his hands held out in a sign of submission till he was very near them. He would speak friendly words – come nearer yet – yet nearer – so near that they could touch him with their hands and stretch them out to make him a captive. That would be the time: with a shout and a leap he would be in the midst of them, kriss in hand, killing, killing, killing, and would die with the shouts of his enemies in his ears, their warm blood spurting before his eyes.

Carried away by his excitement, he snatched the kriss hidden in his sarong and drawing a long breath, rushed forward, struck at the empty air and fell on his face. He lay as if stunned in the sudden reaction from his exaltation, thinking that, even if he died thus gloriously, it would have to be before he saw Nina. Better so. If he saw her again he felt that death would be too terrible. With horror he, the descendant of Rajahs and of conquerors, had to face the doubt of his own bravery. His desire for life tormented him in a paroxysm of agonising remorse. He had not the courage to stir a limb. He had lost faith in himself, and there was nothing else in him of what makes a man. The suffering remained, for it is ordered that it should abide in the human body even to the last breath, and fear remained. Dimly he could look into the depths of his passionate love, see its strength and its weakness, and felt afraid.

The sun went down slowly. The shadow of the western forest marched over the clearing, covered the man's scorched shoulders with its cool mantle, and went on hurriedly to mingle with the shadows of other forests on the eastern side. The sun lingered for a while amongst the light tracery of the higher branches, as if in friendly reluctance to abandon the body stretched in the green paddy-field. Then Dain, revived by the cool of the evening breeze, sat up and stared round him. As he did so the sun dipped sharply, as if ashamed of being detected in a sympathising attitude, and the clearing, which during the day was all light, became suddenly all darkness, where the fire gleamed like an eye. Dain walked slowly towards the creek, and, divesting himself of his torn sarong, his only garment, entered the water cautiously. He had had nothing to eat that day, and had not dared show himself in daylight by the waterside to drink. Now, as he swam silently, he swallowed a few mouthfuls of water that lapped about his lips. This did him good, and he walked with greater confidence in himself and others as he returned

towards the fire. Had he been betrayed by Lakamba all would have
been over by this. He made up a big blaze, and while it lasted dried
himself, and then lay down by the embers. He could not sleep, but he
felt a great numbness in all his limbs. His restlessness was gone, and he
was content to lie still, measuring the time by watching the stars that
rose in endless succession above the forests, while the slight puffs of
wind under the cloudless sky seemed to fan their twinkle into a greater
brightness. Dreamily he assured himself over and over again that she
would come, till the certitude crept into his heart and filled him with a
great peace. Yes, when the next day broke, they would be together on
the great blue sea that was like life – away from the forests that were like
death. He murmured the name of Nina into the silent space with a
tender smile: this seemed to break the spell of stillness, and far away by
the creek a frog croaked loudly as if in answer. A chorus of loud roars
and plaintive calls rose from the mud along the line of bushes. He
laughed heartily; doubtless it was their love-song. He felt affectionate
towards the frogs and listened, pleased with the noisy life near him.

When the moon peeped above the trees he felt the old impatience
and the old restlessness steal over him. Why was she so late? True, it
was a long way to come with a single paddle. With what skill and what
endurance could those small hands manage a heavy paddle! It was very
wonderful – such small hands, such soft little palms that knew how to
touch his cheek with a feel lighter than the fanning of a butterfly's
wing. Wonderful! He lost himself lovingly in the contemplation of this
tremendous mystery, and when he looked at the moon again it had
risen a hand's breadth above the trees. Would she come? He forced
himself to lie still, overcoming the impulse to rise and rush round the
clearing again. He turned this way and that; at last, quivering with the
effort, he lay on his back, and saw her face among the stars looking
down on him.

The croaking of frogs suddenly ceased. With the watchfulness of a
hunted man Dain sat up, listening anxiously, and heard several splashes
in the water as the frogs took rapid headers into the creek. He knew
that they had been alarmed by something, and stood up suspicious and
attentive. A slight grating noise, then the dry sound as of two pieces of
wood struck against each other. Somebody was about to land! He took
up an armful of brushwood, and, without taking his eyes from the path,
held it over the embers of his fire. He waited, undecided, and saw
something gleam amongst the bushes; then a white figure came out of
the shadows and seemed to float towards him in the pale light. His
heart gave a great leap and stood still, then went on shaking his frame in

furious beats. He dropped the brushwood upon the glowing coals, and had an impression of shouting her name – of rushing to meet her; yet he emitted no sound, he stirred not an inch, but he stood silent and motionless like chiselled bronze under the moonlight that streamed over his naked shoulders. As he stood still, fighting with his breath, as if bereft of his senses by the intensity of his delight, she walked up to him with quick, resolute steps and, with the appearance of one about to leap from a dangerous height, threw both her arms round his neck with a sudden gesture. A small blue gleam crept amongst the dry branches, and the crackling of reviving fire was the only sound as they faced each other in the speechless emotion of that meeting; then the dry fuel caught at once, and a bright hot flame shot upwards in a blaze as high as their heads, and in its light they saw each other's eyes.

Neither of them spoke. He was regaining his senses in a slight tremor that ran upwards along his rigid body and hung about his trembling lips. She drew back her head and fastened her eyes on his in one of those long looks that are a woman's most terrible weapon; a look that is more stirring than the closest touch, and more dangerous than the thrust of a dagger, because it also whips the soul out of the body, but leaves the body alive and helpless, to be swayed here and there by the capricious tempests of passion and desire; a look that enwraps the whole body, and that penetrates into the innermost recesses of the being, bringing terrible defeat in the delirious uplifting of accomplished conquest. It has the same meaning for the man of the forests and the sea as for the man threading the paths of the more dangerous wilderness of houses and streets. Men that have felt in their breasts the awful exultation such a look awakens become mere things of today – which is paradise; forget yesterday – which was suffering; care not for tomorrow – which may be perdition. They wish to live under that look for ever. It is the look of woman's surrender.

He understood, and, as if suddenly released from his invisible bonds, fell at her feet with a shout of joy, and embracing her knees, hid his head in the folds of her dress, murmuring disjointed words of gratitude and love. Never before had he felt so proud as now, when at the feet of that woman that half belonged to his enemies. Her fingers played with his hair in an absent-minded caress as she stood absorbed in thought. The thing was done. Her mother was right. The man was her slave. As she glanced down at his kneeling form she felt a great pitying tenderness for that man she was used to call – even in her thoughts – the master of life. She lifted her eyes and looked sadly at the southern heavens under which lay the path of their lives – her own, and that man's at her feet.

Did he not say himself that she was the light of his life? She would be his light and his wisdom; she would be his greatness and his strength; yet hidden from the eyes of all men she would be, above all, his only and lasting weakness. A very woman! In the sublime vanity of her kind she was thinking already of moulding a god from the clay at her feet. A god for others to worship. She was content to see him as he was now, and to feel him quiver at the slightest touch of her light fingers. And while her eyes looked sadly at the southern stars a faint smile seemed to be playing about her firm lips. Who can tell in the fitful light of a camp fire? It might have been a smile of triumph, or of conscious power, or of tender pity, or, perhaps, of love.

She spoke softly to him, and he rose to his feet, putting his arm round her in quiet consciousness of his ownership; she laid her head on his shoulder with a sense of defiance to all the world in the encircling protection of that arm. He was hers with all his qualities and all his faults. His strength and his courage, his recklessness and his daring, his simple wisdom and his savage cunning – all were hers. As they passed together out of the red light of the fire into the silver shower of rays that fell upon the clearing he bent his head over her face, and she saw in his eyes the dreamy intoxication of boundless felicity from the close touch of her slight figure clasped to his side. With a rhythmical swing of their bodies they walked through the light towards the outlying shadows of the forests that seemed to guard their happiness in solemn immobility. Their forms melted in the play of light and shadow at the foot of the big trees, but the murmur of tender words lingered over the empty clearing, grew faint and died out. A sigh as of immense sorrow passed over the land in the last effort of the dying breeze, and in the deep silence which succeeded, the earth and the heavens were suddenly hushed up in the mournful contemplation of human love and human blindness.

They walked slowly back to the fire. He made for her a seat out of the dry branches, and, throwing himself down at her feet, laid his head in her lap and gave himself up to the dreamy delight of the passing hour. Their voices rose and fell, tender or animated as they spoke of their love and of their future. She, with a few skilful words spoken from time to time, guided his thoughts, and he let his happiness flow in a stream of talk, passionate and tender, grave or menacing, according to the mood which she evoked. He spoke to her of his own island, where the gloomy forests and the muddy rivers were unknown. He spoke of its terraced fields, of the murmuring clear rills of sparkling water that flowed down the sides of great mountains, bringing life to the land and joy to its

ALMAYER'S FOLLY   123

tillers. And he spoke also of the mountain peak that rising lonely above
the belt of trees knew the secrets of the passing clouds, and was the
dwelling-place of the mysterious spirit of his race, of the guardian
genius of his house. He spoke of vast horizons swept by fierce winds
that whistled high above the summits of burning mountains. He spoke
of his forefathers that conquered ages ago the island of which he was to
be the future ruler. And then as, in her interest, she brought her face
nearer to his, he, touching lightly the thick tresses of her long hair, felt
a sudden impulse to speak to her of the sea he loved so well; and he told
her of its never-ceasing voice, to which he had listened as a child,
wondering at its hidden meaning that no living man has penetrated
yet; of its enchanting glitter; of its senseless and capricious fury; how its
surface was forever changing, and yet always enticing, while its depths
were forever the same, cold and cruel, and full of the wisdom of
destroyed life. He told her how it held men slaves to its charm for a
lifetime, and then, regardless of their devotion, swallowed them up,
angry at their fear of its mystery, which it would never disclose, not
even to those that loved it most. While he talked, Nina's head had
been gradually sinking lower, and her face almost touched his now.
Her hair was over his eyes, her breath was on his forehead, her arms
were about his body. No two beings could be closer to each other,
yet she guessed rather than understood the meaning of his last words
that came out after a slight hesitation in a faint murmur, dying out
imperceptibly into a profound and significant silence: 'The sea, O Nina,
is like a woman's heart.'

She closed his lips with a sudden kiss, and answered in a steady voice,
'But to the men that have no fear, O master of my life, the sea is ever
true.'

Over their heads a film of dark, threadlike clouds, looking like
immense cobwebs drifting under the stars, darkened the sky with the
presage of the coming thunderstorm. From the invisible hills the first
distant rumble of thunder came in a prolonged roll which, after tossing
about from hill to hill, lost itself in the forests of the Pantai. Dain and
Nina stood up, and the former looked at the sky uneasily.

'It is time for Babalatchi to be here,' he said. 'The night is more than
half gone. Our road is long, and a bullet travels quicker than the best
canoe.'

'He will be here before the moon is hidden behind the clouds,' said
Nina. 'I heard a splash in the water,' she added. 'Did you hear it too?'

'Alligator,' answered Dain shortly, with a careless glance towards the
creek. 'The darker the night,' he continued, 'the shorter will be our

road, for then we could keep in the current of the main stream, but if it is light – even no more than now – we must follow the small channels of sleeping water, with nothing to help our paddles.'

'Dain,' interposed Nina, earnestly, 'it was no alligator. I heard the bushes rustling near the landing-place.'

'Yes,' said Dain, after listening awhile. 'It cannot be Babalatchi, who would come in a big war canoe, and openly. Those that are coming, whoever they are, do not wish to make much noise. But you have heard, and now I can see,' he went on quickly. 'It is but one man. Stand behind me, Nina. If he is a friend he is welcome; if he is an enemy you shall see him die.'

He laid his hand on his kriss, and awaited the approach of his unexpected visitor. The fire was burning very low, and small clouds – precursors of the storm – crossed the face of the moon in rapid succession, and their flying shadows darkened the clearing. He could not make out who the man might be, but he felt uneasy at the steady advance of the tall figure walking on the path with a heavy tread, and hailed it with a command to stop. The man stopped at some little distance, and Dain expected him to speak, but all he could hear was his deep breathing. Through a break in the flying clouds a sudden and fleeting brightness descended upon the clearing. Before the darkness closed in again, Dain saw a hand holding some glittering object extended towards him, heard Nina's cry of 'Father!' and in an instant the girl was between him and Almayer's revolver. Nina's loud cry woke up the echoes in the sleeping woods, and the three stood still as if waiting for the return of silence before they would give expression to their various feelings. At the appearance of Nina, Almayer's arm fell by his side, and he made a step forward. Dain pushed the girl gently aside.

'Am I a wild beast that you should try to kill me suddenly and in the dark, Tuan Almayer?' said Dain, breaking the strained silence. 'Throw some brushwood on the fire,' he went on, speaking to Nina, 'while I watch my white friend, lest harm should come to you or to me, O delight of my heart!'

Almayer ground his teeth and raised his arm again. With a quick bound Dain was at his side: there was a short scuffle, during which one chamber of the revolver went off harmlessly, then the weapon, wrenched out of Almayer's hand, whirled through the air and fell in the bushes. The two men stood close together, breathing hard. The replenished fire threw out an unsteady circle of light and shone on the terrified face of Nina, who looked at them with outstretched hands.

'Dain!' she cried out warningly, 'Dain!'

He waved his hand towards her in a reassuring gesture, and turning to Almayer, said with great courtesy, 'Now we may talk, Tuan. It is easy to send out death, but can your wisdom recall the life? She might have been harmed,' he continued, indicating Nina. 'Your hand shook much; for myself I was not afraid.'

'Nina!' exclaimed Almayer, 'come to me at once. What is this sudden madness? What bewitched you? Come to your father, and together we shall try to forget this horrible nightmare!'

He opened his arms with the certitude of clasping her to his breast in another second. She did not move. As it dawned upon him that she did not mean to obey he felt a deadly cold creep into his heart, and, pressing the palms of his hands to his temples, he looked down on the ground in mute despair. Dain took Nina by the arm and led her towards her father.

'Speak to him in the language of his people,' he said. 'He is grieving – as who would not grieve at losing thee, my pearl! Speak to him the last words he shall hear spoken by that voice, which must be very sweet to him, but is all my life to me.'

He released her, and, stepping back a few paces out of the circle of light, stood in the darkness looking at them with calm interest. The reflection of a distant flash of lightning lit up the clouds over their heads, and was followed after a short interval by the faint rumble of thunder, which mingled with Almayer's voice as he began to speak.

'Do you know what you are doing? Do you know what is waiting for you if you follow that man? Have you no pity for yourself? Do you know that you shall be at first his plaything and then a scorned slave, a drudge, and a servant of some new fancy of that man?'

She raised her hand to stop him, and turning her head slightly, asked, 'You hear this, Dain! Is it true?'

'By all the gods!' came the impassioned answer from the darkness – 'by heaven and earth, by my head and thine I swear: this is a white man's lie. I have delivered my soul into your hands for ever; I breathe with your breath, I see with your eyes, I think with your mind, and I take you into my heart for ever.'

'You thief!' shouted the exasperated Almayer.

A deep silence succeeded this outburst, then the voice of Dain was heard again.

'Nay, Tuan,' he said in a gentle tone, 'that is not true also. The girl came of her own will. I have done no more but to show her my love like a man; she heard the cry of my heart, and she came, and the dowry I have given to the woman you call your wife.'

Almayer groaned in his extremity of rage and shame. Nina laid her hand lightly on his shoulder, and the contact, light as the touch of a falling leaf, seemed to calm him. He spoke quickly, and in English this time.

'Tell me,' he said – 'tell me, what have they done to you, your mother and that man? What made you give yourself up to that savage? For he is a savage. Between him and you there is a barrier that nothing can remove. I can see in your eyes the look of those who commit suicide when they are mad. You are mad. Don't smile. It breaks my heart. If I were to see you drowning before my eyes, and I without the power to help you, I could not suffer a greater torment. Have you forgotten the teaching of so many years?'

'No,' she interrupted, 'I remember it well. I remember how it ended also. Scorn for scorn, contempt for contempt, hate for hate. I am not of your race. Between your people and me there is also a barrier that nothing can remove. You ask why I want to go, and I ask you why I should stay.'

He staggered as if struck in the face, but with a quick, unhesitating grasp she caught him by the arm and steadied him.

'Why you should stay!' he repeated slowly, in a dazed manner, and stopped short, astounded at the completeness of his misfortune.

'You told me yesterday,' she went on again, 'that I could not understand or see your love for me: it is so. How can I? No two human beings understand each other. They can understand but their own voices. You wanted me to dream your dreams, to see your own visions – the visions of life amongst the white faces of those who cast me out from their midst in angry contempt. But while you spoke I listened to the voice of my own self; then this man came, and all was still; there was only the murmur of his love. You call him a savage! What do you call my mother, your wife?'

'Nina!' cried Almayer, 'take your eyes off my face.'

She looked down directly, but continued speaking only a little above a whisper.

'In time,' she went on, 'both our voices, that man's and mine, spoke together in a sweetness that was intelligible to our ears only. You were speaking of gold then, but our ears were filled with the song of our love, and we did not hear you. Then I found that we could see through each other's eyes: that he saw things that nobody but myself and he could see. We entered a land where no one could follow us, and least of all you. Then I began to live.'

She paused. Almayer sighed deeply. With her eyes still fixed on the ground she began speaking again.

'And I mean to live. I mean to follow him. I have been rejected with scorn by the white people, and now I am a Malay! He took me in his arms, he laid his life at my feet. He is brave; he will be powerful, and I hold his bravery and his strength in my hand, and I shall make him great. His name shall be remembered long after both our bodies are laid in the dust. I love you no less than I did before, but I shall never leave him, for without him I cannot live.'

'If he understood what you have said,' answered Almayer, scornfully, 'he must be highly flattered. You want him as a tool for some incomprehensible ambition of yours. Enough, Nina. If you do not go down at once to the creek, where Ali is waiting with my canoe, I shall tell him to return to the settlement and bring the Dutch officers here. You cannot escape from this clearing, for I have cast adrift your canoe. If the Dutch catch this hero of yours they will hang him as sure as I stand here. Now go.'

He made a step towards his daughter and laid hold of her by the shoulder, his other hand pointing down the path to the landing-place.

'Beware!' exclaimed Dain; 'this woman belongs to me!'

Nina wrenched herself free and looked straight at Almayer's angry face.

'No, I will not go,' she said with desperate energy. 'If he dies I shall die too!'

'You die!' said Almayer, contemptuously. 'Oh, no! You shall live a life of lies and deception till some other vagabond comes along to sing – how did you say that? The song of love to you! Make up your mind quickly.'

He waited for a while, and then added meaningly, 'Shall I call out to Ali?'

'Call out,' she answered in Malay, 'you that cannot be true to your own countrymen. Only a few days ago you were selling the powder for their destruction; now you want to give up to them the man that yesterday you called your friend. Oh, Dain,' she said, turning towards the motionless but attentive figure in the darkness, 'instead of bringing you life I bring you death, for he will betray you unless I leave you for ever!'

Dain came into the circle of light, and, throwing his arm around Nina's neck, whispered in her ear – 'I can kill him where he stands, before a sound can pass his lips. For you it is to say yes or no. Babalatchi cannot be far now.'

He straightened himself up, taking his arm off her shoulder, and confronted Almayer, who looked at them both with an expression of concentrated fury.

'No!' she cried, clinging to Dain in wild alarm. 'No! Kill me! Then perhaps he will let you go. You do not know the mind of a white man. He would rather see me dead than standing where I am. Forgive me, your slave, but you must not.' She fell at his feet sobbing violently and repeating, 'Kill me! Kill me!'

'I want you alive,' said Almayer, speaking also in Malay, with sombre calmness. 'You go, or he hangs. Will you obey?'

Dain shook Nina off, and making a sudden lunge, struck Almayer full in the chest with the handle of his kriss, keeping the point towards himself.

'Hai, look! It was easy for me to turn the point the other way,' he said in his even voice. 'Go, Tuan Putih,' he added with dignity. 'I give you your life, my life and her life. I am the slave of this woman's desire, and she wills it so.'

There was not a glimmer of light in the sky now, and the tops of the trees were as invisible as their trunks, being lost in the mass of clouds that hung low over the woods, the clearing and the river.

Every outline had disappeared in the intense blackness that seemed to have destroyed everything but space. Only the fire glimmered like a star forgotten in this annihilation of all visible things, and nothing was heard after Dain ceased speaking but the sobs of Nina, whom he held in his arms, kneeling beside the fire. Almayer stood looking down at them in gloomy thoughtfulness. As he was opening his lips to speak they were startled by a cry of warning by the riverside, followed by the splash of many paddles and the sound of voices.

'Babalatchi!' shouted Dain, lifting up Nina as he got upon his feet quickly.

'Ada! Ada!' came the answer from the panting statesman who ran up the path and stood amongst them. 'Run to my canoe,' he said to Dain excitedly, without taking any notice of Almayer. 'Run! we must go. That woman has told them all!'

'What woman?' asked Dain, looking at Nina. Just then there was only one woman in the whole world for him.

'The she-dog with white teeth; the seven times accursed slave of Bulangi. She yelled at Abdulla's gate till she woke up all Sambir. Now the white officers are coming, guided by her and Reshid. If you want to live, do not look at me, but go!'

'How do you know this?' asked Almayer.

'Oh, Tuan! what matters how I know! I have only one eye, but I saw lights in Abdulla's house and in his campong as we were paddling past. I have ears, and while we lay under the bank I have heard the messengers sent out to the white men's house.'

'Will you depart without that woman who is my daughter?' said Almayer, addressing Dain, while Babalatchi stamped with impatience, muttering, 'Run! Run at once!'

'No,' answered Dain, steadily, 'I will not go; to no man will I abandon this woman.'

'Then kill me and escape yourself,' sobbed out Nina.

He clasped her close, looking at her tenderly, and whispered, 'We will never part, O Nina!'

'I shall not stay here any longer,' broke in Babalatchi, angrily. 'This is great foolishness. No woman is worth a man's life. I am an old man, and I know.'

He picked up his staff, and turning to go, looked at Dain as if offering him his last chance of escape. But Dain's face was hidden amongst Nina's black tresses, and he did not see this last appealing glance.

Babalatchi vanished in the darkness. Shortly after his disappearance they heard the war canoe leave the landing-place in the swish of the numerous paddles dipped in the water together. Almost at the same time Ali came up from the riverside, two paddles on his shoulder.

'Our canoe is hidden up the creek, Tuan Almayer,' he said, 'in the dense bush where the forest comes down to the water. I took it there because I heard from Babalatchi's paddlers that the white men are coming here.'

'Wait for me there,' said Almayer, 'but keep the canoe hidden.'

He remained silent, listening to Ali's footsteps, then turned to Nina. 'Nina,' he said sadly, 'will you have no pity for me?'

There was no answer. She did not even turn her head, which was pressed close to Dain's breast.

He made a movement as if to leave them and stopped. By the dim glow of the burning-out fire he saw their two motionless figures. The woman's back turned to him with the long black hair streaming down over the white dress, and Dain's calm face looking at him above her head.

'I cannot,' he muttered to himself. After a long pause he spoke again a little lower, but in an unsteady voice, 'It would be too great a disgrace. I am a white man.' He broke down completely there, and went on tearfully, 'I am a white man, and of good family. Very good family,' he repeated, weeping bitterly. 'It would be a disgrace . . . all over the islands . . . the only white man on the east coast. No, it cannot be . . . white men finding my daughter with this Malay. My daughter!' he cried aloud, with a ring of despair in his voice.

He recovered his composure after a while and said distinctly, 'I will never forgive you, Nina – never! If you were to come back to me now, the memory of this night would poison all my life. I shall try to forget. I have no daughter. There used to be a half-caste woman in my house, but she is going even now. You, Dain, or whatever your name may be, I shall take you and that woman to the island at the mouth of the river myself. Come with me.'

He led the way, following the bank as far as the forest. Ali answered to his call and, pushing their way through the dense bush, they stepped into the canoe hidden under the overhanging branches. Dain laid Nina in the bottom, and sat holding her head on his knees. Almayer and Ali each took up a paddle. As they were going to push out Ali hissed warningly. All listened.

In the great stillness before the bursting out of the thunderstorm they could hear the sound of oars working regularly in their rowlocks. The sound approached steadily, and Dain, looking through the branches, could see the faint shape of a big white boat. A woman's voice said in a cautious tone, 'There is the place where you may land, white men; a little higher – there!'

The boat was passing them so close in the narrow creek that the blades of the long oars nearly touched the canoe.

'Way enough! Stand by to jump on shore! He is alone and unarmed,' was the quiet order in a man's voice, and in Dutch.

Somebody else whispered, 'I think I can see a glimmer of a fire through the bush.' And then the boat floated past them, disappearing instantly in the darkness.

'Now,' whispered Ali, eagerly, 'let us push out and paddle away.'

The little canoe swung into the stream, and as it sprang forward in response to the vigorous dig of the paddles they could hear an angry shout. 'He is not by the fire. Spread out, men, and search for him!'

Blue lights blazed out in different parts of the clearing, and the shrill voice of a woman cried in accents of rage and pain, 'Too late! O senseless white men! He has escaped!'

Chapter 12

'That is the place,' said Dain, indicating with the blade of his paddle a small islet about a mile ahead of the canoe – 'that is the place where Babalatchi promised that a boat from the prau would come for me when the sun is overhead. We will wait for that boat there.'

Almayer, who was steering, nodded without speaking, and by a slight sweep of his paddle laid the head of the canoe in the required direction.

They were just leaving the southern outlet of the Pantai, which lay behind them in a straight and long vista of water shining between two walls of thick verdure that ran downwards and towards each other, till at last they joined and sank together in the faraway distance. The sun, rising above the calm waters of the Straits, marked its own path by a streak of light that glided upon the sea and darted up the wide reach of the river, a hurried messenger of light and life to the gloomy forests of the coast; and in this radiance of the sun's pathway floated the black canoe heading for the islet which lay bathed in sunshine, the yellow sands of its encircling beach shining like an inlaid golden disc on the polished steel of the unwrinkled sea. To the north and south of it rose other islets, joyous in their brilliant colouring of green and yellow, and on the main coast the sombre line of mangrove bushes ended to the southward in the reddish cliffs of Tanjong Mirrah,[59] advancing into the sea, steep and shadowless under the clear light of the early morning.

The bottom of the canoe grated upon the sand as the little craft ran upon the beach. Ali leaped on shore and held on while Dain stepped out carrying Nina in his arms, exhausted by the events and the long travelling during the night. Almayer was the last to leave the boat, and together with Ali ran it higher up on the beach. Then Ali, tired out by the long paddling, lay down in the shade of the canoe, and incontinently fell asleep. Almayer sat sideways on the gunwale, and with his arms crossed on his breast, looked to the southward upon the sea.

After carefully laying Nina down in the shade of the bushes growing in the middle of the islet, Dain threw himself beside her and watched in silent concern the tears that ran down from under her closed eyelids, and lost themselves in that fine sand upon which they both were lying face to face. These tears and this sorrow were for him a profound and disquieting mystery. Now, when the danger was past, why should she grieve? He doubted her love no more than he would have doubted the fact of his own existence, but as he lay looking ardently in her face, watching her tears, her parted lips, her very breath, he was uneasily conscious of something in her he could not understand. Doubtless she had the wisdom of perfect beings. He sighed. He felt something invisible that stood between them, something that would let him approach her so far, but no farther. No desire, no longing, no effort of will or length of life could destroy this vague feeling of their difference. With awe but also with great pride he concluded that it was her own incomparable perfection. She was his, and yet she was like a woman from another world. His! His! He exulted in the glorious thought; nevertheless her tears pained him.

With a wisp of her own hair which he took in his hand with timid reverence he tried in an access of clumsy tenderness to dry the tears that trembled on her eyelashes. He had his reward in a fleeting smile that brightened her face for the short fraction of a second, but soon the tears fell faster than ever, and he could bear it no more. He rose and walked towards Almayer, who still sat absorbed in his contemplation of the sea. It was a very, very long time since he had seen the sea – that sea that leads everywhere, brings everything, and takes away so much. He had almost forgotten why he was there, and dreamily he could see all his past life on the smooth and boundless surface that glittered before his eyes.

Dain's hand laid on Almayer's shoulder recalled him with a start from some country very far away indeed. He turned round, but his eyes seemed to look rather at the place where Dain stood than at the man himself. Dain felt uneasy under the unconscious gaze.

'What?' said Almayer.

'She is crying,' murmured Dain, softly.

'She is crying! Why?' asked Almayer, indifferently.

'I came to ask you. My Ranee smiles when looking at the man she loves. It is the white woman that is crying now. You would know.'

Almayer shrugged his shoulders and turned away again towards the sea.

'Go, Tuan Putih,' urged Dain. 'Go to her; her tears are more terrible to me than the anger of gods.'

'Are they? You will see them more than once. She told me she could not live without you,' answered Almayer, speaking without the faintest spark of expression in his face, 'so it behoves you to go to her quick, for fear you may find her dead.'

He burst into a loud and unpleasant laugh which made Dain stare at him with some apprehension, but got off the gunwale of the boat and moved slowly towards Nina, glancing up at the sun as he walked.

'And you go when the sun is overhead?' he said.

'Yes, Tuan. Then we go,' answered Dain.

'I have not long to wait,' muttered Almayer. 'It is most important for me to see you go. Both of you. Most important,' he repeated, stopping short and looking at Dain fixedly.

He went on again towards Nina, and Dain remained behind. Almayer approached his daughter and stood for a time looking down on her. She did not open her eyes, but hearing footsteps near her, murmured in a low sob, 'Dain.'

Almayer hesitated for a minute and then sank on the sand by her side. She, not hearing a responsive word, not feeling a touch, opened her eyes – saw her father, and sat up suddenly with a movement of terror.

'Oh, father!' she murmured faintly, and in that word there was expressed regret and fear and dawning hope.

'I shall never forgive you, Nina,' said Almayer, in a dispassionate voice. 'You have torn my heart from me while I dreamt of your happiness. You have deceived me. Your eyes that for me were like truth itself lied to me in every glance – for how long? You know that best. When you were caressing my cheek you were counting the minutes to the sunset that was the signal for your meeting with that man – there!'

He ceased, and they both sat silent side by side, not looking at each other, but gazing at the vast expanse of the sea. Almayer's words had dried Nina's tears, and her look grew hard as she stared before her into the limitless sheet of blue that shone limpid, unwaving and steady like heaven itself. He looked at it also, but his features had lost all expression, and life in his eyes seemed to have gone out. The face was a blank, without a sign of emotion, feeling, reason or even knowledge of itself. All passion, regret, grief, hope or anger – all were gone, erased by the hand of fate, as if after this last stroke everything was over and there was no need for any record. Those few who saw Almayer during the short period of his remaining days were always impressed by the sight of that face that seemed to know nothing of what went on within: like the blank wall of a prison enclosing sin, regrets and pain, and wasted life, in the cold indifference of mortar and stones.

'What is there to forgive?' asked Nina, not addressing Almayer directly, but more as if arguing with herself. 'Can I not live my own life as you have lived yours? The path you would have wished me to follow has been closed to me by no fault of mine.'

'You never told me,' muttered Almayer.

'You never asked me,' she answered, 'and I thought you were like the others and did not care. I bore the memory of my humiliation alone, and why should I tell you that it came to me because I am your daughter? I knew you could not avenge me.'

'And yet I was thinking of that only,' interrupted Almayer, 'and I wanted to give you years of happiness for the short day of your suffering. I only knew of one way.'

'Ah! but it was not my way!' she replied. 'Could you give me happiness without life? Life!' she repeated with sudden energy that sent the word ringing over the sea. 'Life that means power and love,' she added in a low voice.

'That!' said Almayer, pointing his finger at Dain standing close by and looking at them in curious wonder.

'Yes, that!' she replied, looking her father full in the face and noticing for the first time with a slight gasp of fear the unnatural rigidity of his features.

'I would rather have strangled you with my own hands,' said Almayer, in an expressionless voice which was such a contrast to the desperate bitterness of his feelings that it surprised even himself. He asked himself who spoke, and, after looking slowly round as if expecting to see somebody, turned again his eyes towards the sea.

'You say that because you do not understand the meaning of my words,' she said sadly. 'Between you and my mother there never was any love. When I returned to Sambir I found the place which I thought would be a peaceful refuge for my heart, filled with weariness and hatred – and mutual contempt. I have listened to your voice and to her voice. Then I saw that you could not understand me; for was I not part of that woman? Of her who was the regret and shame of your life? I had to choose – I hesitated. Why were you so blind? Did you not see me struggling before your eyes? But, when he came, all doubt disappeared, and I saw only the light of the blue and cloudless heaven – '

'I will tell you the rest,' interrupted Almayer: 'when that man came I also saw the blue and the sunshine of the sky. A thunderbolt has fallen from that sky, and suddenly all is still and dark around me for ever. I will never forgive you, Nina; and tomorrow I shall forget you! I shall never forgive you,' he repeated with mechanical obstinacy while she sat, her head bowed down as if afraid to look at her father.

To him it seemed of the utmost importance that he should assure her of his intention of never forgiving. He was convinced that his faith in her had been the foundation of his hopes, the motive of his courage, of his determination to live and struggle, and to be victorious for her sake. And now his faith was gone, destroyed by her own hands; destroyed cruelly, treacherously, in the dark; in the very moment of success. In the utter wreck of his affections and of all his feelings, in the chaotic disorder of his thoughts, above the confused sensation of physical pain that wrapped him up in a sting as of a whiplash curling round him from his shoulders down to his feet, only one idea remained clear and definite – not to forgive her; only one vivid desire – to forget her. And this must be made clear to her – and to himself – by frequent repetition. That was his idea of his duty to himself – to his race – to his respectable connections; to the whole universe unsettled and shaken by this frightful catastrophe of his life. He saw it clearly and believed he was a strong man. He had always prided himself upon his unflinching firmness. And yet he was afraid. She had been all in all to him. What if he should let the memory of his love for her weaken the sense of his dignity? She was a remarkable woman; he could see that; all the latent greatness of his nature – in which he honestly believed – had been transfused into that slight, girlish figure. Great things could be done! What if he should suddenly take her to his heart, forget his shame, and pain, and anger, and – follow her! What if he changed his heart if not his skin and made her life easier between the two loves that would guard her from any mischance! His heart yearned for her. What if he should say that his love for her was greater than . . .

'I will never forgive you, Nina!' he shouted, leaping up madly in the sudden fear of his dream.

This was the last time in his life that he was heard to raise his voice. Henceforth he spoke always in a monotonous whisper like an instrument of which all the strings but one are broken in a last ringing clamour under a heavy blow.

She rose to her feet and looked at him. The very violence of his cry soothed her in an intuitive conviction of his love, and she hugged to her breast the lamentable remnants of that affection with the unscrupulous greediness of women who cling desperately to the very scraps and rags of love, any kind of love, as a thing that of right belongs to them and is the very breath of their life. She put both her hands on Almayer's shoulders, and looking at him half tenderly, half playfully, she said, 'You speak so because you love me.'

Almayer shook his head.

'Yes, you do,' she insisted softly; then after a short pause she added, 'and you will never forget me.'

Almayer shivered slightly. She could not have said a more cruel thing.

'Here is the boat coming now,' said Dain, his arm outstretched towards a black speck on the water between the coast and the islet.

They all looked at it and remained standing in silence till the little canoe came gently on the beach and a man landed and walked towards them. He stopped some distance off and hesitated.

'What news?' asked Dain.

'We have had orders secretly and in the night to take off from this islet a man and a woman. I see the woman. Which of you is the man?'

'Come, delight of my eyes,' said Dain to Nina. 'Now we go, and your voice shall be for my ears only. You have spoken your last words to the Tuan Putih, your father. Come.'

She hesitated for a while, looking at Almayer, who kept his eyes steadily on the sea, then she touched his forehead in a lingering kiss, and a tear – one of her tears – fell on his cheek and ran down his immovable face, 'Goodbye,' she whispered, and remained irresolute till he pushed her suddenly into Dain's arms.

'If you have any pity for me,' murmured Almayer, as if repeating some sentence learned by heart, 'take that woman away.'

He stood very straight, his shoulders thrown back, his head held high, and looked at them as they went down the beach to the canoe, walking enlaced in each other's arms. He looked at the line of their footsteps marked in the sand. He followed their figures moving in the crude blaze of the vertical sun, in that light violent and vibrating, like a triumphal flourish of brazen trumpets. He looked at the man's brown shoulders, at the red sarong round his waist; at the tall, slender, dazzling white figure he supported. He looked at the white dress, at the falling masses of the long black hair. He looked at them embarking, and at the canoe growing smaller in the distance, with rage, despair and regret in his heart, and on his face a peace as that of a carved image of oblivion. Inwardly he felt himself torn to pieces, but Ali, who – now aroused – stood close to his master, saw on his features the blank expression of those who live in that hopeless calm which sightless eyes only can give.

The canoe disappeared, and Almayer stood motionless with his eyes fixed on its wake. Ali from under the shade of his hand examined the coast curiously. As the sun declined, the sea-breeze sprang up from the northward and shivered with its breath the glassy surface of the water.

'Dapat!'[60] exclaimed Ali, joyously. 'Got him, master! Got prau! Not there! Look more Tanah Mirrah side. Aha! That way! Master, see? Now plain. See?'

Almayer followed Ali's forefinger with his eyes for a long time in vain. At last he sighted a triangular patch of yellow light on the red background of the cliffs of Tanjong Mirrah. It was the sail of the prau that had caught the sunlight and stood out, distinct with its gay tint, on the dark red of the cape. The yellow triangle crept slowly from cliff to cliff, till it cleared the last point of land and shone brilliantly for a fleeting minute on the blue of the open sea. Then the prau bore up to the southward, the light went out of the sail, and all at once the vessel itself disappeared, vanishing in the shadow of the steep headland that looked on, patient and lonely, watching over the empty sea.

Almayer never moved. Round the little islet the air was full of the talk of the rippling water. The crested wavelets ran up the beach audaciously, joyously, with the lightness of young life, and died quickly, unresistingly and graciously, in the wide curves of transparent foam on the yellow sand. Above, the white clouds sailed rapidly southwards as if intent upon overtaking something.

Ali seemed anxious. 'Master,' he said timidly, 'time get home now. Long way off to pull. All ready, sir.'

'Wait,' whispered Almayer.

Now she was gone his business was to forget, and he had a strange notion that it should be done systematically and in order. To Ali's great dismay he fell on his hands and knees, and, creeping along the sand, erased carefully with his hand all traces of Nina's footsteps. He piled up small heaps of sand, leaving behind him a line of miniature graves right down to the water. After burying the last slight imprint of Nina's slipper he stood up, and turning his face towards the headland where he had last seen the prau, he made an effort to shout out loud again his firm resolve never to forgive. Ali watching him uneasily saw only his lips move, but heard no sound. He brought his foot down with a stamp. He was a firm man – firm as a rock. Let her go. He never had a daughter. He would forget. He was forgetting already.

Ali approached him again, insisting on immediate departure, and this time he consented, and they went together towards their canoe, Almayer leading. For all his firmness he looked very dejected and feeble as he dragged his feet slowly through the sand on the beach; and by his side – invisible to Ali – stalked that particular fiend whose mission it is to jog the memories of men, lest they should forget the meaning of life. He whispered into Almayer's ear a childish prattle of many years ago. Almayer, his head bent on one side, seemed to listen to his invisible companion, but his face was like the face of a man that has died struck from behind – a face from which all feelings and all expression are suddenly wiped off by the hand of unexpected death.

*   *   *

They slept on the river that night, mooring their canoe under the bushes and lying down in the bottom side by side, in the absolute exhaustion that kills hunger, thirst, all feeling and all thought in the overpowering desire for that deep sleep which is like the temporary annihilation of the tired body. Next day they started again and fought doggedly with the current all the morning, till about midday they reached the settlement and made fast their little craft to the jetty of Lingard and Co. Almayer walked straight to the house, and Ali followed, paddles on shoulder, thinking that he would like to eat something. As they crossed the front courtyard they noticed the abandoned look of the place. Ali looked in at the different servants' houses: all were empty. In the back courtyard there was the same absence of sound and life. In the cooking-shed the fire was out and the black embers were cold. A tall, lean man came stealthily out of the banana plantation, and went away rapidly across the open space looking at them with big, frightened eyes over his shoulder. Some vagabond without a master; there were many such in the settlement, and they looked upon Almayer as their patron. They prowled about his premises and picked their living there, sure that nothing worse could befall them than a shower of curses when they got in the way of the white man, whom they trusted and liked, and called a fool amongst themselves. In the house, which Almayer entered through the back verandah, the only living thing that met his eyes was his small monkey which, hungry and unnoticed for the last two days, began to cry and complain in monkey language as soon as it caught sight of the familiar face. Almayer soothed it with a few words and ordered Ali to bring in some bananas, then while Ali was gone to get them he stood in the doorway of the front verandah looking at the chaos of overturned furniture. Finally he picked up the table and sat on it while the monkey let itself down from the roof-stick by its chain and perched on his shoulder. When the bananas came they had their breakfast together; both hungry, both eating greedily and showering the skins round them recklessly, in the trusting silence of perfect friendship. Ali went away, grumbling, to cook some rice himself, for all the women about the house had disappeared; he did not know where. Almayer did not seem to care, and, after he finished eating, he sat on the table swinging his legs and staring at the river as if lost in thought.

After some time he got up and went to the door of a room on the right of the verandah. That was the office. The office of Lingard and Co. He very seldom went in there. There was no business now, and he did not want an office. The door was locked, and he stood biting his lower lip, trying to think of the place where the key could be. Suddenly he remembered: in the women's room hung upon a nail. He went over to the doorway where the red curtain hung down in motionless folds, and hesitated for a moment before pushing it aside with his shoulder as if breaking down some solid obstacle. A great square of sunshine entering through the window lay on the floor. On the left he saw Mrs Almayer's big wooden chest, the lid thrown back, empty; near it the brass nails of Nina's European trunk shone in the large initials N. A. on the cover. A few of Nina's dresses hung on wooden pegs, stiffened in a look of offended dignity at their abandonment. He remembered making the pegs himself and noticed that they were very good pegs. Where was the key? He looked round and saw it near the door where he stood. It was red with rust. He felt very much annoyed at that, and directly afterwards wondered at his own feeling. What did it matter? There soon would be no key – no door – nothing! He paused, key in hand, and asked himself whether he knew well what he was about. He went out again on the verandah and stood by the table thinking. The monkey jumped down, and snatching a banana skin absorbed itself in picking it to shreds industriously.

'Forget!' muttered Almayer, and that word started before him a sequence of events, a detailed programme of things to do. He knew perfectly well what was to be done now. First this, then that, and then forgetfulness would come easy. Very easy. He had a fixed idea that if he should not forget before he died he would have to remember to all eternity. Certain things had to be taken out of his life, stamped out of sight, destroyed, forgotten. For a long time he stood in deep thought, lost in the alarming possibilities of unconquerable memory, with the fear of death and eternity before him. 'Eternity!' he said aloud, and the sound of that word recalled him out of his reverie. The monkey started, dropped the skin, and grinned up at him amicably.

He went towards the office door and with some difficulty managed to open it. He entered in a cloud of dust that rose under his feet.

Books open with torn pages bestrewed the floor; other books lay about grimy and black, looking as if they had never been opened. Account books. In those books he had intended to keep day by day a record of his rising fortunes. Long time ago. A very long time. For many years there had been no record to keep on the blue-and-red-ruled pages! In the middle of the room the big office desk, with one of its legs broken, careened over like the hull of a stranded ship; most of the drawers had fallen out, disclosing heaps of paper yellow with age and dirt. The revolving office chair stood in its place, but he found the pivot set fast when he tried to turn it. No matter. He desisted, and his eyes wandered slowly from object to object. All those things had cost a lot of money at the time. The desk, the paper, the torn books and the broken shelves, all under a thick coat of dust. The very dust and bones of a dead and gone business. He looked at all these things, all that was left after so many years of work, of strife, of weariness, of discouragement, conquered so many times. And all for what? He stood thinking mournfully of his past life till he heard distinctly the clear voice of a child speaking amongst all this wreck, ruin and waste. He started with a great fear in his heart, and feverishly began to rake in the papers scattered on the floor, broke the chair into bits, splintered the drawers by banging them against the desk, and made a big heap of all that rubbish in one corner of the room.

He came out quickly, slammed the door after him, turned the key, and, taking it out, ran to the front rail of the verandah and, with a great swing of his arm, sent the key whizzing into the river. This done he went back slowly to the table, called the monkey down, unhooked its chain and induced it to remain quiet in the breast of his jacket. Then he sat again on the table and looked fixedly at the door of the room he had just left. He listened also intently. He heard a dry sound of rustling; sharp cracks as of dry wood snapping; a whirr like that of a bird's wings when it rises suddenly, and then he saw a thin stream of smoke come through the keyhole. The monkey struggled under his coat.

Ali appeared with his eyes starting out of his head. 'Master! House burn!' he shouted.

Almayer stood up holding by the table. He could hear the yells of alarm and surprise in the settlement. Ali wrung his hands, lamenting aloud.

'Stop this noise, fool!' said Almayer, quietly. 'Pick up my hammock and blankets and take them to the other house. Quick, now!'

The smoke burst through the crevices of the door, and Ali, with the hammock in his arms, cleared in one bound the steps of the verandah.

'It has caught well,' muttered Almayer to himself. 'Be quiet, Jack,' he added, as the monkey made a frantic effort to escape from its confinement.

The door split from top to bottom, and a rush of flame and smoke drove Almayer away from the table to the front rail of the verandah. He held on there till a great roar overhead assured him that the roof was ablaze. Then he ran down the steps of the verandah, coughing, half choked with the smoke that pursued him in bluish wreaths curling about his head.

On the other side of the ditch separating Almayer's courtyard from the settlement, a crowd of the inhabitants of Sambir looked at the burning house of the white man. In the calm air the flames rushed up on high, coloured pale brick-red, with violet gleams in the strong sunshine. The thin column of smoke ascended straight and unwavering till it lost itself in the clear blue of the sky, and in the great empty space between the two houses the interested spectators could see the tall figure of the Tuan Putih, with bowed head and dragging feet, walking slowly away from the fire towards the shelter of Almayer's Folly.

In that manner did Almayer move into his new house. He took possession of the new ruin, and in the undying folly of his heart set himself to wait in anxiety and pain for that forgetfulness which was so slow to come. He had done all he could. Every vestige of Nina's existence had been destroyed; and now with every sunrise he asked himself whether the longed-for oblivion would come before sunset, whether it would come before he died? He wanted to live only long enough to be able to forget, and the tenacity of his memory filled him with dread and horror of death; for should it come before he could accomplish the purpose of his life he would have to remember for ever! He also longed for loneliness. He wanted to be alone. But he was not. In the dim light of the rooms with their closed shutters, in the bright sunshine of the verandah, wherever he went, whichever way he turned, he saw the small figure of a little maiden with pretty olive face, with long black hair, her little pink robe slipping off her shoulders, her big eyes looking up at him in the tender trustfulness of a petted child. Ali did not see anything, but he also was aware of the presence of a child in the house. In his long talks by the evening fires of the settlement he used to tell his intimate friends of Almayer's strange doings. His master had turned sorcerer in his old age. Ali said that often when Tuan Putih had retired for the night he could hear him talking to something in his room. Ali thought that it was a spirit in the shape of a child. He knew his master spoke to a child from certain expressions and words his master used. His master spoke in Malay a little, but mostly in English, which he, Ali, could understand. Master spoke to the child at times tenderly, then he would weep over it, laugh at it, scold it, beg of it to go away; curse it. It was a bad and stubborn spirit. Ali thought his master had imprudently called it up, and now could not get rid of it. His master was very brave; he was not afraid to curse this spirit in the very Presence; and once he fought with it. Ali had heard a great noise as of running about inside the room and groans. His master groaned. Spirits do not groan. His master was brave, but foolish. You cannot hurt a spirit. Ali expected to find his master dead next morning, but he came out very early, looking much older than the day before, and had no food all day. So far Ali to the settlement. To Captain Ford he was much more

communicative, for the good reason that Captain Ford had the purse
and gave orders. On each of Ford's monthly visits to Sambir, Ali had to
go on board with a report about the inhabitant of Almayer's Folly. On
his first visit to Sambir after Nina's departure, Ford had taken charge of
Almayer's affairs. They were not cumbersome. The shed for the storage
of goods was empty, the boats had disappeared, appropriated – generally
at night-time – by various citizens of Sambir in need of means of
transport. During a great flood, the jetty of Lingard and Co. left the
bank and floated down the river, probably in search of more cheerful
surroundings; even the flock of geese – 'the only geese on the east
coast' – departed somewhere, preferring the unknown dangers of the
bush to the desolation of their old home. As time went on the grass
grew over the black patch of ground where the old house used to stand,
and nothing remained to mark the place of the dwelling that had
sheltered Almayer's young hopes, his foolish dream of splendid future,
his awakening, and his despair.

Ford did not often visit Almayer, for visiting Almayer was not a
pleasant task. At first he used to respond listlessly to the old seaman's
boisterous enquiries about his health; he even made efforts to talk,
asking for news in a voice that made it perfectly clear that no news
from this world had any interest for him. Then gradually he became
more silent – not sulkily – but as if he was forgetting how to speak. He
used also to hide in the darkest rooms of the house, where Ford had to
seek him out guided by the patter of the monkey galloping before
him. The monkey was always there to receive and introduce Ford.
The little animal seemed to have taken complete charge of its master,
and whenever it wished for his presence on the verandah it would tug
perseveringly at his jacket, till Almayer obediently came out into the
sunshine, which he seemed to dislike so much.

One morning Ford found him sitting on the floor of the verandah,
his back against the wall, his legs stretched stiffly out, his arms hanging
by his sides. His expressionless face, his eyes open wide with immobile
pupils, and the rigidity of his pose, made him look like an immense
man-doll broken and flung there out of the way. As Ford came up the
steps he turned his head slowly.

'Ford,' he murmured from the floor, 'I cannot forget.'

'Can't you?' said Ford, innocently, with an attempt at joviality: 'I wish
I was like you. I am losing my memory – age, I suppose; only the other
day my mate – '

He stopped, for Almayer had got up, stumbled, and steadied himself
on his friend's arm.

'Hallo! You are better today. Soon be all right,' said Ford, cheerfully, but feeling rather scared.

Almayer let go his arm and stood very straight with his head up and shoulders thrown back, looking stonily at the multitude of suns shining in ripples of the river. His jacket and his loose trousers flapped in the breeze on his thin limbs.

'Let her go!' he whispered in a grating voice. 'Let her go. Tomorrow I shall forget. I am a firm man . . . firm as a . . . rock . . . firm . . . '

Ford looked at his face – and fled. The skipper was a tolerably firm man himself – as those who had sailed with him could testify – but Almayer's firmness was altogether too much for his fortitude.

Next time the steamer called at Sambir, Ali came on board early with a grievance. He complained to Ford that Jim-Eng the Chinaman had invaded Almayer's house, and actually had lived there for the last month.

'And they both smoke,' added Ali.

'Phew! Opium, you mean?'

Ali nodded, and Ford remained thoughtful; then he muttered to himself, 'Poor devil! The sooner the better now.' In the afternoon he walked up to the house.

'What are you doing here?' he asked of Jim-Eng, whom he found strolling about on the verandah.

Jim-Eng explained in bad Malay, and speaking in that monotonous, uninterested voice of an opium smoker pretty far gone, that his house was old, the roof leaked and the floor was rotten. So, being an old friend for many, many years, he took his money, his opium and two pipes and came to live in this big house.

'There is plenty of room. He smokes, and I live here. He will not smoke long,' he concluded.

'Where is he now?' asked Ford.

'Inside. He sleeps,' answered Jim-Eng, wearily. Ford glanced in through the doorway. In the dim light of the room he could see Almayer lying on his back on the floor, his head on a wooden pillow, the long white beard scattered over his breast, the yellow skin of the face, the half-closed eyelids showing the whites of the eyes only. . . .

He shuddered and turned away. As he was leaving he noticed a long strip of faded red silk, with some Chinese letters on it, which Jim-Eng had just fastened to one of the pillars.

'What's that?' he asked.

'That,' said Jim-Eng, in his colourless voice, 'that is the name of the house. All the same like my house. Very good name.'

Ford looked at him for awhile and went away. He did not know what the crazy-looking maze of the Chinese inscription on the red silk meant. Had he asked Jim-Eng, that patient Chinaman would have informed him with proper pride that its meaning was: 'House of heavenly delight'.

In the evening of the same day Babalatchi called on Captain Ford. The captain's cabin opened on deck, and Babalatchi sat astride on the high step, while Ford smoked his pipe on the settee inside. The steamer was leaving next morning, and the old statesman came as usual for a last chat.

'We had news from Bali last moon,' remarked Babalatchi. 'A grandson is born to the old Rajah, and there is great rejoicing.'

Ford sat up interested.

'Yes,' went on Babalatchi, in answer to Ford's look. 'I told him. That was before he began to smoke.'

'Well, and what?' asked Ford.

'I escaped with my life,' said Babalatchi, with perfect gravity, 'because the white man is very weak and fell as he rushed upon me.' Then, after a pause, he added, 'She is mad with joy.'

'Mrs Almayer, you mean?'

'Yes, she lives in our Rajah's house. She will not die soon. Such women live a long time,' said Babalatchi, with a slight tinge of regret in his voice. 'She has dollars, and she has buried them, but we know where. We had much trouble with those people. We had to pay a fine and listen to threats from the white men, and now we have to be careful.' He sighed and remained silent for a long while. Then with energy: 'There will be fighting. There is a breath of war on the islands. Shall I live long enough to see? . . . Ah, Tuan!' he went on, more quietly, 'the old times were best. Even I have sailed with Lanun men,[61] and boarded in the night silent ships with white sails. That was before an English Rajah ruled in Kuching.[62] Then we fought amongst ourselves and were happy. Now when we fight with you we can only die!'

He rose to go. 'Tuan,' he said, 'you remember the girl that man Bulangi had? Her that caused all the trouble?'

'Yes,' said Ford. 'What of her?'

'She grew thin and could not work. Then Bulangi, who is a thief and a pig-eater, gave her to me for fifty dollars. I sent her amongst my women to grow fat. I wanted to hear the sound of her laughter, but she must have been bewitched, and . . . she died two days ago. Nay, Tuan. Why do you speak bad words? I am old – that is true – but why should I not like the sight of a young face and the sound of a young voice in my house?' He paused, and then added with a little mournful laugh, 'I am like a white man talking too much of what is not men's talk when they speak to one another.'

And he went off looking very sad.

* * *

The crowd, massed in a semicircle before the steps of Almayer's Folly, swayed silently backwards and forwards and opened out before the group of white-robed and turbaned men advancing through the grass towards the house. Abdulla walked first, supported by Reshid and followed by all the Arabs in Sambir. As they entered the lane made by the respectful throng there was a subdued murmur of voices, where the word 'Mati'[63] was the only one distinctly audible.

Abdulla stopped and looked round slowly. 'Is he dead?' he asked.

'May you live!' answered the crowd in one shout, and then there succeeded a breathless silence.

Abdulla made a few paces forward and found himself for the last time face to face with his old enemy. Whatever he might have been once he was not dangerous now, lying stiff and lifeless in the tender light of the early day. The only white man on the east coast was dead, and his soul, delivered from the trammels of his earthly folly, stood now in the presence of Infinite Wisdom. On the upturned face there was that serene look which follows the sudden relief from anguish and pain, and it testified silently before the cloudless heaven that the man lying there under the gaze of indifferent eyes had been permitted to forget before he died.

Abdulla looked down sadly at this Infidel he had fought so long and had bested so many times. Such was the reward of the Faithful! Yet in the Arab's old heart there was a feeling of regret for that thing gone out of his life. He was leaving fast behind him friendships and enmities, successes and disappointments – all that makes up a life; and before him was only the end. Prayer would fill up the remainder of the days allotted to the True Believer! He took in his hand the beads that hung at his waist.

'I found him here, like this, in the morning,' said Ali, in a low and awed voice.

Abdulla glanced coldly once more at the serene face.

'Let us go,' he said, addressing Reshid.

And as they passed through the crowd that fell back before them, the beads in Abdulla's hand clicked, while in a solemn whisper he breathed out piously the name of Allah! The Merciful! The Compassionate!

(For Notes on *Almayer's Folly*, see pages 341–4 at the end of the book.)

THE ROVER

THE ROVER

———————— ◆ ————————

Joseph Conrad

Sleep after toyle, port after stormie seas,
Ease after warre, death after life, does greatly please.

SPENSER [64]

To

G. JEAN AUBRY

in friendship

this tale of the last days of a
French Brother of the Coast [65]

Chapter 1

After entering at break of day the inner roadstead of the Port of Toulon, exchanging several loud hails with one of the guard boats of the Fleet, which directed him where he was to take up his berth, Master-Gunner Peyrol let go the anchor of the sea-worn and battered ship in his charge, between the arsenal and the town, in full view of the principal quay. The course of his life, which in the opinion of any ordinary person might have been regarded as full of marvellous incidents (only he himself had never marvelled at them), had rendered him undemonstrative to such a degree that he did not even let out a sigh of relief at the rumble of the cable. And yet it ended a most anxious six months of knocking about at sea with valuable merchandise in a damaged hull, most of the time on short rations, always on the lookout for English cruisers, once or twice on the verge of shipwreck and more than once on the verge of capture. But as to that, old Peyrol had made up his mind from the first to blow up his valuable charge – unemotionally, for such was his character, formed under the sun of the Indian Seas in lawless contests with his kind for a little loot that vanished as soon as grasped, but mainly for bare life almost as precarious to hold through its ups and downs, and which now had lasted for fifty-eight years.

While his crew of half-starved scarecrows, hard as nails and ravenous as so many wolves for the delights of the shore, swarmed aloft to furl the sails nearly as thin and as patched as the grimy shirts on their backs, Peyrol took a survey of the quay. Groups were forming along its whole stretch to gaze at the new arrival. Peyrol noted particularly a good many men in red caps and said to himself – 'Here they are.' Amongst the crews of ships that had brought the tricolour into the seas of the East, there were hundreds professing sans-culotte[66] principles; boastful and declamatory beggars he had thought them. But now he was beholding the shore breed. Those who had made the Revolution safe. The real thing. Peyrol, after taking a good long look, went below into his cabin to make himself ready to go ashore.

He shaved his big cheeks with a real English razor, looted years ago from an officer's cabin in an English East Indiaman captured by a ship he was serving in then. He put on a white shirt, a short blue jacket with metal buttons and a high roll-collar, a pair of white trousers which he fastened with a red bandana handkerchief by way of a belt. With a black, shiny low-crowned hat on his head he made a very creditable prize-master. He beckoned from the poop to a boatman and got himself rowed to the quay.

By that time the crowd had grown to a large size. Peyrol's eyes ranged over it with no great apparent interest, though it was a fact that he had never in all his man's life seen so many idle white people massed together to stare at a sailor. He had been a rover of the outer seas; he had grown into a stranger to his native country. During the few minutes it took the boatman to row him to the step, he felt like a navigator about to land on a newly discovered shore.

On putting his foot on it he was mobbed. The arrival of a prize made by a squadron of the Republic in distant seas was not an everyday occurrence in Toulon. The wildest rumours had been already set flying. Peyrol elbowed himself through the crowd somehow, but it continued to move after him. A voice cried out, 'Where do you come from, citoyen?'

'From the other side of the world,' Peyrol boomed out.

He did not get rid of his followers till the door of the Port Office. There he reported himself to the proper officials as master of a prize taken off the Cape by Citoyen Renaud, Commander-in-Chief of the Republican Squadron in the Indian Seas. He had been ordered to make for Dunkerque but, said he, having been chased by the *sacrés Anglais*[67] three times in a fortnight between Cape Verde[68] and Cape Spartel, he had made up his mind to run into the Mediterranean where, he had understood from a Danish brig he had met at sea, there were no English men-of-war just then. And here he was; and there were his ship's papers and his own papers and everything in order. He mentioned also that he was tired of rolling about the seas, and that he longed for a period of repose on shore. But till all the legal business was settled he remained in Toulon roaming about the streets at a deliberate gait, enjoying general consideration as Citizen Peyrol, and looking everybody coldly in the eye.

His reticence about his past was of that kind which starts a lot of mysterious stories about a man. No doubt the maritime authorities of Toulon had a less cloudy idea of Peyrol's past, though it need not necessarily have been more exact. In the various offices connected with the sea where his duties took him, the wretched scribes, and even some of the chiefs, looked very hard at him as he went in and out, dressed very neatly, and always with his cudgel, which he used to leave outside the door of private offices when called in for an interview with one or another of the 'gold-laced lot'. Having, however, cut off his queue[69] and got in touch with some prominent patriots of the Jacobin[70] type, Peyrol cared little for people's stares and whispers. The person that came nearest to trying his composure was a certain naval captain with a patch over one eye and a very threadbare uniform coat who was doing some administrative work at the Port Office. That officer, looking up from some papers, remarked brusquely, 'As a matter of fact you have been the best part of your life skimming the seas, if the truth were known. You must have been a deserter from the navy at one time, whatever you may call yourself now.'

There was not a quiver on the large cheeks of the gunner Peyrol.

'If there was anything of the sort it was in the time of kings and aristocrats,' he said steadily. 'And now I have brought in a prize, and a service letter from Citoyen Renaud, commanding in the Indian Seas. I can also give you the names of good republicans in this town who know my sentiments. Nobody can say I was ever anti-revolutionary in my life. I knocked about the Eastern seas for forty-five years – that's true. But let me observe that it was the seamen who stayed at home that let the English into the Port of Toulon.' He paused a moment and then added: 'When one thinks of that, Citoyen Commandant, any little slips I and fellows of my kind may have made five thousand leagues from here and twenty years ago cannot have much importance in these times of equality and fraternity.'

'As to fraternity,' remarked the post-captain in the shabby coat, 'the only one you are familiar with is the Brotherhood of the Coast,[71] I should say.'

'Everybody in the Indian Ocean except milksops and youngsters had to be,' said the untroubled Citizen Peyrol. 'And we practised republican principles long before a republic was thought of; for the Brothers of the Coast were all equal and elected their own chiefs.'

'They were an abominable lot of lawless ruffians,' remarked the officer venomously, leaning back in his chair. 'You will not dare to deny that.'

Citizen Peyrol refused to take up a defensive attitude. He merely mentioned in a neutral tone that he had delivered his trust to the Port Office all right, and as to his character he had a certificate of civism[72] from his section. He was a patriot and entitled to his discharge. After being dismissed by a nod he took up his cudgel outside the door and walked out of the building with the calmness of rectitude. His large face of the Roman type betrayed nothing to the wretched quill-drivers, who whispered on his passage. As he went along the streets he looked as usual everybody in the eye; but that very same evening he vanished from Toulon. It wasn't that he was afraid of anything. His mind was as calm as the natural set of his florid face. Nobody could know what his forty years or more of sea-life had been, unless he told them himself. And of that he didn't mean to tell more than what he had told the inquisitive captain with the patch over one eye. But he didn't want any bother for certain other reasons; and more than anything else he didn't want to be sent perhaps to serve in the fleet now fitting out in Toulon. So at dusk he passed through the gate on the road to Fréjus in a high two-wheeled cart belonging to a well-known farmer whose habitation lay that way. His personal belongings were brought down and piled up on the tailboard of the cart by some ragamuffin patriots whom he engaged in the street for that purpose. The only indiscretion he committed was to pay them for their trouble with a large handful of assignats.[73] From such a prosperous seaman, however, this generosity was not so very compromising. He himself got into the cart over the wheel with such slow and ponderous movements that the friendly farmer felt called upon to remark: 'Ah, we are not so young as we used to be – you and I.'

'I have also an awkward wound,' said Citizen Peyrol, sitting down heavily.

And so from farmer's cart to farmer's cart, getting lifts all along, jogging in a cloud of dust between stone walls and through little villages well known to him from his boyhood's days, in a landscape of stony hills, pale rocks and dusty green of olive trees, Citizen Peyrol went on unmolested till he got down clumsily in the yard of an inn on the outskirts of the town of Hyères.[74] The sun was setting to his right. Near a clump of dark pines with blood-red trunks in the sunset, Peyrol perceived a rutty track branching off in the direction of the sea.

At that spot Citizen Peyrol had made up his mind to leave the high road. Every feature of the country with the darkly wooded rises, the barren flat expanse of stones and sombre bushes to his left, appealed to him with a sort of strange familiarity, because they had remained unchanged since the days of his boyhood. The very cartwheel tracks scored deep into the stony ground had kept their physiognomy; and far away, like a blue thread, there was the sea of the Hyères roadstead with a lumpy indigo swelling still beyond – which was the island of Porquerolles. He had an idea that he had been born on Porqerolles, but he really did not know. The notion of a father was absent from his mentality. What he remembered of his parents was a tall, lean, brown woman in rags, who was his mother. But then they were working together at a farm which was on the mainland. He had fragmentary memories of her shaking down olives, picking stones out of a field or handling a manure fork like a man, tireless and fierce, with wisps of greyish hair flying about her bony face; and of himself running bare-footed in connection with a flock of turkeys, with hardly any clothes on his back. At night, by the farmer's favour, they were permitted to sleep in a sort of ruinous byre built of stones and with only half a roof on it, lying side by side on some old straw on the ground. And it was on a bundle of straw that his mother had tossed ill for two days and had died in the night. In the darkness, her silence, her cold face had given him an awful scare. He supposed they had buried her but he didn't know, because he had rushed out terror-struck, and never stopped till he got as far as a little place by the sea called Almanarre,[75] where he hid himself on board a tartane[76] that was lying there with no one on board. He went into the hold because he was afraid of some dogs on shore. He found down there a heap of empty sacks, which made a luxurious couch, and being exhausted went to sleep like a stone. Some time during the night the crew came on board and the tartane sailed for Marseilles. That was another awful scare – being hauled out by the scruff of the neck on the deck and being asked who the devil he was and what he was doing there. Only from that one he could not run away. There was water all around him and the whole world, including the coast not very far away, wobbled in a most alarming manner. Three bearded men stood about him and he tried to explain to them that he had been working at Peyrol's. Peyrol was the farmer's name. The boy didn't know that he had one of his own. Moreover, he didn't know very well how to talk to people, and they must have misunderstood him. Thus the name of Peyrol stuck to him for life.

There the memories of his native country stopped, overlaid by other memories, with a multitude of impressions of endless oceans, of the Mozambique Channel,[77] of Arabs and Negroes, of Madagascar, of the coast of India, of islands and channels and reefs; of fights at sea, rows on shore, desperate slaughter and desperate thirst, of all sorts of ships one after another: merchant ships and frigates and privateers; of reckless men and enormous sprees. In the course of years he had learned to speak intelligibly and think connectedly and even to read and write after a fashion. The name of the farmer Peyrol, attached to his person on account of his inability to give a clear account of himself, acquired a sort of reputation, both openly, in the ports of the East, and, secretly, amongst the Brothers of the Coast, that strange fraternity with something masonic and not a little piratical in its constitution. Round the Cape of Storms, which is also the Cape of Good Hope, the words Republic, Nation, Tyranny, Liberty, Equality and Fraternity, and the cult of the Supreme Being,[78] came floating on board ships from home, new cries and new ideas which did not upset the slowly developed intelligence of the gunner Peyrol. They seemed the invention of landsmen, of whom the seaman Peyrol knew very little – nothing, so to speak. Now, after nearly fifty years of lawful and lawless sea-life, Citizen Peyrol, at the yard gate of the roadside inn, looked at the late scene of his childhood. He looked at it without any animosity, but a little puzzled as to his bearings amongst the features of the land. 'Yes, it must be somewhere in that direction,' he thought vaguely. Decidedly he would go no further along the high road . . . A few yards away the woman of the inn stood looking at him, impressed by the good clothes, the great shaven cheeks, the well-to-do air of that seaman; and suddenly Peyrol noticed her. With her anxious brown face, her grey locks, and her rustic appearance she might have been his mother, as he remembered her, only she wasn't in rags.

'Hé! La mère,' hailed Peyrol. 'Have you got a man to lend a hand with my chest into the house?'

He looked so prosperous and so authoritative that she piped without hesitation in a thin voice, 'Mais oui, citoyen. He will be here in a moment.'

In the dusk the clump of pines across the road looked very black against the quiet clear sky; and Citizen Peyrol gazed at the scene of his young misery with the greatest possible placidity. Here he was after nearly fifty years, and to look at things it seemed like yesterday. He felt for all this neither love nor resentment. He felt a little funny as it were, and the funniest thing was the thought which crossed his mind that he could indulge his fancy (if he had a mind to it) to buy up all this land to the farthermost field, away over there where the track lost itself sinking into the flats bordering the sea where the small rise at the end of the Giens peninsula had assumed the appearance of a black cloud.

'Tell me, my friend,' he said in his magisterial way to the farmhand with a tousled head of hair who was awaiting his good pleasure, 'doesn't this track lead to Almanarre?'

'Yes,' said the labourer, and Peyrol nodded. The man continued, mouthing his words slowly as if unused to speech. 'To Almanarre and farther too, beyond the great pond right out to the end of the land, to Cape Esterel.'

Peyrol was lending his big flat hairy ear. 'If I had stayed in this country,' he thought, 'I would be talking like this fellow.' And aloud he asked: 'Are there any houses there, at the end of the land?'

'Why, a hamlet, a hole, just a few houses round a church and a farm where at one time they would give you a glass of wine.'

Chapter 2

Citizen Peyrol stayed at the inn-yard gate till the night had swallowed up all those features of the land to which his eyes had clung as long as the last gleams of daylight. And even after the last gleams had gone he had remained for some time staring into the darkness in which all he could distinguish was the white road at his feet and the black heads of pines where the cart track dipped towards the coast. He did not go indoors till some carters who had been refreshing themselves had departed with their big two-wheeled carts piled up high with empty wine-casks, in the direction of Fréjus. The fact that they did not remain for the night pleased Peyrol. He ate his bit of supper alone, in silence, and with a gravity which intimidated the old woman who had aroused in him the memory of his mother. Having finished his pipe and obtained a bit of candle in a tin candlestick, Citizen Peyrol went heavily upstairs to rejoin his luggage. The crazy staircase shook and groaned under his feet as though he had been carrying a burden. The first thing he did was to close the shutters most carefully as though he had been afraid of a breath of night air. Next he bolted the door of the room. Then sitting on the floor, with the candlestick standing before him between his widely straddled legs, he began to undress, flinging off his coat and dragging his shirt hastily over his head. The secret of his heavy movements was disclosed then in the fact that he had been wearing next his bare skin – like a pious penitent his hair-shirt – a sort of waistcoat made of two thicknesses of old sailcloth and stitched all over in the manner of a quilt with tarred twine. Three horn buttons closed it in front. He undid them, and after he had slipped off the two shoulder-straps which prevented this strange garment from sagging down on his hips he started rolling it up. Notwithstanding all his care there were during this operation several faint chinks of some metal which could not have been lead.

His bare torso thrown backwards and sustained by his rigid big arms heavily tattooed on the white skin above the elbows, Peyrol drew a long breath into his broad chest with a pepper-and-salt pelt down the breastbone. And not only was the breast of Citizen Peyrol relieved to the fullest of its athletic capacity, but a change had also come over his large physiognomy on which the expression of severe stolidity had been simply the result of physical discomfort. It isn't a trifle to have to carry girt about your ribs and hung from your shoulders a mass of mixed foreign coins equal to sixty or seventy thousand francs in hard cash; while as to the paper money of the Republic, Peyrol had had already enough experience of it to estimate the equivalent in cartloads. A thousand of them. Perhaps two thousand. Enough in any case to justify his flight of fancy, while looking at the countryside in the light of the sunset, that what he had on him would buy all that soil from which he had sprung: houses, woods, vines, olives, vegetable gardens, rocks and salt lagoons – in fact, the whole landscape, including the animals in it. But Peyrol did not care for the land at all. He did not want to own any part of the solid earth for which he had no love. All he wanted from it was a quiet nook, an obscure corner out of men's sight where he could dig a hole unobserved.

That would have to be done pretty soon, he thought. One could not live for an indefinite number of days with a treasure strapped round one's chest. Meantime, an utter stranger in his native country the landing on which was perhaps the biggest adventure in his adventurous life, he threw his jacket over the rolled-up waistcoat and laid his head down on it after extinguishing the candle. The night was warm. The floor of the room happened to be of planks, not of tiles. He was no stranger to that sort of couch. With his cudgel laid ready at his hand, Peyrol slept soundly till the noises and the voices about the house and on the road woke him up shortly after sunrise. He threw open the shutter, welcoming the morning light and the morning breeze in the full enjoyment of idleness which, to a seaman of his kind, is inseparable from the fact of being on shore. There was nothing to trouble his thoughts; and though his physiognomy was far from being vacant, it did not wear the aspect of profound meditation.

It had been by the merest accident that he had discovered during the passage, in a secret recess within one of the lockers of his prize, two bags of mixed coins: gold mohurs,[79] Dutch ducats, Spanish pieces, English guineas. After making that discovery he had suffered from no doubts whatever. Loot big or little was a natural fact of his freebooter's life. And now when by the force of things he had become a master-gunner of the navy he was not going to give up his find to confounded landsmen, mere sharks, hungry quill-drivers, who would put it in their own pockets. As to imparting the intelligence to his crew (all bad characters), he was much too wise to do anything of the kind. They would not have been above cutting his throat. An old fighting sea-dog, a Brother of the Coast, had more right to such plunder than anybody on earth. So at odd times, while at sea, he had busied himself within the privacy of his cabin in constructing the ingenious canvas waistcoat in which he could take his treasure ashore secretly. It was bulky, but his garments were of an ample cut, and no wretched customs-guard would dare to lay hands on a successful prize-master going to the Port Admiral's offices to make his report. The scheme had worked perfectly. He found, however, that this secret garment, which was worth precisely its weight in gold, tried his endurance more than he had expected. It wearied his body and even depressed his spirits somewhat. It made him less active and also less communicative. It reminded him all the time that he must not get into trouble of any sort – keep clear of rows, of intimacies, of promiscuous jollities. This was one of the reasons why he had been anxious to get away from the town. Once, however, his head was laid on his treasure he could sleep the sleep of the just.

Nevertheless in the morning he shrank from putting it on again. With a mixture of sailor's carelessness and of old-standing belief in his own luck he simply stuffed the precious waistcoat up the flue of the empty fireplace. Then he dressed and had his breakfast. An hour later, mounted on a hired mule, he started down the track as calmly as though setting out to explore the mysteries of a desert island.

His aim was the end of the peninsula which, advancing like a colossal jetty into the sea, divides the picturesque roadstead of Hyères from the headlands and curves of the coast forming the approaches of the Port of Toulon. The path along which the sure-footed mule took him (for Peyrol, once he had put its head the right way, made no attempt at steering) descended rapidly to a plain of arid aspect, with the white gleam of the Salins [80] in the distance, bounded by bluish hills of no great elevation. Soon all traces of human habitation disappeared from before his roaming eyes. This part of his native country was more foreign to him than the shores of the Mozambique Channel, the coral strands of India, the forests of Madagascar. Before long he found himself on the neck of the Giens peninsula, impregnated with salt and containing a blue lagoon, particularly blue, darker and even more still than the expanses of the sea to the right and left of it from which it was separated by narrow strips of land not a hundred yards wide in places. The track ran indistinct, presenting no wheel-ruts, and with patches of efflorescent salt as white as snow between the tufts of wiry grass and the particularly dead-looking bushes. The whole neck of land was so low that it seemed to have no more thickness than a sheet of paper laid on the sea. Citizen Peyrol saw on the level of his eye, as if from a mere raft, sails of various craft, some white and some brown, while before him his native island of Porquerolles rose dull and solid beyond a wide strip of water. The mule, which knew rather better than Citizen Peyrol where it was going to, took him presently amongst the gentle rises at the end of the peninsula. The slopes were covered with scanty grass; crooked boundary walls of dry stones ran across the fields, and above them, here and there, peeped a low roof of red tiles shaded by the heads of delicate acacias. At a turn of the ravine appeared a village with its few houses, mostly with their blind walls to the path, and, at first, no living soul in sight. Three tall platanes, very ragged as to their bark and very poor as to foliage, stood in a group in an open space; and Citizen Peyrol was cheered by the sight of a dog sleeping in the shade. The mule swerved with great determination towards a massive stone trough under the village fountain. Peyrol, looking round from the saddle while the mule drank, could see no signs of an inn. Then, examining the ground nearer to him, he perceived a ragged man sitting on a stone. He had a broad leathern belt and his legs were bare to the knee. He was contemplating the stranger on the mule with stony surprise. His dark nut-brown face contrasted strongly with his grey shock of hair. At a sign from Peyrol he showed no reluctance and approached him readily without changing the stony character of his stare.

The thought that if he had remained at home he would have probably looked like that man crossed unbidden the mind of Peyrol. With that gravity from which he seldom departed he enquired if there were any inhabitants besides himself in the village. Then, to Peyrol's surprise, that destitute idler smiled pleasantly and said that the people were out looking after their bits of land.

There was enough of the peasant-born in Peyrol, still, to remark that he had seen no man, woman or child or four-footed beast for hours, and that he would hardly have thought that there was any land worth looking after anywhere around. But the other insisted. Well, they were working on it all the same, at least those that had any.

At the sound of the voices the dog got up with a strange air of being all backbone, and, approaching in dismal fidelity, stood with his nose close to his master's calves.

'And you,' said Peyrol, 'you have no land then?'

The man took his time to answer. 'I have a boat.'

Peyrol became interested when the man explained that his boat was on the salt pond, the large, deserted and opaque sheet of water lying dead between the two great bays of the living sea. Peyrol wondered aloud why anyone should want a boat on it.

'There is fish there,' said the man.

'And is the boat all your worldly goods?' asked Peyrol.

The flies buzzed, the mule hung its head, moving its ears and flapping its thin tail languidly.

'I have a sort of hut down by the lagoon and a net or two,' the man confessed, as it were. Peyrol, looking down, completed the list by saying: 'And this dog.'

The man again took his time to say: 'He is company.'

Peyrol sat as serious as a judge. 'You haven't much to make a living of,' he delivered himself at last. 'However! . . . Is there no inn, café or some place where one could put up for a day? I have heard up inland that there was some such place.'

'I will show it to you,' said the man, who then went back to where he had been sitting and picked up a large empty basket before he led the way. His dog followed with his head and tail low, and then came Peyrol dangling his heels against the sides of the intelligent mule, which seemed to know beforehand all that was going to happen. At the corner where the houses ended there stood an old wooden cross stuck into a square block of stone. The lonely boatman of the Lagoon of Pesquiers[81] pointed in the direction of a branching path where the rises terminating the peninsula sank into a shallow pass. There were leaning pines on the skyline, and in the pass itself dull silvery green patches of olive orchards below a long yellow wall backed by dark cypresses, and the red roofs of buildings which seemed to belong to a farm.

'Will they lodge me there?' asked Peyrol.

'I don't know. They will have plenty of room, that's certain. There are no travellers here. But as for a place of refreshment, it used to be that. You have only got to walk in. If he isn't there, the mistress is sure to be there to serve you. She belongs to the place. She was born on it. We know all about her.'

'What sort of woman is she?' asked Citizen Peyrol, who was very favourably impressed by the aspect of the place.

'Well, you are going there. You shall soon see. She is young.'

'And the husband?' asked Peyrol, who, looking down into the other's steady upward stare, detected a flicker in the brown, slightly faded eyes. 'Why are you staring at me like this? I haven't got a black skin, have I?'

The other smiled, showing in the thick pepper-and-salt growth on his face as sound a set of teeth as Citizen Peyrol himself. There was in his bearing something embarrassed, but not unfriendly, and he uttered a phrase from which Peyrol discovered that the man before him, the lonely, hirsute, sunburnt and bare-legged human being at his stirrup, nourished patriotic suspicions as to his character. And this seemed to him outrageous. He wanted to know in a severe voice whether he looked like a confounded landsman of any kind. He swore also without, however, losing any of the dignity of expression inherent in his type of features and in the very modelling of his flesh.

'For an aristocrat you don't look like one, but neither do you look like a farmer or a pedlar or a patriot. You don't look like anything that has been seen here for years and years and years. You look like one, I dare hardly say what. You might be a priest.'

Astonishment kept Peyrol perfectly quiet on his mule. 'Do I dream?' he asked himself mentally. 'You aren't mad?' he asked aloud. 'Do you know what you are talking about? Aren't you ashamed of yourself?'

'All the same,' persisted the other innocently, 'it is much less than ten years ago since I saw one of them of the sort they call bishops, who had a face exactly like yours.'

Instinctively Peyrol passed his hand over his face. What could there be in it? Peyrol could not remember ever having seen a bishop in his life.

The fellow stuck to his point, for he puckered his brow and murmured: 'Others too . . . I remember perfectly . . . It isn't so many years ago. Some of them skulk amongst the villages yet, for all the chasing they got from the patriots.'

The sun blazed on the boulders and stones and bushes in the perfect stillness of the air. The mule, disregarding with republican austerity the neighbourhood of a stable within less than a hundred and twenty yards, dropped its head, and even its ears, and dozed as if in the middle of a desert. The dog, apparently changed into stone at his master's heels, seemed to be dozing too with his nose near the ground. Peyrol had fallen into a deep meditation, and the boatman of the lagoon awaited the solution of his doubts without eagerness and with something like a grin within his thick beard. Peyrol's face cleared. He had solved the problem, but there was a shade of vexation in his tone.

'Well, it can't be helped,' he said. 'I learned to shave from the English. I suppose that's what's the matter.'

At the name of the English the boatman pricked up his ears.

'One can't tell where they are all gone to,' he murmured. 'Only three years ago they swarmed about this coast in their big ships. You saw nothing but them, and they were fighting all round Toulon on land. Then in a week or two, crac! – nobody! Cleared out devil knows where. But perhaps you would know.'

'Oh, yes,' said Peyrol, 'I know all about the English, don't you worry your head.'

'I am not troubling my head. It is for you to think about what's best to say when you speak with him up there. I mean the master of the farm.'

'He can't be a better patriot than I am, for all my shaven face,' said Peyrol. 'That would only seem strange to a savage like you.'

With an unexpected sigh the man sat down at the foot of the cross, and, immediately, his dog went off a little way and curled himself up amongst the tufts of grass.

'We are all savages here,' said the forlorn fisherman from the lagoon. 'But the master up there is a real patriot from the town. If you were ever to go to Toulon and ask people about him they would tell you. He first became busy purveying the guillotine when they were purifying the town from all aristocrats. That was even before the English came in. After the English got driven out there was more of that work than the guillotine could do. They had to kill traitors in the streets, in cellars, in their beds. The corpses of men and women were lying in heaps along the quays. There were a good many of his sort that got the name of drinkers of blood. Well, he was one of the best of them. I am only just telling you.'

Peyrol nodded. 'That will do me all right,' he said. And before he could pick up the reins and hit it with his heels the mule, as though it had just waited for his words, started off along the path.

In less than five minutes Peyrol was dismounting in front of a low, long addition to a tall farmhouse, with very few windows and flanked by walls of stones enclosing not only the yard but apparently a field or two also. A gateway stood open to the left, but Peyrol dismounted at the door, through which he entered a bare room, with rough whitewashed walls and a few wooden chairs and tables, which might have been a rustic café. He tapped with his knuckles on the table. A young woman with a fichu[82] round her neck and a striped white and red skirt, with black hair and a red mouth, appeared in an inner doorway.

'Bonjour, citoyenne,' said Peyrol. She was so startled by the unusual aspect of this stranger that she answered him only by a murmured, 'Bonjour,' but in a moment she came forward and waited expectantly. The perfect oval of her face, the colour of her smooth cheeks, and the whiteness of her throat forced from the Citizen Peyrol a slight hiss through his clenched teeth.

'I am thirsty, of course,' he said, 'but what I really want is to know whether I can stay here.'

The sound of a mule's hoofs outside caused Peyrol to start, but the woman arrested him.

'She is only going to the shed. She knows the way. As to what you said, the master will be here directly. Nobody ever comes here. And how long would you want to stay?'

The old rover of the seas looked at her searchingly.

'To tell you the truth, citoyenne, it may be in a manner of speaking for ever.'

She smiled in a bright flash of teeth, without gaiety or any change in her restless eyes that roamed about the empty room as though Peyrol had come in attended by a mob of shades.

'It's like me,' she said. 'I lived as a child here.'

'You are but little more than that now,' said Peyrol, examining her with a feeling that was no longer surprise or curiosity, but seemed to be lodged in his very breast.

'Are you a patriot?' she asked, still surveying the invisible company in the room.

Peyrol, who had thought that he had 'done with all that damned nonsense', felt angry and also at a loss for an answer.

'I am a Frenchman,' he said bluntly.

'Arlette!' called out an aged woman's voice through the open inner door.

'What do you want?' she answered readily.

'There's a saddled mule come into the yard.'

'All right. The man is here.' Her eyes, which had steadied, began to wander again all round and about the motionless Peyrol. She moved a step nearer to him and asked in a low confidential tone: 'Have you ever carried a woman's head on a pike?'

Peyrol, who had seen fights, massacres on land and sea, towns taken by assault by savage warriors, who had killed men in attack and defence, found himself at first bereft of speech by this simple question, and next moved to speak bitterly.

'No. I have heard men boast of having done so. They were mostly braggarts with craven hearts. But what is all this to you?'

She was not listening to him, the edge of her white even teeth pressing her lower lip, her eyes never at rest. Peyrol remembered suddenly the sans-culotte – the blood-drinker. Her husband. Was it possible? . . . Well, perhaps it was possible. He could not tell. He felt his utter incompetence. As to catching her glance, you might just as well have tried to catch a wild sea-bird with your hands. And altogether she was like a sea-bird – not to be grasped. But Peyrol knew how to be patient, with that patience that is so often a form of courage. He was known for it. It had served him well in dangerous situations. Once it had positively saved his life. Nothing but patience. He could well wait now. He waited. And suddenly as if tamed by his patience this strange creature dropped her eyelids, advanced quite close to him and began to finger the lapel of his coat – something that a child might have done. Peyrol all but gasped with surprise, but he remained perfectly still. He was disposed to hold his breath. He was touched by a soft indefinite emotion, and as her eyelids remained lowered till her black lashes seemed to lie like a shadow on her pale cheek, there was no need for him to force a smile. After the first moment he was not even surprised. It was merely the sudden movement, not the nature of the act itself, that had startled him.

'Yes. You may stay. I think we shall be friends. I'll tell you about the Revolution.'

At these words Peyrol, the man of violent deeds, felt something like a chill breath at the back of his head.

'What's the good of that?' he said.

'It must be,' she said and backed away from him swiftly, and without raising her eyes turned round and was gone in a moment, so lightly that one would have thought her feet had not touched the ground. Peyrol, staring at the open kitchen door, saw after a moment an elderly woman's head, with brown thin cheeks and tied up in a coloured handkerchief, peeping at him fearfully.

'A bottle of wine, please,' he shouted at it.

Chapter 3

The affectation common to seamen of never being surprised at anything that sea or land can produce had become in Peyrol a second
nature. Having learned from childhood to suppress every sign of
wonder before all extraordinary sights and events, all strange people,
all strange customs, and the most alarming phenomena of nature (as
manifested, for instance, in the violence of volcanoes or the fury of
human beings), he had really become indifferent – or only perhaps
utterly inexpressive. He had seen so much that was bizarre or atrocious,
and had heard so many astounding tales, that his usual mental reaction
before a new experience was generally formulated in the words, 'J'en
ai vu bien d'autres.'[83] The last thing which had touched him with the
panic of the supernatural had been the death under a heap of rags of
that gaunt, fierce woman, his mother; and the last thing that had
nearly overwhelmed him at the age of twelve with another kind of
terror was the riot of sound and the multitude of mankind on the
quays in Marseilles, something perfectly inconceivable from which he
had instantly taken refuge behind a stack of wheat sacks after having
been chased ashore from the tartane. He had remained there quaking
till a man in a cocked hat and with a sabre at his side (the boy had
never seen either such a hat or such a sabre in his life) had seized him
by the arm close to the armpit and had hauled him out from there; a
man who might have been an ogre (only Peyrol had never heard of an
ogre), but at any rate in his own way was alarming and wonderful
beyond anything he could have imagined – if the faculty of imagination
had been developed in him then. No doubt all this was enough to
make one die of fright, but that possibility never occurred to him.
Neither did he go mad; but being only a child, he had simply adapted
himself, by means of passive acquiescence, to the new and inexplicable
conditions of life in something like twenty-four hours. After that
initiation the rest of his existence, from flying fishes to whales and on
to black men and coral reefs, to decks running with blood and thirst in
open boats, was comparatively plain sailing. By the time he had heard
of a Revolution in France and of certain Immortal Principles causing
the death of many people, from the mouths of seamen and travellers
and year-old gazettes coming out of Europe, he was ready to appreciate
contemporary history in his own particular way. Mutiny and throwing

officers overboard. He had seen that twice and he was on a different side each time. As to this upset, he took no side. It was too far – too big – also not distinct enough. But he acquired the revolutionary jargon quickly enough and used it on occasion, with secret contempt. What he had gone through, from a spell of crazy love for a yellow girl to the experience of treachery from a bosom friend and shipmate (and both those things Peyrol confessed to himself he could never hope to understand), with all the graduations of varied experience of men and passions between, had put a drop of universal scorn, a wonderful sedative, into the strange mixture which might have been called the soul of the returned Peyrol.

Therefore he not only showed no surprise but did not feel any when he beheld the master, in the right of his wife, of the Escampobar Farm. The homeless Peyrol, sitting in the bare salle with a bottle of wine before him, was in the act of raising the glass to his lips when the man entered, ex-orator in the sections, leader of red-capped mobs, hunter of the ci-devants[84] and priests, purveyor of the guillotine, in short a blood-drinker. And Citizen Peyrol, who had never been nearer than six thousand miles as the crow flies to the realities of the Revolution, put down his glass and in his deep unemotional voice said: 'Salut.'[85]

The other returned a much fainter, 'Salut,' staring at the stranger of whom he had heard already. His almond-shaped, soft eyes were noticeably shiny and so was to a certain extent the skin on his high but rounded cheekbones, coloured red like a mask of which all the rest was but a mass of clipped chestnut hair growing so thick and close around the lips as to hide altogether the design of the mouth which, for all Citizen Peyrol knew, might have been of a quite ferocious character. A careworn forehead and a perpendicular nose suggested a certain austerity proper to an ardent patriot. He held in his hand a long bright knife which he laid down on one of the tables at once. He didn't seem more than thirty years old, a well-made man of medium height, with a lack of resolution in his bearing. Something like disillusion was suggested by the set of his shoulders. The effect was subtle, but Peyrol became aware of it while he explained his case and finished the tale by declaring that he was a seaman of the Republic and that he had always done his duty before the enemy.

The blood-drinker had listened profoundly. The high arches of his eyebrows gave him an astonished look. He came close up to the table and spoke in a trembling voice.

'You may have! But you may all the same be corrupt. The seamen of the Republic were eaten up with corruption paid for with the gold of the tyrants. Who would have guessed it? They all talked like patriots. And yet the English entered the harbour and landed in the town without opposition. The armies of the Republic drove them out, but treachery stalks in the land, it comes up out of the ground, it sits at our hearthstones, lurks in the bosom of the representatives of the people, of our fathers, of our brothers. There was a time when civic virtue flourished, but now it has got to hide its head. And I will tell you why: there has not been enough killing. It seems as if there could never be enough of it. It's discouraging. Look what we have come to.'

His voice died in his throat as though he had suddenly lost confidence in himself.

'Bring another glass, citoyen,' said Peyrol, after a short pause, 'and let's drink together. We will drink to the confusion of traitors. I detest treachery as much as any man, but . . .'

He waited till the other had returned, then poured out the wine, and after they had touched glasses and half emptied them, he put down his own and continued: 'But you see I have nothing to do with your politics. I was at the other side of the world, therefore you can't suspect me of being a traitor. You showed no mercy, you other sans-culottes, to the enemies of the Republic at home, and I killed her enemies abroad, far away. You were cutting off heads without much compunction . . .'

The other most unexpectedly shut his eyes for a moment, then opened them very wide. 'Yes, yes,' he assented very low. 'Pity may be a crime.'

'Yes. And I knocked the enemies of the Republic on the head whenever I had them before me without enquiring about the number. It seems to me that you and I ought to get on together.'

The master of Escampobar farmhouse murmured, however, that in times like these nothing could be taken as proof positive. It behoved every patriot to nurse suspicion in his breast. No sign of impatience escaped Peyrol. He was rewarded for his self-restraint and the unshaken good-humour with which he had conducted the discussion by carrying his point. Citizen Scevola Bron (for that appeared to be the name of the master of the farm), an object of fear and dislike to the other inhabitants of the Giens peninsula, might have been influenced by a wish to have someone with whom he could exchange a few words from time to time. No villagers ever came up to the farm, or were likely to, unless perhaps in a body and animated with hostile intentions. They resented his presence in their part of the world sullenly.

'Where do you come from?' was the last question he asked.

'I left Toulon two days ago.'

Citizen Scevola struck the table with his fist, but this manifestation of energy was very momentary.

'And that was the town of which by a decree not a stone upon another was to be left,' he complained, much depressed.

'Most of it is still standing,' Peyrol assured him calmly. 'I don't know whether it deserved the fate you say was decreed for it. I was there for the last month or so and I know it contains some good patriots. I know because I made friends with them all.' Thereupon Peyrol mentioned a few names which the retired sans-culotte greeted with a bitter smile and an ominous silence, as though the bearers of them had been only good for the scaffold and the guillotine.

'Come along and I will show you the place where you will sleep,' he said with a sigh, and Peyrol was only too ready. They entered the kitchen together. Through the open back door a large square of sunshine fell on the floor of stone flags. Outside one could see quite a mob of expectant chickens, while a yellow hen postured on the very doorstep, darting her head right and left with affectation. All old woman holding a bowl full of broken food put it down suddenly on a table and stared. The vastness and cleanliness of the place impressed Peyrol favourably.

'You will eat with us here,' said his guide, and passed without stopping into a narrow passage giving access to a steep flight of stairs. Above the first landing a narrow spiral staircase led to the upper part of the farmhouse; and when the sans-culotte flung open the solid plank door at which it ended he disclosed to Peyrol a large low room containing a four-poster bedstead piled up high with folded blankets and spare pillows. There were also two wooden chairs and a large oval table.

'We could arrange this place for you,' said the master, 'but I don't know what the mistress will have to say,' he added.

Peyrol, struck by the peculiar expression of his face, turned his head and saw the girl standing in the doorway. It was as though she had floated up after them, for not the slightest sound of rustle or footfall had warned Peyrol of her presence. The pure complexion of her white cheeks was set off brilliantly by her coral lips and the bands of raven-black hair only partly covered by a muslin cap trimmed with lace. She made no sign, uttered no sound, behaved exactly as if there had been nobody in the room; and Peyrol suddenly averted his eyes from that mute and unconscious face with its roaming eyes.

In some way or other, however, the sans-culotte seemed to have ascertained her mind, for he said in a final tone: 'That's all right then,' and there was a short silence, during which the woman shot her dark glances all round the room again and again, while on her lips there was a half-smile, not so much absent-minded as totally unmotived, which Peyrol observed with a side glance, but could not make anything of. She did not seem to know him at all.

'You have a view of salt water on three sides of you,' remarked Peyrol's future host.

The farmhouse was a tall building, and this large attic with its three windows commanded on one side the view of Hyères roadstead on the first plan, with further blue undulations of the coast as far as Fréjus; and on the other the vast semicircle of barren high hills, broken by the entrance to Toulon harbour guarded by forts and batteries, and ending in Cape Cépet, a squat mountain, with sombre folds and a base of brown rocks, with a white spot gleaming on the very summit of it, a ci-devant shrine dedicated to Our Lady, and a ci-devant place of pilgrimage. The noonday glare seemed absorbed by the gemlike surface of the sea, perfectly flawless in the invincible depth of its colour.

'It's like being in a lighthouse,' said Peyrol. 'Not a bad place for a seaman to live in.' The sight of the sails dotted about cheered his heart. The people of landsmen with their houses and animals and activities did not count. What made for him the life of any strange shore were the craft that belonged to it: canoes, catamarans, ballahous,[86] praus, lorchas, mere dugouts, or even rafts of tied logs with a bit of mat for a sail from which naked brown men fished along stretches of white sand crushed under the tropical skyline, sinister in its glare and with a thunder-cloud crouching on the horizon. But here he beheld a perfect serenity, nothing sombre on the shore, nothing ominous in the sunshine. The sky rested lightly on the distant and vaporous outline of the hills; and the immobility of all things seemed poised in the air like a gay mirage. On this tideless sea several tartanes lay becalmed in the Petite Passe between Porquerolles and Cape Esterel, yet theirs was not the stillness of death but of light slumber, the immobility of a smiling enchantment, of a Mediterranean fair day, breathless sometimes but never without life. Whatever enchantment Peyrol had known in his wanderings it had never been so remote from all thoughts of strife and death, so full of smiling security, making all his past appear to him like a chain of lurid days and sultry nights. He thought he would never want to get away from it, as though he had obscurely felt that his old rover's soul had been always rooted there. Yes, this was the place for him; not because expediency dictated, but simply because his instinct of rest had found its home at last.

He turned away from the window and found himself face to face with the sans-culotte, who had apparently come up to him from behind, perhaps with the intention of tapping him on the shoulder, but who now turned away his head. The young woman had disappeared.

'Tell me, patron,' said Peyrol, 'is there anywhere near this house a little dent in the shore with a bit of beach in it perhaps where I could keep a boat?'

'What do you want a boat for?'

'To go fishing when I have a fancy to,' answered Peyrol curtly.

Citizen Bron, suddenly subdued, told him that what he wanted was to be found a couple of hundred yards down the hill from the house. The coast, of course, was full of indentations, but this was a perfect little pool. And the Toulon blood-drinker's almond-shaped eyes became strangely sombre as they gazed at the attentive Peyrol. A perfect little pool, he repeated, opening from a cove that the English knew well. He paused. Peyrol observed without much animosity but in a tone of conviction that it was very difficult to keep off the English whenever there was a bit of salt water anywhere; but what could have brought English seamen to a spot like this he couldn't imagine.

'It was when their fleet first came here,' said the patriot in a gloomy voice, 'and hung round the coast before the anti-revolutionary traitors let them into Toulon, sold the sacred soil of their country for a handful of gold. Yes, in the days before the crime was consummated English officers used to land in that cove at night and walk up to this very house.'

'What audacity!' commented Peyrol, who was really surprised. 'But that's just like what they are.' Still, it was hard to believe. But wasn't it only a tale?

The patriot flung one arm up in a strained gesture. 'I swore to its truth before the tribunal,' he said. 'It was a dark story,' he cried shrilly, and paused. 'It cost her father his life,' he said in a low voice . . . 'her mother too – but the country was in danger,' he added still lower.

Peyrol walked away to the western window and looked towards Toulon. In the middle of the great sheet of water within Cape Cicié a tall two-decker lay becalmed and the little dark dots on the water were her boats trying to tow her head round the right way. Peyrol watched them for a moment, and then walked back to the middle of the room.

'Did you actually drag him from this house to the guillotine?' he asked in his unemotional voice.

The patriot shook his head thoughtfully with downcast eyes. 'No, he came over to Toulon just before the evacuation, this friend of the English . . . sailed over in a tartane he owned that is still lying here at

Madrague. He had his wife with him. They came over to take home their daughter who was living then with some skulking old nuns. The victorious Republicans were closing in and the slaves of tyranny had to fly.'

'Came to fetch their daughter,' mused Peyrol. 'Strange, that guilty people should . . .'

The patriot looked up fiercely. 'It was justice,' he said loudly. 'They were anti-revolutionists, and if they had never spoken to an Englishman in their life the atrocious crime was on their heads.'

'H'm, stayed too long for their daughter,' muttered Peyrol. 'And so it was you who brought her home.'

'I did,' said the patron. For a moment his eyes evaded Peyrol's investigating glance, but in a moment he looked straight into his face. 'No lessons of base superstition could corrupt her soul,' he declared with exaltation. 'I brought home a patriot.'

Peyrol, very calm, gave him a hardly perceptible nod. 'Well,' he said, 'all this won't prevent me sleeping very well in this room. I always thought I would like to live in a lighthouse when I got tired of roving about the seas. This is as near a lighthouse lantern as can be. You will see me with all my little affairs tomorrow,' he added, moving towards the stairs. 'Salut, citoyen.'

There was in Peyrol a fund of self-command amounting to placidity. There were men living in the East who had no doubt whatever that Peyrol was a calmly terrible man. And they would quote illustrative instances which from their own point of view were simply admirable. But all Peyrol had ever done was to behave rationally, as it seemed to him, in all sorts of dangerous circumstances, without ever being led astray by the nature, or the cruelty, or the danger of any given situation. He adapted himself to the character of the event and to the very spirit of it, with a profound responsive feeling of a particularly unsentimental kind. Sentiment in itself was an artificiality of which he had never heard and if he had seen it in action it would have appeared to him too puzzling to make anything of. That sort of genuineness in acceptance made him a satisfactory inmate of the Escampobar Farm. He duly turned up with all his cargo, as he called it, and was met at the door of the farmhouse itself by the young woman with the pale face and wandering eyes. Nothing could hold her attention for long amongst her familiar surroundings. Right and left and far away beyond you, she seemed to be looking for something while you were talking to her, so that you doubted whether she could follow what you said. But as a matter of fact she had all her wits about her. In the midst of this strange search for something that was not there she had enough detachment to smile at Peyrol. Then, withdrawing into the kitchen, she watched, as much as her restless eyes could watch anything, Peyrol's cargo and Peyrol himself passing up the stairs.

The most valuable part of Peyrol's cargo being strapped to his person, the first thing he did after being left alone in that attic room which was like the lantern of a lighthouse was to relieve himself of the burden and lay it on the foot of the bed. Then he sat down and leaning his elbow far on the table he contemplated it with a feeling of complete relief. That plunder had never burdened his conscience. It had merely on occasion oppressed his body; and if it had at all affected his spirits it was not by its secrecy but by its mere weight, which was inconvenient, irritating, and towards the end of a day altogether insupportable. It made a free-limbed, deep-breathing sailor-man feel like a mere overloaded animal, thus extending whatever there was of compassion in Peyrol's nature towards the four-footed beasts that carry men's burdens on the earth. The necessities of a lawless life had taught Peyrol to be ruthless, but he had never been cruel.

Sprawling in the chair, stripped to the waist, robust and grey-haired, his head with a Roman profile propped up on a mighty and tattooed forearm, he remained at ease, with his eyes fixed on his treasure with an air of meditation. Yet Peyrol was not meditating (as a superficial observer might have thought) on the best place of concealment. It was not that he had not had a great experience of that sort of property which had always melted so quickly through his fingers. What made him meditative was its character, not of a share of a hard-won booty in toil, in risk, in danger, in privation, but of a piece of luck personally his own. He knew what plunder was and how soon it went; but this lot had come to stay. He had it with him, away from the haunts of his lifetime, as if in another world altogether. It couldn't be drunk away, gambled away, squandered away in any sort of familiar circumstances, or even given away. In that room, raised a good many feet above his revolutionised native land where he was more of a stranger than anywhere else in the world, in this roomy garret full of light and as it were surrounded by the sea, in a great sense of peace and security, Peyrol didn't see why he should bother his head about it so very much. It came to him that he had never really cared for any plunder that fell into his hands. No, never for any. And to take particular care of this for which no one would seek vengeance or attempt recovery would have been absurd. Peyrol got up and opened his big sandalwood chest secured with an enormous padlock, part, too, of some old plunder gathered in a Chinese town in the Gulf of Tonkin,[87] in company of certain Brothers

of the Coast, who, having boarded at night a Portuguese schooner and
sent her crew adrift in a boat, had taken a cruise on their own account,
years and years and years ago. He was young then, very young, and the
chest fell to his share because nobody else would have anything to do
with the cumbersome thing, and also for the reason that the metal of
the curiously wrought thick hoops that strengthened it was not gold but
mere brass. He, in his innocence, had been rather pleased with the
article. He had carried it about with him into all sorts of places, and also
he had left it behind him – once for a whole year in a dark and noisome
cavern on a certain part of the Madagascar coast. He had left it with
various native chiefs, with Arabs, with a gambling-hell keeper in
Pondicherry,[88] with his various friends in short, and even with his
enemies. Once he had lost it altogether.

That was on the occasion when he had received a wound which laid
him open and gushing like a slashed wine-skin. A sudden quarrel broke
out in a company of Brothers over some matter of policy complicated
by personal jealousies, as to which he was as innocent as a babe unborn.
He never knew who gave him the slash. Another Brother, a chum of
his, an English boy, had rushed in and hauled him out of the fray, and
then he had remembered nothing for days. Even now when he looked
at the scar he could not understand why he had not died. That
occurrence, with the wound and the painful convalescence, was the first
thing that sobered his character somewhat. Many years afterwards,
when in consequence of his altered views of mere lawlessness he was
serving as quartermaster on board the *Hirondelle*, a comparatively
respectable privateer, he caught sight of that chest again in Port Louis,[89]
of all places in the world, in a dark little den of a shop kept by a lone
Hindu. The hour was late, the side street was empty, and so Peyrol
went in there to claim his property, all fair, a dollar in one hand and a
pistol in the other, and was entreated abjectly to take it away. He
carried off the empty chest on his shoulder, and that same night the
privateer went to sea; then only he found time to ascertain that he had
made no mistake, because, soon after he had got it first, he had, in grim
wantonness, scratched inside the lid, with the point of his knife, the
rude outline of a skull and cross-bones into which he had rubbed
afterwards a little Chinese vermilion. And there it was, the whole design,
as fresh as ever.

In the garret full of light of the Escampobar farmhouse, the grey-
haired Peyrol opened the chest, took all the contents out of it, laying
them neatly on the floor, and spread his treasure – pockets downwards –
over the bottom, which it filled exactly. Busy on his knees he repacked

the chest. A jumper or two, a fine cloth jacket, a remnant piece of Madapolam muslin,[90] costly stuff for which he had no use in the world – a quantity of fine white shirts. Nobody would dare to rummage in his chest, he thought, with the assurance of a man who had been feared in his time. Then he rose, and looking round the room and stretching his powerful arms, he ceased to think of the treasure, of the future and even of tomorrow, in the sudden conviction that he could make himself very comfortable there.

Chapter 4

In a tiny bit of a looking-glass hung on the frame of the east window, Peyrol, handling the unwearable English blade, was shaving himself – for the day was Sunday. The years of political changes ending with the proclamation of Napoleon as Consul for life[91] had not touched Peyrol except as to his strong thick head of hair, which was nearly all white now. After putting the razor away carefully, Peyrol introduced his stockinged feet into a pair of sabots[92] of the very best quality and clattered downstairs. His brown cloth breeches were untied at the knee and the sleeves of his shirt rolled up to his shoulders. That sea-rover turned rustic was now perfectly at home in that farm which, like a lighthouse, commanded the view of two roadsteads and of the open sea. He passed through the kitchen. It was exactly as he had seen it first, sunlight on the floor, red copper utensils shining on the walls, the table in the middle scrubbed snowy white; and it was only the old woman, Aunt Catherine, who seemed to have acquired a sharper profile. The very hen manoeuvring her neck pretentiously on the doorstep, might have been standing there for the last eight years.[93] Peyrol shooed her away, and going into the yard washed himself lavishly at the pump. When he returned from the yard he looked so fresh and hale that old Catherine complimented him in a thin voice on his 'bonne mine'.[94] Manners were changing, and she addressed him no longer as citoyen but as Monsieur Peyrol. He answered readily that if her heart was free he was ready to lead her to the altar that very day. This was such an old joke that Catherine took no notice of it whatever, but followed him with her eyes as he crossed the kitchen into the salle, which was cool, with its tables and benches washed clean, and no living soul in it. Peyrol passed through to the front of the house, leaving the outer door open. At the clatter of his clogs a young man sitting outside on a bench turned his head and greeted him by a careless nod. His face was rather long, sunburnt and smooth, with a slightly curved nose and a very well-shaped chin. He wore a dark blue naval jacket open on a white shirt and a black neckerchief tied in a slip-knot with long ends. White breeches and stockings and black shoes with steel buckles completed his costume. A brass-hilted sword in a black scabbard worn on a cross-belt was lying on the ground at his feet. Peyrol, silver-headed and ruddy, sat down on the bench at some little distance. The level piece of rocky ground in front of the house was not very extensive, falling away to the sea in a declivity framed between the rises of two barren hills. The old rover and the young seaman with their arms folded across their chests gazed into space, exchanging no words, like close intimates or like distant strangers. Neither did they stir when the master of the Escampobar Farm appeared out of the yard gate with a manure fork on his shoulder and started to cross the piece of level ground. His grimy hands, his rolled-up shirt sleeves, the fork over the shoulder, the whole of his working-day aspect had somehow an air of being a manifestation; but the patriot dragged his dirty clogs low-spiritedly in the fresh light of the young morning, in a way no real worker on the land would ever do at the end of a day of toil. Yet there were no signs of debility about his person. His oval face with rounded cheek-bones remained unwrinkled except at the corners of his almond-shaped, shiny, visionary's eyes, which had not changed since the day when old Peyrol's gaze had met them for the first time. A few white hairs on his tousled head and in the thin beard alone had marked the passage of years, and you would have had to look for them closely. Amongst the unchangeable rocks at the extreme end of the Peninsula, time seemed to have stood still and idle while the group of people poised at that southernmost point of France had gone about their ceaseless toil, winning bread and wine from a stony-hearted earth.

The master of the farm, staring straight before him, passed before the two men towards the door of the salle, which Peyrol had left open. He leaned his fork against the wall before going in. The sound of a distant bell, the bell of the village where years ago the returned rover had watered his mule and had listened to the talk of the man with the dog, came up faint and abrupt in the great stillness of the upper space. The violent slamming of the salle door broke the silence between the two gazers on the sea.

'Does that fellow never rest?' asked the young man in a low indifferent voice which covered the delicate tinkling of the bell, and without moving his head.

'Not on Sunday anyhow,' answered the rover in the same detached manner. 'What can you expect? The church bell is like poison to him. That fellow, I verily believe, was born a sans-culotte. Every 'décadi'[95] he puts on his best clothes, sticks a red cap on his head and wanders between the buildings like a lost soul in the light of day. A Jacobin, if ever there was one.'

'Yes. There is hardly a hamlet in France where there isn't a sans-culotte or two. But some of them have managed to change their skins if nothing else.'

'This one won't change his skin, and as to his inside he never had anything in him that could be moved. Aren't there some people that remember him in Toulon? It isn't such a long time ago. And yet . . . ' Peyrol turned slightly towards the young man . . . 'And yet to look at him . . . '

The officer nodded, and for a moment his face wore a troubled expression which did not escape the notice of Peyrol who went on speaking easily: 'Some time ago, when the priests began to come back[96] to the parishes, he, that fellow' – Peyrol jerked his head in the direction of the salle door – 'would you believe it? – started for the village with a sabre hanging to his side and his red cap on his head. He made for the church door. What he wanted to do there I don't know. It surely could not have been to say the proper kind of prayers. Well, the people were very much elated about their reopened church, and as he went along some woman spied him out of a window and started the alarm. "Eh, there! look! The Jacobin, the sans-culotte, the blood-drinker! Look at him." Out rushed some of them, and a man or two that were working in their home patches vaulted over the low walls. Pretty soon there was a crowd, mostly women, each with the first thing she could snatch up – stick, kitchen knife, anything. A few men with spades and cudgels joined them by the water-trough. He didn't quite like that. What could he do? He turned and bolted up the hill, like a hare. It takes some pluck to face a mob of angry women. He ran along the cart track without looking behind him, and they after him, yelling: "A mort! A mort le buveur de sang!"[97] He had been a horror and an abomination to the people for years, what with one story and another, and now they thought it was their chance. The priest over in the presbytery hears the noise, comes to the door. One look was enough for him. He is a fellow of about forty but a wiry, long-legged beggar, and agile – what? He just tucked up his skirts and dashed out, taking short cuts over the walls and leaping from boulder to boulder like a blessed goat. I was up in my room when the noise reached me there. I went to the window and saw the chase in full cry after him. I was beginning to think the fool would fetch all those furies along with him up here and that they would carry the house by boarding and do for the lot of us, when the priest cut in just in the nick of time. He could have tripped Scevola as easy as anything, but he lets him pass and stands in front of his parishioners with his arms extended. That did it. He saved the patron all right. What he could say to quieten them I don't know, but these were early days and they were very fond of their new priest. He could have turned them round his little finger. I had my head and shoulders out of the window – it was interesting enough. They would have massacred all the accursed lot, as they used to call us down there – and when I drew in, behold there was the patronne standing behind me looking on too. You have been here often enough to know how she roams about the grounds and about the house, without a sound. A leaf doesn't pose itself lighter on the ground than her feet do. Well, I suppose she didn't know that I was upstairs, and came into the room just in her way of always looking for something that isn't there, and noticing me with my head stuck out, naturally came up to see what I was looking at. Her face wasn't any paler than usual, but she was clawing the dress over her chest with her ten fingers – like this. I was confounded. Before I could find my tongue she just turned round and went out with no more sound than a shadow.'

When Peyrol ceased, the ringing of the church bell went on faintly and then stopped as abruptly as it had begun.

'Talking about her shadow,' said the young officer indolently, 'I know her shadow.'

Old Peyrol made a really pronounced movement. 'What do you mean?' he asked. 'Where?'

'I have got only one window in the room where they put me to sleep last night and I stood at it looking out. That's what I am here for – to look out, am I not? I woke up suddenly, and being awake I went to the window and looked out.'

'One doesn't see shadows in the air,' growled old Peyrol.

'No, but you see them on the ground, pretty black too when the moon is full. It fell across this open space here from the corner of the house.'

'The patronne,' exclaimed Peyrol in a low voice, 'impossible!'

'Does the old woman that lives in the kitchen roam, do the village women roam as far as this?' asked the officer composedly. 'You ought to know the habits of the people. It was a woman's shadow. The moon being to the west, it glided slanting from that corner of the house and glided back again. I know her shadow when I see it.'

'Did you hear anything?' asked Peyrol after a moment of visible hesitation.

'The window being open I heard somebody snoring. It couldn't have been you, you are too high. Moreover, from the snoring,' he added grimly, 'it must have been somebody with a good conscience. Not like you, old skimmer of the seas, because, you know, that's what you are, for all your gunner's warrant.' He glanced out of the corner of his eyes at old Peyrol. 'What makes you look so worried?'

'She roams, that cannot be denied,' murmured Peyrol, with an uneasiness which he did not attempt to conceal.

'Evidently. I know a shadow when I see it, and when I saw it, it did not frighten me, not a quarter as much as the mere tale of it seems to have frightened you. However, that sans-culotte friend of yours must be a hard sleeper. Those purveyors of the guillotine all have a first-class fireproof Republican conscience. I have seen them at work up north when I was a boy running barefoot in the gutters . . . '

'The fellow always sleeps in that room,' said Peyrol earnestly.

'But that's neither here nor there,' went on the officer, 'except that it may be convenient for roaming shadows to hear his conscience taking its ease.'

Peyrol, excited, lowered his voice forcibly. 'Lieutenant,' he said, 'if I had not seen from the first what was in your heart I would have contrived to get rid of you a long time ago in some way or other.'

The lieutenant glanced sideways again and Peyrol let his raised fist fall heavily on his thigh. 'I am old Peyrol and this place, as lonely as a ship at sea, is like a ship to me and all in it are like shipmates. Never mind the patron. What I want to know is whether you heard anything? Any sound at all? Murmur, footstep?'

A bitterly mocking smile touched the lips of the young man. 'Not a fairy footstep. Could you hear the fall of a leaf – and with that terrorist cur trumpeting right above my head?' Without unfolding his arms he turned towards Peyrol, who was looking at him anxiously. 'You want to know, do you? Well, I will tell you what I heard and you can make the best of it. I heard the sound of a stumble. It wasn't a fairy either that stubbed its toe. It was something in a heavy shoe. Then a stone went rolling down the ravine in front of us interminably, then a silence as of death. I didn't see anything moving. The way the moon was then, the ravine was in black shadow. And I didn't try to see.'

Peyrol, with his elbow on his knee, leaned his head in the palm of his hand. The officer repeated through his clenched teeth: 'Make the best of it.'

Peyrol shook his head slightly. After having spoken, the young officer leaned back against the wall, but next moment the report of a piece of ordnance reached them as it were from below, travelling around the rising ground to the left in the form of a dull thud followed by a sighing sound that seemed to seek an issue amongst the stony ridges and rocks near by.

'That's the English corvette which has been dodging in and out of Hyères roads for the last week,' said the young officer, picking up his sword hastily. He stood up and buckled the belt on, while Peyrol rose more deliberately from the bench, and said: 'She can't be where we saw her at anchor last night. That gun was near. She must have crossed over. There has been enough wind for that at various times during the night. But what could she be firing at down there in the Petite Passe? We had better go and see.'

He strode off, followed by Peyrol. There was not a human being in sight about the farm and not a sound of life except for the lowing of a cow coming faintly from behind a wall. Peyrol kept close behind the quickly moving officer who followed the footpath marked faintly on the stony slope of the hill.

'That gun was not shotted,' he observed suddenly in a deep steady voice.

The officer glanced over his shoulder.

'You may be right. You haven't been a gunner for nothing. Not shotted, eh? Then a signal gun. But who to? We have been observing that corvette now for days and we know she has no companion.'

He moved on, Peyrol following him on the awkward path without losing his wind and arguing in a steady voice: 'She has no companion but she may have seen a friend at daylight this morning.'

'Bah!' retorted the officer without checking his pace. 'You talk now like a child or else you take me for one. How far could she have seen? What view could she have had at daylight if she was making her way to the Petite Passe where she is now? Why, the islands would have masked for her two-thirds of the sea and just in the direction too where the English inshore squadron is hovering below the horizon. Funny blockade that! You can't see a single English sail for days and days together, and then when you least expect them they come down all in a crowd as if ready to eat us alive. No, no! There was no wind to bring her up a companion. But tell me, gunner, you who boast of knowing the bark of every English piece, what sort of gun was it?'

Peyrol growled in answer: 'Why, a twelve. The heaviest she carries. She is only a corvette.'

'Well, then, it was fired as a recall for one of her boats somewhere out of sight along the shore. With a coast like this, all points and bights, there would be nothing very extraordinary in that, would there?'

'No,' said Peyrol, stepping out steadily. 'What is extraordinary is that she should have had a boat away at all.'

'You are right there.' The officer stopped suddenly. 'Yes, it is really remarkable that she should have sent a boat away. And there is no other way to explain that gun.'

Peyrol's face expressed no emotion of any sort.

'There is something there worth investigating,' continued the officer with animation.

'If it is a matter of a boat,' Peyrol said without the slightest excitement, 'there can be nothing very deep in it. What could there be? As likely as not they sent her inshore early in the morning with lines to try to catch some fish for the captain's breakfast. Why do you open your eyes like this? Don't you know the English? They have enough cheek for anything.'

After uttering those words with a deliberation made venerable by his white hair, Peyrol made the gesture of wiping his brow, which was barely moist.

'Let us push on,' said the lieutenant abruptly.

'Why hurry like this?' argued Peyrol without moving. 'Those heavy clogs of mine are not adapted for scrambling on loose stones.'

'Aren't they?' burst out the officer. 'Well, then, if you are tired you can sit down and fan yourself with your hat. Goodbye.' And he strode away before Peyrol could utter a word.

The path following the contour of the hill took a turn towards its sea-face and very soon the lieutenant passed out of sight with startling suddenness. Then his head reappeared for a moment, only his head, and that too vanished suddenly. Peyrol remained perplexed. After gazing in the direction in which the officer had disappeared, he looked down at the farm buildings, now below him but not at a very great distance. He could see distinctly the pigeons walking on the roof ridges. Somebody was drawing water from the well in the middle of the yard. The patron, no doubt; but that man, who at one time had the power to send so many luckless persons to their death, did not count for old Peyrol. He had even ceased to be an offence to his sight and a disturber of his feelings. By himself he was nothing. He had never been anything but a creature of the universal blood-lust of the time. The very doubts about him had died out by now in old Peyrol's breast. The fellow was so insignificant that had Peyrol in a moment of particular attention discovered that he cast no shadow, he would not have been surprised. Below there he was reduced to the shape of a dwarf lugging a bucket away from the well. But where was she? Peyrol asked himself, shading his eyes with his hand. He knew that the patronne could not be very far away, because he had a sight of her during the morning; but that was before he had learned she had taken to roaming at night. His growing uneasiness came suddenly to an end when, turning his eyes away from the farm buildings, where obviously she was not, he saw her appear, with nothing but the sky full of light at her back, coming down round the very turn of the path which had taken the lieutenant out of sight.

Peyrol moved briskly towards her. He wasn't a man to lose time in idle wonder, and his sabots did not seem to weigh heavy on his feet. The fermière,[98] whom the villagers down there spoke of as Arlette as though she had been a little girl, but in a strange tone of shocked awe, walked with her head drooping and her feet (as Peyrol used to say) touching the ground as lightly as falling leaves. The clatter of the clogs made her raise her black, clear eyes that had been smitten on the very verge of womanhood by such sights of bloodshed and terror as to leave in her a fear of looking steadily in any direction for long, lest she should see coming through the empty air some mutilated vision of the dead. Peyrol called it trying not to see something that was not there; and this evasive yet frank mobility was so much a part of her being that the steadiness with which she met his inquisitive glance surprised old Peyrol for a moment.

He asked without beating about the bush: 'Did he speak to you?'

She answered with something airy and provoking in her voice, which also struck Peyrol as a novelty: 'He never stopped. He passed by as though he had not seen me' – and then they both looked away from each other.

'Now, what is it you took into your head to watch for at night?'

She did not expect that question. She hung her head and took a pleat of her skirt between her fingers, embarrassed like a child.

'Why should I not,' she murmured in a low shy note, as if she had two voices within her.

'What did Catherine say?'

'She was asleep, or perhaps, only lying on her back with her eyes shut.'

'Does she do that?' asked Peyrol with incredulity.

'Yes.' Arlette gave Peyrol a queer, meaningless smile with which her eyes had nothing to do. 'Yes, she often does. I have noticed that before. She lies there trembling under her blankets till I come back.'

'What drove you out last night?' Peyrol tried to catch her eyes, but they eluded him in the usual way. And now her face looked as though it couldn't smile.

'My heart,' she said. For a moment Peyrol lost his tongue and even all power of motion. The fermière having lowered her eyelids, all her life seemed to have gone into her coral lips, vivid and without a quiver in the perfection of their design, and Peyrol, giving up the conversation with an upward fling of his arm, hurried up the path without looking behind him. But once round the turn of the path, he approached the lookout at an easier gait. It was a piece of smooth ground below the summit of the hill. It had quite a pronounced slope, so that a short and robust pine growing true out of the soil yet leaned well over the edge of the sheer drop of some fifty feet or so. The first thing that Peyrol's eyes took in was the water of the Petite Passe with the enormous shadow of the Porquerolles Island darkening more than half of its width at this still early hour. He could not see the whole of it, but on the part his glance embraced there was no ship of any kind. The lieutenant, leaning with his chest along the inclined pine, addressed him irritably.

'Squat! Do you think there are no glasses on board the Englishman?'

Peyrol obeyed without a word and for the space of a minute or so presented the bizarre sight of a rather bulky peasant with venerable white locks crawling on his hands and knees on a hillside for no visible reason. When he got to the foot of the pine he raised himself on his knees.

The lieutenant, flattened against the inclined trunk and with a pocket-glass glued to his eye, growled angrily: 'You can see her now, can't you?'

Peyrol in his kneeling position could see the ship now. She was less than a quarter of a mile from him up the coast, almost within hailing effort of his powerful voice. His unaided eyes could follow the movements of the men on board like dark dots about her decks. She had drifted so far within Cape Esterel that the low projecting mass of it seemed to be in actual contact with her stern. Her unexpected nearness made Peyrol draw a sharp breath through his teeth.

The lieutenant murmured, still keeping the glass to his eye: 'I can see the very epaulettes of the officers on the quarterdeck.'

Chapter 5

As Peyrol and the lieutenant had surmised from the report of the gun, the English ship which the evening before was lying in Hyères roads had got under way after dark. The light airs had taken her as far as the Petite Passe in the early part of the night, and then had abandoned her to the breathless moonlight in which, bereft of all motion, she looked more like a white monument of stone dwarfed by the darkling masses of land on either hand than a fabric famed for its swiftness in attack or in flight.

Her captain was a man of about forty, with clean-shaven, full cheeks and mobile thin lips which he had a trick of compressing mysteriously before he spoke and sometimes also at the end of his speeches. He was alert in his movements and nocturnal in his habits.

Directly he found that the calm had taken complete possession of the night and was going to last for hours, Captain Vincent[99] assumed his favourite attitude of leaning over the rail. It was then some time after midnight and in the pervading stillness the moon, riding on a speckless sky, seemed to pour her enchantment on an uninhabited planet. Captain Vincent did not mind the moon very much. Of course it made his ship visible from both shores of the Petite Passe. But after nearly a year of constant service in command of the extreme lookout ship of Admiral Nelson's blockading fleet he knew the emplacement of almost every gun of the shore defences. Where the breeze had left him he was safe from the biggest gun of the few that were mounted on Porquerolles. On the Giens side of the pass he knew for certain there was not even a popgun mounted anywhere. His long familiarity with that part of the coast had imbued him with the belief that he knew the habits of its population thoroughly. The gleams of light in their houses went out very early and Captain Vincent felt convinced that they were all in their beds, including the gunners of the batteries who belonged to the local militia. Their interest in the movements of HM's twenty-two-gun sloop *Amelia* had grown stale by custom. She never interfered with their private affairs, and allowed the small coasting craft to go to and fro unmolested. They would have wondered if she had been more than two days away. Captain Vincent used to say grimly that the Hyères roadstead had become like a second home to him.

For an hour or so Captain Vincent mused a bit on his real home, on matters of service and other unrelated things, then getting into motion in a very wide-awake manner, he superintended himself the dispatch of that boat the existence of which had been acutely surmised by Lieutenant Réal and was a matter of no doubt whatever to old Peyrol. As to her mission, it had nothing to do with catching fish for the captain's breakfast. It was the captain's own gig, a very fast-pulling boat. She was already alongside with her crew in her when the officer, who was going in charge, was beckoned to by the captain. He had a cutlass at his side and a brace of pistols in his belt, and there was a businesslike air about him that showed he had been on such service before.

'This calm will last a good many hours,' said the captain. 'In this tideless sea you are certain to find the ship very much where she is now, but closer inshore. The attraction of the land – you know.'

'Yes, sir. The land does attract.'

'Yes. Well, she may be allowed to put her side against any of these rocks. There would be no more danger than alongside a quay with a sea like this. Just look at the water in the pass, Mr Bolt. Like the floor of a ballroom. Pull close along shore when you return. I'll expect you back at dawn.'

Captain Vincent paused suddenly. A doubt crossed his mind as to the wisdom of this nocturnal expedition. The hammer-head of the peninsula with its sea-face invisible from both sides of the coast was an ideal spot for a secret landing. Its lonely character appealed to his imagination, which in the first instance had been stimulated by a chance remark of Mr Bolt himself.

The fact was that the week before, when the *Amelia* was cruising off the peninsula, Bolt, looking at the coast, mentioned that he knew that part of it well; he had actually been ashore there a good many years ago, while serving with Lord Howe's[100] fleet. He described the nature of the path, the aspect of a little village on the reverse slope, and had much to say about a certain farmhouse where he had been more than once, and had even stayed for twenty-four hours at a time on more than one occasion.

This had aroused Captain Vincent's curiosity. He sent for Bolt and had a long conversation with him. He listened with great interest to Bolt's story – how one day a man was seen, from the deck of the ship in which Bolt was serving then, waving a white sheet or tablecloth amongst the rocks at the water's edge. It might have been a trap; but, as the man seemed alone and the shore was within range of the ship's guns, a boat was sent to take him off.

'And that, sir,' Bolt pursued impressively, 'was, I verily believe, the very first communication that Lord Howe had from the royalists in Toulon.' Afterwards Bolt described to Captain Vincent the meetings of the Toulon royalists with the officers of the fleet. From the back of the farm he, Bolt himself, had often watched for hours the entrance of the Toulon harbour on the lookout for the boat bringing over the royalist emissaries. Then he would make an agreed signal to the advanced squadron and some English officers would land on their side and meet the Frenchmen at the farmhouse. It was as simple as that. The people of the farmhouse, husband and wife, were well-to-do, good class altogether, and staunch royalists. He had got to know them well.

Captain Vincent wondered whether the same people were still living there. Bolt could see no reason why they shouldn't be. It wasn't more than ten years ago, and they were by no means an old couple. As far as he could make out, the farm was their own property. He, Bolt, knew only very few French words at that time. It was much later, after he had been made a prisoner and kept inland in France till the Peace of Amiens,[101] that he had picked up a smattering of the lingo. His captivity had done away with his feeble chance of promotion, he could not help remarking. Bolt was a master's mate still.

Captain Vincent, in common with a good many officers of all ranks in Lord Nelson's fleet, had his misgivings about the system of distant blockade from which the Admiral apparently would not depart. Yet one could not blame Lord Nelson. Everybody in the fleet understood that what was in his mind was the destruction of the enemy; and if the enemy was closely blockaded he would never come out to be destroyed. On the other hand it was clear that as things were conducted the French had too many chances left them to slip out unobserved and vanish from all human knowledge for months. Those possibilities were a constant worry to Captain Vincent, who had thrown himself with the ardour of passion into the special duty with which he was entrusted. Oh, for a pair of eyes fastened night and day on the entrance of the harbour of Toulon! Oh, for the power to look at the very state of French ships and into the very secrets of French minds!

But he said nothing of this to Bolt. He only observed that the character of the French Government was changed and that the minds of the royalist people in the farmhouse might have changed too, since they had got back the exercise of their religion. Bolt's answer was that he had had a lot to do with royalists, in his time, on board Lord Howe's fleet, both before and after Toulon was evacuated. All sorts, men and women, barbers and noblemen, sailors and tradesmen; almost every kind of royalist one could think of; and his opinion was that a royalist never changed. As to the place itself, he only wished the captain had seen it. It was the sort of spot that nothing could change. He made bold to say that it would be just the same a hundred years hence.

The earnestness of his officer caused Captain Vincent to look hard at him. He was a man of about his own age, but while Vincent was a comparatively young captain, Bolt was an old master's mate. Each understood the other perfectly. Captain Vincent fidgeted for a while and then observed abstractedly that he was not a man to put a noose round a dog's neck, let alone a good seaman's.

This cryptic pronouncement caused no wonder to appear in Bolt's attentive gaze. He only became a little thoughtful before he said in the same abstracted tone that an officer in uniform was not likely to be hanged for a spy. The service was risky, of course. It was necessary, for its success, that, assuming the same people were there, it should be undertaken by a man well known to the inhabitants. Then he added that he was certain of being recognised. And while he enlarged on the extremely good terms he had been on with the owners of the farm, especially the farmer's wife, a comely motherly woman, who had been very kind to him, and had all her wits about her, Captain Vincent, looking at the master's mate's bushy whiskers, thought that these in themselves were enough to ensure recognition. This impression was so strong that he asked point-blank: 'You haven't altered the growth of the hair on your face, Mr Bolt, since then?'

There was just a touch of indignation in Bolt's negative reply; for he was proud of his whiskers. He declared he was ready to take the most desperate chances for the service of his king and his country.

Captain Vincent added: 'For the sake of Lord Nelson, too.' One understood well what his Lordship wished to bring about by that blockade at sixty leagues off. He was talking to a sailor, and there was no need to say any more. Did Bolt think that he could persuade those people to conceal him in their house on that lonely shore end of the peninsula for some considerable time? Bolt thought it was the easiest thing in the world. He would simply go up there and renew the old acquaintance, but he did not mean to do that in a reckless manner. It would have to be done at night, when of course there would be no one about. He would land just where he used to before, wrapped up in a Mediterranean sailor's cloak – he had one of his own – over his uniform, and simply go straight to the door, at which he would knock. Ten to one the farmer himself would come down to open it. He knew enough French by now, he hoped, to persuade those people to conceal him in some room having a view in the right direction; and there he would stick day after day on the watch, taking a little exercise in the middle of the night, ready to live on mere bread and water if necessary, so as not to arouse suspicion amongst the farmhands. And who knows if, with the farmer's help, he could not get some news of what was going on actually within the port. Then from time to time he could go down in the dead of night, signal to the ship and make his report. Bolt expressed the hope that the *Amelia* would remain as much as possible in sight of the coast. It would cheer him up to see her about. Captain Vincent naturally assented. He pointed out to Bolt, however, that his post would become most important exactly when the ship had been chased away or driven by the weather off her station, as could very easily happen. 'You would be then the eyes of Lord Nelson's fleet, Mr Bolt – think of that. The actual eyes of Lord Nelson's fleet!'

After dispatching his officer, Captain Vincent spent the night on deck. The break of day came at last, much paler than the moonlight which it replaced. And still no boat. And again Captain Vincent asked himself if he had not acted indiscreetly. Impenetrable, and looking as fresh as if he had just come up on deck, he argued the point with himself till the rising sun clearing the ridge on Porquerolles Island flashed its level rays upon his ship with her dew-darkened sails and dripping rigging. He roused himself then to tell his first lieutenant to get the boats out to tow the ship away from the shore. The report of the gun he ordered to be fired expressed simply his irritation. The *Amelia*, pointing towards the middle of the Passe, was moving at a snail's pace behind her string of boats. Minutes passed. And then suddenly Captain Vincent perceived his boat pulling back, in shore according to orders. When nearly abreast of the ship, she darted away, making for the side. Mr Bolt clambered on board, alone, ordering the gig to go ahead and help with the towing. Captain Vincent, standing apart on the quarter-deck, received him with a grimly questioning look.

Mr Bolt's first words were to the effect that he believed the confounded spot to be bewitched. Then he glanced at the group of officers on the other side of the quarterdeck. Captain Vincent led the way to his cabin. There he turned and looked at his officer, who, with an air of distraction, mumbled: 'There are night-walkers there.'

'Come, Bolt, what the devil have you seen? Did you get near the house at all?'

'I got within twenty yards of the door, sir,' said Bolt. And encouraged by the captain's much less ferocious – 'Well?' began his tale. He did not pull up to the path which he knew, but to a little bit of beach on which he told his men to haul up the boat and wait for him. The beach was concealed by a thick growth of bushes on the landward side and by some rocks from the sea. Then he went to what he called the ravine, still avoiding the path, so that as a matter of fact he made his way up on his hands and knees mostly, very carefully and slowly amongst the loose stones, till by holding on to a bush he brought his eyes on a level with the piece of flat ground in front of the farmhouse.

The familiar aspect of the buildings, totally unchanged from the time when he had played his part in what appeared as a most successful operation at the beginning of the war, inspired Bolt with great confidence in the success of his present enterprise, vague as it was, but the great charm of which lay, no doubt, in mental associations with his younger years. Nothing seemed easier than to stride across the forty yards of open ground and rouse the farmer whom he remembered so well, the well-to-do man, a grave sagacious royalist in his humble way; certainly, in Bolt's view, no traitor to his country, and preserving so well his dignity in ambiguous circumstances. To Bolt's simple vision neither that man nor his wife could have changed.

In this view of Arlette's parents Bolt was influenced by the consciousness of there having been no change in himself. He was the same Jack Bolt, and everything around him was the same as if he had left the spot only yesterday. Already he saw himself in the kitchen which he knew so well, seated by the light of a single candle before a glass of wine and talking his best French to that worthy farmer of sound principles. The whole thing was as well as done. He imagined himself a secret inmate of that building, closely confined indeed, but sustained by the possible great results of his watchfulness, in many ways more comfortable than on board the *Amelia* and with the glorious consciousness that he was, in Captain Vincent's phrase, the actual physical eyes of the fleet.

He didn't, of course, talk of his private feelings to Captain Vincent. All those thoughts and emotions were compressed in the space of not much more than a minute or two while, holding on with one hand to his bush and having got a good foothold for one of his feet, he indulged in that pleasant anticipatory sense of success. In the old days the farmer's wife used to be a light sleeper. The farmhands who, he remembered, lived in the village or were distributed in stables and outhouses, did not give him any concern. He wouldn't need to knock heavily. He pictured to himself the farmer's wife sitting up in bed, listening, then rousing her husband, who, as likely as not, would take the gun standing against the dresser downstairs and come to the door.

And then everything would be all right . . . But perhaps . . . Yes! It was just as likely the farmer would simply open the window and hold a parley. That really was most likely. Naturally. In his place Bolt felt he would do that very thing. Yes, that was what a man in a lonely house, in the middle of the night, would do most naturally. And he imagined himself whispering mysteriously his answers up the wall to the obvious questions – 'Ami' – 'Bolt' – 'Ouvrez-moi' – 'Vive le roi' [102] – or things of that sort. And in sequence to those vivid images it occurred to Bolt that the best thing he could do would be to throw small stones against the window shutter, the sort of sound most likely to rouse a light sleeper. He wasn't quite sure which window on the floor above the ground floor was that of those people's bedroom, but there were anyhow only three of them. In a moment he would have sprung up from his foothold on to the level if, raising his eyes for another look at the front of the house, he had not perceived that one of the windows was already open. How he could have failed to notice that before he couldn't explain.

He confessed to Captain Vincent in the course of his narrative, 'This open window, sir, checked me dead. In fact, sir, it shook my confidence, for you know, sir, that no native of these parts would dream of sleeping with his window open. It struck me that there was something wrong there; and I remained where I was.'

That fascination of repose, of secretive friendliness, which houses present at night, was gone. By the power of an open window, a black square in the moon-lighted wall, the farmhouse took on the aspect of a man-trap. Bolt assured Captain Vincent that the window would not have stopped him; he would have gone on all the same, though with an uncertain mind. But while he was thinking it out, there glided without a sound before his irresolute eyes from somewhere a white vision – a woman. He could see her black hair flowing down her back. A woman whom anybody would have been excused for taking for a ghost. 'I won't say that she froze my blood, sir, but she made me cold all over for a moment. Lots of people have seen ghosts, at least they say so, and I have an open mind about that. She was a weird thing to look at in the moonlight. She did not act like a sleep-walker either. If she had not come out of a grave, then she had jumped out of bed. But when she stole back and hid herself round the corner of the house I knew she was not a ghost. She could not have seen me. There she stood in the black shadow watching for something – or waiting for somebody,' added Bolt in a grim tone. 'She looked crazy,' he conceded charitably.

One thing was clear to him: there had been changes in that farmhouse since his time. Bolt resented them, as if that time had been only last week. The woman concealed round the corner remained in his full view, watchful, as if only waiting for him to show himself in the open to run off screeching and rouse all the countryside. Bolt came quickly to the conclusion that he must withdraw from the slope. On lowering himself from his first position he had the misfortune to dislodge a stone. This circumstance precipitated his retreat. In a very few minutes he found himself by the shore. He paused to listen. Above him, up the ravine and all round amongst the rocks, everything was perfectly still. He walked along in the direction of his boat. There was nothing for it but to get away quietly and perhaps . . .

'Yes, Mr Bolt, I fear we shall have to give up our plan,' interrupted Captain Vincent at that point. Bolt's assent came reluctantly, and then he braced himself to confess that this was not the worst. Before the astonished face of Captain Vincent he hastened to blurt it out. He was very sorry, he could in no way account for it, but – he had lost a man.

Captain Vincent seemed unable to believe his ears. 'What do you say? Lost a man out of my boat's crew!' He was profoundly shocked. Bolt was correspondingly distressed. He narrated that, shortly after he had left them, the seamen had heard, or imagined they had heard, some faint and peculiar noises somewhere within the cove. The coxswain sent one of the men, the oldest of the boat's crew, along the shore to ascertain whether their boat hauled on the beach could be seen from the other side of the cove. The man – it was Symons – departed crawling on his hands and knees to make the circuit and, well – he had not returned. This was really the reason why the boat was so late in getting back to the ship. Of course Bolt did not like to give up the man. It was inconceivable that Symons should have deserted. He had left his cutlass behind and was completely unarmed, but had he been suddenly pounced upon he surely would have been able to let out a yell that could have been heard all over the cove. But till daybreak a profound stillness, in which it seemed a whisper could have been heard for miles, had reigned over the coast. It was as if Symons had been spirited away by some supernatural means, without a scuffle, without a cry. For it was inconceivable that he should have ventured inland and got captured there. It was equally inconceivable that there should have been on that particular night men ready to pounce upon Symons and knock him on the head so neatly as not to let him give a groan even.

Captain Vincent said: 'All this is very fantastical, Mr Bolt,' and compressed his lips firmly for a moment before he continued: 'But not much more than your woman. I suppose you did see something real . . .'

'I tell you, sir, she stood there in full moonlight for ten minutes within a stone's throw of me,' protested Bolt with a sort of desperation. 'She seemed to have jumped out of bed only to look at the house. If she had a petticoat over her night-shift, that was all. Her back was to me. When she moved away I could not make out her face properly. Then she went to stand in the shadow of the house.'

'On the watch,' suggested Captain Vincent.

'Looked like it, sir,' confessed Bolt.

'So there must have been somebody about,' concluded Captain Vincent with assurance.

Bolt murmured a reluctant, 'Must have been.' He had expected to get into enormous trouble over this affair and was much relieved by the captain's quiet attitude. 'I hope, sir, you approve of my conduct in not attempting to look for Symons at once?'

'Yes. You acted prudently by not advancing inland,' said the captain.

'I was afraid of spoiling our chances to carry out your plan, sir, by disclosing our presence on shore. And that could not have been avoided. Moreover, we were only five in all and not properly armed.'

'The plan has gone down before your night-walker, Mr Bolt,' Captain Vincent declared dryly. 'But we must try to find out what has become of our man if it can be done without risking too much.'

'By landing a large party this very next night we could surround the house,' Bolt suggested. 'If we find friends there, well and good. If enemies, then we could carry off some of them on board for exchange perhaps. I am almost sorry I did not go back and kidnap that wench – whoever she was,' he added recklessly. 'Ah! If it had only been a man!'

'No doubt there was a man not very far off,' said Captain Vincent equably. 'That will do, Mr Bolt. You had better go and get some rest now.'

Bolt was glad to obey, for he was tired and hungry after his dismal failure. What vexed him most was its absurdity. Captain Vincent, though he too had passed a sleepless night, felt too restless to remain below. He followed his officer on deck.

Chapter 6

By that time the *Amelia* had been towed half a mile or so away from
Cape Esterel. This change had brought her nearer to the two watchers
on the hillside, who would have been plainly visible to the people on
her deck, but for the head of the pine which concealed their movements.
Lieutenant Réal, bestriding the rugged trunk as high as he could get,
had the whole of the English ship's deck open to the range of his
pocket-glass which he used between the branches. He said to Peyrol
suddenly: 'Her captain has just come on deck.'

Peyrol, sitting at the foot of the tree, made no answer for a long
while. A warm drowsiness lay over the land and seemed to press down
his eyelids. But inwardly the old rover was intensely awake. Under the
mask of his immobility, with half-shut eyes and idly clasped hands, he
heard the lieutenant, perched up there near the head of the tree, mutter,
counting something: 'One, two, three,' and then a loud, 'Parbleu!'[103]
after which the lieutenant in his trunk-bestriding attitude began to jerk
himself backwards.

Peyrol got up out of his way, but could not restrain himself from
asking: 'What's the matter now?'

'I will tell you what's the matter,' said the other excitedly. As soon as
he got his footing he walked up to old Peyrol and when quite close to
him folded his arms across his chest. 'The first thing I did was to count
the boats in the water. There was not a single one left on board. And
now I just counted them again and found one more there. That ship
had a boat out last night. How I missed seeing her pull out from under
the land I don't know. I was watching the decks, I suppose, and she
seems to have gone straight up to the tow-rope. But I was right. That
Englishman had a boat out.'

He seized Peyrol by both shoulders suddenly. 'I believe you knew it
all the time. You knew it, I tell you.'

Peyrol, shaken violently by the shoulders, raised his eyes to look
at the angry face within a few inches of his own. In his worn gaze
there was no fear or shame, but a troubled perplexity and obvious
concern. He remained passive, merely remonstrating softly: 'Doucement. Doucement.'[104]

The lieutenant suddenly desisted with a final jerk which failed to
stagger old Peyrol, who, directly he had been released, assumed an

explanatory tone. 'For the ground is slippery here. If I had lost my footing I would not have been able to prevent myself from grabbing at you, and we would have gone down that cliff together; which would have told those Englishmen more than twenty boats could have found out in as many nights.'

Secretly Lieutenant Réal was daunted by Peyrol's mildness. It could not be shaken. Even physically he had an impression of the utter futility of his effort, as though he had tried to shake a rock. He threw himself on the ground carelessly saying: 'As for instance?'

Peyrol lowered himself with a deliberation appropriate to his grey hairs. 'You don't suppose that out of a hundred and twenty or so pairs of eyes on board that ship there wouldn't be a dozen at least scanning the shore. Two men falling down a cliff would have been a startling sight. The English would have been interested enough to send a boat ashore to go through our pockets, and whether dead or only half dead we wouldn't have been in a state to prevent them. It wouldn't matter so much as to me, and I don't know what papers you may have in your pockets, but there are your shoulder-straps, your uniform coat.'

'I carry no papers in my pocket, and . . . ' A sudden thought seemed to strike the lieutenant, a thought so intense and far-fetched as to give his mental effort a momentary aspect of vacancy. He shook it off and went on in a changed tone: 'The shoulder-straps would not have been much of a revelation by themselves.'

'No. Not much. But enough to let her captain know that he had been watched. For what else could the dead body of a naval officer with a spyglass in his pocket mean? Hundreds of eyes may glance carelessly at that ship every day from all parts of the coast, though I fancy those landsmen hardly take the trouble to look at her now. But that's a very different thing from being kept under observation. However, I don't suppose all this matters much.'

The lieutenant was recovering from the spell of that sudden thought. 'Papers in my pocket,' he muttered to himself. 'That would be a perfect way.' His parted lips came together in a slightly sarcastic smile with which he met Peyrol's puzzled, sidelong glance provoked by the inexplicable character of these words.

'I bet,' said the lieutenant, 'that ever since I came here first you have been more or less worrying your old head about my motives and intentions.'

Peyrol said simply: 'You came here on service at first and afterwards you came again because even in the Toulon fleet an officer may get a few days' leave. As to your intentions, I won't say anything about them.

Especially as regards myself. About ten minutes ago anybody looking on would have thought they were not friendly to me.'

The lieutenant sat up suddenly. By that time the English sloop, getting away from under the land, had become visible even from the spot on which they sat.

'Look!' exclaimed Réal. 'She seems to be forging ahead in this calm.'

Peyrol, startled, raised his eyes and saw the *Amelia* clear of the edge of the cliff and heading across the Passe. All her boats were already alongside, and yet, as a minute or two of steady gazing was enough to convince Peyrol, she was not stationary.

'She moves! There is no denying that. She moves. Watch the white speck of that house on Porquerolles. There! The end of her jib-boom touches it now. In a moment her head sails will mask it from us.'

'I would never have believed it,' muttered the lieutenant, after a pause of intent gazing. 'And look, Peyrol, look, there is not a wrinkle on the water.'

Peyrol, who had been shading his eyes from the sun, let his hand fall. 'Yes,' he said, 'she would answer to a child's breath quicker than a feather, and the English very soon found it out when they got her. She was caught in Genoa[105] only a few months after I came home and got my moorings here.'

'I didn't know,' murmured the young man.

'Aha, lieutenant,' said Peyrol, pressing his finger to his breast, 'it hurts here, doesn't it? There is nobody but good Frenchmen here. Do you think it is a pleasure to me to watch that flag out there at her peak? Look, you can see the whole of her now. Look at her ensign hanging down as if there were not a breath of wind under the heavens . . . ' He stamped his foot suddenly. 'And yet she moves! Those in Toulon that may be thinking of catching her dead or alive would have to think hard and make long plans and get good men to carry them out.'

'There was some talk of it at the Toulon Admiralty,' said Réal.

The rover shook his head. 'They need not have sent you on the duty,' he said. 'I have been watching her now for a month, her and the man who has got her now. I know all his tricks and all his habits and all his dodges by this time. The man is a seaman, that must be said for him, but I can tell beforehand what he will do in any given case.'

Lieutenant Réal lay down on his back again, his clasped hands under his head. He thought that this old man was not boasting. He knew a lot about the English ship, and if an attempt to capture her was to be made, his ideas would be worth having. Nevertheless, in his relations with old Peyrol Lieutenant Réal suffered from contradictory feelings. Réal was

the son of a ci-devant couple – small provincial gentry – who had both
lost their heads on the scaffold, within the same week. As to their boy,
he was apprenticed by order of the Delegate of the Revolutionary
Committee of his town to a poor but pure-minded joiner, who could
not provide him with shoes to run his errands in, but treated this
aristocrat not unkindly. Nevertheless, at the end of the year the orphan
ran away and volunteered as a boy on board one of the ships of the
Republic about to sail on a distant expedition. At sea he found another
standard of values. In the course of some eight years, suppressing his
faculties of love and hatred, he arrived at the rank of an officer by sheer
merit, and had accustomed himself to look at men sceptically, without
much scorn or much respect. His principles were purely professional
and he had never formed a friendship in his life – more unfortunate in
that respect than old Peyrol, who at least had known the bonds of
the lawless Brotherhood of the Coast. He was, of course, very self-
contained. Peyrol, whom he had found unexpectedly settled on the
peninsula, was the first human being to break through that schooled
reserve which the precariousness of all things had forced on the orphan
of the Revolution. Peyrol's striking personality had aroused Réal's
interest, a mistrustful liking mixed with some contempt of a purely
doctrinaire kind. It was clear that the fellow had been next thing to a
pirate at one time or another – a sort of past which could not commend
itself to a naval officer.

Still, Peyrol had broken through: and, presently, the peculiarities of
all those people at the farm, each individual one of them, had entered
through the breach.

Lieutenant Réal, on his back, closing his eyes to the glare of the sky,
meditated on old Peyrol, while Peyrol himself, with his white head bare
in the sunshine, seemed to be sitting by the side of a corpse. What in
that man impressed Lieutenant Réal was the faculty of shrewd insight.
The facts of Réal's connection with the farmhouse on the peninsula
were much as Peyrol had stated. First on specific duty about establishing
a signal station, then, when that project had been given up, voluntary
visits. Not belonging to any ship of the fleet but doing shore duty at the
Arsenal, Lieutenant Réal had spent several periods of short leave at the
farm, where indeed nobody could tell whether he had come on duty or
on leave. He personally could not – or perhaps would not – tell even to
himself why it was that he came there. He had been growing sick of his
work. He had no place in the world to go to, and no one either. Was it
Peyrol he was coming to see? A mute, strangely suspicious, defiant
understanding had established itself imperceptibly between him and

that lawless old man who might have been suspected to have come there only to die, if the whole robust personality of Peyrol with its quiet vitality had not been antagonistic to the notion of death. That rover behaved as though he had all the time in the world at his command.

Peyrol spoke suddenly, with his eyes fixed in front of him as if he were addressing the Island of Porquerolles, eight miles away.

'Yes – I know all her moves, though I must say that this trick of dodging close to our peninsula is something new.'

'H'm! Fish for the captain's breakfast,' mumbled Réal without opening his eyes. 'Where is she now?'

'In the middle of the Passe, busy hoisting in her boats. And still moving! That ship will keep her way as long as the flame of a candle on her deck will not stand upright.'

'That ship is a marvel.'

'She has been built by French shipwrights,' said old Peyrol bitterly.

This was the last sound for a long time. Then the lieutenant said in an indifferent tone: 'You are very positive about that. How do you know?'

'I have been looking at her for a month, whatever name she might have had or whatever name the English call her by now. Did you ever see such a bow on an English-built ship?'

The lieutenant remained silent, as though he had lost all interest and there had been no such thing as an English man-of-war within a mile. But all the time he was thinking hard. He had been told confidentially of a certain piece of service to be performed on instructions received from Paris. Not an operation of war, but service of the greatest importance. The risk of it was not so much deadly as particularly odious. A brave man might well have shrunk from it; and there are risks (not death) from which a resolute man might shrink without shame.

'Have you ever tasted of prison, Peyrol?' he asked suddenly, in an affectedly sleepy voice.

It roused Peyrol nearly into a shout. 'Heavens! No! Prison! What do you mean by prison? . . . I have been a captive to savages,' he added, calming down, 'but that's a very old story. I was young and foolish then. Later, when a grown man, I was a slave to the famous Ali-Kassim. I spent a fortnight with chains on my legs and arms in the yard of a mud fort on the shores of the Persian Gulf. There was nearly a score of us Brothers of the Coast in the same predicament in consequence of a shipwreck.'

'Yes . . . ' The lieutenant was very languid indeed . . . 'And I dare say you all took service with that bloodthirsty old pirate.'

'There was not a single one of his thousands of blackamoors[106] that could lay a gun properly. But Ali-Kassim made war like a prince. We sailed, a regular fleet, across the Gulf, took a town on the coast of Arabia somewhere, and looted it. Then I and the others managed to get hold of an armed dhow, and we fought our way right through the blackamoors' fleet. Several of us died of thirst later. All the same, it was a great affair. But don't you talk to me of prisons. A proper man if given a chance to fight can always get himself killed. You understand me?'

'Yes, I understand you,' drawled the lieutenant. 'I think I know you pretty well. I suppose an English prison . . . '

'That is a horrible subject of conversation,' interrupted Peyrol in a loud, emotional tone. 'Naturally, any death is better than a prison. Any death! What is it you have in your mind, lieutenant?'

'Oh, it isn't that I want you to die,' drawled Réal in an uninterested manner.

Peyrol, his entwined fingers clasping his legs, gazed fixedly at the English sloop floating idly in the Passe while he gave up all his mind to the consideration of these words that had floated out, idly too, into the peace and silence of the morning. Then he asked in a low tone: 'Do you want to frighten me?'

The lieutenant laughed harshly. Neither by word, gesture nor glance did Peyrol acknowledge the enigmatic and unpleasant sound. But when it ceased the silence grew so oppressive between the two men that they got up by a common impulse. The lieutenant sprang to his feet lightly. The uprising of Peyrol took more time and had more dignity. They stood side by side unable to detach their longing eyes from the enemy ship below their feet.

'I wonder why he put himself into this curious position,' said the officer.

'I wonder,' growled Peyrol curtly. 'If there had been only a couple of eighteen-pounders placed on the rocky ledge to the left of us, we could have unrigged her in about ten minutes.'

'Good old gunner,' commented Réal ironically. 'And what afterwards? Swim off, you and I, with our cutlasses in our teeth and take her by boarding, what?'

This sally provoked in Peyrol an austere smile. 'No! No!' he protested soberly. 'But why not let Toulon know? Bring out a frigate or two and catch him alive. Many a time have I planned his capture just to ease my heart. Often I have stared at night out of my window upstairs across the bay to where I knew he was lying at anchor, and thinking of a little surprise I could arrange for him if I were not only old Peyrol, the gunner.'

'Yes. And keeping out of the way at that, with a bad note against his name in the books of the Admiralty in Toulon.'

'You can't say I have tried to hide myself from you who are a naval officer,' struck in Peyrol quickly. 'I fear no man. I did not run. I simply went away from Toulon. Nobody had given me an order to stay there. And you can't say I ran very far either.'

'That was the cleverest move of all. You knew what you were doing.'

'Here you go again, hinting at something crooked like that fellow with big epaulettes at the Port Office that seemed to be longing to put me under arrest just because I brought a prize from the Indian Ocean, eight thousand miles, dodging clear of every Englishmen that came in my way, which was more perhaps than he could have done. I have my gunner's warrant signed by Citoyen Renaud, a chef d'escadre.[107] It wasn't given me for twirling my thumbs or hiding in the cable tier when the enemy was about. There were on board our ships some patriots that weren't above doing that sort of thing, I can tell you. But republic or no republic, that kind wasn't likely to get a gunner's warrant.'

'That's all right,' said Réal, with his eyes fixed on the English ship, the head of which was swung to the northward now . . . 'Look, she seems to have lost her way at last,' he remarked parenthetically to Peyrol, who also glanced that way and nodded . . . 'That's all right. But it's on record that you managed in a very short time to get very thick with a lot of patriots ashore. Section leaders. Terrorists . . . '

'Why, yes. I wanted to hear what they had to say. They talked like a drunken crew of scallywags that had stolen a ship. But at any rate it wasn't such as they that had sold the Port to the English. They were a lot of bloodthirsty landlubbers. I did get out of town as soon as I could. I remembered I was born around here. I knew no other bit of France, and I didn't care to go any farther. Nobody came to look for me.'

'No, not here. I suppose they thought it was too near. They did look for you, a little, but they gave it up. Perhaps if they had persevered and made an admiral of you we would not have been beaten at Aboukir.'[108]

At the mention of that name Peyrol shook his fist at the serene Mediterranean sky. 'And yet we were no worse men than the English,' he cried, 'and there are no such ships as ours in the world. You see, lieutenant, the republican god of these talkers would never give us seamen a chance of fair play.'

The lieutenant looked round in surprise. 'What do you know about a republican god?' he asked. 'What on earth do you mean?'

'I have heard of and seen more gods than you could ever dream of in a long night's sleep, in every corner of the earth, in the very heart of forests, which is an inconceivable thing. Figures, stones, sticks. There must be something in the idea . . . And what I meant,' he continued in a resentful tone, 'is that their republican god, which is neither stick nor stone, but seems to be some kind of lubber, has never given us seamen a chief like that one the soldiers have got ashore.'

Lieutenant Réal looked at Peyrol with unsmiling attention, then remarked quietly, 'Well, the god of the aristocrats is coming back again and it looks as if he were bringing an emperor[109] along with him. You've heard something of that, you people in the farmhouse? Haven't you?'

'No,' said Peyrol. 'I have heard no talk of an emperor. But what does it matter? Under one name or another a chief can be no more than a chief, and that general whom they have been calling consul is a good chief – nobody can deny that.'

After saying those words in a dogmatic tone, Peyrol looked up at the sun and suggested that it was time to go down to the farmhouse 'pour manger la soupe'.[110] With a suddenly gloomy face Réal moved off, followed by Peyrol. At the first turn of the path they got the view of the Escampobar buildings with the pigeons still walking on the ridges of the roofs, of the sunny orchards and yards without a living soul in them. Peyrol remarked that everybody no doubt was in the kitchen waiting for his and the lieutenant's return. He himself was properly hungry. 'And you, lieutenant?'

The lieutenant was not hungry. Hearing this declaration made in a peevish tone, Peyrol gave a sagacious movement of his head behind the lieutenant's back. Well, whatever happened, a man had to eat. He, Peyrol, knew what it was to be altogether without food; but even half-rations was a poor show, very poor show for anybody who had to work or to fight. For himself he couldn't imagine any conjuncture that would prevent him having a meal as long as there was something to eat within reach.

His unwonted garrulity provoked no response, but Peyrol continued to talk in that strain as though his thoughts were concentrated on food, while his eyes roved here and there and his ears were open for the slightest sound. When they arrived in front of the house Peyrol stopped to glance anxiously down the path to the coast, letting the lieutenant enter the café. The Mediterranean, in that part which could be seen from the door of the café, was as empty of all sail as a yet undiscovered sea. The dull tinkle of a cracked bell on the neck of some wandering cow was the only sound that reached him, accentuating the Sunday peace of the farm. Two goats were lying down on the western slope of the hill. It all had a very reassuring effect and the anxious expression on Peyrol's face was passing away when suddenly one of the goats leaped to its feet. The rover gave a start and became rigid in a pose of tense apprehension. A man who is in such a frame of mind that a leaping goat makes him start cannot be happy. However, the other goat remained lying down. There was really no reason for alarm, and Peyrol, composing his features as near as possible to their usual placid expression, followed the lieutenant into the house.

A single cover having been laid at the end of a long table in the salle for the lieutenant, he had his meal there while the others sat down to theirs in the kitchen, the usual strangely assorted company served by the anxious and silent Catherine. Peyrol, thoughtful and hungry, faced Citizen Scevola in his working clothes and very much withdrawn within himself. Scevola's aspect was more feverish than usual, with the red patches on his cheekbones very marked above the thick beard. From time to time the mistress of the farm would get up from her place by the side of old Peyrol and go out into the salle to attend to the lieutenant. The other three people seemed unconscious of her absences. Towards the end of the meal Peyrol leaned back in his wooden chair and let his gaze rest on the ex-terrorist who had not finished yet, and was still busy over his plate with the air of a man who had done a long morning's work. The door leading from the kitchen to the salle stood wide open, but no sound of voices ever came from there.

Till lately Peyrol had not concerned himself very much with the mental states of the people with whom he lived. Now, however, he wondered to himself what could be the thoughts of the ex-terrorist patriot, that sanguinary and extremely poor creature occupying the position of master of the Escampobar Farm. But when Citizen Scevola raised his head at last to take a long drink of wine there was nothing new on that face which in its high colour resembled so much a painted mask. Their eyes met.

'Sacré bleu!'[111] exclaimed Peyrol at last. 'If you never say anything to anybody like this you will forget how to speak at last.'

The patriot smiled from the depths of his beard, a smile which Peyrol for some reason, mere prejudice perhaps, always thought resembled the defensive grin of some small wild animal afraid of being cornered.

'What is there to talk about?' he retorted. 'You live with us; you haven't budged from here; I suppose you have counted the bunches of grapes in the enclosure and the figs on the fig tree on the west wall many times over . . . ' He paused to lend an ear to the dead silence in the salle, and then said with a slight rise of tone, 'You and I know everything that is going on here.'

Peyrol wrinkled the corners of his eyes in a keen, searching glance. Catherine clearing the table bore herself as if she had been completely deaf. Her face, of a walnut colour, with sunken cheeks and lips, might have been a carving in the marvellous immobility of its fine wrinkles. Her carriage was upright and her hands swift in their movements. Peyrol said: 'We don't want to talk about the farm. Haven't you heard any news lately?'

The patriot shook his head violently. Of public news he had a horror. Everything was lost. The country was ruled by perjurers and renegades. All the patriotic virtues were dead. He struck the table with his fist and then remained listening as though the blow could have roused an echo in the silent house. Not the faintest sound came from anywhere. Citizen Scevola sighed. It seemed to him that he was the only patriot left, and even in his retirement his life was not safe.

'I know,' said Peyrol. 'I saw the whole affair out of the window. You can run like a hare, citizen.'

'Was I to allow myself to be sacrificed by those superstitious brutes?' argued Citizen Scevola in a high-pitched voice and with genuine indignation which Peyrol watched coldly. He could hardly catch the mutter of, 'Perhaps it would have been just as well if I had let those reactionary dogs kill me that time.'

The old woman washing up at the sink glanced uneasily towards the door of the salle.

'No!' shouted the lonely sans-culotte. 'It isn't possible! There must be plenty of patriots left in France. The sacred fire is not burnt out yet.'

For a short time he presented the appearance of a man who is sitting with ashes on his head[112] and desolation in his heart. His almond-shaped eyes looked dull, extinguished. But after a moment he gave a sidelong look at Peyrol as if to watch the effect and began declaiming in a low voice and apparently as if rehearsing a speech to himself: 'No, it isn't possible. Some day tyranny will stumble and then it will be time to pull it down again. We will come out in our thousands and – ça ira!'[113]

Those words, and even the passionate energy of the tone, left Peyrol unmoved. With his head sustained by his thick brown hand he was thinking of something else so obviously as to depress again the feebly struggling spirit of terrorism in the lonely breast of Citizen Scevola. The glow of reflected sunlight in the kitchen became darkened by the body of the fisherman of the lagoon, mumbling a shy greeting to the company from the frame of the doorway. Without altering his position Peyrol turned his eyes on him curiously. Catherine, wiping her hands on her apron, remarked: 'You come late for your dinner, Michel.' He stepped in then, took from the old woman's hand an earthenware pot and a large hunk of bread and carried them out at once into the yard.

Peyrol and the sans-culotte got up from the table. The latter, after hesitating like somebody who has lost his way, went brusquely into the passage, while Peyrol, avoiding Catherine's anxious stare, made for the back-yard. Through the open door of the salle he obtained a glimpse of Arlette sitting upright with her hands in her lap gazing at somebody he could not see, but who could be no other than Lieutenant Réal.

In the blaze and heat of the yard the chickens, broken up into small groups, were having their siesta in patches of shade. But Peyrol cared nothing for the sun. Michel, who was eating his dinner under the pent roof of the cart shed, put the earthenware pot down on the ground and joined his master at the well encircled by a low wall of stones and topped by an arch of wrought iron on which a wild fig tree had twined a slender offshoot. After his dog's death the fisherman had abandoned the salt lagoon, leaving his rotting punt exposed on the dismal shore and his miserable nets shut up in the dark hut. He did not care for another dog, and besides, who was there to give him a dog? He was the last of men. Somebody must be last. There was no place for him in the life of the village. So one fine morning he had walked up to the farm in order to see Peyrol. More correctly, perhaps, to let himself be seen by Peyrol. That was exactly Michel's only hope. He sat down on a stone outside the gate with a small bundle, consisting mainly of an old blanket, and a crooked stick lying on the ground near him, and looking the most lonely, mild and harmless creature on this earth. Peyrol had listened gravely to his confused tale of the dog's death. He, personally, would not have made a friend of a dog like Michel's dog, but he understood perfectly the sudden breaking up of the establishment on the shore of the lagoon. So when Michel had concluded with the words, 'I thought I would come up here,' Peyrol, without waiting for a plain request, had said: 'Très bien.[114] You will be my crew,' and had pointed down the path leading to the seashore. And as Michel, picking up his bundle and stick, started off, waiting for no further directions, he had shouted after him: 'You will find a loaf of bread and a bottle of wine in a locker aft, to break your fast on.'

These had been the only formalities of Michel's engagement to serve as 'crew' on board Peyrol's boat. The rover indeed had tried without loss of time to carry out his purpose of getting something of his own that would float. It was not so easy to find anything worthy. The miserable population of Madrague, a tiny fishing hamlet facing towards Toulon, had nothing to sell. Moreover, Peyrol looked with contempt on all their possessions. He would have as soon bought a catamaran of three logs of wood tied together with rattans as one of their boats; but lonely and prominent on the beach, lying on her side in weather-beaten melancholy, there was a two-masted tartane with her sun-whitened cordage hanging in festoons and her dry masts showing long cracks. No man was ever seen dozing under the shade of her hull on which the Mediterranean gulls made themselves very much at home. She looked a wreck thrown high up on the land by a disdainful sea. Peyrol, having surveyed her from a distance, saw that the rudder still hung in its place. He ran his eye along her body and said to himself that a craft with such lines would sail well. She was much bigger than anything he had thought of, but in her size, too, there was a fascination. It seemed to bring all the shores of the Mediterranean within his reach, Baleares[115] and Corsica, Barbary[116] and Spain. Peyrol had sailed over hundreds of leagues of ocean in craft that were no bigger. At his back in silent wonder a knot of fishermen's wives, bareheaded and lean, with a swarm of ragged children clinging to their skirts, watched the first stranger they had seen for years.

Peyrol borrowed a short ladder in the hamlet (he knew better than to trust his weight to any of the ropes hanging over the side) and carried it down to the beach, followed at a respectful distance by the staring women and children: a phenomenon and a wonder to the natives, as it had happened to him before on more than one island in distant seas. He clambered on board the neglected tartane and stood on the decked forepart, the centre of all eyes. A gull flew away with an angry scream. The bottom of the open hold contained nothing but a little sand, a few broken pieces of wood, a rusty hook and some few stalks of straw which the wind must have carried for miles before they found their rest in there. The decked after-part had a small skylight and a companion, and Peyrol's eyes rested fascinated on an enormous padlock which secured its sliding door. It was as if there had been secrets or treasures inside – and yet most probably it was empty.

Peyrol turned his head away and with the whole strength of his lungs shouted in the direction of the fishermen's wives who had been joined by two very old men and a hunchbacked cripple swinging between two crutches: 'Is there anybody looking after this tartane – a caretaker?'

At first the only answer was a movement of recoil. Only the hunchback held his ground and shouted back in an unexpectedly strong voice: 'You are the first man that has been on board her for years.'

The wives of the fishermen admired his boldness, for Peyrol indeed appeared to them a very formidable being.

'I might have guessed that,' thought Peyrol. 'She is in a dreadful mess.' The disturbed gull had brought some friends as indignant as itself and they circled at different levels uttering wild cries over Peyrol's head. He shouted again: 'Who does she belong to?'

The being on crutches lifted a finger towards the circling birds and answered in a deep tone: 'They are the only ones I know.' Then, as Peyrol gazed down at him over the side, he went on: 'This craft used to belong to Escampobar. You know Escampobar? It's a house in the hollow between the hills there.'

'Yes, I know Escampobar,' yelled Peyrol, turning away and leaning against the mast in a pose which he did not change for a long time. His immobility tired out the crowd. They moved slowly in a body towards their hovels, the hunchback bringing up the rear with long swings between his crutches, and Peyrol remained alone with the angry gulls. He lingered on board the tragic craft which had taken Arlette's parents to their death in the vengeful massacre of Toulon and had brought the youthful Arlette and Citizen Scevola back to Escampobar where old Catherine, left alone all that time, had waited for days for somebody's return. Days of anguish and prayer, while she listened to the booming of guns about Toulon – and with an almost greater but different terror to the dead silence which ensued.

Peyrol, enjoying the sensation of some sort of craft under his feet, indulged in no images of horror connected with that desolate tartane. It was late in the evening before he returned to the farm, so that he had to have his supper alone. The women had retired, only the sans-culotte, smoking a short pipe out of doors, had followed him into the kitchen and asked where he had been and whether he had lost his way. This question gave Peyrol an opening. He had been to Madrague and had seen a very fine tartane lying perishing on the beach.

'They told me down there that she belonged to you, citoyen.'

At this the terrorist only blinked.

'What's the matter? Isn't she the craft you came here in? Won't you sell her to me?' Peyrol waited a little. 'What objection can you have?'

It appeared that the patriot had no positive objections. He mumbled something about the tartane being very dirty. This caused Peyrol to look at him with intense astonishment.

'I am ready to take her off your hands as she stands.'

'I will be frank with you, citoyen. You see, when she lay at the quay in Toulon a lot of fugitive traitors, men and women, and children too, swarmed on board of her, and cut the ropes with a view to escaping, but the avengers were not far behind and made short work of them. When we discovered her behind the Arsenal, I and another man, we had to throw a lot of bodies overboard, out of the hold and the cabin. You will find her very dirty all over. We had no time to clear up.' Peyrol felt inclined to laugh. He had seen decks swimming in blood and had himself helped to throw dead bodies overboard after a fight; but he eyed the citizen with an unfriendly eye. He thought to himself: 'He had a hand in that massacre, no doubt,' but he made no audible remark. He only thought of the enormous padlock securing that emptied charnel house at the stern. The terrorist insisted. 'We really had not a moment to clean her up. The circumstances were such that it was necessary for me to get away quickly lest some of the false patriots should do me some carmagnole[117] or other. There had been bitter quarrelling in my section. I was not alone in getting away, you know.'

Peyrol waved his arm to cut short the explanation. But before he and the terrorist had parted for the night Peyrol could regard himself as the owner of the tragic tartane.

Next day he returned to the hamlet and took up his quarters there for a time. The awe he had inspired wore off, though no one cared to come very near the tartane. Peyrol did not want any help. He wrenched off the enormous padlock himself with a bar of iron and let the light of day into the little cabin which did indeed bear the traces of the massacre in the stains of blood on its woodwork, but contained nothing else except a wisp of long hair and a woman's earring, a cheap thing which Peyrol picked up and looked at for a long time. The associations of such finds were not foreign to his past. He could without very strong emotion figure to himself the little place choked with corpses. He sat down and looked about at the stains and splashes which had been untouched by sunlight for years. The cheap little earring lay before him on the rough-hewn table between the lockers, and he shook his head at it weightily. He, at any rate, had never been a butcher.

Peyrol unassisted did all the cleaning. Then he turned *con amore* to the fitting out of the tartane. The habits of activity still clung to him. He welcomed something to do; this congenial task had all the air of preparation for a voyage, which was a pleasing dream, and it brought every evening the satisfaction of something achieved to that illusory end. He rove new gear, scraped the masts himself, did all the sweeping, scrubbing and painting single-handed, working steadily and hopefully as though he had been preparing his escape from a desert island; and directly he had cleaned and renovated the dark little hole of a cabin he took to sleeping on board. Once only he went up on a visit to the farm for a couple of days, as if to give himself a holiday. He passed them mostly in observing Arlette. She was perhaps the first problematic human being he had ever been in contact with. Peyrol had no contempt for women. He had seen them love, suffer, endure, riot, and even fight for their own hand, very much like men. Generally with men and women you had to be on your guard, but in some ways women were more to be trusted. As a matter of fact, his country-women were to him less known than any other kind. From his experience of many different races, however, he had a vague idea that women were very much alike everywhere. This one was a lovable creature. She produced on him the effect of a child, aroused a kind of intimate emotion which he had not known before to exist by itself in a man. He was startled by its detached character. 'Is it that I am getting old?' he asked himself suddenly one evening, as he sat on the bench against the wall looking straight before him, after she had crossed his line of sight.

He felt himself an object of observation to Catherine, whom he used to detect peeping at him round corners or through half-opened doors. On his part he would stare at her openly – aware of the impression he produced on her: mingled curiosity and awe. He had the idea she did not disapprove of his presence at the farm, where, it was plain to him, she had a far from easy life. This had no relation to the fact that she did all the household work. She was a woman of about his own age, straight as a dart but with a wrinkled face. One evening as they were sitting alone in the kitchen Peyrol said to her: 'You must have been a handsome girl in your day, Catherine. It's strange you never got married.'

She turned to him under the high mantel of the fireplace and seemed struck all of a heap, unbelieving, amazed, so that Peyrol was quite provoked. 'What's the matter? If the old moke[118] in the yard had spoken you could not look more surprised. You can't deny that you were a handsome girl.'

She recovered from her scare to say: 'I was born here, grew up here, and early in my life I made up my mind to die here.'

'A strange notion,' said Peyrol, 'for a young girl to take into her head.'

'It's not a thing to talk about,' said the old woman, stooping to get a pot out of the warm ashes. 'I did not think, then,' she went on, with her back to Peyrol, 'that I would live long. When I was eighteen I fell in love with a priest.'

'Ah, bah!' exclaimed Peyrol under his breath.

'That was the time when I prayed for death,' she pursued in a quiet voice. 'I spent nights on my knees upstairs in that room where you sleep now. I shunned everybody. People began to say I was crazy. We have always been hated by the rabble about here. They have poisonous tongues. I got the nickname of 'la fiancée du prêtre'.[119] Yes, I was handsome, but who would have looked at me if I had wanted to be looked at? My only luck was to have a fine man for a brother. He understood. No word passed his lips, but sometimes when we were alone, and not even his wife was by, he would lay his hand on my shoulder gently. From that time to this I have not been to church and I never will go. But I have no quarrel with God now.'

There were no signs of watchfulness and care in her bearing now. She stood straight as an arrow before Peyrol and looked at him with a confident air. The rover was not yet ready to speak. He only nodded twice and Catherine turned away to put the pot to cool in the sink. 'Yes, I wished to die. But I did not, and now I have got something to do,' she said, sitting down near the fireplace and taking her chin in her hand. 'And I dare say you know what that is,' she added.

Peyrol got up deliberately.

'Well! bonsoir,'[120] he said. 'I am off to Madrague. I want to begin work again on the tartane at daylight.'

'Don't talk to me about the tartane! She took my brother away for ever. I stood on the shore watching her sails growing smaller and smaller. Then I came up alone to this farmhouse.'

Moving calmly her faded lips which no lover or child had ever kissed, old Catherine told Peyrol of the days and nights of waiting, with the distant growl of the big guns in her ears. She used to sit outside on the bench longing for news, watching the flickers in the sky and listening to heavy bursts of gunfire coming over the water. Then came a night as if the world were coming to an end. All the sky was lighted up, the earth shook to its foundations, and she felt the house rock, so that jumping up from the bench she screamed with fear. That night she never went to bed. Next morning she saw the sea covered with sails, while a black and yellow cloud of smoke hung over Toulon. A man coming up from Madrague told her that he believed that the whole town had been blown up. She gave him a bottle of wine and he helped her to feed the stock that evening. Before going home he expressed the opinion that there could not be a soul left alive in Toulon, because the few that survived would have gone away in the English ships. Nearly a week later she was dozing by the fire when voices outside woke her up, and she beheld standing in the middle of the salle,[121] pale like a corpse out of a grave, with a blood-soaked blanket over her shoulders and a red cap on her head, a ghastly-looking young girl in whom she suddenly recognised her niece. She screamed in her terror: 'François, François!' This was her brother's name, and she thought he was outside. Her scream scared the girl, who ran out of the door. All was still outside. Once more she screamed 'François!' and, tottering as far as the door, she saw her niece clinging to a strange man in a red cap and with a sabre by his side who yelled excitedly: 'You won't see François again. Vive la République!'

'I recognised the son Bron,' went on Catherine. 'I knew his parents. When the troubles began he left his home to follow the Revolution. I walked straight up to him and took the girl away from his side. She didn't want much coaxing. The child always loved me,' she continued, getting up from the stool and moving a little closer to Peyrol. 'She remembered her Aunt Catherine. I tore the horrid blanket off her shoulders. Her hair was clotted with blood and her clothes all stained with it. I took her upstairs. She was as helpless as a little child. I undressed her and examined her all over. She had no hurt anywhere. I was sure of that – but of what more could I be sure? I couldn't make sense of the things she babbled at me. Her very voice distracted me. She fell asleep directly I had put her into my bed, and I stood there looking down at her, nearly going out of my mind with the thought of what that child may have been dragged through. When I went downstairs I found that good-for-nothing inside the house. He was ranting up and down the salle, vapouring and boasting till I thought all this must be an awful dream. My head was in a whirl. He laid claim to her, and God knows what. I seemed to understand things that made my hair stir on my head. I stood there clasping my hands with all the strength I had, for fear I should go out of my senses.'

'He frightened you,' said Peyrol, looking at her steadily. Catherine moved a step nearer to him.

'What? The son Bron, frighten me! He was the butt of all the girls, mooning about amongst the people outside the church on feast days in the time of the King. All the countryside knew about him. No. What I said to myself was that I mustn't let him kill me. There upstairs was the child I had just got away from him, and there was I, all alone with that man with the sabre and unable to get hold of a kitchen knife even.'

'And so he remained,' said Peyrol.

'What would you have had me do?' asked Catherine steadily. 'He had brought the child back out of those shambles. It was a long time before I got an idea of what had happened. I don't know everything even yet and I suppose I will never know. In a very few days my mind was more at ease about Arlette, but it was a long time before she would speak and then it was never anything to the purpose. And what could I have done single-handed? There was nobody I would condescend to call to my help. We of the Escampobar have never been in favour with the peasants here,' she said, proudly. 'And this is all I can tell you.'

Her voice faltered, she sat down on the stool again and took her chin in the palm of her hand. As Peyrol left the house to go to the hamlet he saw Arlette and the patron come round the corner of the yard wall walking side by side but as if unconscious of each other.

That night he slept on board the renovated tartane and the rising sun found him at work about the hull. By that time he had ceased to be the object of awed contemplation to the inhabitants of the hamlet, who still, however, kept up a mistrustful attitude. His only intermediary for communicating with them was the miserable cripple. He was Peyrol's only company, in fact, during his period of work on the tartane. He had more activity, audacity and intelligence, it seemed to Peyrol, than all the rest of the inhabitants put together. Early in the morning he could be seen making his way on his crutches with a pendulum motion towards the hull on which Peyrol would have been already an hour or so at work. Peyrol then would throw him over a sound rope's end and the cripple, leaning his crutches against the side of the tartane, would pull his wretched little carcass, all withered below the waist, up the rope, hand over hand, with extreme ease. There, sitting on the small foredeck, with his back against the mast and his thin, twisted legs folded in front of him, he would keep Peyrol company, talking to him along the whole length of the tartane in a strained voice and sharing his midday meal, as of right, since it was he generally who brought the provisions slung round his neck in a quaint flat basket. Thus were the hours of labour shortened for Peyrol by shrewd remarks and bits of local gossip. How the cripple got hold of it it was difficult to imagine, and the rover had not enough knowledge of European superstitions to suspect him of flying through the night on a broomstick like a sort of male witch – for there was a manliness in that twisted scrap of humanity which struck Peyrol from the first. His very voice was manly and the character of his gossip was not feminine. He did indeed mention to Peyrol that people used to take him about the neighbourhood in carts for the purpose of playing a fiddle at weddings and other festive occasions; but this seemed hardly adequate, and even he himself confessed that there was not much of that sort of thing going on during the Revolution when people didn't like to attract attention and everything was done in a hole-and-corner manner. There were no priests to officiate at weddings, and if there were no ceremonies how could there be rejoicings? Of course children were born as before, but there were no christenings – and people got to look funny somehow or other. Their countenances got changed somehow; the very boys and girls seemed to have something on their minds.

Peyrol, busy about one thing and another, listened without appearing to pay much attention to the story of the Revolution, as if to the tale of an intelligent islander on the other side of the world talking of bloody rites and amazing hopes of some religion unknown to the rest of mankind. But there was something biting in the speech of that cripple which confused his thoughts a little. Sarcasm was a mystery which he could not understand. On one occasion he remarked to his friend the cripple as they sat together on the foredeck munching the bread and figs of their midday meal: 'There must have been something in it. But it doesn't seem to have done much for you people here.'

'To be sure,' retorted the scrap of man vivaciously, 'it hasn't straightened my back or given me a pair of legs like yours.'

Peyrol, whose trousers were rolled up above the knee because he had been washing the hold, looked at his calves complacently. 'You could hardly have expected that,' he remarked with simplicity.

'Ah, but you don't know what people with properly made bodies expected or pretended to,' said the cripple. 'Everything was going to be changed. Everybody was going to tie up his dog with a string of sausages for the sake of principles.' His long face, which, in repose, had an expression of suffering peculiar to cripples, was lighted up by an enormous grin. 'They must feel jolly well sold by this time,' he added. 'And of course that vexes them, but I am not vexed. I was never vexed with my father and mother. While the poor things were alive I never went hungry – not very hungry. They couldn't have been very proud of me.' He paused and seemed to contemplate himself mentally. 'I don't know what I would have done in their place. Something very different. But then, don't you see, I know what it means to be like I am. Of course they couldn't know, and I don't suppose the poor people had very much sense. A priest from Almanarre – Almanarre is a sort of village up there where there is a church . . . '

Peyrol interrupted him by remarking that he knew all about Almanarre. This, on his part, was a simple delusion because in reality he knew much less of Almanarre than of Zanzibar or any pirate village from there up to Cape Guardafui.[122] And the cripple contemplated him with his brown eyes which had an upward cast naturally.

'You know . . . ! For me,' he went on, in a tone of quiet decision, 'you are a man fallen from the sky. Well, a priest from Almanarre came to bury them. A fine man with a stern face. The finest man I have seen from that time till you dropped on us here. There was a story of a girl having fallen in love with him some years before. I was old enough then to have heard something of it, but that's neither here nor there.

Moreover, many people wouldn't believe the tale.'

Peyrol, without looking at the cripple, tried to imagine what sort of child he might have been – what sort of youth? The rover had seen staggering deformities, dreadful mutilations which were the cruel work of man; but it was amongst people with dusky skins. And that made a great difference. But what he had heard and seen since he had come back to his native land, the tales, the facts, and also the faces, reached his sensibility with a particular force, because of that feeling that came to him so suddenly after a whole lifetime spent amongst Indians, Malagashes,[123] Arabs, blackamoors of all sorts, that he belonged there, to this land, and had escaped all those things by a mere hair's breadth.

His companion completed his significant silence, which seemed to have been occupied with thoughts very much like his own, by saying: 'All this was in the King's time. They didn't cut off his head till several years afterwards. It didn't make my life any easier for me, but since those Republicans had deposed God and flung Him out of all the churches I have forgiven Him all my troubles.'

'Spoken like a man,' said Peyrol. Only the misshapen character of the cripple's back prevented Peyrol from giving him a hearty slap. He got up to begin his afternoon's work. It was a bit of inside painting and from the foredeck the cripple watched him at it with dreamy eyes and something ironic on his lips.

It was not till the sun had travelled over Cape Cicié, which could be seen across the water like dark mist in the glare, that he opened his lips to ask: 'And what do you propose to do with this tartane, citoyen?'

Peyrol answered simply that the tartane was fit to go anywhere now, the very moment she took the water.

'You could go as far as Genoa and Naples and even farther,' suggested the cripple.

'Much farther,' said Peyrol.

'And you have been fitting her out like this for a voyage?'

'Certainly,' said Peyrol, using his brush steadily.

'Somehow I fancy it will not be a long one.'

Peyrol never checked the to-and-fro movement of his brush, but it was with an effort. The fact was that he had discovered in himself a distinct reluctance to go away from the Escampobar Farm. His desire to have something of his own that could float was no longer associated with any desire to wander. The cripple was right. The voyage of the renovated tartane would not take her very far. What was surprising was the fellow being so very positive about it. He seemed able to read people's thoughts.

The dragging of the renovated tartane into the water was a great affair. Everybody in the hamlet, including the women, did a full day's work and there was never so much coin passed from hand to hand in the hamlet in all the days of its obscure history. Swinging between his crutches on a low sand-ridge, the cripple surveyed the whole of the beach. It was he that had persuaded the villagers to lend a hand and had arranged the terms for their assistance. It was he also who through a very miserable-looking pedlar (the only one who frequented the peninsula) had got in touch with some rich persons in Fréjus who had changed for Peyrol a few of his gold pieces for current money. He had expedited the course of the most exciting and interesting experience of his life, and now planted on the sand on his two sticks in the manner of a beacon he watched the last operation. The rover, as if about to launch himself upon a track of a thousand miles, walked up to shake hands with him and look once more at the soft eyes and the ironic smile.

'There is no denying it – you are a man.'

'Don't talk like this to me, citoyen,' said the cripple in a trembling voice. Till then, suspended between his two sticks and with his shoulders as high as his ears, he had not looked towards the approaching Peyrol. 'This is too much of a compliment!'

'I tell you,' insisted the rover roughly, and as if the insignificance of mortal envelopes had presented itself to him for the first time at the end of his roving life, 'I tell you that there is that in you which would make a chum one would like to have alongside one in a tight place.'

As he went away from the cripple towards the tartane, while the whole population of the hamlet disposed around her waited for his word, some on land and some waist-deep in the water holding ropes in their hands, Peyrol had a slight shudder at the thought: 'Suppose I had been born like that.' Ever since he had put his foot on his native land such thoughts had haunted him. They would have been impossible anywhere else. He could not have been like any blackamoor, good, bad or indifferent, hale or crippled, king or slave; but here, on this Southern shore that had called to him irresistibly as he had approached the Straits of Gibraltar on what he had felt to be his last voyage, any woman, lean and old enough, might have been his mother; he might have been any Frenchman of them all, even one of those he pitied, even one of those he despised. He felt the grip of his origins from the crown of his head to the soles of his feet while he clambered on board the tartane as if for a long and distant voyage. As a matter of fact he knew very well that with a bit of luck it would be over in about an hour. When the tartane took the water the feeling of being afloat plucked at his very heart. Some

Madrague fishermen had been persuaded by the cripple to help old
Peyrol to sail the tartane round to the cove below the Escampobar
Farm. A glorious sun shone upon that short passage and the cove itself
was full of sparkling light when they arrived. The few Escampobar
goats wandering on the hillside pretending to feed where no grass was
visible to the naked eye never even raised their heads. A gentle breeze
drove the tartane, as fresh as paint could make her, opposite a narrow
crack in the cliff which gave admittance to a tiny basin, no bigger than a
village pond, concealed at the foot of the southern hill. It was there that
old Peyrol, aided by the Madrague men, who had their boat with them,
towed his ship, the first really that he ever owned.

Once in, the tartane nearly filled the little basin, and the fishermen,
getting into their boat, rowed away for home. Peyrol, by spending the
afternoon in dragging ropes ashore and fastening them to various
boulders and dwarf trees, moored her to his complete satisfaction. She
was as safe from the tempests there as a house ashore.

After he had made everything fast on board and had furled the sails
neatly, a matter of some time for one man, Peyrol contemplated his
arrangements which savoured of rest much more than of wandering,
and found them good. Though he never meant to abandon his room at
the farmhouse he felt that his true home was in the tartane, and he
rejoiced at the idea that it was concealed from all eyes except perhaps
the eyes of the goats when their arduous feeding took them on the
southern slope. He lingered on board, he even threw open the sliding
door of the little cabin, which now smelt of fresh paint, not of stale
blood. Before he started for the farm the sun had travelled far beyond
Spain and all the sky to the west was yellow, while on the side of Italy it
presented a sombre canopy pierced here and there with the light of
stars. Catherine put a plate on the table, but nobody asked him any
questions.

He spent a lot of his time on board, going down early, coming up at
midday 'pour manger la soupe', and sleeping on board almost every
night. He did not like to leave the tartane alone for so many hours.
Often, having climbed a little way up to the house, he would turn round
for a last look at her in the gathering dusk, and actually would go back
again. After Michel had been enlisted for a crew and had taken his
abode on board for good, Peyrol found it a much easier matter to spend
his nights in the lantern-like room at the top of the farmhouse.

Often waking up at night he would get up to look at the starry sky out
of all his three windows in succession, and think: 'Now there is nothing
in the world to prevent me getting out to sea in less than an hour.' As a

matter of fact it was possible for two men to manage the tartane. Thus Peyrol's thought was comfortingly true in every way, for he loved to feel himself free, and Michel of the lagoon, after the death of his depressed dog, had no tie on earth. It was a fine thought which somehow made it quite easy for Peyrol to go back to his four-poster and resume his slumbers.

Chapter 8

Perched sideways on the circular wall bordering the well, in the full blaze of the midday sun, the rover of the distant seas and the fisherman of the lagoon, sharing between them a most surprising secret, had the air of two men conferring in the dark. The first word that Peyrol said was, 'Well?'

'All quiet,' said the other.

'Have you fastened the cabin door properly?'

'You know what the fastenings are like.'

Peyrol could not deny that. It was a sufficient answer. It shifted the responsibility on to his shoulders and all his life he had been accustomed to trust to the work of his own hands, in peace and in war. Yet he looked doubtfully at Michel before he remarked: 'Yes, but I know the man too.'

There could be no greater contrast than those two faces: Peyrol's clean, like a carving of stone, and only very little softened by time, and that of the owner of the late dog, hirsute, with many silver threads, with something elusive in the features and the vagueness of expression of a baby in arms.

'Yes, I know the man,' repeated Peyrol.

Michel's mouth fell open at this, a small oval set a little crookedly in the innocent face. 'He will never wake,' he suggested timidly.

The possession of a common and momentous secret drawing the men together, Peyrol condescended to explain.

'You don't know the thickness of his skull. I do.'

He spoke as though he had made it himself. Michel, who in the face of that positive statement had forgotten to shut his mouth, had nothing to say.

'He breathes all right?' asked Peyrol.

'Yes. After I got out and locked the door I listened for a bit and I thought I heard him snore.'

Peyrol looked interested and also slightly anxious.

'I had to come up and show myself this morning as if nothing had happened,' he said. 'The officer has been here for two days and he might have taken it into his head to go down to the tartane. I have been on the stretch all the morning. A goat jumping up was enough to give me a turn. Fancy him running up here with his broken head all bandaged up, with you after him.'

This seemed to be too much for Michel. He said almost indignantly: 'The man's half killed.'

'It takes a lot to even half kill a Brother of the Coast. There are men and men. You, for instance,' Peyrol continued placidly, 'you would have been altogether killed if it had been your head that got in the way. And there are animals, beasts twice your size, regular monsters, that may be killed with nothing more than just a tap on the nose. That's well known. I was really afraid he would overcome you in some way or other . . . '

'Come, maître! One isn't a little child,' protested Michel against this accumulation of improbabilities. He did it, however, only in a whisper and with childlike shyness.

Peyrol folded his arms on his breast: 'Go, finish your soup,' he commanded in a low voice, 'and then go down to the tartane. You locked the cabin door properly, you said?'

'Yes, I have,' protested Michel, staggered by this display of anxiety. 'He could sooner burst the deck above his head, as you know.'

'All the same, take a small spar and shore up that door against the heel of the mast. And then watch outside. Don't you go in to him on any account. Stay on deck and keep a lookout for me. There is a tangle here that won't be easily cleared and I must be very careful. I will try to slip away and get down as soon as I get rid of that officer.'

The conference in the sunshine being ended, Peyrol walked leisurely out of the yard gate, and protruding his head beyond the corner of the house, saw Lieutenant Réal sitting on the bench. This he had expected to see. But he had not expected to see him there alone. It was just like this: wherever Arlette happened to be, there were worrying possibilities. But she might have been helping her aunt in the kitchen with her sleeves rolled up on such white arms as Peyrol had never seen on any woman before. The way she had taken to dressing her hair in a plait with a broad black velvet ribbon and an Arlesian[124] cap was very becoming. She was wearing now her mother's clothes of which there were chestfuls, altered for her of course. The late mistress of the Escampobar Farm had been an Arlesienne. Well-to-do, too. Yes, even for women's clothes the Escampobar natives could do without intercourse with the outer world. It was quite time that this confounded lieutenant went back to Toulon. This was the third day. His short leave must be up. Peyrol's attitude towards naval officers had been always guarded and suspicious. His relations with them had been very mixed. They had been his enemies and his superiors. He had been chased by them. He had been trusted by them. The Revolution had made a clean cut across the consistency of his wild life – Brother of the Coast and gunner in the national navy – and yet he was always the same man. It was like that, too, with them. Officers of the King, officers of the Republic, it was only changing the skin. All alike looked askance at a free rover. Even this one could not forget his epaulettes when talking to him. Scorn and mistrust of epaulettes were rooted deeply in old Peyrol. Yet he did not absolutely hate Lieutenant Réal. Only the fellow's coming to the farm was generally a curse and his presence at that particular moment a confounded nuisance and to a certain extent even a danger. 'I have no mind to be hauled to Toulon by the scruff of my neck,' Peyrol said to himself. There was no trusting those epaulette-wearers. Any one of them was capable of jumping on his best friend on account of some officer-like notion or other.

Peyrol, stepping round the corner, sat down by the side of Lieutenant Réal with the feeling somehow of coming to grips with a slippery customer. The lieutenant, as he sat there, unaware of Peyrol's survey of his person, gave no notion of slipperiness. On the contrary, he looked rather immovably established. Very much at home. Too much at home. Even after Peyrol sat down by his side he continued to look immovable – or at least difficult to get rid of. In the still noonday heat the faint shrilling of cicadas was the only sound of life heard for quite a long time. Delicate, evanescent, cheerful, careless sort of life, yet not without passion. A sudden gloom seemed to be cast over the joy of the cicadas by the lieutenant's voice, though the words were the most perfunctory possible.

'Tiens! Vous voilà.'[125]

In the stress of the situation Peyrol at once asked himself: 'Now why does he say that? Where did he expect me to be?' The lieutenant need not have spoken at all. He had known him now for about two years off and on, and it had happened many times that they had sat side by side on that bench in a sort of 'at arm's length' equality without exchanging a single word. And why could he not have kept quiet now? That naval officer never spoke without an object, but what could one make of words like that?

Peyrol achieved an insincere yawn and suggested mildly: 'A bit of siesta wouldn't be amiss. What do you think, lieutenant?'

And to himself he thought: 'No fear, he won't go to his room.' He would stay there and thereby keep him, Peyrol, from going down to the cove. He turned his eyes on that naval officer, and if extreme and concentrated desire and mere force of will could have had any effect Lieutenant Réal would certainly have been removed suddenly from that bench. But he didn't move. And Peyrol was astonished to see that man smile, but what astonished him still more was to hear him say: 'The trouble is that you have never been frank with me, Peyrol.'

'Frank with you,' repeated the rover. 'You want me to be frank with you? Well, I have wished you to the devil many times.'

'That's better,' said Lieutenant Réal. 'But why? I never tried to do you any harm.'

'Me harm,' cried Peyrol, 'harm to me?' But he faltered in his indignation as if frightened at it and ended in a very quiet tone: 'You have been nosing in a lot of dirty papers to find something against a man who was not doing *you* any harm and was a seaman before you were born.'

'Quite a mistake. There was no nosing amongst papers. I came on them quite by accident. I won't deny I was *intrigué* finding a man of your sort living in this place. But don't be uneasy. Nobody would trouble his head about you. It's a long time since you have been forgotten. Have no fear.'

'You! You talk to me of fear . . . ? No,' cried the rover, 'it's enough to turn a fellow into a sans-culotte if it weren't for the sight of that specimen sneaking around here.'

The lieutenant turned his head sharply, and for a moment the naval officer and the free sea-rover looked at each other gloomily. When Peyrol spoke again he had changed his mood.

'Why should I fear anybody? I owe nothing to anybody. I have given them up the prize ship in order and everything else, except my luck; and for that I account to nobody,' he added darkly.

'I don't know what you are driving at,' the lieutenant said after a moment of thought. 'All I know is that you seem to have given up your share of the prize money. There is no record of you ever claiming it.'

Peyrol did not like the sarcastic tone. 'You have a nasty tongue,' he said, 'with your damned trick of talking as if you were made of different clay.'

'No offence,' said the lieutenant, grave but a little puzzled. 'Nobody will drag out that against you. It has been paid years ago to the Invalides' fund. All this is buried and forgotten.'

Peyrol was grumbling and swearing to himself with such concentration that the lieutenant stopped and waited till he had finished.

'And there is no record of desertion or anything like that,' he continued then. 'You stand there as *disparu*.[126] I believe that after searching for you a little they came to the conclusion that you had come by your death somehow or other.'

'Did they? Well, perhaps old Peyrol is dead. At any rate he has buried himself here.' The rover suffered from great instability of feelings for he passed in a flash from melancholy into fierceness. 'And he was quiet enough till you came sniffing around this hole. More than once in my life I had occasion to wonder how soon the jackals would have a chance to dig up my carcass; but to have a naval officer come scratching round here was the last thing . . . ' Again a change came over him. 'What can you want here?' he whispered, suddenly depressed.

The lieutenant fell into the humour of that discourse. 'I don't want to disturb the dead,' he said, turning full to the rover who after his last words had fixed his eyes on the ground. 'I want to talk to the gunner Peyrol.'

Peyrol, without raising his eyes from the ground, growled: 'He isn't here. He is *disparu*. Go and look at the papers again. Vanished. Nobody here.'

'That,' said Lieutenant Réal, in a conversational tone, 'that is a lie. He was talking to me this morning on the hillside as we were looking at the English ship. He knows all about her. He told me he spent nights making plans for her capture. He seemed to be a fellow with his heart in the right place. *Un homme de coeur*. You know him.'

Peyrol raised his big head slowly and looked at the lieutenant.

'Humph,' he grunted. A heavy, non-committal grunt. His old heart was stirred, but the tangle was such that he had to be on his guard with any man who wore epaulettes. His profile preserved the immobility of a head struck on a medal while he listened to the lieutenant assuring him that this time he had come to Escampobar on purpose to speak with the gunner Peyrol. That he had not done so before was because it was a very confidential matter. At this point the lieutenant stopped and Peyrol made no sign. Inwardly he was asking himself what the lieutenant was driving at. But the lieutenant seemed to have shifted his ground. His tone, too, was slightly different. More practical.

'You say you have made a study of that English ship's movements. Well, for instance, suppose a breeze springs up, as it very likely will towards the evening, could you tell me where she will be tonight? I mean, what her captain is likely to do.'

'No, I couldn't,' said Peyrol.

'But you said you have been observing him minutely for weeks. There aren't so many alternatives, and taking the weather and everything into consideration, you can judge almost with certainty.'

'No,' said Peyrol again. 'It so happens that I can't.'

'Can't you? Then you are worse than any of the old admirals that you think so little of. Why can't you?'

'I will tell you why,' said Peyrol after a pause and with a face more like a carving than ever. 'It's because the fellow has never come so far this way before. Therefore I don't know what he has got in his mind, and in consequence I can't guess what he will do next. I may be able to tell you some other day but not today. Next time when you come . . . to see the old gunner.'

'No, it must be this time.'

'Do you mean you are going to stay here tonight?'

'Did you think I was here on leave? I tell you I am on service. Don't you believe me?'

Peyrol let out a heavy sigh. 'Yes, I believe you. And so they are thinking of catching her alive. And you are sent on service. Well, that doesn't make it any easier for me to see you here.'

'You are a strange man, Peyrol,' said the lieutenant. 'I believe you wish me dead.'

'No. Only out of this. But you are right, Peyrol is no friend either to your face or to your voice. They have done harm enough already.'

They had never attained to such intimate terms before. There was no need for them to look at each other. The lieutenant thought: 'Ah! He can't keep his jealousy in.' There was no scorn or malice in that thought. It was much more like despair. He said mildly: 'You snarl like an old dog, Peyrol.'

'I have felt sometimes as if I could fly at your throat,' said Peyrol in a sort of calm whisper. 'And it amuses you the more.'

'Amuses me? Do I look light-hearted?'

Again Peyrol turned his head slowly for a long, steady stare. And again the naval officer and the rover gazed at each other with a searching and sombre frankness. This new-born intimacy could go no further.

'Listen to me, Peyrol . . . '

'No,' said the other. 'If you want to talk, talk to the gunner.'

Though he seemed to have adopted the notion of a double personality the rover did not seem to be much easier in one character than in the other. Furrows of perplexity appeared on his brow, and as the lieutenant did not speak at once, Peyrol the gunner asked impatiently: 'So they are thinking of catching her alive?'

It did not please him to hear the lieutenant say that it was not exactly this that the chiefs in Toulon had in their minds. Peyrol at once expressed the opinion that of all the naval chiefs that ever were, Citizen Renaud was the only one that was worth anything. Lieutenant Réal, disregarding the challenging tone, kept to the point.

'What they want to know is whether that English corvette interferes much with the coast traffic.'

'No, she doesn't,' said Peyrol: 'she leaves poor people alone, unless, I suppose, some craft acts suspiciously. I have seen her give chase to one or two. But even those she did not detain. Michel – you know Michel – has heard from the mainland people that she has captured several at various times. Of course, strictly speaking, nobody is safe.'

'Well, no. I wonder now what that Englishman would call "acting suspiciously".'

'Ah, now you are asking something. Don't you know what an Englishman is? One day easy and casual, next day ready to pounce on you like a tiger. Hard in the morning, careless in the afternoon, and only reliable in a fight, whether with or against you, but for the rest perfectly fantastic. You might think a little touched in the head, and there again it would not do to trust to that notion either.'

The lieutenant lending an attentive ear, Peyrol smoothed his brow and discoursed with gusto on Englishmen as if they had been a strange, very little-known tribe. 'In a manner of speaking,' he concluded, 'the oldest bird of them all can be caught with chaff, but not every day.' He shook his head, smiling to himself faintly as if remembering a quaint passage or two.

'You didn't get all that knowledge of the English while you were a gunner,' observed the lieutenant dryly.

'There you go again,' said Peyrol. 'And what's it to you where I learned it all? Suppose I learned it all from a man who is dead now. Put it down to that.'

'I see. It amounts to this, that one can't get at the back of their minds very easily.'

'No,' said Peyrol, then added grumpily, 'and some Frenchmen are not much better. I wish I could get at the back of your mind.'

'You would find a service matter there, gunner, that's what you would find there, and a matter that seems nothing much at first sight, but when you look into it, is about as difficult to manage properly as anything you ever undertook in your life. It puzzled all the big-wigs. It must have, since I was called in. Of course I work on shore at the Admiralty and I was in the way. They showed me the order from Paris and I could see at once the difficulty of it. I pointed it out and I was told . . . '

'To come here,' struck in Peyrol.

'No. To make arrangements to carry it out.'

'And you began by coming here. You are always coming here.'

'I began by looking for a man,' said the naval officer with emphasis.

Peyrol looked at him searchingly. 'Do you mean to say that in the whole fleet you couldn't have found a man?'

'I never attempted to look for one there. My chief agreed with me that it isn't a service for navy men.'

'Well, it must be something nasty for a naval man to admit that much. What is the order? I don't suppose you came over here without being ready to show it to me.'

The lieutenant plunged his hand into the inside pocket of his naval jacket and then brought it out empty.

'Understand, Peyrol,' he said earnestly, 'this is not a service of fighting. Good men are plentiful for that. The object is to play the enemy a trick.'

'Trick?' said Peyrol in a judicial tone, 'that's all right. I have seen in the Indian seas Monsieur Surcouf[127] play tricks on the English . . . seen them with my own eyes, deceptions, disguises and suchlike . . . That's quite sound in war.'

'Certainly. The order for this one comes from the First Consul himself, for it is no small matter. It's to deceive the English Admiral.'

'What – that Nelson? Ah! but he is a cunning one.'

After expressing that opinion the old rover pulled out a red bandana handkerchief and after rubbing his face with it repeated his opinion deliberately: 'Celui-là est un malin.'

This time the lieutenant really brought out a paper from his pocket and saying, 'I have copied the order for you to see,' handed it to the rover, who took it from him with a doubtful air.

Lieutenant Réal watched old Peyrol handling it at arm's length, then with his arm bent trying to adjust the distance to his eyesight, and wondered whether he had copied it in a hand big enough to be read easily by the gunner Peyrol. The order ran like this:

> You will make up a packet of dispatches and pretended private letters, as if from officers, containing a clear statement besides hints calculated to convince the enemy that the destination of the fleet now fitting in Toulon is for Egypt and generally for the East. That packet you will send by sea in some small craft to Naples, taking care that the vessel shall fall into the enemy's hands.

The Préfet Maritime[128] had called Réal, had shown him the paragraph of the letter from Paris, had turned the page over and laid his finger on the signature, 'Bonaparte'. Then after giving him a meaning glance, the admiral locked up the paper in a drawer and put the key in his pocket. Lieutenant Réal had written the passage down from memory directly the notion of consulting Peyrol had occurred to him.

The rover, screwing his eyes and pursing his lips, had come to the end of it. The lieutenant extended his hand negligently and took the paper away: 'Well, what do you think?' he asked. 'You understand that there can be no question of any ship of war being sacrificed to that dodge. What do you think of it?'

'Easier said than done,' opined Peyrol curtly.

'That's what I told my admiral.'

'Is he a lubber, so that you had to explain it to him?'

'No, gunner, he is not. He listened to me, nodding his head.'

'And what did he say when you finished?'

'He said: "Parfaitement. Have you got any ideas about it?" And I said – listen to me, gunner – I said: "Oui, Amiral, I think I've got a man," and the admiral interrupted me at once: "All right, you don't want to talk to me about him. I put you in charge of that affair and give you a week to arrange it. When it's done, report to me. Meantime you may just as well take this packet." They were already prepared, Peyrol, all those faked letters and dispatches. I carried it out of the admiral's room, a parcel done up in sailcloth, properly corded and sealed. I have had it in my possession for three days. It's upstairs in my valise.'

'That doesn't advance you very much,' growled old Peyrol.

'No,' admitted the lieutenant. 'I can also dispose of a few thousand francs.'

'Francs,' repeated Peyrol. 'Well, you had better get back to Toulon and try to bribe some man to put his head into the jaws of the English lion.'

Réal reflected, then said slowly, 'I wouldn't tell any man that. Of course a service of danger, that would be understood.'

'It would be. And if you could get a fellow with some sense in his caboche, he would naturally try to slip past the English fleet and maybe do it, too. And then where's your trick?'

'We could give him a course to steer.'

'Yes. And it may happen that your course would just take him clear of all Nelson's fleet, for you never can tell what the English are doing. They might be watering in Sardinia.'

'Some cruisers are sure to be out and pick him up.'

'Maybe. But that's not doing the job, that's taking a chance. Do you think you are talking to a toothless baby – or what?'

'No, my gunner. It will take a strong man's teeth to undo that knot.' A moment of silence followed. Then Peyrol assumed a dogmatic tone.

'I will tell you what it is, lieutenant. This seems to me just the sort of order that a landlubber would give to good seamen. You daren't deny that.'

'I don't deny it,' the lieutenant admitted. 'And look at the whole difficulty. For supposing even that the tartane blunders right into the English fleet, as if it had been indeed arranged, they would just look into her hold or perhaps poke their noses here and there but it would never occur to them to search for dispatches, would it? Our man, of course, would have them well hidden, wouldn't he? He is not to know. And if he were ass enough to leave them lying about the decks the English would at once smell a rat there. But what I think he would do would be to throw the dispatches overboard.'

'Yes – unless he is told the nature of the job,' said Peyrol.

'Evidently. But where's the bribe big enough to induce a man to taste of the English pontoons?'

'The man will take the bribe all right and then will do his best not to be caught; and if he can't avoid that, he will take jolly good care that the English should find nothing on board his tartane. Oh no, lieutenant, any damn scallywag that owns a tartane will take a couple of thousand francs from your hand as tame as can be; but as to deceiving the English Admiral, it's the very devil of an affair. Didn't you think of all that before you spoke to the big epaulettes that gave you the job?'

'I did see it, and I put it all before him,' the lieutenant said, lowering his voice still more, for their conversation had been carried on in undertones though the house behind them was silent and solitude reigned round the approaches of Escampobar Farm. It was the hour of siesta – for those that could sleep. The lieutenant, edging closer towards the old man, almost breathed the words in his ear.

'What I wanted was to hear you say all those things. Do you understand now what I meant this morning on the lookout? Don't you remember what I said?'

Peyrol, gazing into space, spoke in a level murmur.

'I remember a naval officer trying to shake old Peyrol off his feet and not managing to do it. I may be *disparu* but I am too solid yet for any blancbec[129] that loses his temper, devil only knows why. And it's a good thing that you didn't manage it, else I would have taken you down with me, and we would have made our last somersault together for the amusement of an English ship's company. A pretty end that!'

'Don't you remember me saying, when you mentioned that the English would have sent a boat to go through our pockets, that this would have been the perfect way?' In his stony immobility with the other man leaning towards his ear, Peyrol seemed a mere insensible receptacle for whispers, and the lieutenant went on forcibly: 'Well, it was in allusion to this affair, for, look here, gunner, what could be more convincing, if they had found the packet of dispatches on me! What would have been their surprise, their wonder! Not the slightest doubt could enter their heads. Could it, gunner? Of course it couldn't. I can imagine the captain of that corvette crowding sail on her to get this packet into the Admiral's hands. The secret of the Toulon fleet's destination found on the body of a dead officer. Wouldn't they have exulted at their enormous piece of luck! But they wouldn't have called it accidental. Oh, no! They would have called it providential. I know the English a little too. They like to have God on their side – the only ally they never need pay a subsidy to. Come, gunner, would it not have been a perfect way?'

Lieutenant Réal threw himself back and Peyrol, still like a carven image of grim dreaminess, growled softly: 'Time yet. The English ship is still in the Passe.' He waited a little in his uncanny living-statue manner before he added viciously: 'You don't seem in a hurry to go and take that leap.'

'Upon my word, I am almost sick enough of life to do it,' the lieutenant said in a conversational tone.

'Well, don't forget to run upstairs and take that packet with you before you go,' said Peyrol as before. 'But don't wait for me; I am not sick of life. I am *disparu*, and that's good enough. There's no need for me to die.'

And at last he moved in his seat, swung his head from side to side as if to make sure that his neck had not been turned to stone, emitted a short laugh, and grumbled: '*Disparu*! Hein![130] Well, I am damned!' as if the word 'vanished' had been a gross insult to enter against a man's name in a register. It seemed to rankle, as Lieutenant Réal observed with some surprise; or else it was something inarticulate that rankled, manifesting itself in that funny way. The lieutenant, too, had a moment of anger which flamed and went out at once in the deadly cold philosophic reflection: 'We are victims of the destiny which has brought us together.' Then again his resentment flamed. Why should he have stumbled against that girl or that woman, he didn't know how he must think of her, and suffer so horribly for it? He who had endeavoured almost from a boy to destroy all the softer feelings within himself. His changing moods of distaste, of wonder at himself and at the unexpected turns of life, wore the aspect of profound abstraction from which he was recalled by an outburst of Peyrol's, not loud but fierce enough.

'No,' cried Peyrol, 'I am too old to break my bones for the sake of a lubberly soldier in Paris who fancies he has invented something clever.'

'I don't ask you to,' the lieutenant said, with extreme severity, in what

Peyrol would call an epaulette-wearer's voice. 'You old sea-bandit. And it wouldn't be for the sake of a soldier anyhow. You and I are Frenchmen after all.'

'You have discovered that, have you?'

'Yes,' said Réal. 'This morning, listening to your talk on the hillside with that English corvette within one might say a stone's throw.'

'Yes,' groaned Peyrol. 'A French-built ship!' He struck his breast a resounding blow. 'It hurts one there to see her. It seemed to me I could jump down on her deck single-handed.'

'Yes, there you and I understood each other,' said the lieutenant. 'But look here, this affair is a much bigger thing than getting back a captured corvette. In reality it is much more than merely playing a trick on an admiral. It's a part of a deep plan, Peyrol! It's another stroke to help us on the way towards a great victory at sea.'

'Us!' said Peyrol. 'I am a sea-bandit and you are a sea-officer. What do you mean by us?'

'I mean all Frenchmen,' said the lieutenant. 'Or, let us say simply France, which you too have served.'

Peyrol, whose stone-effigy bearing had become humanised almost against his will, gave an appreciative nod, and said: 'You've got something in your mind. Now what is it? If you will trust a sea-bandit.'

'No, I will trust a gunner of the Republic. It occurred to me that for this great affair we could make use of this corvette that you have been observing so long. For to count on the capture of any old tartane by the fleet in a way that would not arouse suspicion is no use.'

'A lubberly notion,' assented Peyrol, with more heartiness than he had ever displayed towards Lieutenant Réal.

'Yes, but there's that corvette. Couldn't something be arranged to make them swallow the whole thing, somehow, some way? You laugh . . . Why?'

'I laugh because it would be a great joke,' said Peyrol, whose hilarity was very short-lived. 'That fellow on board, he thinks himself very clever. I never set my eyes on him, but I used to feel that I knew him as if he were my own brother; but now . . . ' He stopped short.

Lieutenant Réal, after observing the sudden change on his countenance, said in an impressive manner: 'I think you have just had an idea.'

'Not the slightest,' said Peyrol, turning suddenly into stone as if by enchantment. The lieutenant did not feel discouraged and he was not surprised to hear the effigy of Peyrol pronounce: 'All the same one could see.' Then very abruptly: 'You meant to stay here tonight?'

'Yes. I will only go down to Madrague and leave word with the sailing barge which was to come today from Toulon to go back without me.'

'No, lieutenant. You must return to Toulon today. When you get there you must turn out some of those damned quill-drivers at the Port Office if it were midnight and have papers made out for a tartane – oh, any name you like. Some sort of papers. And then you must come back as soon as you can. Why not go down to Madrague now and see whether the barge isn't already there? If she is, then by starting at once you may get back here some time about midnight.'

He got up impetuously and the lieutenant stood up too. Hesitation was imprinted on his whole attitude. Peyrol's aspect was not animated, but his Roman face with its severe aspect gave him a great air of authority.

'Won't you tell me something more?' asked the lieutenant.

'No,' said the rover. 'Not till we meet again. If you return during the night don't you try to get into the house. Wait outside. Don't rouse anybody. I will be about, and if there is anything to say I will say it to you then. What are you looking about you for? You don't want to go up for your valise. Your pistols up in your room too? What do you want with pistols, only to go to Toulon and back with a naval boat's crew?' He actually laid his hand on the lieutenant's shoulder and impelled him gently towards the track leading to Madrague. Réal turned his head at the touch and their eyes met with the strained closeness of a wrestler's hug. It was the lieutenant who gave way before the unflinchingly direct stare of the old Brother of the Coast. He gave way under the cover of a sarcastic smile and a very airy, 'I see you want me out of the way for some reason or other,' which produced not the slightest effect upon Peyrol, who stood with his arm pointing towards Madrague. When the lieutenant turned his back on him Peyrol's pointing arm fell down by his side; but he watched the lieutenant out of sight before he turned too and moved in a contrary direction.

Chapter 9

On losing sight of the perplexed lieutenant, Peyrol discovered that his own mind was a perfect blank. He started to get down to his tartane after one sidelong look at the face of the house which contained quite a different problem. Let that wait. His head feeling strangely empty, he felt the pressing necessity of furnishing it with some thought without loss of time. He scrambled down steep places, caught at bushes, stepped from stone to stone, with the assurance of long practice, with mechanical precision and without for a moment relaxing his efforts to capture some definite scheme which he could put into his head. To his right the cove lay full of pale light, while the rest of the Mediterranean extended beyond it in a dark, unruffled blue. Peyrol was making for the little basin where his tartane had been hidden for years, like a jewel in a casket meant only for the secret rejoicing of his eye, of no more practical use than a miser's hoard – and as precious! Coming upon a hollow in the ground where grew a few bushes and even a few blades of grass, Peyrol sat down to rest. In that position his visible world was limited to a stony slope, a few boulders, the bush against which he leaned and the vista of a piece of empty sea-horizon. He perceived that he detested that lieutenant much more when he didn't see him. There was something in the fellow. Well, at any rate he had got rid of him for say eight or ten hours. An uneasiness came over the old rover, a sense of the endangered stability of things, which was anything but welcome. He wondered at it, and the thought 'I am growing old' intruded on him again. And yet he was aware of his sturdy body. He could still creep stealthily like an Indian and with his trusty cudgel knock a man over with a certain aim at the back of his head, and with force enough to fell him like a bullock. He had done that thing no further back than two o'clock the night before, not twelve hours ago, as easy as easy and without an undue sense of exertion. This fact cheered him up. But still he could not find an idea for his head. Not what one could call a real idea. It wouldn't come. It was no use sitting there.

He got up and after a few strides came to a stony ridge from which he could see the two white blunt mastheads of his tartane. Her hull was hidden from him by the formation of the shore, in which the most prominent feature was a big flat piece of rock. That was the spot on which not twelve hours before Peyrol, unable to rest in his bed and coming to seek sleep in his tartane, had seen by moonlight a man standing above his vessel and looking down at her, a characteristic forked black shape that certainly had no business to be there. Peyrol, by a sudden and logical deduction, had said to himself, 'Landed from an English boat.' Why, how, wherefore, he did not stay to consider. He acted at once like a man accustomed for many years to meet emergencies of the most unexpected kind. The dark figure, lost in a sort of attentive amazement, heard nothing, suspected nothing. The impact of the thick end of the cudgel came down on its head like a thunderbolt from the blue. The sides of the little basin echoed the crash. But he could not have heard it. The force of the blow flung the senseless body over the edge of the flat rock and down headlong into the open hold of the tartane, which received it with the sound of a muffled drum. Peyrol could not have done the job better at the age of twenty. No. Not so well. There was swiftness, mature judgement – and the sound of the muffled drum was followed by a perfect silence, without a sigh, without a moan. Peyrol ran round a little promontory to where the shore shelved down to the level of the tartane's rail and got on board. And still the silence remained perfect in the cold moonlight and amongst the deep shadows of the rocks. It remained perfect because Michel, who always slept under the half-deck forward, being wakened by the thump which had made the whole tartane tremble, had lost the power of speech. With his head just protruding from under the half-deck, arrested on all fours and shivering violently like a dog that had been washed with hot water, he was kept from advancing farther by his terror of this bewitched corpse that had come on board flying through the air. He would not have touched it for anything.

The, 'You there, Michel,' pronounced in an undertone, acted like a moral tonic. This then was not the doing of the Evil One; it was no sorcery! And even if it had been, now that Peyrol was there, Michel had lost all fear. He ventured not a single question while he helped Peyrol to turn over the limp body. Its face was covered with blood from the cut on the forehead which it had got by striking the sharp edge of the keelson. What accounted for the head not being completely smashed and for no limbs being broken was the fact that on its way through the air the victim of undue curiosity had come in contact with and had snapped like a carrot one of the foremast shrouds. Raising his eyes casually Peyrol noticed the broken rope, and at once put his hand on the man's breast.

'His heart beats yet,' he murmured. 'Go and light the cabin lamp, Michel.'

'You going to take that thing into the cabin?'

'Yes,' said Peyrol. 'The cabin is used to that kind of thing,' and suddenly he felt very bitter. 'It has been a deathtrap for better people than this fellow, whoever he is.'

While Michel was away executing that order Peyrol's eyes roamed all over the shores of the basin, for he could not divest himself of the idea that there must be more Englishmen dodging about. That one of the corvette's boats was still in the cove he had not the slightest doubt. As to the motive of her coming, it was incomprehensible. Only that senseless form lying at his feet could perhaps have told him: but Peyrol had little hope that it would ever speak again. If his friends started to look for their shipmate there was just a bare chance that they would not discover the existence of the basin. Peyrol stooped and felt the body all over. He found no weapon of any kind on it. There was only a common clasp-knife on a lanyard round its neck.

That soul of obedience, Michel, returning from aft, was directed to throw a couple of bucketfuls of salt water upon the bloody head with its face upturned to the moon. The lowering of the body down into the cabin was a matter of some little difficulty. It was heavy. They laid it full length on a locker and after Michel with a strange tidiness had arranged its arms along its sides it looked incredibly rigid. The dripping head with soaked hair was like the head of a drowned man with a gaping pink gash on the forehead.

'Go on deck to keep a lookout,' said Peyrol. 'We may have to fight yet before the night's out.'

After Michel left him Peyrol began by flinging off his jacket and, without a pause, dragging his shirt off over his head. It was a very fine shirt. The Brothers of the Coast in their hours of ease were by no means a ragged crowd, and Peyrol the gunner had preserved a taste for fine linen. He tore the shirt into long strips, sat down on the locker and took the wet head on his knees. He bandaged it with some skill, working as calmly as though he had been practising on a dummy. Then the experienced Peyrol sought the lifeless hand and felt the pulse. The spirit had not fled yet. The rover, stripped to the waist, his powerful arms folded on the grizzled pelt of his bare breast, sat gazing down at the inert face in his lap with the eyes closed peacefully under the white band covering the forehead. He contemplated the heavy jaw combined oddly with a certain roundness of cheek, the noticeably broad nose with a sharp tip and a faint dent across the bridge, either natural or the result of some old injury. A face of brown clay, roughly modelled, with a lot of black eyelashes stuck on the closed lids and looking artificially youthful on that physiognomy forty years old or more. And Peyrol thought of his youth. Not his own youth; that he was never anxious to recapture. It was of that man's youth that he thought, of how that face had looked twenty years ago.

Suddenly he shifted his position, and putting his lips to the ear of that inanimate head, yelled with all the force of his lungs: 'Hello! Hello! Wake up, shipmate!'

It seemed enough to wake up the dead. A faint, 'Voilà! Voilà!' was the answer from a distance, and presently Michel put his head into the cabin with an anxious grin and a gleam in the round eyes.

'You called, maître?'

'Yes,' said Peyrol. 'Come along and help me to shift him.'

'Overboard?' murmured Michel readily.

'No,' said Peyrol, 'into that bunk. Steady! Don't bang his head,' he cried with unexpected tenderness. 'Throw a blanket over him. Stay in the cabin and keep his bandages wetted with salt water. I don't think anybody will trouble you tonight. I am going to the house.'

'The day is not very far off,' remarked Michel.

This was one reason the more why Peyrol was in a hurry to get back to the house and steal up to his room unseen. He drew on his jacket over his bare skin, picked up his cudgel, recommended Michel not to let that strange bird get out of the cabin on any account. As Michel was convinced that the man would never walk again in his life, he received those instructions without particular emotion.

The dawn had broken some time before Peyrol, on his way up to Escampobar, happened to look round and had the luck actually to see with his own eyes the English man-of-war's boat pulling out of the cove. This confirmed his surmises but did not enlighten him a bit as to the causes. Puzzled and uneasy, he approached the house through the farmyard – Catherine, always the first up, stood at the open kitchen door. She moved aside and would have let him pass without remark, if Peyrol himself had not asked in a whisper: 'Anything new?' She answered him in the same tone: 'She has taken to roaming at night.' Peyrol stole silently up to his bedroom, from which he descended an hour later as though he had spent all the night in his bed up there.

It was this nocturnal adventure which had affected the character of Peyrol's forenoon talk with the lieutenant. What with one thing and another he found it very trying. Now that he had got rid of Réal for several hours, the rover had to turn his attention to that other invader of the strained, questionable, and ominous in its origins, peace of the Escampobar Farm. As he sat on the flat rock with his eyes fixed idly on the few drops of blood betraying his last night's work to the high heaven, and trying to get hold of something definite that he could think about, Peyrol became aware of a faint thundering noise. Faint as it was it filled the whole basin. He soon guessed its nature, and his face lost its perplexity. He picked up his cudgel, got on his feet briskly, muttering to himself, 'He's anything but dead,' and hurried on board the tartane.

On the after-deck Michel was keeping a lookout. He had carried out the orders he had received by the well. Besides being secured by the very obvious padlock, the cabin door was shored up by a spar which made it stand as firm as a rock. The thundering noise seemed to issue from its immovable substance magically. It ceased for a moment, and a sort of distracted continuous growling could be heard. Then the thundering began again.

Michel reported: 'This is the third time he starts this game.'

'Not much strength in this,' remarked Peyrol gravely.

'That he can do it at all is a miracle,' said Michel, showing a certain excitement. 'He stands on the ladder and beats the door with his fists. He is getting better. He began about half an hour after I got back on board. He drummed for a bit and then fell off the ladder. I heard him. I had my ear against the scuttle. He lay there and talked to himself for a long time. Then he went at it again.' Peyrol approached the scuttle while Michel added his opinion: 'He will go on like that for ever. You can't stop him.'

'Easy there,' said Peyrol in a deep authoritative voice. 'Time you finish that noise.'

These words brought instantly a deathlike silence. Michel ceased to grin. He wondered at the power of these few words of a foreign language.

Peyrol himself smiled faintly. It was ages since he had uttered a sentence of English. He waited complacently until Michel had unbarred and unlocked the door of the cabin. After it was thrown open he boomed out a warning: 'Stand clear!' and, turning about, went down with great deliberation, ordering Michel to go forward and keep a lookout.

Down there the man with the bandaged head was hanging on to the table and swearing feebly without intermission. Peyrol, after listening for a time with an air of interested recognition as one would to a tune heard many years ago, stopped it by a deep-voiced: 'That will do.' After a short silence he added: 'You look bien malade, hein? What you call sick,' in a tone which if not tender was certainly not hostile. 'We will remedy that.'

'Who are you?' asked the prisoner, looking frightened and throwing his arm up quickly to guard his head against the coming blow. But Peyrol's uplifted hand fell only on his shoulder in a hearty slap which made him sit down suddenly on a locker in a partly collapsed attitude and unable to speak. But though very much dazed he was able to watch Peyrol open a cupboard and produce from there a small demijohn[131] and two tin cups. He took heart to say plaintively: 'My throat's like tinder,' and then suspiciously: 'Was it you who broke my head?'

'It was me,' admitted Peyrol, sitting down on the opposite side of the table and leaning back to look at his prisoner comfortably.

'What the devil did you do that for?' enquired the other with a sort of faint fierceness which left Peyrol unmoved.

'Because you put your nose where you no business.[132] Understand? I see you there under the moon, penché,[133] eating my tartane with your eyes. You never hear me, hein?'

'I believe you walked on air. Did you mean to kill me?'

'Yes, in preference to letting you go and make a story of it on board your cursed corvette.'

'Well then, now's your chance to finish me. I am as weak as a kitten.'

'How did you say that? Kitten? Ha, ha, ha!' laughed Peyrol. 'You make a nice petit chat.' He seized the demijohn by the neck and filled the mugs. 'There,' he went on, pushing one towards the prisoner – 'it's good drink – that.'

Symons' state was as though the blow had robbed him of all power of resistance, of all faculty of surprise and generally of all the means by which a man may assert himself, except bitter resentment. His head was aching, it seemed to him enormous, too heavy for his neck and as if full of hot smoke. He took a drink under Peyrol's fixed gaze and with uncertain movements put down the mug. He looked drowsy for a moment. Presently a little colour deepened his bronze; he hitched himself up on the locker and said in a strong voice: 'You played a damned dirty trick on me. Call yourself a man, walking on air behind a fellow's back and felling him like a bullock?'

Peyrol nodded calmly and sipped from his mug.

'If I had met you anywhere else but looking at my tartane I would have done nothing to you. I would have permitted you to go back to your boat. Where was your damned boat?'

'How can I tell you? I can't tell where I am. I've never been here before. How long have I been here?'

'Oh, about fourteen hours,' said Peyrol.

'My head feels as if it would fall off if I moved,' grumbled the other . . . 'You are a damned bungler, that's what you are.'

'What for – bungler?'

'For not finishing me off at once.'

He seized the mug and emptied it down his throat. Peyrol drank too, observing him all the time. He put the mug down with extreme gentleness and said slowly: 'How could I know it was you? I hit hard enough to crack the skull of any other man.'

'What do you mean? What do you know about my skull? What are you driving at? I don't know you, you white-headed villain, going about at night knocking people on the head from behind. Did you do for our officer, too?'

'Oh yes! Your officer. What was he up to? What trouble did you people come to make here, anyhow?'

'Do you think they tell a boat's crew? Go and ask our officer. He went up the gully and our coxswain got the jumps. He says to me: 'You are light-footed, Sam, says he; 'you just creep round the head of the cove and see if our boat can be seen across from the other side. Well, I couldn't see anything. That was all right. But I thought I would climb a little higher amongst the rocks . . . '

He paused drowsily.

'That was a silly thing to do,' remarked Peyrol in an encouraging voice.

'I would've sooner expected to see an elephant inland than a craft lying in a pool that seemed no bigger than my hand. Could not understand how she got there. Couldn't help going down to find out – and the next thing I knew I was lying on my back with my head tied up, in a bunk in this kennel of a cabin here. Why couldn't you have given me a hail and engaged me properly, yardarm to yardarm? You would have got me all the same, because all I had in the way of weapons was the clasp-knife which you have looted off me.'

'Up on the shelf there,' said Peyrol, looking round. 'No, my friend, I wasn't going to take the risk of seeing you spread your wings and fly.'

'You need not have been afraid for your tartane. Our boat was after no tartane. We wouldn't have taken your tartane for a gift. Why, we see them by dozens every day – those tartanes.'

Peyrol filled the two mugs again. 'Ah,' he said, 'I dare say you see many tartanes, but this one is not like the others. You a sailor – and you couldn't see that she was something extraordinary.'

'Hellfire and gunpowder!' cried the other. 'How can you expect me to have seen anything? I just noticed that her sails were bent before your club hit me on the head.' He raised his hands to his head and groaned. 'Oh Lord, I feel as though I had been drunk for a month.'

Peyrol's prisoner did look somewhat as though he had got his head broken in a drunken brawl. But to Peyrol his appearance was not repulsive. The rover preserved a tender memory of his freebooter's life, with its lawless spirit and its spacious scene of action, before the change in the state of affairs in the Indian Ocean, the astounding rumours from the outer world, made him reflect on its precarious character. It was true that he had deserted the French flag when quite a youngster; but at that time that flag was white; and now it was a flag of three colours. He had known the practice of liberty, equality and fraternity as understood in the haunts open or secret of the Brotherhood of the Coast. So the change, if one could believe what people talked about, could not be very great. The rover had also his own positive notions as to what these three words were worth. Liberty – to hold your own in the world if you could. Equality – yes! But no body of men ever accomplished anything without a chief. All this was worth what it was worth. He regarded fraternity somewhat differently. Of course brothers would quarrel amongst themselves; it was during a fierce quarrel that flamed up suddenly in a company of Brothers that he had received the most dangerous wound of his life. But for that Peyrol nursed no grudge against anybody. In his view the claim of the Brotherhood was a claim for help against the outside world. And here he was sitting opposite a Brother whose head he had broken on sufficient grounds. There he was across the table looking dishevelled and dazed, uncomprehending and aggrieved, and that head of his proved as hard as ages ago when the nickname of Testa Dura[134] had been given to him by a Brother of Italian origin on some occasion or other, some butting match no doubt; just as he, Peyrol himself, was known for a time on both sides of the Mozambique Channel as Poigne-de-Fer,[135] after an incident when in the presence of the Brothers he played at arm's length with the windpipe of an obstreperous Negro sorcerer with an enormous girth of chest. The villagers brought out food with alacrity, and the sorcerer was never the same man again. It had been a great display.

Yes, no doubt it was Testa Dura, the young neophyte of the order (where and how picked up Peyrol never heard), strange to the camp, simple-minded and much impressed by the swaggering cosmopolitan company in which he found himself. He had attached himself to Peyrol in preference to some of his own countrymen, of whom there were several in that band, and used to run after him like a little dog, and certainly had acted a good shipmate's part on the occasion of that wound which had neither killed nor cowed Peyrol but merely had given him an opportunity to reflect at leisure on the conduct of his own life.

The first suspicion of that amazing fact had intruded on Peyrol while he was bandaging that head by the light of the smoky lamp. Since the fellow still lived, it was not in Peyrol to finish him off or let him lie unattended like a dog. And then this was a sailor. His being English was no obstacle to the development of Peyrol's mixed feelings in which hatred certainly had no place. Amongst the members of the Brotherhood it was the Englishmen whom he preferred. He had also found amongst them that particular and loyal appreciation, which a Frenchman of character and ability will receive from Englishmen sooner than from any other nation. Peyrol had at times been a leader, without ever trying for it very much, for he was not ambitious. The lead used to fall to him mostly at a time of crisis of some sort; and when he had got the lead it was on the Englishmen that he used to depend most.

And so that youngster had turned into this English man-of-war's man! In the fact itself there was nothing impossible. You found Brothers of the Coast in all sorts of ships and in all sorts of places. Peyrol had found one once in a very ancient and hopeless cripple practising the profession of a beggar on the steps of Manila cathedral; and had left him the richer by two broad gold pieces to add to his secret hoard. There was a tale of a Brother of the Coast having become a mandarin in China, and Peyrol believed it. One never knew where and in what position one would find a Brother of the Coast. The wonderful thing was that this one should have come to seek him out, to put himself in the way of his cudgel. Peyrol's greatest concern had been all through that Sunday morning to conceal the whole adventure from Lieutenant Réal. As against a wearer of epaulettes, mutual protection was the first duty between Brothers of the Coast. The unexpectedness of that claim coming to him after twenty years invested it with an extraordinary strength. What he would do with the fellow he didn't know. But since that morning the situation had changed. Peyrol had received the lieutenant's confidence and had got on terms with him in a special way. He fell into profound thought.

'Sacrée tête dure,' he muttered without rousing himself. Peyrol was annoyed a little at not having been recognised. He could not conceive how difficult it would have been for Symons to identify this portly deliberate person with a white head of hair as the object of his youthful admiration, the black-ringleted French Brother in the prime of life of whom everybody thought so much.

Peyrol was roused by hearing the other declare suddenly: 'I am an Englishman, I am. I am not going to knuckle under to anybody. What are you going to do with me?'

'I will do what I please,' said Peyrol, who had been asking himself exactly the same question.

'Well, then, be quick about it, whatever it is. I don't care a damn what you do, but – be – quick – about it.' He tried to be emphatic, but as a matter of fact the last words came out in a faltering tone.

And old Peyrol was touched. He thought that if he were to let him drink the mugful standing there, it would make him dead drunk. But he took the risk. So he said only: 'Allons. Drink.'

The other did not wait for a second invitation but could not control very well the movements of his arm extended towards the mug.

Peyrol raised his on high. 'Trinquons,[136] eh?' he proposed.

But in his precarious condition the Englishman remained unforgiving.'I'm damned if I do,' he said indignantly, but so low that Peyrol had to turn his ear to catch the words. 'You will have to explain to me first what you meant by knocking me on the head.'

He drank, staring all the time at Peyrol in a manner which was meant to give offence but which struck Peyrol as so childlike that he burst into a laugh.

'Sacré imbécile, va![137] Did I not tell you it was because of the tartane? If it hadn't been for the tartane I would have hidden from you. I would have crouched behind a bush like a – what do you call them? – lièvre.'[138]

The other, who was feeling the effect of the drink, stared with frank incredulity.

'You are of no account,' continued Peyrol. 'Ah! if you had been an officer I would have gone for you anywhere. Did you say your officer went up the gully?'

Symons sighed deeply and easily. 'That's the way he went. We had heard on board of a house thereabouts.'

'Oh, he went to the house!' said Peyrol. 'Well, if he did get there he must be very sorry for himself. There is half a company of infantry billeted in the farm.'

This inspired fib went down easily with the English sailor. Soldiers were stationed in many parts of the coast as any seaman of the blockading fleet knew very well. To the many expressions which had passed over the face of that man recovering from a long period of unconsciousness, there was added the shade of dismay.

'What the devil have they stuck soldiers on this piece of rock for?' he asked.

'Oh, signalling post and things like that. I am not likely to tell you everything. Why! you might escape.'

That phrase reached the soberest spot in the whole of Symons' individuality. Things were happening, then. Mr Bolt was a prisoner. But the main idea evoked in his confused mind was that he would be given up to those soldiers before very long. The prospect of captivity made his heart sink and he resolved to give as much trouble as he could.

'You will have to get some of these soldiers to carry me up. I won't walk. I won't. Not after having had my brains nearly knocked out from behind. I tell you straight! I won't walk. Not a step. They will have to carry me ashore.'

Peyrol only shook his head deprecatingly.

'Now you go and get a corporal with a file of men,' insisted Symons obstinately. 'I want to be made a proper prisoner of. Who the devil are you? You had no right to interfere. I believe you are a civilian. A common marinero, whatever you may call yourself. You look to me a pretty fishy marinero at that. Where did you learn English? In prison – eh? You ain't going to keep me in this damned dog-hole, on board your rubbishy tartane. Go and get that corporal, I tell you.' He looked suddenly very tired and only murmured: 'I am an Englishman, I am.'

Peyrol's patience was positively angelic.

'Don't you talk about the tartane,' he said impressively, making his words as distinct as possible. 'I told you she was not like the other tartanes. That is because she is a courier boat. Every time she goes to sea she makes a *pied-de-nez*, what you call thumb to the nose, to all your English cruisers. I do not mind telling you because you are my prisoner. You will soon learn French now.'

'Who are you? The caretaker of this thing or what?' asked the undaunted Symons. But Peyrol's mysterious silence seemed to intimidate him at last. He became dejected and began to curse in a languid tone all boat expeditions, the coxswain of the gig and his own infernal luck.

Peyrol sat alert and attentive like a man interested in an experiment, while after a moment Symons' face began to look as if he had been hit with a club again, but not as hard as before. A film came over his round eyes and the words 'fishy marinero' made their way out of his lips in a sort of deathbed voice. Yet such was the hardness of his head that he actually rallied enough to address Peyrol in an ingratiating tone.

'Come, grandfather!' He tried to push the mug across the table and upset it. 'Come! Let us finish what's in that tiny bottle of yours.'

'No,' said Peyrol, drawing the demijohn to his side of the table and putting the cork in.

'No?' repeated Symons in an unbelieving voice and looking at the demijohn fixedly. 'You must be a tinker . . . ' He tried to say something more under Peyrol's watchful eyes, failed once or twice, and suddenly pronounced the word 'cochon'[139] so correctly as to make old Peyrol start. After that it was no use looking at him any more. Peyrol busied himself in locking up the demijohn and the mugs. When he turned round most of his prisoner's body was extended over the table and no sound came from it, not even a snore.

When Peyrol got outside, pulling to the door of the cuddy behind him, Michel hastened from forward to receive the master's orders. But Peyrol stood so long on the after-deck meditating profoundly with his hand over his mouth that Michel became fidgety and ventured a cheerful: 'It looks as if he were not going to die.'

'He is dead,' said Peyrol with grim jocularity. 'Dead drunk. And you very likely will not see me till tomorrow sometime.'

'But what am I to do?' asked Michel timidly.

'Nothing,' said Peyrol. 'Of course you must not let him set fire to the tartane.'

'But suppose,' insisted Michel, 'he should give signs of escaping.'

'If you see him trying to escape,' said Peyrol with mock solemnity, 'then, Michel, it will be a sign for you to get out of his way as quickly as you can. A man who would try to escape with a head like this on him would just swallow you at one mouthful.'

He picked up his cudgel and, stepping ashore, went off without as much as a look at his faithful henchman. Michel listened to him scrambling amongst the stones, and his habitual amiably vacant face acquired a sort of dignity from the utter and absolute blankness that came over it.

Chapter 10

It was only after reaching the level ground in front of the farmhouse that Peyrol took time to pause and resume his contact with the exterior world.

While he had been closeted with his prisoner the sky had got covered with a thin layer of cloud, in one of those swift changes of weather that are not unusual in the Mediterranean. This grey vapour, drifting high up, close against the disc of the sun, seemed to enlarge the space behind its veil, add to the vastness of a shadowless world no longer hard and brilliant but all softened in the contours of its masses and in the faint line of the horizon, as if ready to dissolve in the immensity of the Infinite.

Familiar and indifferent to his eyes, material and shadowy, the extent of the changeable sea had gone pale under the pale sun in a mysterious and emotional response. Mysterious too was the great oval patch of dark water to the west; and also a broad blue lane traced on the dull silver of the waters in a parabolic curve described magistrally by an invisible finger for a symbol of endless wandering. The face of the farmhouse might have been the face of a house from which all the inhabitants had fled suddenly. In the high part of the building the window of the lieutenant's room remained open, both glass and shutter. By the door of the salle the stable fork leaning against the wall seemed to have been forgotten by the sans-culotte. This aspect of abandonment struck Peyrol with more force than usual. He had been thinking so hard of all these people that to find no one about seemed unnatural and even depressing. He had seen many abandoned places in his life, grass huts, mud forts, kings' palaces – temples from which every white-robed soul had fled. Temples, however, never looked quite empty. The gods clung to their own. Peyrol's eyes rested on the bench against the wall of the salle. In the usual course of things it should have been occupied by the lieutenant who had the habit of sitting there with hardly a movement, for hours, like a spider watching for the coming of a fly. This paralysing comparison held Peyrol motionless, with a twisted mouth and a frown on his brow, before the evoked vision, coloured and precise, of the man more troubling than the reality had ever been.

He came to himself with a start. What sort of occupation was this, 'cré nom de nom,[140] staring at a silly bench with no one on it? Was he going wrong in his head? Or was it that he was getting really old? He had noticed old men losing themselves like that. But he had something to do. First of all he had to go and see what the English sloop in the Passe was doing.

While he was making his way towards the lookout on the hill where the inclined pine hung peering over the cliff as if an insatiable curiosity were holding it in that precarious position, Peyrol had another view from above of the farmyard and of the buildings and was again affected by their deserted appearance. Not a soul, not even an animal seemed to have been left; only on the roofs the pigeons walked with smart elegance. Peyrol hurried on and presently saw the English ship well over on the Porquerolles side with her yards braced up and her head to the southward. There was a little wind in the Passe, while the dull silver of the open had a darkling rim of rippled water far away to the east in that quarter where, far or near, but mostly out of sight, the British Fleet kept its endless watch. Not a shadow of a spar or gleam of sail on the horizon betrayed its presence; but Peyrol would not have been surprised to see a crowd of ships surge up, people the horizon with hostile life, come in running, and dot the sea with their ordered groups all about Cape Cicié, parading their damned impudence. Then indeed that corvette, the big factor of everyday life on that stretch of coast, would become very small potatoes indeed; and the man in command of her (he had been Peyrol's personal adversary in many imaginary encounters fought to a finish in the room upstairs) – then indeed that Englishman would have to mind his steps. He would be ordered to come within hail of the Admiral, be sent here and there, made to run like a little dog and as likely as not get called on board the flagship and get a dressing down for something or other.

Peyrol thought for a moment that the impudence of this Englishman was going to take the form of running along the peninsula and looking into the very cove; for the corvette's head was falling off slowly. A fear for his tartane clutched Peyrol's heart till he remembered that the Englishman did not know of her existence. Of course not. His cudgel had been absolutely effective in stopping that bit of information. The only Englishman who knew of the existence of the tartane was that fellow with the broken head. Peyrol actually laughed at his momentary scare. Moreover, it was evident that the Englishman did not mean to parade in front of the peninsula. He did not mean to be impudent. The sloop's yards were swung right round and she came again to the wind but now heading to the northward back from where she came. Peyrol saw at once that the Englishman meant to pass to windward of Cape

Esterel, probably with the intention of anchoring for the night off the long white beach which in a regular curve closes the roadstead of Hyères on that side.

Peyrol pictured her to himself, on the clouded night, not so very dark since the full moon was but a day old, lying at anchor within hail of the low shore, with her sails furled and looking profoundly asleep, but with the watch on deck lying by the guns. He gnashed his teeth. It had come to this at last, that the captain of the *Amelia* could do nothing with his ship without putting Peyrol into a rage. Oh, for forty Brothers, or sixty, picked ones, he thought, to teach the fellow what it might cost him taking liberties along the French coast! Ships had been carried by surprise before, on nights when there was just light enough to see the whites of each other's eyes in a close tussle. And what would be the crew of that Englishman? Something between ninety and a hundred altogether, boys and landsman included . . . Peyrol shook his fist for a goodbye, just when Cape Esterel shut off the English sloop from his sight. But in his heart of hearts that seaman of cosmopolitan associations knew very well that no forty or sixty, not any given hundred Brothers of the Coast would have been enough to capture that corvette making herself at home within ten miles of where he had first opened his eyes to the world.

He shook his head dismally at the leaning pine, his only companion. The disinherited soul of that rover, ranging for so many years a lawless ocean with the coasts of two continents for a raiding ground, had come back to its crag, circling like a sea-bird in the dusk and longing for a great sea victory for its people: that inland multitude of which Peyrol knew nothing except the few individuals on that peninsula cut off from the rest of the land by the dead water of a salt lagoon; and where only a strain of manliness in a miserable cripple and an unaccountable charm of a half-crazed woman had found response in his heart.

This scheme of false dispatches was but a detail in a plan for a great, a destructive victory. Just a detail, but not a trifle all the same. Nothing connected with the deception of an admiral could be called trifling. And such an admiral too. It was, Peyrol felt vaguely, a scheme that only a confounded landsman would invent. It behoved the sailors, however, to make a workable thing of it. It would have to be worked through that corvette.

And here Peyrol was brought up by the question that all his life had not been able to settle for him – and that was whether the English were really very stupid or very acute. That difficulty had presented itself with every fresh case. The old rover had enough genius in him to have arrived at a general conclusion that if they were to be deceived at all it could not be done very well by words but rather by deeds; not by mere wriggling, but by deep craft concealed under some sort of straight-forward action. That conviction, however, did not take him forward in this case, which was one in which much thinking would be necessary.

The *Amelia* had disappeared behind Cape Esterel, and Peyrol wondered with a certain anxiety whether this meant that the Englishman had given up his man for good. 'If he has,' said Peyrol to himself, 'I am bound to see him pass out again from beyond Cape Esterel before it gets dark.' If, however, he did not see the ship again within the next hour or two, then she would be anchored off the beach, to wait for the night before making some attempt to discover what had become of her man. This could be done only by sending out one or two boats to explore the coast, and no doubt to enter the cove – perhaps even to land a small search party.

After coming to this conclusion Peyrol began deliberately to charge his pipe. Had he spared a moment for a glance inland he might have caught a whisk of a black skirt, the gleam of a white fichu – Arlette running down the faint track leading from Escampobar to the village in the hollow; the same track in fact up which Citizen Scevola, while indulging in the strange freak to visit the church, had been chased by the incensed faithful. But Peyrol, while charging and lighting his pipe, had kept his eyes fastened on Cape Esterel. Then, throwing his arm affectionately over the trunk of the pine, he had settled himself to watch. Far below him the roadstead, with its play of grey and bright gleams, looked like a plaque of mother-of-pearl in a frame of yellow rocks and dark green ravines set off inland by the masses of the hills displaying the tint of the finest purple; while above his head the sun, behind a cloud-veil, hung like a silver disc.

That afternoon, after waiting in vain for Lieutenant Réal to appear outside in the usual way, Arlette, the mistress of Escampobar, had gone unwillingly into the kitchen where Catherine sat upright in a heavy capacious wooden armchair, the back of which rose above the top of her white muslin cap. Even in her old age, even in her hours of ease, Catherine preserved the upright carriage of the family that had held Escampobar for so many generations. It would have been easy to believe that, like some characters famous in the world, Catherine would have wished to die standing up and with unbowed shoulders.

With her sense of hearing undecayed she detected the light footsteps in the salle long before Arlette entered the kitchen. That woman, who had faced alone and unaided (except for her brother's comprehending silence) the anguish of passion in a forbidden love, and of terrors comparable to those of the Judgement Day, neither turned her face, quiet without serenity, nor her eyes, fearless but without fire, in the direction of her niece.

Arlette glanced on all sides, even at the walls, even at the mound of ashes under the big overmantel, nursing in its heart a spark of fire, before she sat down and leaned her elbow on the table.

'You wander about like a soul in pain,' said her aunt, sitting by the hearth like an old queen on her throne.

'And you sit here eating your heart out.'

'Formerly,' remarked Catherine, 'old women like me could always go over their prayers, but now . . . '

'I believe you have not been to church for years. I remember Scevola telling me that a long time ago. Was it because you didn't like people's eyes? I have fancied sometimes that most people in the world must have been massacred long ago.'

Catherine turned her face away. Arlette rested her head on her half-closed hand, and her eyes, losing their steadiness, began to tremble amongst cruel visions. She got up suddenly and caressed the thin, half-averted, withered cheek with the tips of her fingers, and in a low voice, with that marvellous cadence that plucked at one's heart-strings, she said coaxingly: 'Those were dreams, weren't they?'

In her immobility the old woman called with all the might of her will for the presence of Peyrol. She had never been able to shake off a superstitious fear of that niece restored to her from the terrors of a Judgement Day in which the world had been given over to the devils. She was always afraid that this girl, wandering about with restless eyes and a dim smile on her silent lips, would suddenly say something atrocious, unfit to be heard, calling for vengeance from heaven, unless Peyrol were by. That stranger come from 'par dela les mers'[141] was out of it altogether, cared probably for no one in the world but had struck her imagination by his massive aspect, his deliberation suggesting a mighty force like the reposeful attitude of a lion. Arlette desisted from caressing the irresponsive cheek, exclaimed petulantly: 'I am awake now!' and went out of the kitchen without having asked her aunt the question she had meant to ask, which was whether she knew what had become of the lieutenant.

Her heart had failed her. She let herself drop on the bench outside the door of the salle. 'What is the matter with them all?' she thought. 'I can't make them out. What wonder is it that I have not been able to sleep?' Even Peyrol, so different from all mankind, who from the first moment when he stood before her had the power to soothe her aimless unrest, even Peyrol would now sit for hours with the lieutenant on the bench, gazing into the air and keeping him in talk about things without sense, as if on purpose to prevent him from thinking of her. Well, he could not do that. But the enormous change implied in the fact that every day had a tomorrow now, and that all the people around her had ceased to be mere phantoms for her wandering glances to glide over without concern, made her feel the need of support from somebody, from somewhere. She could have cried aloud for it.

She sprang up and walked along the whole front of the farm building. At the end of the wall enclosing the orchard she called out in a modulated undertone: 'Eugène,' not because she hoped that the lieutenant was anywhere within earshot, but for the pleasure of hearing the sound of the name uttered for once above a whisper. She turned about and at the end of the wall on the yard side she repeated her call, drinking in the sound that came from her lips, 'Eugène, Eugène,' with a sort of half-exulting despair. It was in such dizzy moments that she wanted a steadying support. But all was still. She heard no friendly murmur, not even a sigh. Above her head under the thin grey sky a big mulberry tree stirred no leaf. Step by step, as if unconsciously, she began to move down the track. At the end of fifty yards she opened the inland view, the roofs of the village between the green tops of the platanes overshadowing the fountain, and just beyond the flat blue-grey level of the salt lagoon, smooth and dull like a slab of lead. But what drew her on was the church-tower, where, in a round arch, she could see the black speck of the bell which escaping the requisitions of the Republican wars, and dwelling mute above the locked-up empty church, had only lately recovered its voice. She ran on, but when she had come near enough to make out the figures moving about the village fountain, she checked herself, hesitated a moment and then took the footpath leading to the presbytery.

She pushed open the little gate with the broken latch. The humble building of rough stones, from between which much mortar had crumbled out, looked as though it had been sinking slowly into the ground. The beds of the plot in front were choked with weeds, because the abbé had no taste for gardening. When the heiress of Escampobar opened the door, he was walking up and down the largest room which was his bedroom and sitting-room and where he also took his meals. He was a gaunt man with a long, as if convulsed, face. In his young days he had been tutor to the sons of a great noble, but he did not emigrate with his employer. Neither did he submit to the Republic. He had lived in his native land like a hunted wild beast, and there had been many tales of his activities, warlike and others. When the hierarchy was re-established he found no favour in the eyes of his superiors. He had remained too much of a Royalist. He had accepted, without a word, the charge of this miserable parish, where he had acquired influence quickly enough. His sacerdotalism lay in him like a cold passion. Though accessible enough, he never walked abroad without his breviary, acknowledging the solemnly bared heads by a curt nod. He was not exactly feared, but some of the oldest inhabitants who remembered the previous incumbent, an old man who died in the garden after having been dragged out of bed by some patriots anxious to take him to prison in Hyères, jerked their heads sideways in a knowing manner when their curé was mentioned.

On seeing this apparition in an Arlesian cap and silk skirt, a white fichu, and otherwise as completely different as any princess could be from the rustics with whom he was in daily contact, his face expressed the blankest astonishment. Then – for he knew enough of the gossip of his community – his straight, thick eyebrows came together inimically. This was no doubt the woman of whom he had heard his parishioners talk with bated breath as having given herself and her property up to a Jacobin, a Toulon sans-culotte who had either delivered her parents to execution or had murdered them himself during the first three days of massacres. No one was very sure which it was, but the rest was current knowledge. The abbé, though persuaded that any amount of moral turpitude was possible in a godless country, had not accepted all that tale literally. No doubt those people were republican and impious, and the state of affairs up there was scandalous and horrible. He struggled with his feelings of repulsion and managed to smooth his brow and waited. He could not imagine what that woman with mature form and a youthful face could want at the presbytery. Suddenly it occurred to him that perhaps she wanted to thank him – it was a very old occurrence – for interposing between the fury of the villagers and that man. He couldn't call him, even in his thoughts, her husband, for apart from all other circumstances, that connection could not imply any kind of marriage to a priest, even had there been legal form observed. His visitor was apparently disconcerted by the expression of his face, the austere aloofness of his attitude, and only a low murmur escaped her lips. He bent his head and was not very certain what he had heard.

'You come to seek my aid?' he asked in a doubting tone.

She nodded slightly, and the abbé went to the door she had left half open and looked out. There was not a soul in sight between the presbytery and the village, or between the presbytery and the church.

He went back to face her, saying: 'We are as alone as we can well be. The old woman in the kitchen is as deaf as a post.'

Now that he had been looking at Arlette closer the abbé felt a sort of dread. The carmine of those lips, the pellucid, unstained, unfathomable blackness of those eyes, the pallor of her cheeks, suggested to him something provokingly pagan, something distastefully different from the common sinners of this earth. And now she was ready to speak. He arrested her with a raised hand.

'Wait,' he said. 'I have never seen you before. I don't even know properly who you are. None of you belong to my flock – for you are from Escampobar, are you not?' Sombre under their bony arches, his eyes, fastened on her face, noticed the delicacy of features, the naïve pertinacity of her stare.

She said: 'I am the daughter.'

'The daughter! . . . Oh! I see . . . Much evil is spoken of you.'

She said a little impatiently: 'By that rabble?' and the priest remained mute for a moment. 'What do they say? In my father's time they wouldn't have dared to say anything. The only thing I saw of them for years and years was when they were yelping like curs on the heels of Scevola.'

The absence of scorn in her tone was perfectly annihilating. Gentle sounds flowed from her lips and a disturbing charm from her strange equanimity. The abbé frowned heavily at these fascinations, which seemed to have in them something diabolic.

'They are simple souls, neglected, fallen back into darkness. It isn't their fault. They have natural feelings of humanity which were outraged. I saved him from their indignation. There are things that must be left to divine justice.'

He was exasperated by the unconsciousness of that fair face.

'That man whose name you have just pronounced and which I have heard coupled with the epithet of 'blood-drinker' is regarded as the master of Escampobar Farm. He has been living there for years. How is that?'

'Yes, it is a long time ago since he brought me back to the house. Years ago. Catherine let him stay.'

'Who is Catherine?' the abbé asked harshly.

'She is my father's sister who was left at home to wait. She had given up all hope of seeing any of us again, when one morning Scevola came with me to the door. Then she let him stay. He is a poor creature. What else could Catherine have done? And what is it to us up there how the people in the village regard him?' She dropped her eyes and seemed to fall into deep thought, then added, 'It was only later that I discovered that he was a poor creature, even quite lately. They call him blood-drinker, do they? What of that? All the time he was afraid of his own shadow.'

She ceased but did not raise her eyes.

'You are no longer a child,' began the abbé in a severe voice, frowning at her downcast eyes, and he heard a murmur: 'Not very long.' He disregarded it and continued: 'I ask you, is this all that you have to tell me about that man? I hope that at least you are no hypocrite.'

'Monsieur l'Abbé,' she said, raising her eyes fearlessly, 'what more am I to tell you about him? I can tell you things that will make your hair stand on end, but it wouldn't be about him.'

For all answer the abbé made a weary gesture and turned away to walk up and down the room. His face expressed neither curiosity nor pity, but a sort of repugnance which he made an effort to overcome. He dropped into a deep and shabby old armchair, the only object of luxury in the room, and pointed to a wooden straight-backed stool. Arlette sat down on it and began to speak. The abbé listened, but looking far away; his big bony hands rested on the arms of the chair. After the first words he interrupted her: 'This is your own story you are telling me.'

'Yes,' said Arlette.

'Is it necessary that I should know?'

'Yes, Monsieur l'Abbé.'

'But why?'

He bent his head a little, without, however, ceasing to look far away. Her voice now was very low.

Suddenly the abbé threw himself back. 'You want to tell me your story because you have fallen in love with a man?'

'No, because that has brought me back to myself. Nothing else could have done it.'

He turned his head to look at her grimly, but he said nothing and looked away again. He listened. At the beginning he muttered once or twice, 'Yes, I have heard that,' and then kept silent, not looking at her at all. Once he interrupted her by a question: 'You were confirmed before the convent was forcibly entered and the nuns dispersed?'[142]

'Yes,' she said, 'a year before that or more.'

'And then two of those ladies took you with them towards Toulon.'

'Yes, the other girls had their relations near by. They took me with them thinking to communicate with my parents, but it was difficult. Then the English came and my parents sailed over to try and get some news of me. It was safe for my father to be in Toulon then. Perhaps you think that he was a traitor to his country?' she asked, and waited with parted lips. With an impassible face the abbé murmured: 'He was a good Royalist,' in a tone of bitter fatalism, which seemed to absolve that man and all the other men of whose actions and errors he had ever heard.

For a long time, Arlette continued, her father could not discover the house where the nuns had taken refuge. He only obtained some information on the very day before the English evacuated Toulon. Late in the day he appeared before her and took her away. The town was full of retreating foreign troops. Her father left her with her mother and went out again to make preparations for sailing home that very night; but the tartane was no longer in the place where he had left her lying. The two Madrague men that he had for a crew had disappeared also. Thus the family was trapped in that town full of tumult and confusion. Ships and houses were bursting into flames. Appalling explosions of gunpowder shook the earth. She spent that night on her knees with her face hidden in her mother's lap, while her father kept watch by the barricaded door with a pistol in each hand.

In the morning the house was filled with savage yells. People were heard rushing up the stairs, and the door was burst in. She jumped up at the crash and flung herself down on her knees in a corner with her face to the wall. There was a murderous uproar, she heard two shots fired, then somebody seized her by the arm and pulled her up to her feet. It was Scevola. He dragged her to the door. The bodies of her father and mother were lying across the doorway. The room was full of gunpowder smoke. She wanted to fling herself on the bodies and cling to them, but Scevola took her under the arms and lifted her over them. He seized her hand and made her run with him, or rather dragged her downstairs. Outside on the pavement some dreadful men and many fierce women with knives joined them. They ran along the streets brandishing pikes and sabres, pursuing other groups of unarmed people, who fled round corners with loud shrieks.

'I ran in the midst of them, Monsieur l'Abbé,' Arlette went on in a breathless murmur. 'Whenever I saw any water I wanted to throw myself into it, but I was surrounded on all sides, I was jostled and pushed and most of the time Scevola held my hand very tight. When they stopped at a wine shop, they would offer me some wine. My tongue stuck to the roof of my mouth and I drank. The wine, the pavements, the arms and faces, everything was red. I had red splashes all over me. I had to run with them all day, and all the time I felt as if I were falling down, and down, and down. The houses were nodding at me. The sun would go out at times. And suddenly I heard myself yelling exactly like the others. Do you understand, Monsieur l'Abbé? The very same words!'

The eyes of the priest in their deep orbits glided towards her and then resumed their faraway fixity. Between his fatalism and his faith he was not very far from the belief of Satan taking possession of rebellious mankind, exposing the nakedness of hearts like flint and of the homicidal souls of the Revolution.

'I have heard something of that,' he whispered stealthily.

She affirmed with quiet earnestness: 'Yet at that time I resisted with all my might.'

That night Scevola put her under the care of a woman called Perose. She was young and pretty and was a native of Arles, her mother's country. She kept an inn. That woman locked her up in her own room, which was next to the room where the patriots kept on shouting, singing and making speeches far into the night. Several times the woman would look in for a moment, make a hopeless gesture at her with both arms, and vanish again. Later, on many other nights when all the band lay asleep on benches and on the floor, Perose would steal into the room, fall on her knees by the bed on which Arlette sat upright, open-eyed, and raving silently to herself, embrace her feet and cry herself to sleep. But in the morning she would jump up briskly and say: 'Come. The great affair is to keep our life in our bodies. Come along to help in the work of justice'; and they would join the band that was making ready for another day of traitor hunting. But after a time the victims, of which the streets were full at first, had to be sought for in back-yards, ferreted out of their hiding-places, dragged up out of the cellars or down from the garrets of the houses, which would be entered by the band with howls of death and vengeance.

'Then, Monsieur l'Abbé,' said Arlette, 'I let myself go at last. I could resist no longer. I said to myself, "If it is so then it must be right." But most of the time I was like a person half asleep and dreaming things that it is impossible to believe. About that time, I don't know why, the woman Perose hinted to me that Scevola was a poor creature. Next night while all the band lay fast asleep in the big room Perose and Scevola helped me out of the window into the street and led me to the quay behind the arsenal. Scevola had found our tartane lying at the pontoon and one of the Madrague men with her. The other had disappeared. Perose fell on my neck and cried a little. She gave me a kiss and said: "My time will come soon. You, Scevola, don't you show yourself in Toulon, because nobody believes in you any more. Adieu, Arlette. Vive la Nation!" and she vanished in the night. I waited on the pontoon shivering in my torn clothes, listening to Scevola and the man throwing dead bodies overboard out of the tartane. Splash, splash, splash. And suddenly I felt I must run away, but they were after me in a moment, dragged me back and threw me down into that cabin which smelt of blood. But when I got back to the farm all feeling had left me. I did not feel myself exist. I saw things round me here and there, but I couldn't look at anything for long. Something was gone out of me. I know now that it was not my heart, but then I didn't mind what it was. I felt light and empty, and a little cold all the time, but I could smile at people. Nothing could matter. Nothing could mean anything. I cared for no one. I wanted nothing. I wasn't alive at all, Monsieur l'Abbé. People seemed to see me and would talk to me, and it seemed funny – till one day I felt my heart beat.'

'Why precisely did you come to me with this tale?' asked the abbé in a low voice.

'Because you are a priest. Have you forgotten that I have been brought up in a convent? I have not forgotten how to pray. But I am afraid of the world now. What must I do?'

'Repent!' thundered the abbé, getting up. He saw her candid gaze uplifted and lowered his voice forcibly. 'You must look with fearless sincerity into the darkness of your soul. Remember whence the only true help can come. Those whom God has visited by a trial such as yours cannot be held guiltless of their enormities. Withdraw from the world. Descend within yourself and abandon the vain thoughts of what people call happiness. Be an example to yourself of the sinfulness of our nature and of the weakness of our humanity. You may have been possessed. What do I know? Perhaps it was permitted in order to lead your soul to saintliness through a life of seclusion and prayer. To that it would be my duty to help you. Meantime you must pray to be given strength for a complete renunciation.'

Arlette, lowering her eyes slowly, appealed to the abbé as a symbolic figure of spiritual mystery.

'What can be God's designs on this creature?' he asked himself.

'Monsieur le Curé,' she said quietly, 'I felt the need to pray today for the first time in many years. When I left home it was only to go to your church.'

'The church stands open to the worst of sinners,' said the abbé.

'I know. But I would have had to pass before all those villagers: and you, abbé, know well what they are capable of.'

'Perhaps,' murmured the abbé, 'it would be better not to put their charity to the test.'

'I must pray before I go back again. I thought you would let me come in through the sacristy.'

'It would be inhuman to refuse your request,' he said, rousing himself and taking down a key that hung on the wall. He put on his broad-brimmed hat and without a word led the way through the wicket gate and along the path which he always used himself and which was out of sight of the village fountain. After they had entered the damp and dilapidated sacristy he locked the door behind them and only then opened another, a smaller one, leading into the church. When he stood aside, Arlette became aware of the chilly odour as of freshly turned-up earth mingled with a faint scent of incense. In the deep dusk of the nave a single little flame glimmered before an image of the virgin.

The abbé whispered as she passed on: 'There before the great altar abase yourself and pray for grace and strength and mercy in this world full of crimes against God and men.'

She did not look at him. Through the thin soles of her shoes she could feel the chill of the flagstones. The abbé left the door ajar, sat down on a rush-bottomed chair, the only one in the sacristy, folded his arms and let his chin fall on his breast. He seemed to be sleeping profoundly, but at the end of half an hour he got up and, going to the doorway, stood looking at the kneeling figure sunk low on the altar steps. Arlette's face was buried in her hands in a passion of piety and prayer.

The abbé waited patiently for a good many minutes more, before he raised his voice in a grave murmur which filled the whole dark place. 'It is time for you to leave. I am going to ring for vespers.'

The view of her complete absorption before the Most High had touched him. He stepped back into the sacristy and after a time heard the faintest possible swish of the black silk skirt of the Escampobar daughter in her Arlesian costume. She entered the sacristy lightly with shining eyes, and the abbé looked at her with some emotion.

'You have prayed well, my daughter,' he said. 'No forgiveness will be refused to you, for you have suffered much. Put your trust in the grace of God.'

She raised her head and stayed her footsteps for a moment. In the dark little place he could see the gleam of her eyes swimming in tears.

'Yes, Monsieur l'Abbé,' she said in her clear seductive voice. 'I have prayed and I feel answered. I entreated the merciful God to keep the heart of the man I love always true to me or else to let me die before I set my eyes on him again.'

The abbé paled under his tan of a village priest and leaned his shoulders against the wall without a word.

After leaving the church by the sacristy door Arlette never looked back. The abbé saw her flit past the presbytery, and the building hid her from his sight. He did not accuse her of duplicity. He had deceived himself. A heathen. White as her skin was, the blackness of her hair and of her eyes, the dusky red of her lips, suggested a strain of Saracen[143] blood. He gave her up without a sigh.

Arlette walked rapidly towards Escampobar as if she could not get there soon enough; but as she neared the first enclosed field her steps became slower and after hesitating awhile she sat down between two olive trees, near a wall bordered by a growth of thin grass at the foot. 'And if I have been possessed,' she argued to herself, 'as the abbé said, what is it to me as I am now? That evil spirit cast my true self out of my body and then cast away the body too. For years I have been living empty. There has been no meaning in anything.'

But now her true self had returned matured, in its mysterious exile, hopeful and eager for love. She was certain that it had never been far away from that outcast body which Catherine had told her lately was fit for no man's arms. That was all that old woman knew about it, thought Arlette, not in scorn but rather in pity. She knew better, she had gone to heaven for truth in that long prostration with its ardent prayers and its moment of ecstasy before an unlighted altar.

She knew its meaning well, and also the meaning of another – of a terrestrial revelation which had come to her that day at noon while she waited on the lieutenant. Everybody else was in the kitchen; she and Réal were as much alone together as had ever happened to them in their lives. That day she could not deny herself the delight to be near him, to watch him covertly, to hear him perhaps utter a few words, to experience that strange satisfying consciousness of her own existence which nothing but Réal's presence could give her; a sort of unimpassioned but all-absorbing bliss, warmth, courage, confidence! . . . She backed away from Réal's table, seated herself facing him and cast down her eyes. There was a great stillness in the salle except for the murmur of the voices in the kitchen. She had at first stolen a glance or two and then peeping again through her eyelashes, as it were, she saw his eyes rest on her with a peculiar meaning. This had never happened before. She jumped up, thinking that he wanted something, and while she stood in front of him with her hand resting on the table he stooped suddenly, pressed it to the table with his lips and began kissing it passionately without a sound, endlessly . . . More startled than surprised at first, then infinitely happy, she was beginning to breathe quickly, when he left off and threw himself back in the chair. She walked away from the table and sat down again to gaze at him openly, steadily, without a smile. But he was not looking at her. His passionate lips were set hard now and his face had an expression of stern despair. No word passed between them. Brusquely he got up with averted eyes and went outside, leaving the food before him unfinished.

In the usual course of things, on any other day, she would have got up and followed him, for she had always yielded to the fascination that had first roused her faculties. She would have gone out just to pass in front of him once or twice. But this time she had not obeyed what was stronger than fascination, something within herself which at the same time prompted and restrained her. She only raised her arm and looked at her hand. It was true. It had happened. He had kissed it. Formerly she cared not how gloomy he was as long as he remained somewhere where she could look at him – which she would do at every opportunity with an open and unbridled innocence. But now she knew better than to do that. She had got up, had passed through the kitchen, meeting without embarrassment Catherine's inquisitive glance, and had gone upstairs. When she came down after a time, he was nowhere to be seen, and everybody else too seemed to have gone into hiding: Michel, Peyrol, Scevola . . . But if she had met Scevola she would not have spoken to him. It was now a very long time since she had volunteered a conversation with Scevola. She guessed, however, that Scevola had simply gone to lie down in his lair, a narrow shabby room lighted by one glazed little window high up in the end wall. Catherine had put him in there on the very day he had brought her niece home and he had retained it for his own ever since. She could even picture him to herself in there stretched on his pallet. She was capable of that now. Formerly, for years after her return, people that were out of her sight were out of her mind also. Had they run away and left her she would not have thought of them at all. She would have wandered in and out of the empty house and round the empty fields without giving anybody a thought. Peyrol was the first human being she had noticed for years. Peyrol, since he had come, had always existed for her. And as a matter of fact the rover was generally very much in evidence about the farm. That afternoon, however, even Peyrol was not to be seen. Her uneasiness began to grow, but she felt a strange reluctance to go into the kitchen where she knew her aunt would be sitting in the armchair like a presiding genius of the house taking its rest and unreadable in her immobility. And yet she felt she must talk about Réal to somebody. This was how the idea of going down to the church had come to her. She would talk of him to the priest and to God. The force of old associations asserted itself. She had been taught to believe that one could tell everything to a priest, and that the omnipotent God who knew everything could be prayed to, asked for grace, for strength, for mercy, for protection, for pity. She had done it and felt she had been heard.

Her heart had quietened down while she rested under the wall. Pulling out a long stalk of grass she twined it round her fingers absently. The veil of cloud had thickened over her head, early dusk had descended upon the earth, and she had not found out what had become of Réal. She jumped to her feet wildly. But directly she had done that she felt the need of self-control. It was with her usual light step that she approached the front of the house and for the first time in her life perceived how barren and sombre it looked when Réal was not about. She slipped in quietly through the door of the main building and ran upstairs. It was dark on the landing. She passed by the door leading into the room occupied by her aunt and herself. It had been her father and mother's bedroom. The other big room was the lieutenant's during his visits to Escampobar. Without even a rustle of her dress, like a shadow, she glided along the passage, turned the handle without noise and went in. After shutting the door behind her she listened. There was no sound in the house. Scevola was either already down in the yard or still lying open-eyed on his tumbled pallet in raging sulks about something. She had once accidentally caught him at it, down on his face, one eye and cheek of which were buried in the pillow, the other eye glaring savagely, and had been scared away by a thick mutter: 'Keep off. Don't approach me.' And all this had meant nothing to her then.

Having ascertained that the inside of the house was as still as the grave, Arlette walked across to the window, which when the lieutenant was occupying the room stood always open and with the shutter pushed right back against the wall. It was of course uncurtained, and as she came near to it Arlette caught sight of Peyrol coming down the hill on his return from the lookout. His white head gleamed like silver against the slope of the ground and by and by passed out of her sight, while her ear caught the sound of his footsteps below the window. They passed into the house, but she did not hear him come upstairs. He had gone into the kitchen. To Catherine. They would talk about her and Eugène.

But what would they say? She was so new to life that everything appeared dangerous: talk, attitudes, glances. She felt frightened at the mere idea of silence between those two. It was possible. Suppose they didn't say anything to each other. That would be awful.

Yet she remained calm like a sensible person who knows that rushing about in excitement is not the way to meet unknown dangers. She swept her eyes over the room and saw the lieutenant's valise in a corner. That was really what she had wanted to see. He wasn't gone then. But it didn't tell her, though she opened it, what had become of him. As to his return, she had no doubt whatever about that. He had always returned. She noticed particularly a large packet sewn up in sailcloth and with three large red seals on the seam. It didn't, however, arrest her thoughts. Those were still hovering about Catherine and Peyrol downstairs. How changed they were. Had they ever thought that she was mad? She became indignant. 'How could I have prevented that?' she asked herself with despair. She sat down on the edge of the bed in her usual attitude, her feet crossed, her hands lying in her lap. She felt on one of them the impress off Réal's lips, soothing, reassuring like every certitude, but she was aware of a still remaining confusion in her mind, an indefinite weariness like the strain of an imperfect vision trying to discern shifting outlines, floating shapes, incomprehensible signs. She could not resist the temptation of resting her tired body, just for a little while.

She lay down on the very edge of the bed, the kissed hand tucked under her cheek. The faculty of thinking abandoned her altogether, but she remained open-eyed, wide awake. In that position, without hearing the slightest sound, she saw the door handle move down as far as it would go, perfectly noiseless, as though the lock had been oiled not long before. Her impulse was to leap right out into the middle of the room, but she restrained herself and only swung herself into a sitting posture. The bed had not creaked. She lowered her feet gently to the ground, and by the time when holding her breath she put her ear against the door, the handle had come back into position. She had detected no sound outside. Not the faintest. Nothing. It never occurred to her to doubt her own eyes, but the whole thing had been so noiseless that it could not have disturbed the lightest sleeper. She was sure that had she been lying on her other side, that is with her back to the door, she would have known nothing. It was some time before she walked away from the door and sat on a chair which stood near a heavy and much-carved table, an heirloom more appropriate to a château than to a farmhouse. The dust of many months covered its smooth oval surface of dark, finely grained wood.

'It must have been Scevola,' thought Arlette. It could have been no one else. What could he have wanted? She gave herself up to thought, but really she did not care. The absent Réal occupied all her mind. With an unconscious slowness her finger traced in the dust on the table the initials E A and achieved a circle round them. Then she jumped up, unlocked the door and went downstairs. In the kitchen, as she fully expected, she found Scevola with the others. Directly she appeared he got up and ran upstairs, but returned almost immediately looking as if he had seen a ghost, and when Peyrol asked him some insignificant question his lips and even his chin trembled before he could command his voice. He avoided looking anybody in the face. The others too seemed shy of meeting each other's eyes, and the evening meal of the Escampobar seemed haunted by the absent lieutenant. Peyrol, besides, had his prisoner to think of. His existence presented a most interesting problem, and the proceedings of the English ship were another, closely connected with it and full of dangerous possibilities. Catherine's black and ungleaming eyes seemed to have sunk deeper in their sockets, but her face wore its habitual severe aloofness of expression. Suddenly Scevola spoke as if in answer to some thought of his own.

'What has lost us was moderation.'

Peyrol swallowed the piece of bread and butter which he had been masticating slowly and asked: 'What are you alluding to, citoyen?'

'I am alluding to the republic,' answered Scevola, in a more assured tone than usual. 'Moderation I say. We patriots held our hand too soon. All the children of the ci-devants and all the children of traitors should have been killed together with their fathers and mothers. Contempt for civic virtues and love of tyranny were inborn in them all. They grow up and trample on all the sacred principles . . . The work of the Terror is undone!'

'What do you propose to do about it?' growled Peyrol. 'No use declaiming here or anywhere for that matter. You wouldn't find anybody to listen to you – you cannibal,' he added in a good-humoured tone. Arlette, leaning her head on her left hand, was tracing with the forefinger of her right invisible initials on the tablecloth. Catherine, stooping to light a four-beaked oil lamp mounted on a brass pedestal, turned her finely carved face over her shoulder. The sans-culotte jumped up, flinging his arms about. His hair was tousled from his sleepless tumbling on his pallet. The unbuttoned sleeves of his shirt flapped against his thin hairy forearms. He no longer looked as though he had seen a ghost. He opened a wide black mouth, but Peyrol raised his finger at him calmly.

'No, no. The time when your own people up La Boyère way – don't they live up there? – trembled at the idea of you coming to visit them with a lot of patriot scallywags at your back is past. You have nobody at your back; and if you started spouting like this at large, people would rise up and hunt you down like a mad dog.'

Scevola, who had shut his mouth, glanced over his shoulder, and as if impressed by his unsupported state went out of the kitchen, reeling, like a man who had been drinking. He had drunk nothing but water. Peyrol looked thoughtfully at the door which the indignant sans-culotte had slammed after him. During the colloquy between the two men, Arlette had disappeared into the salle. Catherine, straightening her long back, put the oil lamp with its four smoky flames on the table. It lighted her face from below. Peyrol moved it slightly aside before he spoke.

'It was lucky for you,' he said, gazing upwards, 'that Scevola hadn't even one other like himself when he came here.'

'Yes,' she admitted. 'I had to face him alone from first to last. But can you see me between him and Arlette? In those days he raved terribly, but he was dazed and tired out. Afterwards I recovered myself and I could argue with him firmly. I used to say to him, "Look, she is so young and she has no knowledge of herself." Why, for months the only thing she would say that one could understand was, "Look how it spurts, look how it splashes!" He talked to me of his republican virtue. He was not a profligate. He could wait. She was, he said, sacred to him, and things like that. He would walk up and down for hours talking of her and I would sit there listening to him with the key of the room the child was locked in, in my pocket. I temporised, and, as you say yourself, it was perhaps because he had no one at his back that he did not try to kill me, which he might have done any day. I temporised. And after all, why should he want to kill me? He told me more than once he was sure to have Arlette for his own. Many a time he made me shiver explaining why it must be so. She owed her life to him. Oh! that dreadful crazy life. You know he is one of those men that can be patient as far as women are concerned.'

Peyrol nodded understandingly. 'Yes, some are like that. That kind is more impatient sometimes to spill blood. Still I think that your life was one long narrow escape, at least till I turned up here.'

'Things had settled down, somehow,' murmured Catherine. 'But all the same I was glad when you appeared here, a grey-headed man, serious.'

'Grey hairs will come to any sort of man,' observed Peyrol acidly, 'and you did not know me. You don't know anything of me even now.'

'There have been Peyrols living less than half a day's journey from here,' observed Catherine in a reminiscent tone.

'That's all right,' said the rover in such a peculiar tone that she asked him sharply: 'What's the matter? Aren't you one of them? Isn't Peyrol your name?'

'I have had many names and this was one of them. So this name and my grey hair pleased you, Catherine? They gave you confidence in me, hein?'

'I wasn't sorry to see you come. Scevola, too, I believe. He heard that patriots were being hunted down, here and there, and he was growing quieter every day. You roused the child wonderfully.'

'And did that please Scevola too?'

'Before you came she never spoke to anybody unless first spoken to. She didn't seem to care where she was. At the same time,' added Catherine after a pause, 'she didn't care what happened to her either. Oh, I have had some heavy hours thinking it all over, in the daytime doing my work, and at night while I lay awake, listening to her breathing. And I growing older all the time, and, who knows, with my last hour ready to strike. I often thought that when I felt it coming I would speak to you as I am speaking to you now.'

'Oh, you did think,' said Peyrol in an undertone. 'Because of my grey hairs, I suppose.'

'Yes. And because you came from beyond the seas,' Catherine said with unbending mien and in an unflinching voice. 'Don't you know that the first time Arlette saw you she spoke to you and that it was the first time I heard her speak of her own accord since she had been brought back by that man, and I had to wash her from head to foot before I put her into her mother's bed?'

'The first time,' repeated Peyrol.

'It was like a miracle happening,' said Catherine, 'and it was you that had done it.'

'Then it must be that some Indian witch has given me the power,' muttered Peyrol, so low that Catherine could not hear the words.

But she did not seem to care, and presently went on again: 'And the child took to you wonderfully. Some sentiment was aroused in her at last.'

'Yes,' assented Peyrol grimly. 'She did take to me. She learned to talk to – the old man.'

'It's something in you that seems to have opened her mind and unloosed her tongue,' said Catherine, speaking with a sort of regal composure down at Peyrol, like a chieftainess of a tribe. 'I often used to look from afar at you two talking and wonder what she . . . '

'She talked like a child,' struck in Peyrol abruptly. 'And so you were going to speak to me before your last hour came. Why, you are not making ready to die yet?'

'Listen, Peyrol. If anybody's last hour is near it isn't mine. You just look about you a little. It was time I spoke to you.'

'Why, I am not going to kill anybody,' muttered Peyrol. 'You are getting strange ideas into your head.'

'It is as I said,' insisted Catherine without animation. 'Death seems to cling to her skirts. She has been running with it madly. Let us keep her feet out of more human blood.'

Peyrol, who had let his head fall on his breast, jerked it up suddenly. 'What on earth are you talking about?' he cried angrily. 'I don't understand you at all.'

'You have not seen the state she was in when I got her back into my hands,' remarked Catherine . . . 'I suppose you know where the lieutenant is. What made him go off like that? Where did he go to?'

'I know,' said Peyrol. 'And he may be back tonight.'

'You know where he is! And of course you know why he has gone away and why he is coming back,' pronounced Catherine in an ominous voice. 'Well, you had better tell him that unless he has a pair of eyes at the back of his head he had better not return here – not return at all; for if he does, nothing can save him from a treacherous blow.'

'No man was ever safe from treachery,' opined Peyrol after a moment's silence. 'I won't pretend not to understand what you mean.'

'You heard as well as I what Scevola said just before he went out. The lieutenant is the child of some ci-devant and Arlette of a man they called a traitor to his country. You can see yourself what was in his mind.'

'He is a chicken-hearted spouter,' said Peyrol contemptuously, but it did not affect Catherine's attitude of an old sibyl[144] risen from the tripod to prophesy calmly atrocious disasters. 'It's all his republicanism,' commented Peyrol with increased scorn. 'He has got a fit of it on.'

'No, that's jealousy,' said Catherine. 'Maybe he has ceased to care for her in all these years. It is a long time since he has left off worrying me. With a creature like that I thought that if I let him be master here . . . But no! I know that after the lieutenant started coming here his awful fancies have come back. He is not sleeping at night. His republicanism is always there. But don't you know, Peyrol, that there may be jealousy without love?'

'You think so,' said the rover profoundly. He pondered, full of his own experience. 'And he has tasted blood too,' he muttered after a pause. 'You may be right.'

'I may be right,' repeated Catherine in a slightly indignant tone. 'Every time I see Arlette near him I tremble lest it should come to words and to a bad blow. And when they are both out of my sight it is still worse. At this moment I am wondering where they are. They may be together and I daren't raise my voice to call her away for fear of rousing his fury.'

'But it's the lieutenant he is after,' observed Peyrol in a lowered voice. 'Well, I can't stop the lieutenant coming back.'

'Where is she? Where is he?' whispered Catherine in a tone betraying her secret anguish.

Peyrol rose quietly and went into the salle, leaving the door open. Catherine heard the latch of the outer door being lifted cautiously. In a few moments Peyrol returned as quietly as he had gone out.

'I stepped out to look at the weather. The moon is about to rise and the clouds have thinned down. One can see a star here and there.' He lowered his voice considerably. 'Arlette is sitting on the bench humming a little song to herself. I really wonder whether she knew I was standing within a few feet of her.'

'She doesn't want to hear or see anybody except one man,' affirmed Catherine, now in complete control of her voice. 'And she was humming a song, did you say? She who would sit for hours without making a sound. And God knows what song it could have been!'

'Yes, there's a great change in her,' admitted Peyrol with a heavy sigh. 'This lieutenant,' he continued after a pause, 'has always behaved coldly to her. I noticed him many times turn his face away when he saw her coming towards us. You know what these epaulette-wearers are, Catherine. And then this one has some worm of his own that is gnawing at him. I doubt whether he has ever forgotten that he was a ci-devant boy. Yet I do believe that she does not want to see and hear anybody but him. Is it because she has been deranged in her head for so long?'

'No, Peyrol,' said the old woman. 'It isn't that. You want to know how I can tell? For years nothing could make her either laugh or cry. You know that yourself. You have seen her every day. Would you believe that within the last month she has been both crying and laughing on my breast without knowing why?'

'This I don't understand,' said Peyrol.

'But I do. That lieutenant has got only to whistle to make her run after him. Yes, Peyrol. That is so. She has no fear, no shame, no pride. I myself have been nearly like that.' Her fine brown face seemed to grow more impassive before she went on much lower and as if arguing with herself: 'Only I at least was never blood-mad. I was fit for any man's arms . . . But then that man is not a priest.'

The last words made Peyrol start. He had almost forgotten that story. He said to himself: 'She knows, she has had the experience.'

'Look here, Catherine,' he said decisively, 'the lieutenant is coming back. He will be here probably about midnight. But one thing I can tell you: he is not coming back to whistle her away. Oh, no! It is not for her sake that he will come back.'

'Well, if it isn't for her that he is coming back then it must be because death has beckoned to him,' she announced in a tone of solemn un-emotional conviction. 'A man who has received a sign from death – nothing can stop him!'

Peyrol, who had seen death face to face many times, looked at Catherine's fine brown profile curiously.

'It is a fact,' he murmured, 'that men who rush out to seek death do not often find it. So one must have a sign? What sort of sign would it be?'

'How is anybody to know?' asked Catherine, staring across the kitchen at the wall. 'Even those to whom it is made do not recognise it for what it is. But they obey all the same. I tell you, Peyrol, nothing can stop them. It may be a glance, or a smile, or a shadow on the water, or a thought that passes through the head. For my poor brother and sister-in-law it was the face of their child.'

Peyrol folded his arms on his breast and dropped his head. Melancholy was a sentiment to which he was a stranger; for what has melancholy to do with the life of a sea-rover, a Brother of the Coast, a simple, venturesome, precarious life, full of risks and leaving no time for introspection or for that momentary self-forgetfulness which is called gaiety. Sombre fury, fierce merriment, he had known in passing gusts, coming from outside; but never this intimate inward sense of the vanity of all things, that doubt of the power within himself.

'I wonder what the sign for me will be,' he thought; and concluded with self-contempt that for him there would be no sign, that he would have to die in his bed like an old yard dog in his kennel. Having reached that depth of despondency, there was nothing more before him but a black gulf into which his consciousness sank like a stone.

The silence which had lasted perhaps a minute after Catherine had finished speaking was traversed suddenly by a clear high voice saying: 'What are you two plotting here?'

Arlette stood in the doorway of the salle. The gleam of light in the whites of her eyes set off her black and penetrating glance. The surprise was complete. The profile of Catherine, who was standing by the table, became if possible harder; a sharp carving of an old prophetess of some desert tribe. Arlette made three steps forward. In Peyrol even extreme astonishment was deliberate. He had been famous for never looking as though he had been caught unprepared. Age had accentuated that trait of a born leader. He only slipped off the edge of the table and said in his deep voice: 'Why, patronne! We haven't said a word to each other for ever so long.'

Arlette moved nearer still. 'I know,' she cried. 'It was horrible. I have been watching you two. Scevola came and dumped himself on the bench close to me. He began to talk to me, and so I went away. That man bores me. And here I find you people saying nothing. It's insupportable. What has come to you both? Say, you, Papa Peyrol – don't you like me any more?' Her voice filled the kitchen.

Peyrol went to the salle door and shut it. While coming back he was staggered by the brilliance of life within her that seemed to pale the flames of the lamp. He said half in jest: 'I don't know whether I didn't like you better when you were quieter.'

'And you would like best to see me still quieter in my grave.'

She dazzled him. Vitality streamed out of her eyes, her lips, her whole person, enveloped her like a halo and . . . yes, truly, the faintest possible flush had appeared on her cheeks, played on them faintly rosy like the light of a distant flame on the snow. She raised her arms up in the air and let her hands fall from on high on Peyrol's shoulders, captured his desperately dodging eyes with her black and compelling glance, put out all her instinctive seduction – while he felt a growing fierceness in the grip of her fingers.

'No! I can't hold it in! Monsieur Peyrol, Papa Peyrol, old gunner, you horrid sea-wolf, be an angel and tell me where he is.'

The rover, whom only that morning the powerful grasp of Lieutenant Réal found as unshakable as a rock, felt all his strength vanish under the hands of that woman. He said thickly: 'He has gone to Toulon. He had to go.'

'What for? Speak the truth to me!'

'Truth is not for everybody to know,' mumbled Peyrol, with a sinking sensation as though the very ground were going soft under his feet. 'On service,' he added in a growl.

Her hands slipped suddenly from his big shoulders. 'On service?' she repeated. 'What service?' Her voice sank and the words, 'Oh, yes! His service,' were hardly heard by Peyrol, who as soon as her hands had left his shoulders felt his strength returning to him and the yielding earth grow firm again under his feet. Right in front of him Arlette, silent, with her arms hanging down before her with entwined fingers, seemed stunned because Lieutenant Réal was not free from all earthly connections, like a visiting angel from heaven depending only on God to whom she had prayed. She had to share him with some service that could order him about. She felt in herself a strength, a power, greater than any service.

'Peyrol,' she cried low, 'don't break my heart, my new heart, that has just begun to beat. Feel how it beats. Who could bear it?' She seized the rover's thick hairy paw and pressed it hard against her breast. 'Tell me when he will be back.'

'Listen, patronne, you had better go upstairs,' began Peyrol with a great effort and snatching his captured hand away.

He staggered backwards a little while Arlette shouted at him: 'You can't order me about as you used to do.' In all the changes from entreaty to anger she never struck a false note, so that her emotional outburst had the heart-moving power of inspired art. She turned round with a tempestuous swish to Catherine who had neither stirred nor emitted a sound: 'Nothing you two can do will make any difference now.' The next moment she was facing Peyrol again. 'You frighten me with your white hairs. Come! . . . am I to go on my knees to you? . . . There!'

The rover caught her under the elbows, swung her up clear of the ground, and set her down on her feet as if she had been a child.

Directly he had let her go, she stamped her foot at him. 'Are you stupid?' she cried. 'Don't you understand that something has happened today?'

Through all this scene Peyrol had kept his head as creditably as could have been expected, in the manner of a seaman caught by a white squall in the tropics. But at those words a dozen thoughts tried to rush together through his mind, in chase of that startling declaration. Something had happened! Where? How? Whom to? What thing? It couldn't be anything between her and the lieutenant. He had, it seemed to him, never lost sight of the lieutenant from the first hour when they met in the morning till he had sent him off to Toulon by an actual push on the shoulder; except while he was having his dinner in the next room with the door open, and for the few minutes spent in talking with Michel in the yard. But that was only a very few minutes, and directly afterwards the first sight of the lieutenant sitting gloomily on the bench like a lonely crow did not suggest either elation or excitement or any emotion connected with a woman. In the face of these difficulties Peyrol's mind became suddenly a blank. 'Voyons,[145] patronne,' he began, unable to think of anything else to say. 'What's all this fuss about? I expect him to be back here about midnight.'

He was extremely relieved to notice that she believed him. It was the truth. For indeed he did not know what he could have invented on the spur of the moment that would get her out of the way and induce her to go to bed. She treated him to a sinister frown and a terribly menacing, 'If you have lied . . . Oh!'

He produced an indulgent smile. 'Compose yourself. He will be here soon after midnight. You may go to sleep with an easy mind.'

She turned her back on him contemptuously, and said curtly, 'Come along, aunt,' and went to the door leading to the passage. There she turned for a moment with her hand on the door handle.

'You are changed. I can't trust either of you. You are not the same people.'

She went out. Only then did Catherine detach her gaze from the wall to meet Peyrol's eyes. 'Did you hear what she said? We! Changed! It is she herself . . . '

Peyrol nodded twice and there was a long pause, during which even the flames of the lamp did not stir.

'Go after her, Mademoiselle Catherine,' he said at last with a shade of sympathy in his tone. She did not move. 'Allons – du courage,'[146] he urged her deferentially as it were. 'Try to put her to sleep.'

Chapter 12

Upright and deliberate, Catherine left the kitchen, and in the passage outside found Arlette waiting for her with a lighted candle in her hand. Her heart was filled with sudden desolation by the beauty of that young face enhaloed in the patch of light, with the profound darkness as of a dungeon for a background. At once her niece led the way upstairs muttering savagely through her pretty teeth: 'He thinks I could go to sleep. Old imbecile!'

Peyrol did not take his eyes off Catherine's straight back till the door had closed after her. Only then he relieved himself by letting the air escape through his pursed lips and rolling his eyes freely about. He picked up the lamp by the ring on the top of the central rod and went into the salle, closing behind him the door of the dark kitchen. He stood the lamp on the very table on which Lieutenant Réal had had his midday meal. A small white cloth was still spread on it and there was his chair askew as he had pushed it back when he got up. Another of the many chairs in the salle was turned round conspicuously to face the table. These things made Peyrol remark to himself bitterly: 'She sat and stared at him as if he had been gilt all over, with three heads and seven arms on his body' – a comparison reminiscent of certain idols he had seen in an Indian temple. Though not an iconoclast, Peyrol felt positively sick at the recollection, and hastened to step outside. The great cloud had broken up and the mighty fragments were moving to the westward in stately flight before the rising moon. Scevola, who had been lying extended full length on the bench, swung himself up suddenly, very upright.

'Had a little nap in the open?' asked Peyrol, letting his eyes roam through the luminous space under the departing rearguard of the clouds jostling each other up there.

'I did not sleep,' said the sans-culotte. 'I haven't closed my eyes – not for one moment.'

'That must be because you weren't sleepy,' suggested the deliberate Peyrol, whose thoughts were far away with the English ship. His mental eye contemplated her black image against the white beach of the Salins describing a sparkling curve under the moon, and meantime he went on slowly: 'For it could not have been noise that kept you awake.' On the level of Escampobar the shadows lay long on the ground while the side of the lookout hill remained yet black but edged with an increasing brightness. And the amenity of the stillness was such that it softened for a moment Peyrol's hard inward attitude towards all mankind, including even the captain of the English ship. The old rover savoured a moment of serenity in the midst of his cares.

'This is an accursed spot,' declared Scevola suddenly.

Peyrol, without turning his head, looked at him sideways. Though he had sprung up from his reclining posture smartly enough, the citizen had gone slack all over and was sitting all in a heap. His shoulders were hunched up, his hands reposed on his knees. With his staring eyes he resembled a sick child in the moonlight.

'It's the very spot for hatching treacheries. One feels steeped in them up to the neck.' He shuddered and yawned a long irresistible nervous yawn with the gleam of unexpected long canines in a retracted, gaping mouth giving away the restless panther lurking in the man. 'Oh, yes, there's treachery about right enough. You couldn't conceive that, citoyen?'

'Of course I couldn't,' assented Peyrol with serene contempt. 'What is this treachery that you are concocting?' he added carelessly, in a social way, while enjoying the charm of a moonlit evening.

Scevola, who did not expect that turn, managed, however, to produce a rattling sort of laugh almost at once. 'That's a good one. Ha! ha! ha! . . . Me! . . . concocting! . . . Why me?'

'Well,' said Peyrol carelessly, 'there are not many of us to carry out treacheries about here. The women are gone upstairs; Michel is down at the tartane. There's me, and you would not dare suspect me of treachery. Well, there remains only you.'

Scevola roused himself. 'This is not much of a jest,' he said. 'I have been a treason-hunter. I . . . '

He checked that strain. He was full of purely emotional suspicions. Peyrol was talking like this only to annoy him and to get him out of the way; but in the particular state of his feelings Scevola was acutely aware of every syllable of these offensive remarks. 'Aha,' he thought to himself, 'he doesn't mention the lieutenant.' This omission seemed to the patriot of immense importance. If Peyrol had not mentioned the lieutenant it was because those two had been plotting some treachery together, all the afternoon on board that tartane. That's why nothing had been seen of them for the best part of the day. As a matter of fact, Scevola too had observed Peyrol returning to the farm in the evening, only he had observed him from another window than Arlette. This was a few minutes before his attempt to open the lieutenant's door, in order to find out whether Réal was in his room. He had tiptoed away, uncertain, and going into the kitchen had found only Catherine and Peyrol there. Directly Arlette joined them a sudden inspiration made him run upstairs and try the door again. It was open now! A clear proof that it was Arlette who had been locked up in there. The discovery that she made herself at home like this in the lieutenant's room gave Scevola such a sickening shock that he thought he would die of it. It was beyond doubt now that the lieutenant had been conspiring with Peyrol down on board that tartane; for what else could they have been doing there? But why had not Réal come up in the evening with Peyrol? Scevola asked himself, sitting on the bench with his hands clasped between his knees . . . 'It's their cunning,' he concluded suddenly. 'Conspirators always avoid being seen together. Ha!'

It was as if somebody had let off a lot of fireworks in his brain. He was illuminated, dazzled, confused, with a hissing in his ears and showers of sparks before his eyes. Peyrol had vanished. Scevola seemed to remember that he had heard somebody pronounce the word 'good-night' and the door of the salle slam. And sure enough the door of the salle was shut now. A dim light shone in the window that was next to it. Peyrol had extinguished three of the lamp flames and was now reclining on one of the long tables with that faculty of accommodating himself to a plank an old sea-dog never loses. He had decided to remain below simply to be handy, and he didn't lie down on one of the benches along the wall because they were too narrow. He left one wick burning, so that the lieutenant should know where to look for him, and he was tired enough to think that he would snatch a couple of hours' sleep before Réal could return from Toulon. He settled himself with one arm under his head as if he were on the deck of a privateer, and it never occurred to him that Scevola was looking through the panes; but they were so small and dusty that the patriot could see nothing. His movement had been purely instinctive. He wasn't even aware that he had looked in. He went away from there, walked to the end of the building, spun round and walked back again to the other end; and it was as if he had been afraid of going beyond the wall against which he reeled sometimes. 'Conspiracy, conspiracy,' he thought. He was now absolutely certain that the lieutenant was still hiding in that tartane, and was only waiting till all was quiet to sneak back to his room in which Scevola had proof positive that Arlette was in the habit of making herself at home. To rob him of his right to Arlette was part of the conspiracy no doubt.

'Have I been a slave to those two women, have I waited all those years, only to see that corrupt creature go off infamously with a ci-devant, with a conspiring aristocrat?'

He became giddy with virtuous fury. There was enough evidence there for any revolutionary tribunal to cut all their heads off. Tribunal! There was no tribunal! No revolutionary justice! No patriots! He hit his shoulder against the wall in his distress with such force that he rebounded. This world was no place for patriots.

'If I had betrayed myself in the kitchen they would have murdered me in there.'

As it was he thought that he had said too much. Too much. 'Prudence! Caution!' he repeated to himself, gesticulating with both arms. Suddenly he stumbled and there was an amazing metallic clatter made by something that fell at his feet.

'They are trying to kill me now,' he thought, shaking with fright. He gave himself up for dead. Profound silence reigned all round. Nothing more happened. He stooped fearfully to look and recognised his own stable fork lying on the ground. He remembered he had left it at noon leaning against the wall. His own foot had made it fall. He threw himself upon it greedily. 'Here's what I need,' he muttered feverishly. 'I suppose that by now the lieutenant would think I am gone to bed.'

He flattened himself upright against the wall with the fork held along his body like a grounded musket. The moon clearing the hilltop flooded suddenly the front of the house with its cold light, but he didn't know it; he imagined himself still to be ambushed in the shadow and remained motionless, glaring at the path leading towards the cove. His teeth chattered with savage impatience.

He was so plainly visible in his deathlike rigidity that Michel, coming up out of the ravine, stopped dead short, believing him an apparition not belonging to this earth. Scevola, on his side, noticed the moving shadow cast by a man – that man! – and charged forward without reflection, the prongs of the fork lowered like a bayonet. He didn't shout. He came straight on, growling like a dog, and lunged headlong with his weapon.

Michel, a primitive, untroubled by anything so uncertain as intelligence, executed an instantaneous sideways leap with the precision of a wild animal; but he was enough of a man to become afterwards paralysed with astonishment. The impetus of the rush carried Scevola several yards down the hill before he could turn round and assume an offensive attitude. Then the two adversaries recognised each other. The terrorist exclaimed: 'Michel?' and Michel hastened to pick up a large stone from the ground.

'Hey, you, Scevola,' he cried, not very loud but very threatening. 'What are these tricks? . . . Keep away, or I will heave that piece of rock at your head, and I am good at that.'

Scevola grounded the fork with a thud. 'I didn't recognise you,' he said.

'That's a story. Who did you think I was? Not the other! I haven't got a bandaged head, have I?'

Scevola began to scramble up. 'What's this?' he asked. 'What head, did you say?'

'I say that if you come near I will knock you over with that stone,' answered Michel. 'You aren't to be trusted when the moon is full. Not recognise! There's a silly excuse for flying at people like this. You haven't got anything against me, have you?'

'No,' said the ex-terrorist in a dubious tone and keeping a watchful eye on Michel, who was still holding the stone in his hand.

'People have been saying for years that you are a kind of lunatic,' Michel criticised fearlessly, because the other's discomfiture was evident enough to put heart into the timid hare. 'If a fellow cannot come up now to get a snooze in the shed without being run at with a fork, well . . . '

'I was only going to put this fork away,' Scevola burst out volubly. 'I had left it leaning against the wall, and as I was passing along I suddenly saw it, so I thought I would put it in the stable before I went to bed. That's all.'

Michel's mouth fell open a bit.

'Now what do you think I would want with a stable fork at this time of night, if it wasn't to put it away?' argued Scevola.

'What indeed!' mumbled Michel, who began to doubt the evidence of his senses.

'You go about mooning like a fool and imagine a lot of silly things, you great, stupid imbecile. All I wanted to do was to ask whether everything was all right down there, and you, idiot, bound to one side like a goat and pick up a stone. The moon has affected your head, not mine. Now drop it.'

Michel, accustomed to do what he was told, opened his fingers slowly, not quite convinced but thinking there might be something in it.

Scevola, perceiving his advantage, scolded on: 'You are dangerous. You ought to have your feet and hands tied every full moon. What did you say about a head just now? What head?'

'I said that I didn't have a broken head.'

'Was that all?' said Scevola. He was asking himself what on earth could have happened down there during the afternoon to cause a broken head. Clearly, it must have been either a fight or an accident, but in any case he considered that it was for him a favourable circumstance, for obviously a man with a bandaged head is at a disadvantage. He was inclined to think it must have been some silly accident, and he regretted profoundly that the lieutenant had not killed himself outright. He turned sourly to Michel.

'Now you may go into the shed. And don't try any of your tricks with me any more, because next time you pick up a stone I will shoot you like a dog.'

He began to move towards the yard gate which stood always open, throwing over his shoulder an order to Michel: 'Go into the salle. Somebody has left a light in there. They all seem to have gone crazy today. Take the lamp into the kitchen and put it out and see that the door into the yard is shut. I am going to bed.' He passed through the gateway, but he did not penetrate into the yard very far. He stopped to watch Michel obeying the order. Scevola, advancing his head cautiously beyond the pillar of the gate, waited till he had seen Michel open the door of the salle and then bounded out again across the level space and down the ravine path. It was a matter of less than a minute. His fork was still on his shoulder. His only desire was not to be interfered with, and for the rest he did not care what they all did, what they would think and how they would behave. The fixed idea had taken complete possession of him. He had no plan, but he had a principle on which to act; and that was to get at the lieutenant unawares, and if the fellow died without knowing what hand had struck him, so much the better. Scevola was going to act in the cause of virtue and justice. It was not to be a matter of personal contest at all. Meantime, Michel, having gone into the salle, had discovered Peyrol fast asleep on a table. Though his reverence for Peyrol was unbounded, his simplicity was such that he shook his master by the shoulder as he would have done any common mortal. The rover passed from a state of inertia into a sitting posture so quickly that Michel stepped back a pace and waited to be addressed. But as Peyrol only stared at him, Michel took the initiative in a concise phrase: 'He's at it!'

Peyrol did not seem completely awake: 'What is it you mean?' he asked.

'He is making motions to escape.'

Peyrol was wide awake now. He even swung his feet off the table.

'Is he? Haven't you locked the cabin door?'

Michel, very frightened, explained that he had never been told to do that.

'No?' remarked Peyrol placidly. 'I must have forgotten.' But Michel remained agitated and murmured: 'He is escaping.'

'That's all right,' said Peyrol. 'What are you fussing about? How far can he escape, do you think?'

A slow grin appeared on Michel's face. 'If he tries to scramble over the top of the rocks, he will get a broken neck in a very short time,' he said. 'And he certainly won't get very far, that's a fact.'

'Well – you see,' said Peyrol.

'And he doesn't seem strong either. He crawled out of the cabin door and got as far as the little water cask and he dipped and dipped into it. It must be half empty by now. After that he got on to his legs. I cleared out ashore directly I heard him move,' he went on in a tone of intense self-approval. 'I hid myself behind a rock and watched him.'

'Quite right,' observed Peyrol. After that word of commendation, Michel's face wore a constant grin.

'He sat on the after-deck,' he went on as if relating an immense joke, 'with his feet dangling down the hold, and may the devil take me if I don't think he had a nap with his back against the cask. He was nodding and catching himself up, with that big white head of his. Well, I got tired of watching that, and as you told me to keep out of his way, I thought I would come up here and sleep in the shed. That was right, wasn't it?'

'Quite right,' repeated Peyrol. 'Well, you go now into the shed. And so you left him sitting on the after-deck?'

'Yes,' said Michel. 'But he was rousing himself. I hadn't got away more than ten yards when I heard an awful thump on board. I think he tried to get up and fell down the hold.'

'Fell down the hold?' repeated Peyrol sharply.

'Yes, notre maître. I thought at first I would go back and see, but you had warned me against him, hadn't you? And I really think that nothing can kill him.'

Peyrol got down from the table with an air of concern which would have astonished Michel, if he had not been utterly incapable of observing things.

'This must be seen to,' murmured the rover, buttoning the waistband of his trousers. 'My cudgel there, in the corner. Now you go to the shed. What the devil are you doing at the door? Don't you know the way to the shed?' This last observation was caused by Michel remaining in the doorway of the salle with his head out and looking to right and left along the front of the house. 'What's come to you? You don't suppose he has been able to follow you so quick as this up here?'

'Oh no, notre maître, quite impossible. I saw that sacré Scevola promenading up and down here. I don't want to meet him again.'

'Was he promenading outside?' asked Peyrol, with annoyance. 'Well, what do you think he can do to you? What notions have you got in your silly head? You are getting worse and worse. Out you go.'

Peyrol extinguished the lamp and, going out, closed the door without the slightest noise. The intelligence about Scevola being on the move did not please him very much, but he reflected that probably the sans-culotte had fallen asleep again and after waking up was on his way to bed when Michel caught sight of him. He had his own view of the patriot's psychology and did not think the women were in any danger. Nevertheless he went to the shed and heard the rustling of straw as Michel settled himself for the night.

'Debout,'[147] he cried low. 'Sh, don't make any noise. I want you to go into the house and sleep at the bottom of the stairs. If you hear voices, go up, and if you see Scevola about, knock him down. You aren't afraid of him, are you?'

'No, if you tell me not to be,' said Michel, who, picking up his shoes, a present from Peyrol, walked barefoot towards the house. The rover watched him slipping noiselessly through the salle door. Having thus, so to speak, guarded his base, Peyrol proceeded down the ravine with a very deliberate caution. When he got as far as the little hollow in the ground from which the mastheads of the tartane could be seen, he squatted and waited. He didn't know what his prisoner had done or was doing and he did not want to blunder into the way of his escape. The day-old moon was high enough to have shortened the shadows almost to nothing and all the rocks were inundated by a yellow sheen, while the bushes by contrast looked very black. Peyrol reflected that he was not very well concealed. The continued silence impressed him in the end. 'He has got away,' he thought. Yet he was not sure. Nobody could be sure. He reckoned it was about an hour since Michel had left the tartane; time enough for a man, even on all fours, to crawl down to the shore of the cove. Peyrol wished he had not hit so hard. His object could have been attained with half the force. On the other hand all the proceedings of his prisoner, as reported by Michel, seemed quite rational. Naturally the fellow was badly shaken. Peyrol felt as though he wanted to go on board and give him some encouragement, and even active assistance.

The report of a gun from seaward cut his breath short as he lay there meditating. Within a minute there was a second report, sending another wave of deep sound among the crags and hills of the peninsula. The ensuing silence was so profound that it seemed to extend to the very inside of Peyrol's head, and lull all his thoughts for a moment. But he had understood. He said to himself that after this his prisoner, if he had life enough left in him to stir a limb, would rather die than not try to make his way to the seashore. The ship was calling to her man.

In fact those two gunshots had proceeded from the *Amelia*. After passing beyond Cape Esterel, Captain Vincent dropped an anchor underfoot off the beach just as Peyrol had surmised he would do. From about six o'clock till nine the *Amelia* lay there with her unfurled sails hanging in the gear. Just before the moon rose the captain came up on deck and after a short conference with his first lieutenant, directed the master to get the ship under way and put her head again for the Petite Passe. Then he went below, and presently word was passed on deck that the captain wanted Mr Bolt. When the master's mate appeared in his cabin, Captain Vincent motioned him to a chair.

'I don't think I ought to have listened to you,' he said. 'Still, the idea was fascinating, but how it would strike other people it is hard to say. The losing of our man is the worst feature. I have an idea that we might recover him. He may have been captured by the peasants or have met with an accident. It's unbearable to think of him lying at the foot of some rock with a broken leg. I have ordered the first and second cutters to be manned, and I propose that you should take command of them, enter the cove and, if necessary, advance a little inland to investigate. As far as we know there have never been any troops on that peninsula. The first thing you will do is to examine the coast.'

He talked for some time, giving more minute instructions, and then went on deck. The *Amelia*, with the two cutters towing alongside, reached about halfway down the Passe and then the boats were ordered to proceed. Just before they shoved off, two guns were fired in quick succession.

'Like this, Bolt,' explained Captain Vincent, 'Symons will guess that we are looking for him; and if he is hiding anywhere near the shore he will be sure to come down where he can be seen by you.'

The motive force of a fixed idea is very great. In the case of Scevola it was great enough to launch him down the slope and to rob him for the moment of all caution. He bounded amongst the boulders, using the handle of the stable fork for a staff. He paid no regard to the nature of the ground, till he got a fall and found himself sprawling on his face, while the stable fork went clattering down until it was stopped by a bush. It was this circumstance which saved Peyrol's prisoner from being caught unawares. Since he had got out of the little cabin, simply because after coming to himself he had perceived it was open, Symons had been greatly refreshed by long drinks of cold water and by his little nap in the fresh air. Every moment he was feeling in better command of his limbs. As to the command of his thoughts, that was coming to him too rather quickly. The advantage of having a very thick skull became evident in the fact that as soon as he had dragged himself out of that cabin he knew where he was. The next thing he did was to look at the moon, to judge of the passage of time. Then he gave way to an immense surprise at the fact of being alone aboard the tartane. As he sat with his legs dangling into the open hold he tried to guess how it came about that the cabin had been left unlocked and unguarded.

He went on thinking about this unexpected situation. What could have become of that white-headed villain? Was he dodging about somewhere watching for a chance to give him another tap on the head? Symons felt suddenly very unsafe sitting there on the after-deck in the full light of the moon. Instinct rather than reason suggested to him that he ought to get down into the dark hold. It seemed a great undertaking at first, but once he started he accomplished it with the greatest ease, though he could not avoid knocking down a small spar which was leaning up against the deck. It preceded him into the hold with a loud crash which gave poor Symons an attack of palpitation of the heart. He sat on the keelson[148] of the tartane and gasped, but after a while reflected that all this did not matter. His head felt very big, his neck was very painful and one shoulder was certainly very stiff. He could never stand up against that old ruffian. But what had become of him? Why! He had gone to fetch the soldiers! After that conclusion Symons became more composed. He began to try to remember things. When he had last seen that old fellow it was daylight, and now –

Symons looked up at the moon again – it must be near six bells in the first watch.[149] No doubt the old scoundrel was sitting in a wine shop drinking with the soldiers. They would be here soon enough! The idea of being a prisoner of war made his heart sink a little. His ship appeared to him invested with an extraordinary number of lovable features which included Captain Vincent and the first lieutenant. He would have been glad to shake hands even with the corporal, a surly and malicious marine acting as master-at-arms of the ship. 'I wonder where she is now,' he thought dismally, feeling his distaste for captivity grow with the increase of his strength.

It was at this moment that he heard the noise of Scevola's fall. It was pretty close; but afterwards he heard no voices and footsteps heralding the approach of a body of men. If this was the old ruffian coming back, then he was coming back alone. At once Symons started on all fours for the fore-end of the tartane. He had an idea that ensconced under the foredeck he would be in a better position to parley with the enemy and that perhaps he could find there a handspike or some piece of iron to defend himself with. Just as he had settled himself in his hiding-place Scevola stepped from the shore on to the after-deck.

At the very first glance Symons perceived that this one was very unlike the man he expected to see. He felt rather disappointed. As Scevola stood still in full moonlight Symons congratulated himself on having taken up a position under the foredeck. That fellow, who had a beard, was like a sparrow in body compared with the other; but he was armed dangerously with something that looked to Symons like either a trident or fishgrains[150] on a staff. 'A devil of a weapon that,' he thought, appalled. And what on earth did that beggar want on board? What could he be after?

The newcomer acted strangely at first. He stood stock-still, craning his neck here and there, peering along the whole length of the tartane, then crossing the deck he repeated all those performances on the other side. 'He has noticed that the cabin door is open. He's trying to see where I've got to. He will be coming forward to look for me,' said Symons to himself. 'If he corners me here with that beastly pronged affair I am done for.' For a moment he debated within himself whether it wouldn't be better to make a dash for it and scramble ashore; but in the end he mistrusted his strength. 'He would run me down for sure,' he concluded. 'And he means no good, that's certain. No man would go about at night with a confounded thing like that if he didn't mean to do for somebody.'

Scevola, after keeping perfectly still, straining his ears for any sound from below where he supposed Lieutenant Réal to be, stooped down to the cabin scuttle and called in a low voice: 'Are you there, lieutenant?' Symons saw these motions and could not imagine their purport. That excellent able seaman of proved courage in many cutting-out expeditions broke into a slight perspiration. In the light of the moon the prongs of the fork polished by much use shone like silver, and the whole aspect of the stranger was weird and dangerous in the extreme. Whom could that man be after but him, himself?

Scevola, receiving no answer, remained in a stooping position. He could not detect the slightest sound of breathing down there. He remained in this position so long that Symons became quite interested. 'He must think I am still down there,' he whispered to himself. The next proceeding was quite astonishing. The man, taking up a position on one side of the cuddy scuttle and holding his horrid weapon as one would a boarding pike, uttered a terrific whoop and went on yelling in French with such volubility that he quite frightened Symons. Suddenly he left off, moved away from the scuttle and looked at a loss what to do next. Anybody who could have seen then Symons protruded head with his face turned aft would have seen on it an expression of horror. 'The cunning beast,' he thought. 'If I had been down there, with the row he made I would have surely rushed on deck and then he would have had me.' Symons experienced the feeling of a very narrow escape; yet it brought not much relief. It was simply a matter of time. The fellow's homicidal purpose was evident. He was bound before long to come forward. Symons saw him move, and thought, 'Now he's coming,' and prepared himself for a dash. 'If I can dodge past those blamed prongs I might be able to take him by the throat,' he reflected, without, however, feeling much confidence in himself.

But to his great relief Scevola's purpose was simply to conceal the fork in the hold in such a manner that the handle of it just reached the edge of the after-deck. In that position it was of course invisible to anybody coming from the shore. Scevola had made up his mind that the lieutenant was out of the tartane. He had wandered away along the shore and would probably be back in a moment. Meantime it had occurred to him to see if he could discover anything compromising in the cabin. He did not take the fork down with him because in that confined space it would have been useless and rather a source of embarrassment than otherwise, should the returning lieutenant find him there. He cast a circular glance around the basin and then prepared to go down.

Every movement of his was watched by Symons. He guessed Scevola's purpose by his movements and said to himself: 'Here's my only chance, and not a second to be lost either.' Directly Scevola turned his back on the forepart of the tartane in order to go down the little cabin ladder, Symons crawled out from his concealment. He ran along the hold on all fours for fear the other should turn his head round before disappearing below, but directly he judged that the man had touched bottom, he stood on his feet and catching hold of the main rigging swung himself on the after-deck and, as it were in the same movement, flung himself on the doors of the cabin which came together with a crash. How he could secure them he had not thought, but as a matter of fact he saw the padlock hanging on a staple on one side; the key was in it, and it was a matter of a fraction of a second to secure the doors effectually.

Almost simultaneously with the crash of the cabin door there was a shrill exclamation of surprise down there, and just as Symons had turned the key the man he had trapped made an effort to break out. That, however, did not disturb Symons. He knew the strength of that door. His first action was to get possession of the stable fork. At once he felt himself a match for any single man or even two men unless they had firearms. He had no hope, however, of being able to resist the soldiers and really had no intention of doing so. He expected to see them appear at any moment led by that confounded marinero. As to what the farmer man had come for on board the tartane he had not the slightest doubt about it. Not being troubled by too much imagination, it seemed to him obvious that it was to kill an Englishman and for nothing else. 'Well, I am jiggered,' he exclaimed mentally. 'The damned savage! I haven't done anything to him. They must be a murderous lot hereabouts.' He looked anxiously up the slope. He would have welcomed the arrival of soldiers. He wanted more than ever to be made a proper prisoner, but a profound stillness reigned on the shore and a most absolute silence down below in the cabin. Absolute. No word, no movement. The silence of the grave. 'He's scared to death,' thought Symons, hitting in his simplicity on the exact truth. 'It would serve him jolly well right if I went down there and ran him through with that thing. I would do it for a shilling, too.' He was getting angry. It occurred to him also that there was some wine down there too. He discovered he was very thirsty and he felt rather faint. He sat down on the little skylight to think the matter over while awaiting the soldiers. He even gave a friendly thought to Peyrol himself. He was quite aware that he could have gone ashore and hidden himself for a time, but that meant in the end being hunted among the rocks and, certainly, captured; with the additional risk of getting a musket ball through his body.

The first gun of the *Amelia* lifted him to his feet as though he had
been snatched up by the hair of his head. He intended to give a
resounding cheer, but produced only a feeble gurgle in his throat. His
ship was talking to him. They hadn't given him up. At the second
report he scrambled ashore with the agility of a cat – in fact, with so
much agility that he had a fit of giddiness. After it passed off he returned
deliberately to the tartane to get hold of the stable fork. Then trembling
with emotion, he staggered off quietly and resolutely with the only
purpose of getting down to the seashore. He knew that as long as he
kept downhill he would be all right. The ground in this part being a
smooth rocky surface and Symons being barefooted, he passed at no
great distance from Peyrol without being heard. When he got on rough
ground he used the stable fork for a staff. Slowly as he moved, he was
not really strong enough to be sure-footed. Ten minutes later or so
Peyrol, lying ensconced behind a bush, heard the noise of a rolling
stone far away in the direction of the cove. Instantly the patient Peyrol
got on his feet and started towards the cove himself. Perhaps he would
have smiled if the importance and gravity of the affair in which he was
engaged had not given all his thoughts a serious cast. Pursuing a higher
path than the one followed by Symons, he had presently the satisfaction
of seeing the fugitive, made very noticeable by the white bandages
about his head, engaged in the last part of the steep descent. No nurse
could have watched with more anxiety the adventure of a little boy than
Peyrol the progress of his former prisoner. He was very glad to perceive
that he had had the sense to take what looked like the tartane's boathook
to help himself with. As Symons' figure sank lower and lower in his
descent Peyrol moved on, step by step, till at last he saw him from
above sitting down on the seashore, looking very forlorn and lonely,
with his bandaged head between his hands. Instantly Peyrol sat down
too, protected by a projecting rock. And it is safe to say that with that
there came a complete cessation of all sound and movement on the
lonely head of the peninsula for a full half-hour.

Peyrol was not in doubt as to what was going to happen. He was as
certain that the corvette's boat or boats were now on the way to the
cove as though he had seen them leave the side of the *Amelia*. But he
began to get a little impatient. He wanted to see the end of this episode.
Most of the time he was watching Symons. 'Sacré tête dure,' he thought.
'He has gone to sleep.' Indeed Symons' immobility was so complete
that he might have been dead from his exertions: only Peyrol had a
conviction that his once youthful chum was not the sort of person that
dies easily. The part of the cove he had reached was all right for Peyrol's

purpose. But it would have been quite easy for a boat or boats to fail to notice Symons, and the consequence of that would be that the English would probably land in several parties for a search and discover the tartane. Peyrol shuddered.

Suddenly he made out a boat just clear of the eastern point of the cove. Mr Bolt had been hugging the coast and progressing very slowly, according to his instructions, till he had reached the edge of the point's shadow where it lay ragged and black on the moonlit water. Peyrol could see the oars rise and fall. Then another boat glided into view. Peyrol's alarm for his tartane grew intolerable. 'Wake up, animal, wake up,' he mumbled through his teeth. Slowly they glided on, and the first cutter was on the point of passing by the man on the shore when Peyrol was relieved by the hail of 'Boat ahoy!' reaching him faintly where he knelt leaning forward, an absorbed spectator.

He saw the boat heading for Symons, who was standing up now and making desperate signs with both arms. Then he saw him dragged in over the bows, the boat back out, and then both of them tossed oars and floated side by side on the sparkling water of the cove.

Peyrol got up from his knees. They had their man now. But perhaps they would persist in landing since there must have been some other purpose at first in the mind of the captain of the English corvette. This suspense did not last long. Peyrol saw the oars fall in the water, and in a very few minutes the boats, pulling round, disappeared one after another behind the eastern point of the cove.

'That's done,' muttered Peyrol to himself. 'I will never see the silly hard-head again.' He had a strange notion that those English boats had carried off something belonging to him, not a man but a part of his own life, the sensation of a regained touch with the far-off days in the Indian Ocean. He walked down quickly as if to examine the spot from which Testa Dura had left the soil of France. He was in a hurry now to get back to the farmhouse and meet Lieutenant Réal, who would be due back from Toulon. The way by the cove was as short as any other. When he got down he surveyed the empty shore and wondered at a feeling of emptiness within himself. While walking up towards the foot of the ravine he saw an object lying on the ground. It was a stable fork. He stood over it asking himself, 'How on earth did this thing come here?' as though he had been too surprised to pick it up. Even after he had done so he remained motionless, meditating on it. He connected it with some activity of Scevola, since he was the man to whom it belonged, but that was no sort of explanation of its presence on that spot, unless . . .

'Could he have drowned himself?' thought Peyrol, looking at the smooth and luminous water of the cove. It could give him no answer. Then at arm's length he contemplated his find. At last he shook his head, shouldered the fork, and with slow steps continued on his way.

Chapter 14

The midnight meeting of Lieutenant Réal and Peyrol was perfectly silent. Peyrol, sitting on the bench outside the salle, had heard the footsteps coming up the Madrague track long before the lieutenant became visible. But he did not move. He did not even look at him. The lieutenant, unbuckling his sword-belt, sat down without uttering a word. The moon, the only witness of the meeting, seemed to shine on two friends so identical in thought and feeling that they could commune with each other without words.

It was Peyrol who spoke first. 'You are up to time.'

'I had the deuce of a job to hunt up the people and get the certificate stamped. Everything was shut up. The Port-Admiral was giving a dinner-party, but he came out to speak to me when I sent in my name. And all the time, do you know, gunner, I was wondering whether I would ever see you again in my life. Even after I had the certificate, such as it is, in my pocket, I wondered whether I would.'

'What the devil did you think was going to happen to me?' growled Peyrol perfunctorily. He had thrown the incomprehensible stable fork under the narrow bench, and with his feet drawn in he could feel it there, lying against the wall.

'No, the question with me was whether I would ever come here again.'

Réal drew a folded paper from his pocket and dropped it on the bench. Peyrol picked it up carelessly. That thing was meant only to throw dust into Englishmen's eyes. The lieutenant, after a moment's silence, went on with the sincerity of a man who suffered too much to keep his trouble to himself.

'I had a hard struggle.'

'That was too late,' said Peyrol, very positively. 'You had to come back here for very shame; and now you have come, you don't look very happy.'

'Never mind my looks, gunner. I have made up my mind.'

A ferocious, not unpleasing thought flashed through Peyrol's mind. It was that this intruder on the Escampobar sinister solitude, in which he, Peyrol, kept order, was under a delusion. Mind! Pah! His mind had nothing to do with his return. He had returned because in Catherine's words, 'death had made a sign to him'.

Meantime, Lieutenant Réal raised his hat to wipe his moist brow. 'I made up my mind to play the part of dispatch-bearer. As you have said yourself, Peyrol, one could not bribe a man – I mean an honest man – so you will have to find the vessel and leave the rest to me. In two or three days . . . You are under a moral obligation to let me have your tartane.'

Peyrol did not answer. He was thinking that Réal had got his sign, but whether it meant death from starvation or disease on board an English prison hulk, or in some other way, it was impossible to say. This naval officer was not a man he could trust; to whom he could, for instance, tell the story of his prisoner and what he had done with him. Indeed, the story was altogether incredible. The Englishman commanding that corvette had no visible, conceivable or probable reason for sending a boat ashore to the cove of all places in the world. Peyrol himself could hardly believe that it had happened. And he thought: 'If I were to tell that lieutenant he would only think that I was an old scoundrel who had been in treasonable communication with the English for God knows how long. No words of mine could persuade him that this was as unforeseen to me as the moon falling from the sky.'

'I wonder,' he burst out, but not very loud, 'what made you keep on coming back here time after time!' Réal leaned his back against the wall and folded his arms in the familiar attitude of their leisurely talks.

'Ennui, Peyrol,' he said in a faraway tone. 'Confounded boredom.'

Peyrol also, as if unable to resist the force of example, assumed the same attitude, and said: 'You seem to be a man that makes no friends.'

'True, Peyrol. I think I am that sort of man.'

'What, no friends at all? Not even a little friend of any sort?'

Lieutenant Réal leaned the back of his head against the wall and made no answer.

Peyrol got on his legs. 'Oh, then, it wouldn't matter to anybody if you were to disappear for years in an English hulk. And so if I were to give you my tartane you would go?'

'Yes, I would go this moment.'

Peyrol laughed quite loud, tilting his head back. All at once the laugh stopped short and the lieutenant was amazed to see him reel as though he had been hit in the chest. While giving way to his bitter mirth, the rover had caught sight of Arlette's face at the open window of the lieutenant's room. He sat heavily on the bench and was unable to make a sound. The lieutenant was startled enough to detach the back of his head from the wall to look at him. Peyrol stooped low suddenly, and began to drag the stable fork from its concealment. Then he got on his feet and stood leaning on it, glaring down at Réal, who gazed upwards with languid surprise. Peyrol was asking himself, 'Shall I pick him up on that pair of prongs, carry him down and fling him in the sea?' He felt suddenly overcome by a heaviness of arms and a heaviness of heart that made all movement impossible. His stiffened and powerless limbs refused all service . . . Let Catherine look after her niece. He was sure that the old woman was not very far away. The lieutenant saw him absorbed in examining the points of the prongs carefully. There was something queer about all this.

'Hello, Peyrol! What's the matter?' he couldn't help asking.

'I was just looking,' said Peyrol. 'One prong is chipped a little. I found this thing in a most unlikely place.'

The lieutenant still gazed at him curiously. 'I know! It was under the bench.'

'H'm,' said Peyrol, who had recovered some self-control. 'It belongs to Scevola.'

'Does it?' said the lieutenant, falling back again.

His interest seemed exhausted, but Peyrol didn't move.

'You go about with a face fit for a funeral,' he remarked suddenly in a deep voice. 'Hang it all, lieutenant, I have heard you laugh once or twice, but the devil take me if I ever saw you smile. It is as if you had been bewitched in your cradle.'

Lieutenant Réal got up as if moved by a spring. 'Bewitched,' he repeated, standing very stiff. 'In my cradle, eh? . . . No, I don't think it was so early as that.'

He walked forward with a tense still face straight at Peyrol as though he had been blind. Startled, the rover stepped out of the way and, turning on his heels, followed him with his eyes. The lieutenant paced on, as if drawn by a magnet, in the direction of the door of the house. Peyrol, his eyes fastened on Réal's back, let him nearly reach it before he called out tentatively: 'I say, lieutenant!' To his extreme surprise, Réal swung round as if to a touch.

'Oh, yes,' he answered, also in an undertone. 'We will have to discuss that matter tomorrow.'

Peyrol, who had approached him close, said in a whisper which sounded quite fierce: 'Discuss? No! We will have to carry it out tomorrow. I have been waiting half the night just to tell you that.'

Lieutenant Réal nodded. The expression on his face was so stony that Peyrol doubted whether he had understood.

He added: 'It isn't going to be child's play.'

The lieutenant was about to open the door when Peyrol said: 'A moment,' and again the lieutenant turned about silently.

'Michel is sleeping somewhere on the stairs. Will you just stir him up and tell him I am waiting outside? We two will have to finish our night on board the tartane, and start work at break of day to get her ready for sea. Yes, lieutenant, by noon. In twelve hours' time you will be saying goodbye to la belle France.'

Lieutenant Réal's eyes, staring over his shoulder, seemed glazed and motionless in the moonlight like the eyes of a dead man. But he went in. Peyrol heard presently sounds within of somebody staggering in the passage and Michel projected himself outside headlong, but after a stumble or two pulled up, scratching his head and looking on every side in the moonlight without perceiving Peyrol, who was regarding him from a distance of five feet.

At last Peyrol said: 'Come, wake up! Michel! Michel!'

'Voilà, notre maître.'

'Look at what I have picked up,' said Peyrol. 'Take it and put it away.' Michel didn't offer to touch the stable fork extended to him by Peyrol.

'What's the matter with you?' asked Peyrol.

'Nothing, nothing! Only last time I saw it, it was on Scevola's shoulder.' He glanced up at the sky. 'A little better than an hour ago.'

'What was he doing?'

'Going into the yard to put it away.'

'Well, now *you* go into the yard to put it away,' said Peyrol, 'and don't be long about it.' He waited with his hand over his chin till his henchman reappeared before him.

But Michel had not got over his surprise. 'He was going to bed, you know,' he said.

'Eh, what? He was going . . . He hasn't gone to sleep in the stable, perchance? He does sometimes, you know.'

'I know. I looked. He isn't there,' said Michel, very awake and round-eyed.

Peyrol started towards the cove. After three or four steps he turned round and found Michel motionless where he had left him.

'Come on,' he cried, 'we will have to fit the tartane for sea directly the day breaks.'

Standing in the lieutenant's room just clear of the open window, Arlette listened to their voices and to the sound of their footsteps diminishing down the slope. Before they had quite died out she became aware of a light tread approaching the door of the room.

Lieutenant Réal had spoken the truth. While in Toulon he had more than once said to himself that he could never go back to that fatal farmhouse. His mental state was quite pitiable. Honour, decency, every principle forbade him to trifle with the feelings of a poor creature with her mind darkened by a very terrifying, atrocious and, as it were, guilty experience. And suddenly he had given way to a base impulse and had betrayed himself by kissing her hand! He recognised with despair that this was no trifling, but that the impulse had come from the very depths of his being. It was an awful discovery for a man who on emerging from boyhood had laid for himself a rigidly straight line of conduct amongst the unbridled passions and the clamouring falsehoods of revolution which seemed to have destroyed in him all capacity for the softer emotions. Taciturn and guarded, he had formed no intimacies. Relations he had none. He had kept clear of social connections. It was in his character. At first he visited Escampobar because when he took his leave he had no place in the world to go to, and a few days there were a complete change from the odious town. He enjoyed the sense of remoteness from ordinary mankind. He had developed a liking for old Peyrol, the only man who had nothing to do with the Revolution – who had not even seen it at work. The sincere lawlessness of the ex-Brother of the Coast was refreshing. That one was neither a hypocrite nor a fool. When he robbed or killed it was not in the name of the sacred revolutionary principles or for the love of humanity.

Of course Réal had remarked at once Arlette's black, profound and unquiet eyes and the persistent dim smile on her lips, her mysterious silences and the rare sound of her voice which made a caress of every word. He heard something of her story from the reluctant Peyrol who did not care to talk about it. It awakened in Réal more bitter indignation than pity. But it stimulated his imagination, confirmed him in that scorn and angry loathing for the Revolution he had felt as a boy and had nursed secretly ever since. She attracted him by her unapproachable aspect. Later he tried not to notice that, in common parlance, she was inclined to hang about him. He used to catch her gazing at him stealthily. But he was free from masculine vanity. It was one day in Toulon that it suddenly dawned on him what her mute interest in his person might mean. He was then sitting outside a café sipping some drink or other with three or four officers, and not listening to their uninteresting conversation. He marvelled that this sort of illumination should come to him like this, under these circumstances; that he should have thought of her while seated in the street with these men round him, in the midst of more or less professional talk! And then it suddenly dawned on him that he had been thinking of nothing but that woman for days.

He got up brusquely, flung the money for his drink on the table, and without a word left his companions. But he had the reputation of an eccentric man and they did not even comment on his abrupt departure. It was a clear evening. He walked straight out of town, and that night wandered beyond the fortifications, not noticing the direction he took. All the countryside was asleep. There was not a human being stirring, and his progress in that desolate part of the country between the forts could have been traced only by the barking of dogs in the rare hamlets and scattered habitations.

'What has become of my rectitude, of my self-respect, of the firmness of my mind?' he asked himself pedantically. 'I have let myself be mastered by an unworthy passion for a mere mortal envelope, stained with crime and without a mind.'

His despair at this awful discovery was so profound that if he had not been in uniform he would have tried to commit suicide with the small pistol he had in his pocket. He shrank from the act, and the thought of the sensation it would produce, from the gossip and comments it would raise, the dishonouring suspicions it would provoke. 'No,' he said to himself, 'what I will have to do is to unmark my linen, put on civilian old clothes and walk out much farther away, miles beyond the forts, hide myself in some wood or in an overgrown hollow and put an end to my life there. The gendarmes or a garde-champêtre[151] discovering my body after a few days, a complete stranger without marks of identity, and being unable to find out anything about me, will give me an obscure burial in some village churchyard.'

On that resolution he turned back abruptly and at daybreak found himself outside the gate of the town. He had to wait till it was opened, and then the morning was so far advanced that he had to go straight to work at his office at the Toulon Admiralty. Nobody noticed anything peculiar about him that day. He went through his routine tasks with outward composure, but all the same he never ceased arguing with himself. By the time he returned to his quarters he had come to the conclusion that as an officer in wartime he had no right to take his own life. His principles would not permit him to do that. In this reasoning he was perfectly sincere. During a deadly struggle against an irreconcilable enemy his life belonged to his country. But there were moments when his loneliness, haunted by the forbidden vision of Escampobar with the figure of that distracted girl, mysterious, awful, pale, irresistible in her strangeness, passing along the walls, appearing on the hill-paths, looking out of the window, became unbearable. He spent hours of solitary anguish shut up in his quarters, and the opinion amongst his comrades was that Réal's misanthropy was getting beyond all bounds.

One day it dawned upon him clearly that he could not stand this. It affected his power of thinking. 'I shall begin to talk nonsense to people,' he said to himself. 'Hasn't there been once a poor devil who fell in love with a picture or a statue?[152] He used to go and contemplate it. His misfortune cannot be compared with mine! Well, I will go to look at her as at a picture too; a picture as untouchable as if it had been under glass.' And he went on a visit to Escampobar at the very first opportunity. He made up for himself a repellent face, he clung to Peyrol for society, out there on the bench, both with their arms folded and gazing into space. But whenever Arlette crossed his line of sight it was as if something had moved in his breast. Yet these visits made life just bearable; they enabled him to attend to his work without beginning to talk nonsense to people. He said to himself that he was strong enough to rise above temptation, that he would never overstep the line; but it happened that upstairs in his room at the farm he wept tears of sheer tenderness while thinking of his fate. These tears would put out for a while the gnawing fire of his passion. He assumed austerity like an armour and in his prudence he, as a matter of fact, looked very seldom at Arlette for fear of being caught in the act.

The discovery that she had taken to wandering at night had upset him all the same, because that sort of thing was unaccountable. It gave him a shock which unsettled, not his resolution, but his fortitude. That morning he had allowed himself, while she was waiting on him, to be caught looking at her, and then, losing his self-control, he had given her that kiss on the hand. Directly he had done it he was appalled. He had overstepped the line. Under the circumstances this was an absolute moral disaster. The full consciousness of it came to him slowly. In fact this moment of fatal weakness was one of the reasons why he had let himself be sent off so unceremoniously by Peyrol to Toulon. Even while crossing over he thought the only thing was not to come back any more. Yet while battling with himself he went on with the execution of the plan. A bitter irony presided over his dual state. Before leaving the Admiral, who had received him in full uniform in a room lighted by a single candle, he was suddenly moved to say: 'I suppose if there is no other way I am authorised to go myself,' and the Admiral had answered: 'I didn't contemplate that, but if you are willing I don't see any objection. I would only advise you to go in uniform in the character of an officer entrusted with dispatches. No doubt in time the Government would arrange for your exchange. But bear in mind that it would be a long captivity, and you must understand it might affect your promotion.'

At the foot of the grand staircase in the lighted hall of the official building Réal suddenly thought: 'And now I must go back to Escampobar.' Indeed he had to go to Escampobar because the false dispatches were there in the valise he had left behind. He couldn't go back to the Admiral and explain that he had lost them. They would look on him as an unutterable idiot or a man gone mad. While walking to the quay where the naval boat was waiting for him he said to himself: 'This, in truth, is my last visit for years – perhaps for life.'

Going back in the boat, notwithstanding that the breeze was very light, he would not let the men take to the oars. He didn't want to return before the women had gone to bed. He said to himself that the proper and honest thing to do was not to see Arlette again. He even managed to persuade himself that his uncontrolled impulse had had no meaning for that witless and unhappy creature. She had neither started nor exclaimed; she had made no sign. She had remained passive and then she had backed away and sat down quietly. He could not even remember that she had coloured at all. As to himself, he had enough self-control to rise from the table and go out without looking at her again. Neither did she make a sign. What could startle that body without mind? She had made nothing of it, he thought with self-contempt. 'Body without mind! Body without mind!' he repeated with angry derision directed at himself. And all at once he thought: 'No. It isn't that. All in her is mystery, seduction, enchantment. And then – what do I care for her mind!'

This thought wrung from him a faint groan so that the coxswain asked respectfully: 'Are you in pain, lieutenant?' 'It's nothing,' he muttered and set his teeth with the desperation of a man under torture.

While talking with Peyrol outside the house, the words 'I won't see her again' and 'body without mind' rang through his head. By the time he had left Peyrol and walked up the stairs his endurance was absolutely at an end. All he wanted was to be alone. Going along the dark passage he noticed that the door of Catherine's room was standing ajar. But that did not arrest his attention. He was approaching a state of insensibility. As he put his hand on the door handle of his room he said to himself: 'It will soon be over!'

He was so tired out that he was almost unable to hold up his head, and on going in he didn't see Arlette, who stood against the wall on one side of the window, out of the moonlight and in the darkest corner of the room. He only became aware of somebody's presence in the room as she flitted past him with the faintest possible rustle, when he staggered back two paces and heard behind him the key being turned in the lock. If the whole house had fallen into ruins, bringing him to the ground, he could not have been more overwhelmed and, in a manner, more utterly bereft of all his senses. The first that came back to him was the sense of touch when Arlette seized his hand. He regained his hearing next. She was whispering to him: 'At last. At last! But you are careless. If it had been Scevola instead of me in this room you would have been dead now. I have seen him at work.' He felt a significant pressure on his hand, but he couldn't see her properly yet, though he was aware of her nearness with every fibre of his body. 'It wasn't yesterday though,' she added in a low tone. Then suddenly: 'Come to the window so that I may look at you.'

A great square of moonlight lay on the floor. He obeyed the tug like a little child. She caught hold of his other hand as it hung by his side. He was rigid all over, without joints, and it did not seem to him that he was breathing. With her face a little below his she stared at him closely, whispering gently: 'Eugène, Eugène,' and suddenly the livid immobility of his face frightened her. 'You say nothing. You look ill. What is the matter? Are you hurt?' She let go his insensitive hands and began to feel him all over for evidence of some injury. She even snatched off his hat and flung it away in her haste to discover that his head was unharmed; but finding no sign of bodily damage, she calmed down like a sensible, practical person. With her hands clasped round his neck she hung back a little. Her little even teeth gleamed, her black eyes, immensely profound, looked into his, not with a transport of passion or fear but with a sort of reposeful satisfaction, with a searching and appropriating expression. He came back to life with a low and reckless exclamation, felt horribly insecure at once as if he were standing on a lofty pinnacle above a noise as of breaking waves in his ears, in fear lest her fingers should part and she would fall off and be lost to him for ever. He flung his arms round her waist and hugged her close to his breast. In the great silence, in the bright moonlight falling through the window, they stood like that for a long, long time. He looked at her head resting on his shoulder. Her eyes were closed and the expression of her unsmiling face was that of a delightful dream, something infinitely ethereal, peaceful and, as it were, eternal. Its appeal pierced his heart with a pointed sweetness. 'She is exquisite. It's a miracle,' he thought with a sort of terror. 'It's impossible.'

She made a movement to disengage herself, and instinctively he resisted, pressing her closer to his breast. She yielded for a moment and then tried again. He let her go. She stood at arm's length, her hands on his shoulders, and her charm struck him suddenly as funny in the seriousness of expression as of a very capable, practical woman.

'All this is very well,' she said in a businesslike undertone. 'We will have to think how to get away from here. I don't mean now, this moment,' she added, feeling his slight start. 'Scevola is thirsting for your blood.' She detached one hand to point a finger at the inner wall of the room, and lowered her voice. 'He's there, you know. Don't trust Peyrol either. I was looking at you two out there. He has changed. I can trust him no longer.' Her murmur vibrated. 'He and Catherine behave strangely. I don't know what came to them. He doesn't talk to me. When I sit down near him he turns his shoulder to me . . .'

She felt Réal sway under her hands, paused in concern and said: 'You are tired.' But as he didn't move, she actually led him to a chair, pushed him into it, and sat on the floor at his feet. She rested her head against his knees and kept possession of one of his hands. A sigh escaped her. 'I knew this was going to be,' she said very low. 'But I was taken by surprise.'

'Oh, you knew it was going to be,' he repeated faintly.

'Yes! I had prayed for it. Have you ever been prayed for, Eugène?' she asked, lingering on his name.

'Not since I was a child,' answered Réal in a sombre tone.

'Oh yes! You have been prayed for today. I went down to the church . . .'

Réal could hardly believe his ears . . .

'The abbé let me in by the sacristy door. He told me to renounce the world. I was ready to renounce anything for you.'

Réal, turning his face to the darkest part of the room, seemed to see the spectre of fatality awaiting its time to move forward and crush that calm, confident joy. He shook off the dreadful illusion, raised her hand to his lips for a lingering kiss, and then asked: 'So you knew that it was going to be? Everything? Yes! And of me, what did you think?'

She pressed strongly the hand to which she had been clinging all the time. 'I thought this.'

'But what did you think of my conduct at times? You see, I did not know what was going to be. I . . . I was afraid,' he added under his breath.

'Conduct? What conduct? You came, you went. When you were not here I thought of you, and when you were here I could look my fill at you. I tell you I knew how it was going to be. I was not afraid then.'

'You went about with a little smile,' he whispered, as one would mention an inconceivable marvel.

'I was warm and quiet,' murmured Arlette, as if on the borders of dreamland. Tender murmurs flowed from her lips describing a state of blissful tranquillity in phrases that sounded like the veriest nonsense, incredible, convincing and soothing to Réal's conscience.

'You were perfect,' it went on. 'Whenever you came near me everything seemed different.'

'What do you mean? How different?'

'Altogether. The light, the very stones of the house, the hills, the little flowers amongst the rocks! Even Nanette was different.'

Nanette was a white Angora with long silken hair, a pet that lived mostly in the yard.

'Oh, Nanette was different too,' said Réal, whom delight in the modulations of that voice had cut off from all reality, and even from a consciousness of himself, while he sat stooping over that head resting against his knee, the soft grip of her hand being his only contact with the world.

'Yes. Prettier. It's only the people . . . ' She ceased on an uncertain note. The crested wave of enchantment seemed to have passed over his head ebbing out faster than the sea, leaving the dreary expanses of the sand. He felt a chill at the roots of his hair.

'What people?' he asked.

'They are so changed. Listen, tonight while you were away – why did you go away? – I caught those two in the kitchen, saying nothing to each other. That Peyrol – he is terrible.'

He was struck by the tone of awe, by its profound conviction. He could not know that Peyrol, unforeseen, unexpected, inexplicable, had given by his mere appearance at Escampobar a moral and even a physical jolt to all her being, that he was to her an immense figure, like a messenger from the unknown entering the solitude of Escampobar; something immensely strong, with inexhaustible power, unaffected by familiarity and remaining invincible.

'He will say nothing, he will listen to nothing. He can do what he likes.'

'Can he?' muttered Réal.

She sat up on the floor, moved her head up and down several times as if to say that there could be no doubt about that.

'Is he, too, thirsting for my blood?' asked Réal bitterly.

'No, no. It isn't that. You could defend yourself. I could watch over you. I have been watching over you. Only two nights ago I thought I heard noises outside and I went downstairs, fearing for you; your window was open but I could see nobody, and yet I felt . . . No, it isn't that! It's worse. I don't know what he wants to do. I can't help being fond of him, but I begin to fear him now. When he first came here and I saw him he was just the same – only his hair was not so white – big, quiet. It seemed to me that something moved in my head. He was gentle, you know. I had to smile at him. It was as if I had recognised him. I said to myself: "That's he, the man himself." '

'And when I came?' asked Réal with a feeling of dismay.

'You! You were expected,' she said in a low tone with a slight tinge of surprise at the question, but still evidently thinking of the Peyrol mystery. 'Yes, I caught them at it last evening, he and Catherine in the kitchen, looking at each other and as quiet as mice. I told him he couldn't order me about. Oh, mon chéri, mon chéri, don't you listen to Peyrol – don't let him . . . '

With only a slight touch on his knee she sprang to her feet. Réal stood up too.

'He can do nothing to me,' he mumbled.

'Don't tell him anything. Nobody can guess what he thinks, and now even I cannot tell what he means when he speaks. It was as if he knew a secret.' She put an accent into those words which made Réal feel moved almost to tears. He repeated that Peyrol could have no influence over him, and he felt that he was speaking the truth. He was in the power of his own word. Ever since he had left the Admiral in a gold-embroidered uniform, impatient to return to his guests, he was on a service for which he had volunteered. For a moment he had the sensation of an iron hoop very tight round his chest. She peered at his face closely, and it was more than he could bear.

'All right. I'll be careful,' he said. 'And Catherine, is she also dangerous?'

In the sheen of the moonlight Arlette, her neck and head above the gleams of the fichu, visible and elusive, smiled at him and moved a step closer.

'Poor Aunt Catherine,' she said . . . 'Put your arm round me, Eugéne . . . She can do nothing. She used to follow me with her eyes always. She thought I didn't notice, but I did. And now she seems unable to look me in the face. Peyrol too, for that matter. He used to follow me with his eyes. Often I wondered what made them look at me like that. Can you tell, Eugéne? But it's all changed now.'

'Yes, it is all changed,' said Réal in a tone which he tried to make as light as possible. 'Does Catherine know you are here?'

'When we went upstairs this evening I lay down all dressed on my bed and she sat on hers. The candle was out, but in the moonlight I could see her quite plainly with her hands on her lap. When I could lie still no longer I simply got up and went out of the room. She was still sitting at the foot of her bed. All I did was to put my finger on my lips and then she dropped her head. I don't think I quite closed the door . . . Hold me tighter, Eugène, I am tired . . . Strange, you know! Formerly, a long time ago, before I ever saw you, I never rested and never felt tired.' She stopped her murmur suddenly and lifted a finger recommending silence. She listened and Réal listened too, he did not know for what; and in this sudden concentration on a point, all that had happened since he had entered the room seemed to him a dream in its improbability and in the more than lifelike force dreams have in their inconsequence. Even the woman letting herself go on his arm seemed to have no weight as it might have happened in a dream.

'She is there,' breathed Arlette suddenly, rising on tiptoe to reach up to his ear. 'She must have heard you go past.'

'Where is she?' asked Réal with the same intense secrecy.

'Outside the door. She must have been listening to the murmur of our voices . . . ' Arlette breathed into his ear as if relating an enormity. 'She told me one day that I was one of those who are fit for no man's arms.'

At this he flung his other arm round her and looked into her enlarged as if frightened eyes, while she clasped him with all her strength and they stood like that a long time, lips pressed on lips without a kiss, and breathless in the closeness of their contact. To him the stillness seemed to extend to the limits of the universe. The thought 'Am I going to die?' flashed through that stillness and lost itself in it like a spark flying in an everlasting night. The only result of it was the tightening of his hold on Arlette.

An aged and uncertain voice was heard uttering the word 'Arlette'. Catherine, who had been listening to their murmurs, could not bear the long silence. They heard her trembling tones as distinctly as though she had been in the room. Réal felt as if it had saved his life. They separated silently.

'Go away,' called out Arlette.

'Arl – '

'Be quiet,' she cried louder. 'You can do nothing.'

'Arlette,' came through the door, tremulous and commanding.

'She will wake up Scevola,' remarked Arlette to Réal in a conversational tone. And they both waited for sounds that did not come. Arlette pointed her finger at the wall. 'He is there, you know.'

'He is asleep,' muttered Réal. But the thought 'I am lost' which he formulated in his mind had no reference to Scevola.

'He is afraid,' said Arlette contemptuously in an undertone. 'But that means little. He would quake with fright one moment and rush out to do murder the next.'

Slowly, as if drawn by the irresistible authority of the old woman, they had been moving towards the door. Réal thought with the sudden enlightenment of passion: 'If she does not go now I won't have the strength to part from her in the morning.' He had no image of death before his eyes but of a long and intolerable separation. A sigh verging upon a moan reached them from the other side of the door and made the air around them heavy with sorrow against which locks and keys will not avail.

'You had better go to her,' he whispered in a penetrating tone.

'Of course I will,' said Arlette with some feeling. 'Poor old thing. She and I have only each other in the world, but I am the daughter here, she must do what I tell her.' With one of her hands on Réal's shoulder she put her mouth close to the door and said distinctly: 'I am coming directly. Go back to your room and wait for me,' as if she had no doubt of being obeyed.

A profound silence ensued. Perhaps Catherine had gone already. Réal and Arlette stood still for a whole minute as if both had been changed into stone.

'Go now,' said Réal in a hoarse, hardly audible voice.

She gave him a quick kiss on the lips and again they stood like a pair of enchanted lovers bewitched into immobility.

'If she stays on,' thought Réal, 'I shall never have the courage to tear myself away, and then I shall have to blow my brains out.' But when at last she moved he seized her again and held her as if she had been his very life. When he let her go he was appalled by hearing a very faint laugh of her secret joy.

'Why do you laugh?' he asked in a scared tone.

She stopped to answer him over her shoulder. 'I laughed because I thought of all the days to come. Days and days and days. Have you thought of them?'

'Yes,' Réal faltered, like a man stabbed to the heart, holding the door half open. And he was glad to have something to hold on to.

She slipped out with a soft rustle of her silk skirt, but before he had time to close the door behind her she put back her arm for an instant. He had just time to press the palm of her hand to his lips. It was cool. She snatched it away and he had the strength of mind to shut the door after her. He felt like a man chained to the wall and dying of thirst, from whom a cold drink is snatched away. The room became dark suddenly.

He thought, 'A cloud over the moon, a cloud over the moon, an enormous cloud,' while he walked rigidly to the window, insecure and swaying as if on a tight rope. After a moment he perceived the moon in a sky on which there was no sign of the smallest cloud anywhere. He said to himself, 'I suppose I nearly died just now. But no,' he went on thinking with deliberate cruelty, 'Oh, no, I shall not die. I shall only suffer, suffer, suffer . . . '

'Suffer, suffer.' Only by stumbling against the side of the bed did he discover that he had gone away from the window. At once he flung himself violently on the bed with his face buried in the pillow, which he bit to restrain the cry of distress about to burst through his lips. Natures schooled into insensibility when once overcome by a mastering passion are like vanquished giants ready for despair. He, a man on service, felt himself shrinking from death and that doubt contained in itself all possible doubts of his own fortitude. The only thing he knew was that he would be gone tomorrow morning. He shuddered along his whole extended length, then lay still gripping a handful of bedclothes in each hand to prevent himself from leaping up in panicky restlessness. He was saying to himself pedantically, 'I must lie down and rest, I must rest to have strength for tomorrow, I must rest,' while the tremendous struggle to keep still broke out in waves of perspiration on his forehead. At last sudden oblivion must have descended on him because he turned over and sat up suddenly with the sound of the word 'Ecoutez'[153] in his ears.

A strange, dim, cold light filled the room; a light he did not recognise for anything he had known before, and at the foot of his bed stood a figure in dark garments[154] with a dark shawl over its head, with a fleshless predatory face and dark hollows for its eyes, silent, expectant, implacable . . . Is this death?' he asked himself, staring at it terrified. It resembled Catherine. It said again: 'Ecoutez.'

He took away his eyes from it and glancing down noticed that his clothes were torn open on his chest. He would not look up at that thing, whatever it was, spectre or old woman, and said: 'Yes, I hear you.'

'You are an honest man.' It was Catherine's unemotional voice. 'The day has broken. You will go away.'

'Yes,' he said without raising his head.

'She is asleep,' went on Catherine or whoever it was, 'exhausted, and you would have to shake her hard before she would wake. You will go. You know,' the voice continued inflexibly, 'she is my niece, and you know that there is death in the folds of her skirt and blood about her feet. She is for no man.'

Réal felt all the anguish of an unearthly experience. This thing that looked like Catherine and spoke like a cruel fate had to be faced. He raised his head in this light that seemed to him appalling and not of this world.

'Listen well to me, you too,' he said. 'If she had all the madness of the world and the sin of all the murders of the Revolution on her shoulders, I would still hug her to my breast. Do you understand?'

The apparition which resembled Catherine lowered and raised its hooded head slowly. 'There was a time when I could have hugged l'enfer même[155] to my breast. He went away. He had his vow.[156] You have only your honesty. You will go.'

'I have my duty,' said Lieutenant Réal in measured tones, as if calmed by the excess of horror that old woman inspired him with.

'Go without disturbing her, without looking at her.'

'I will carry my shoes in my hand,' he said. He sighed deeply and felt as if sleepy. 'It is very early,' he muttered.

'Peyrol is already down at the well,' announced Catherine. 'What can he be doing there all this time?' she added in a troubled voice. Réal, with his feet now on the ground, gave her a side glance; but she was already gliding away, and when he looked again she had vanished from the room and the door was shut.

Chapter 15

Catherine, going downstairs, found Peyrol still at the well. He seemed to be looking into it with extreme interest.

'Your coffee is ready, Peyrol,' she shouted to him from the doorway.

He turned very sharply like a man surprised and came along smiling.

'That's pleasant news, Mademoiselle Catherine,' he said. 'You are down early.'

'Yes,' she admitted, 'but you too, Peyrol. Is Michel about? Let him come and have some coffee too.'

'Michel's at the tartane. Perhaps you don't know that she is going to make a little voyage.' He drank a mouthful of coffee and took a bite out of a slice of bread. He was hungry. He had been up all night and had even had a conversation with Citizen Scevola. He had also done some work with Michel after daylight; however, there had not been much to do because the tartane was always kept ready for sea. Then, after having again locked up Citizen Scevola, who was extremely concerned as to what was going to happen to him but was left in a state of uncertainty, he had come up to the farm, had gone upstairs where he was busy with various things for a time, and then had stolen down very cautiously to the well, where Catherine, whom he had not expected downstairs so early, had seen him before she went into Lieutenant Réal's room. While he enjoyed his coffee he listened without any signs of surprise to Catherine's comments upon the disappearance of Scevola. She had looked into his den. He had not slept on his pallet last night, of that she was certain, and he was nowhere to be seen, not even in the most distant field, from the points of vantage around the farm. It was inconceivable that he should have slipped away to Madrague, where he disliked to go, or to the village, where he was afraid to go. Peyrol remarked that whatever had happened to him he was no great loss, but Catherine was not to be soothed.

'It frightens a body,' she said. 'He may be hiding somewhere to jump on one treacherously. You know what I mean, Peyrol.'

'Well, the lieutenant will have nothing to fear, as he's going away. As to myself, Scevola and I are good friends. I had a long talk with him quite recently. You two women can manage him perfectly; and then, who knows, perhaps he has gone away for good.'

Catherine stared at him, if such a word as stare can be applied to a profound contemplative gaze. 'The lieutenant has nothing to fear from him,' she repeated cautiously.

'No, he is going away. Didn't you know it?' The old woman continued to look at him profoundly. 'Yes, he is on service.'

For another minute or so Catherine continued silent in her contemplative attitude. Then her hesitation came to an end. She could not resist the desire to inform Peyrol of the events of the night. As she went on Peyrol forgot the half-full bowl of coffee and his half-eaten piece of bread. Catherine's voice flowed with austerity. She stood there, imposing and solemn like a peasant-priestess. The relation of what had been to her a soul-shaking experience did not take much time, and she finished with the words, 'The lieutenant is an honest man.' And after a pause she insisted further: 'There is no denying it. He has acted like an honest man.'

For a moment longer Peyrol continued to look at the coffee in the bowl, then without warning got up with such violence that the chair behind him was thrown back upon the flagstones.

'Where is he, that honest man?' he shouted suddenly in stentorian tones which not only caused Catherine to raise her hands but frightened himself, and he dropped at once to a mere forcible utterance. 'Where is that man? Let me see him.'

Even Catherine's hieratic composure was disturbed. 'Why,' she said, looking really disconcerted, 'he will be down here directly. This bowl of coffee is for him.'

Peyrol made as if to leave the kitchen, but Catherine stopped him. 'For God's sake, Monsieur Peyrol,' she said, half in entreaty and half in command, 'don't wake up the child. Let her sleep. Oh, let her sleep! Don't wake her up. God only knows how long it is since she has slept properly. I could not tell you. I daren't think of it.' She was shocked by hearing Peyrol declare: 'All this is confounded nonsense.' But he sat down again, seemed to catch sight of the coffee bowl and emptied what was left in it down his throat.

'I don't want her on my hands more crazy than she has been before,' said Catherine, in a sort of exasperation but in a very low tone. This phrase in its selfish form expressed a real and profound compassion for her niece. She dreaded the moment when that fatal Arlette would wake up and the dreadful complications of life which her slumbers had suspended would have to be picked up again.

Peyrol fidgeted on his seat. 'And so he told you he was going? He actually did tell you that?' he asked.

'He promised to go before the child wakes up . . . At once.'

'But, sacré nom d'un chien,[157] there is never any wind before eleven o'clock,' Peyrol exclaimed in a tone of profound annoyance, yet trying to moderate his voice, while Catherine, indulgent to his changing moods, only compressed her lips and nodded at him soothingly. 'It is impossible to work with people like that,' he mumbled.

'Do you know, Monsieur Peyrol, that she has been to see the priest?' Catherine was heard suddenly, towering above her end of the table. The two women had had a talk before Arlette had been induced by her aunt to lie down.

Peyrol gave a start. 'What? Priest? . . . Now look here, Catherine,' he went on with repressed ferocity, 'do you imagine that all this interests me in the least?'

'I can think of nothing but that niece of mine. We two have nobody but each other in the world,' she went on, reproducing the very phrase Arlette had used to Réal. She seemed to be thinking aloud, but noticed that Peyrol was listening with attention. 'He wanted to shut her up from everybody,' and the old woman clasped her meagre hands with a sudden gesture. 'I suppose there are still some convents about the world.'

'You and the patronne are mad together,' declared Peyrol. 'All this only shows what an ass the curé is. I don't know much about these things, though I have seen some nuns in my time, and some very queer ones too, but it seems to me that they don't take crazy people into convents. Don't you be afraid. I tell you that.' He stopped because the inner door of the kitchen came open and Lieutenant Réal stepped in. His sword hung on his forearm by the belt, his hat was on his head. He dropped his little valise on the floor and sat down in the nearest chair to put on his shoes which he had brought down in his other hand. Then he came up to the table. Peyrol, who had kept his eyes on him, thought: 'Here is one who looks like a moth scorched in the fire.' Réal's eyes were sunk, his cheeks seemed hollowed and the whole face had an arid and dry aspect.

'Well, you are in a fine state for the work of deceiving the enemy,' Peyrol observed. 'Why, to look at you, nobody would believe a word you said. You are not going to be ill, I hope. You are on service. You haven't got the right to be ill. I say, Mademoiselle Catherine, produce the bottle – you know, my private bottle . . . ' He snatched it from Catherine's hand, poured some brandy into the lieutenant's coffee, pushed the bowl towards him and waited. 'Nom de nom!' he said forcibly, 'don't you know what this is for? It's for you to drink.' Réal obeyed with a strange, automatic docility. 'And now,' said Peyrol, getting up, 'I will go to my room and shave. This is a great day – the day we are going to see the lieutenant off.'

Till then Réal had not uttered a word, but directly the door closed behind Peyrol he raised his head.

'Catherine!' His voice was like a rustle in his throat. She was looking at him steadily and he continued: 'Listen, when she finds I am gone you tell her I will return soon. Tomorrow. Always tomorrow.'

'Yes, my good monsieur,' said Catherine in an unmoved voice but clasping her hands convulsively. 'There is nothing else I would dare tell her!'

'She will believe you,' whispered Réal wildly.

'Yes! She will believe me,' repeated Catherine in a mournful tone.

Réal got up, put the sword-belt over his head, picked up the valise. There was a little flush on his cheeks.

'Adieu,'[158] he said to the silent old woman. She made no answer, but as he turned away she raised her hand a little, hesitated, and let it fall again. It seemed to her that the women of Escampobar had been singled out for divine wrath. Her niece appeared to her like the scapegoat charged with all the murders and blasphemies of the Revolution. She herself too had been cast out from the grace of God. But that had been a long time ago. She had made her peace with Heaven since. Again she raised her hand and, this time, made in the air the sign of the cross at the back of Lieutenant Réal.

Meanwhile upstairs Peyrol, scraping his big flat cheek with an English razor-blade at the window, saw Lieutenant Réal on the path to the shore; and high above there, commanding a vast view of sea and land, he shrugged his shoulders impatiently with no visible provocation. One could not trust those epaulette-wearers. They would cram a fellow's head with notions either for their own sake or for the sake of the service. Still, he was too old a bird to be caught with chaff; and besides, that long-legged stiff beggar going down the path, with all his officer airs, was honest enough. At any rate he knew a seaman when he saw one, though he was as cold-blooded as a fish. Peyrol had a smile which was a little awry.

Cleaning the razor-blade (one of a set of twelve in a case) he had a vision of a brilliantly hazy ocean and an English Indiaman with her yards braced all ways, her canvas blowing loose above her bloodstained decks overrun by a lot of privateersmen, and with the island of Ceylon swelling like a thin blue cloud on the far horizon. He had always wished to own a set of English blades and there he had got it, fell over it as it were, lying on the floor of a cabin which had been already ransacked. 'For good steel – it was good steel,' he thought looking at the blade fixedly. And there it was, nearly worn out. The others too. That steel! And here he was holding the case in his hand as though he had just picked it up from the floor. Same case. Same man. And the steel worn out.

He shut the case brusquely, flung it into his sea-chest which was standing open, and slammed the lid down. The feeling which was in his breast and had been known to more articulate men than himself, was that life was a dream less substantial than the vision of Ceylon lying like a cloud on the sea. Dream left astern. Dream straight ahead. This disenchanted philosophy took the shape of fierce swearing. 'Sacré nom de nom de nom . . . Tonnerre de bon Dieu!'[159]

While tying his neckcloth he handled it with fury as though he meant to strangle himself with it. He rammed a soft cap on to his venerable locks recklessly, seized his cudgel – but before leaving the room walked up to the window giving on the east. He could not see the Petite Passe on account of the lookout hill, but to the left a great portion of the Hyères roadstead lay spread out before him, pale grey in the morning light, with the land about Cape Blanc swelling in the distance with all its details blurred as yet and only one conspicuous object presenting to his sight something that might have been a lighthouse by its shape, but which Peyrol knew very well was the English corvette already under way and with all her canvas set.

This sight pleased Peyrol mainly because he had expected it. The Englishman was doing exactly what he had expected he would do, and Peyrol looked towards the English cruiser with a smile of malicious triumph as if he were confronting her captain. For some reason or other he imagined Captain Vincent as long-faced, with yellow teeth and a wig, whereas that officer wore his own hair and had a set of teeth which would have done honour to a London belle – and was really the hidden cause of Captain Vincent appearing so often wreathed in smiles.

That ship at this great distance and steering in his direction held Peyrol at the window long enough for the increasing light of the morning to burst into sunshine, colouring and filling in the flat outline of the land with tints of wood and rock and field, with clear dots of buildings enlivening the view. The sun threw a sort of halo around the ship. Recollecting himself, Peyrol left the room and shut the door quietly. Quietly too he descended the stairs from his garret. On the landing he underwent a short inward struggle, at the end of which he approached the door of Catherine's room and, opening it a little, put his head in. Across the whole width of it he saw Arlette fast asleep. Her aunt had thrown a light coverlet over her. Her low shoes stood at the foot of the bed. Her black hair lay loose on the pillow; and Peyrol's gaze became arrested by the long eyelashes on her pale cheek. Suddenly he fancied she moved, and he withdrew his head sharply, pulling the door to. He listened for a moment as if tempted to open it again, but judging it too risky, continued on his way downstairs. At his reappearance in the kitchen Catherine turned sharply. She was dressed for the day, with a big white cap on her head, a black bodice and a brown skirt with ample folds. She had a pair of varnished sabots on her feet over her shoes.

'No signs of Scevola,' she said, advancing towards Peyrol. 'And Michel too has not been here yet.'

Peyrol thought that if she had been only shorter, what with her black eyes and slightly curved nose she would have looked like a witch. But witches can read people's thoughts, and he looked openly at Catherine with the pleasant conviction that she could not read his thoughts. He said: 'I took good care not to make any noise upstairs, Mademoiselle Catherine. When I am gone the house will be empty and quiet enough.'

She had a curious expression. She struck Peyrol suddenly as if she were lost in that kitchen in which she had reigned for many years. He continued: 'You will be alone all the morning.'

She seemed to be listening to some distant sound, and after Peyrol had added, 'Everything is all right now,' she nodded and after a moment said in a manner that for her was unexpectedly impulsive: 'Monsieur Peyrol, I am tired of life.'

He shrugged his shoulders and with somewhat sinister jocosity remarked: 'I will tell you what it is; you ought to have been married.'

She turned her back on him abruptly.

'No offence,' Peyrol excused himself in a tone of gloom rather than of apology. 'It is no use to attach any importance to things. What is this life? Phew! Nobody can remember one-tenth of it. Here I am; and, you know, I would bet that if one of my old-time chums came along and saw me like this, here with you – I mean one of those chums that stand up for a fellow in a scrimmage and look after him should he be hurt – well, I bet,' he repeated, 'he wouldn't know me. He would say to himself perhaps, "Hello! here's a comfortable married couple." '

He paused. Catherine, with her back to him and calling him not 'Monsieur' but 'Peyrol', *tout court*,[160] remarked, not exactly with displeasure, but rather with an ominous accent, that this was no time for idle talk.

Peyrol, however, continued, though his tone was very far from being that of idle talk: 'But you see, Mademoiselle Catherine, you were not like the others. You allowed yourself to be struck all of a heap, and at the same time you were too hard on yourself.'

Her long thin frame bent low to work the bellows under the enormous overmantel, she assented: 'Perhaps! We Escampobar women were always hard on ourselves.'

'That's what I say. If you had had things happen to you which happened to me . . . '

'But you men, you are different. It doesn't matter what you do. You have got your own strength. You need not be hard on yourselves. You go from one thing to another thoughtlessly.'

He remained looking at her searchingly with something like a hint of a smile on his shaven lips, but she turned away to the sink where one of the women working about the farm had deposited a great pile of vegetables. She started on them with a broken-bladed knife, preserving her sibylline air even in that homely occupation.

'It will be a good soup, I see, at noon today,' said the rover suddenly. He turned on his heels and went out through the salle. The whole world lay open to him, or at any rate the whole of the Mediterranean, viewed down the ravine between the two hills. The bell of the farm's milch-cow, which had a talent for keeping herself invisible, reached him from the right, but he could not see as much as the tips of her horns, though he looked for them. He stepped out sturdily. He had not gone twenty yards down the ravine when another sound made him stand still as if changed into stone. It was a faint noise resembling very much the hollow rumble an empty farm-cart would make on a stony road, but Peyrol looked up at the sky, and though it was perfectly clear, he did not seem pleased with its aspect. He had a hill on each side of him and the placid cove below his feet. He muttered, 'H'm! Thunder at sunrise. It must be in the west. It only wanted that!' He feared it would first kill the little breeze there was and then knock the weather up altogether. For a moment all his faculties seemed paralysed by that faint sound. On that sea ruled by the gods of Olympus he might have been a pagan mariner subject to Jupiter's caprices; but like a defiant pagan he shook his fist vaguely at space which answered him by a short and threatening mutter. Then he swung on his way till he caught sight of the two mastheads of the tartane, when he stopped to listen. No sound of any sort reached him from there, and he went on his way thinking, 'Go from one thing to another thoughtlessly! Indeed! . . . That's all old Catherine knows about it.' He had so many things to think of that he did not know which to lay hold of first. He just let them lie jumbled up in his head. His feelings too were in a state of confusion, and vaguely he felt that his conduct was at the mercy of an internal conflict. The consciousness of that fact accounted perhaps for his sardonic attitude towards himself and outwardly towards those whom he perceived on board the tartane; and especially towards the lieutenant whom he saw sitting on the deck leaning against the head of the rudder, characteristically aloof from the two other persons on board. Michel, also characteristically, was standing on the top of the little cabin scuttle, obviously looking out for his 'maître'. Citizen Scevola, sitting on deck, seemed at first sight to be at liberty, but as a matter of fact he was not. He was loosely tied up to a stanchion by three turns of the mainsheet, with the knot in such a position that he could not get at it without attracting attention; and that situation seemed also somewhat characteristic of Citizen Scevola with its air of half liberty, half suspicion and, as it were, contemptuous restraint. The sans-culotte, whose late experiences had nearly unsettled his reason, first by their utter incomprehensibility and afterwards by the enigmatical attitude of Peyrol, had dropped his head and folded his arms on his breast. And that attitude was dubious too. It might have been resignation or it might have been profound sleep.

The rover addressed himself first to the lieutenant. 'Le moment approche,' said Peyrol with a queer twitch at a corner of his lip, while under his soft woollen cap his venerable locks stirred in the breath of a suddenly warm air. 'The great moment – eh?'

He leaned over the big tiller, and seemed to be hovering above the lieutenant's shoulder.

'What's this infernal company?' murmured the latter without even looking at Peyrol.

'All old friends – quoi?'[161] said Peyrol in a homely tone. 'We will keep that little affair amongst ourselves. The fewer the men the greater the glory. Catherine is getting the vegetables ready for the noonday soup and the Englishman is coming down towards the Passe where he will arrive about noon too, ready to have his eye put out. You know, lieutenant, that will be your job. You may depend on me for sending you off when the moment comes. For what is it to you? You have no friends, you have not even a petite amie.[162] As to expecting an old rover like me – oh no, lieutenant! Of course liberty is sweet, but what do you know of it, you epaulette-wearers? Moreover, I am no good for quarter-deck talks and all that politeness.'

'I wish, Peyrol, you would not talk so much,' said Lieutenant Réal, turning his head slightly. He was struck by the strange expression on the old rover's face. 'And I don't see what the actual moment matters. I am going to look for the fleet. All you have to do is to hoist the sails for me and then scramble ashore.'

'Very simple,' observed Peyrol through his teeth, and then began to sing:

> 'Quoique leurs chapeaux sont bien laids
> God-damn! Moi, j'aime les Anglais.
> Ils ont un si bon caractère!'[163]

but interrupted himself suddenly to hail Scevola: 'Hé! Citoyen!' and then remarked confidentially to Réal: 'He isn't asleep, you know, but he isn't like the English, he has a sacré mauvais caractère. He got into his head,' continued Peyrol, in a loud and innocent tone, 'that you locked him up in this cabin last night. Did you notice the venomous glance he gave you just now?'

Both Lieutenant Réal and the innocent Michel appeared surprised at his boisterousness; but all the time Peyrol was thinking: 'I wish to goodness I knew how that thunderstorm is getting on and what course it is shaping. I can't find that out unless I go up to the farm and get a view to the westward. It may be as far as the Rhône Valley; no doubt it is and it will come out of it too, curses on it. One won't be able to reckon on half an hour of steady wind from any quarter.' He directed a look of ironic gaiety at all the faces in turn. Michel met it with a faithful-dog gaze and innocently open mouth. Scevola kept his chin buried on his chest. Lieutenant Réal was insensible to outward impressions and his absent stare made nothing of Peyrol. The rover himself presently fell into thought. The last stir of air died out in the little basin, and the sun clearing Porquerolles inundated it with a sudden light in which Michel blinked like an owl.

'It's hot early,' he announced aloud but only because he had formed the habit of talking to himself. He would not have presumed to offer an opinion unless asked by Peyrol.

Michael's voice having recalled Peyrol to himself, he proposed to masthead the yards and even asked Lieutenant Réal to help in that operation which was accomplished in silence except for the faint squeaking of the blocks. The sails, however, were kept hauled up in the gear.

'Like this,' said Peyrol, 'you have only to let go the ropes and you will be under canvas at once.'

Without answering Réal returned to his position by the rudder-head. He was saying to himself – 'I am sneaking off. No, there is honour, duty. And of course I will return. But when? They will forget all about me and I shall never be exchanged. This war may last for years – ' and illogically he wished he could have had a God to whom he could pray for relief in his anguish. 'She will be in despair,' he thought, writhing inwardly at the mental picture of a distracted Arlette. Life, however, had embittered his spirit early, and he said to himself: 'But in a month's time will she even give me a thought?' Instantly he felt remorseful with a remorse strong enough to lift him to his feet as if he were morally obliged to go up again and confess to Arlette this sacrilegious cynicism of thought. 'I am mad,' he muttered, perching himself on the low rail. His lapse from faith plunged him into such a depth of unhappiness that he felt all his strength of will go out of him. He sat there apathetic and suffering. He meditated dully: 'Young men have been known to die suddenly; why should not I? I am, as a matter of fact, at the end of my endurance. I am half dead already. Yes! but what is left of that life does not belong to me now.'

'Peyrol,' he said in such a piercing tone that even Scevola jerked his head up; but he made an effort to reduce his shrillness and went on speaking very carefully: 'I have left a letter for the Secretary General at the Majorité[164] to pay twenty-five hundred francs to Jean – you are Jean, are you not? – Peyrol, price of the tartane in which I sail. Is that right?'

'What did you do that for?' asked Peyrol with an extremely stony face. 'To get me into trouble?'

'Don't be a fool, gunner, nobody remembers your name. It is buried under a stack of blackened paper. I must ask you to go there and tell them that you have seen with your own eyes Lieutenant Réal sail away on his mission.'

The stoniness of Peyrol persisted but his eyes were full of fury. 'Oh, yes, I see myself going there. Twenty-five hundred francs! Twenty-five hundred fiddlesticks.' His tone changed suddenly. 'I heard someone say that you were an honest man, and I suppose this is a proof of it. Well, to the devil with your honesty.' He glared at the lieutenant and then thought: 'He doesn't even pretend to listen to what I say' – and another sort of anger, partly contemptuous and with something of dim sympathy in it, replaced his downright fury. 'Pah!' he said, spat over the side, and walking up to Réal with great deliberation, slapped him on the shoulder. The only effect of this proceeding was to make Réal look up at him without any expression whatever.

Peyrol then picked up the lieutenant's valise and carried it down into the cuddy. As he passed by, Citizen Scevola uttered the word, 'Citoyen,' but it was only when he came back again that Peyrol condescended to say, 'Well?'

'What are you going to do with me?' asked Scevola.

'You would not give me an account of how you came on board this tartane,' said Peyrol in a tone that sounded almost friendly, 'therefore I need not tell you what I will do with you.'

A low muttering of thunder followed so close upon his words that it might have come out of Peyrol's own lips. The rover gazed uneasily at the sky. It was still clear overhead, and at the bottom of that little basin surrounded by rocks there was no view in any other direction; but even as he gazed there was a sort of flicker in the sunshine succeeded by a mighty but distant clap of thunder. For the next half-hour Peyrol and Michel were busy ashore taking a long line from the tartane to the entrance of the little basin where they fastened the end of it to a bush. This was for the purpose of hauling the tartane out into the cove. Then they came aboard again. The bit of sky above their heads was still clear, but while walking with the hauling line near the cove Peyrol had got a glimpse of the edge of the cloud. The sun grew scorching all of a sudden, and in the stagnating air a mysterious change seemed to come over the quality and the colour of the light. Peyrol flung his cap on the deck, baring his head to the subtle menace of the breathless stillness of the air.

'Phew! Ça chauffe,'[165] he muttered, rolling up the sleeves of his jacket. He wiped his forehead with his mighty forearm upon which a mermaid with an immensely long fishtail was tattooed. Perceiving the lieutenant's belted sword lying on the deck, he picked it up and without any ceremony threw it down the cabin stairs. As he was passing again near Scevola, the sans-culotte raised his voice.

'I believe you are one of those wretches corrupted by English gold,' he cried like one inspired. His shining eyes, his red cheeks, testified to the fire of patriotism burning in his breast, and he used that conventional phrase of revolutionary time, a time when, intoxicated with oratory, he used to run about dealing death to traitors of both sexes and all ages. But his denunciation was received in such profound silence that his own belief in it wavered. His words had sunk into an abysmal stillness and the next sound was Peyrol speaking to Réal.

'I am afraid you will get very wet, lieutenant, before long,' and then, looking at Réal, he thought with great conviction: 'Wet! He wouldn't mind getting drowned.' Standing stock-still, he fretted and fumed inwardly, wondering where precisely the English ship was by this time and where the devil that thunderstorm had got to: for the sky had become as mute as the oppressed earth.

Réal asked: 'Is it not time to haul out, gunner?'

And Peyrol said: 'There is not a breath of wind anywhere for miles.' He was gratified by the fairly loud mutter rolling apparently along the inland hills. Over the pool a little ragged cloud torn from the purple robe of the storm floated, arrested and thin like a bit of dark gauze.

Above at the farm Catherine had heard too the ominous mutter and came to the door of the salle. From there she could see the purple cloud itself, convoluted and solid, and its sinister shadow lying over the hills. The oncoming of the storm added to her sense of uneasiness at finding herself all alone in the house. Michel had not come up. She would have welcomed Michel, to whom she hardly ever spoke, simply as a person belonging to the usual order of things. She was not talkative, but somehow she would have liked somebody to speak to just for a moment. This cessation of all sound, voices or footsteps around the buildings was not welcome; but looking at the cloud, she thought that there would be noise enough presently. However, stepping back into the kitchen, she was met by a sound that made her regret the oppressive silence, by its piercing and terrifying character; it was a shriek in the upper part of the house where, as far as she knew, there was only Arlette asleep. In her attempt to cross the kitchen to the foot of the stairs the weight of her accumulated years fell upon the old woman. She felt suddenly very feeble and hardly able to breathe. And all at once the thought, 'Scevola! Was he murdering her up there?' paralysed the last remnant of her physical powers. What else could it be? She fell, as if shot, into a chair under the first shock and found herself unable to move. Only her brain remained active, and she raised her hands to her eyes as if to shut out the image of the horrors upstairs. She heard nothing more from above. Arlette was dead. She thought that now it was her turn. While her body quailed before the brutal violence, her weary spirit longed ardently for the end. Let him come! Let all this be over at last, with a blow on the head or a stab in the breast. She had not the courage to uncover her eyes. She waited. But after about a minute – it seemed to her interminable – she heard rapid footsteps overhead. Arlette was running here and there. Catherine uncovered her eyes and was about to rise when she heard at the top of the stairs the name of Peyrol shouted with a desperate accent. Then, again, after the shortest of pauses, the cry of: 'Peyrol, Peyrol!' and then the sound of feet running downstairs. There was another shriek, 'Peyrol!' just outside the door before it flew open. Who was pursuing her? Catherine managed to stand up. Steadying herself with one hand on the table she presented an undaunted front to her niece who ran into the kitchen with loose hair flying and the appearance of wildest distraction in her eyes.

The staircase door had slammed to behind her. Nobody was pursuing her; and Catherine, putting forth her lean brown arm, arrested Arlette's flight with such a jerk that the two women swung against each other. She seized her niece by the shoulders.

'What is this, in heaven's name? Where are you rushing to?' she cried, and the other, as if suddenly exhausted, whispered: 'I woke up from an awful dream.'

The kitchen grew dark under the cloud that hung over the house now. There was a feeble flicker of lightning and a faint crash, far away.

The old woman gave her niece a little shake.

'Dreams are nothing,' she said. 'You are awake now . . . ' And indeed Catherine thought that no dream could be so bad as the realities which kept hold of one through the long waking hours.

'They were killing him,' moaned Arlette, beginning to tremble and struggle in her aunt's arms. 'I tell you they were killing him.'

'Be quiet. Were you dreaming of Peyrol?'

She became still in a moment and then whispered: 'No. Eugène.'

She had seen Réal set upon by a mob of men and women, all dripping with blood, in a livid cold light, in front of a stretch of mere shells of houses with cracked walls and broken windows, and going down in the midst of a forest of raised arms brandishing sabres, clubs, knives, axes. There was also a man flourishing a red rag on a stick, while another was beating a drum which boomed above the sickening sound of broken glass falling like rain on the pavement. And away round the corner of an empty street came Peyrol whom she recognised by his white head, walking without haste, swinging his cudgel regularly. The terrible thing was that Peyrol looked straight at her, not noticing anything, composed, without a frown or a smile, unseeing and deaf, while she waved her arms and shrieked desperately to him for help. She woke up with the piercing sound of his name in her ears and with the impression of the dream so powerful that even now, looking distractedly into her aunt's face, she could see the bare arms of that murderous crowd raised above Réal's sinking head. Yet the name that had sprung to her lips on waking was the name of Peyrol. She pushed her aunt away with such force that the old woman staggered backwards and to save herself had to catch hold of the overmantel above her head. Arlette ran to the door of the salle, looked in, came back to her aunt and shouted: 'Where is he?'

Catherine really did not know which path the lieutenant had taken. She understood very well that 'he' meant Réal.

She said: 'He went away a long time ago,' grasped her niece's arm and added with an effort to steady her voice: 'He is coming back, Arlette – for nothing will keep him away from you.'

Arlette, as if mechanically, was whispering to herself the magic name, 'Peyrol, Peyrol!' then cried: 'I want Eugène now. This moment.'

Catherine's face wore a look of unflinching patience. 'He has departed on service,' she said. Her niece looked at her with enormous eyes, coal-black, profound and immovable, while in a forcible and distracted tone she said: 'You and Peyrol have been plotting to rob me of my reason. But I will know how to make that old man give him up. He is mine!' She spun round wildly, like a person looking for a way of escape from a deadly peril, and rushed out blindly.

About Escampobar the air was murky but calm, and the silence was so profound that it was possible to hear the first heavy drops of rain striking the ground. In the intimidating shadow of the storm-cloud, Arlette stood irresolute for a moment, but it was to Peyrol, the man of mystery and power, that her thoughts turned. She was ready to embrace his knees, to entreat and to scold. 'Peyrol, Peyrol!' she cried twice, and lent her ear as if expecting an answer. Then she shouted: 'I want him back.'

Catherine, alone in the kitchen, moving with dignity, sat down in the armchair with the tall back, like a senator in his curule chair[166] awaiting the blow of a barbarous fate.

Arlette flew down the slope. The first sign of her coming was a faint thin scream which really the rover alone heard and understood. He pressed his lips in a particular way, showing his appreciation of the coming difficulty. The next moment he saw, poised on a detached boulder and thinly veiled by the first perpendicular shower, Arlette, who, catching sight of the tartane with the men on board of her, let out a prolonged shriek of mingled triumph and despair: 'Peyrol! Help! Pey—rol!'

Réal jumped to his feet with an extremely scared face, but Peyrol extended an arresting arm. 'She is calling to me,' he said, gazing at the figure poised on the rock. 'Well leaped! Sacré nom! . . . Well leaped!' And he muttered to himself soberly: 'She will break her legs or her neck.'

'I see you, Peyrol,' screamed Arlette, who seemed to be flying through the air. 'Don't you dare.'

'Yes, here I am,' shouted the rover, striking his breast with his fist.

Lieutenant Réal put both his hands over his face. Michel looked on open-mouthed, very much as if watching a performance in a circus; but Scevola cast his eyes down. Arlette came on board with such an impetus that Peyrol had to step forward and save her from a fall which would have stunned her. She struggled in his arms with extreme violence. The heiress of Escampobar with her loose black hair seemed the incarnation of pale fury. 'Misérable![167] Don't you dare!' A roll of thunder covered her voice, but when it had passed away she was heard again in suppliant tones. 'Peyrol, my friend, my dear old friend. Give him back to me,' and all the time her body writhed in the arms of the old seaman. 'You used to love me, Peyrol,' she cried without ceasing to struggle, and suddenly struck the rover twice in the face with her clenched fist. Peyrol's head received the two blows as if it had been made of marble, but he felt with fear her body become still, grow rigid in his arms. A heavy squall enveloped the group of people on board the tartane. Peyrol laid Arlette gently on the deck. Her eyes were closed, her hands remained clenched; every sign of life had left her white face. Peyrol stood up and looked at the tall rocks streaming with water. The rain swept over the tartane with an angry swishing roar to which was added the sound of water rushing violently down the folds and seams of the precipitous shore vanishing gradually from his sight, as if this had been the beginning of a destroying and universal deluge – the end of all things.

Lieutenant Réal, kneeling on one knee, contemplated the pale face of Arlette. Distinct, yet mingling with the faint growl of distant thunder, Peyrol's voice was heard saying: 'We can't put her ashore and leave her lying in the rain. She must be taken up to the house.' Arlette's soaked clothes clung to her limbs while the lieutenant, his bare head dripping with rain water, looked as if he had just saved her from drowning. Peyrol gazed down inscrutably at the woman stretched on the deck and at the kneeling man. 'She has fainted from rage at her old Peyrol,' he went on rather dreamily. 'Strange things do happen. However, lieutenant, you had better take her under the arms and step ashore first. I will help you. Ready? Lift.'

The movements of the two men had to be careful and their progress was slow on the lower, steep part of the slope. After going up more than two-thirds of the way, they rested their insensible burden on a flat stone. Réal continued to sustain the shoulders but Peyrol lowered the feet gently.

'Ha!' he said. 'You will be able to carry her yourself the rest of the way and give her up to old Catherine. Get a firm footing and I will lift her and place her in your arms. You can walk the distance quite easily. There . . . Hold her a little higher, or her feet will be catching on the stones.'

Arlette's hair was hanging far below the lieutenant's arm in an inert and heavy mass. The thunderstorm was passing away, leaving a cloudy sky. And Peyrol thought with a profound sigh: 'I am tired.'

'She is light,' said Réal.

'Parbleu, she is light. If she were dead, you would find her heavy enough. Allons, mon lieutenant. No! I am not coming. What's the good? I'll stay down here. I have no mind to listen to Catherine's scolding.'

The lieutenant, looking absorbed into the face resting in the hollow of his arm, never averted his gaze – not even when Peyrol, stooping over Arlette, kissed the white forehead near the roots of the hair, black as a raven's wing.

'What am I to do?' muttered Réal.

'Do? Why, give her up to old Catherine. And you may just as well tell her that I will be coming along directly. That will cheer her up. I used to count for something in that house. Allez. For our time is very short.'

With these words he turned away and walked slowly down to the tartane. A breeze had sprung up. He felt it on his wet neck and was grateful for the cool touch which recalled him to himself, to his old wandering self which had known no softness and no hesitation in the face of any risk offered by life.

As he stepped on board, the shower passed away. Michel, wet to the skin, was still in the very same attitude gazing up the slope. Citizen Scevola had drawn his knees up and was holding his head in his hands; whether because of rain or cold or for some other reason, his teeth were chattering audibly with a continuous and distressing rattle. Peyrol flung off his jacket, heavy with water, with a strange air as if it was of no more use to his mortal envelope, squared his broad shoulders and directed Michel in a deep, quiet voice to let go the lines holding the tartane to the shore. The faithful henchman was taken aback and required one of Peyrol's authoritative 'Allez!' to put him in motion. Meantime the rover cast off the tiller lines and laid his hand with an air of mastery on the stout piece of wood projecting horizontally from the rudder-head about the level of his hip. The voices and the movements of his companions caused Citizen Scevola to master the desperate trembling of his jaw. He wriggled a little in his bonds and the question that had been on his lips for a good many hours was uttered again.

'What are you going to do with me?'

'What do you think of a little promenade at sea?' Peyrol asked in a tone that was not unkindly.

Citizen Scevola, who had seemed totally and completely cast down and subdued, let out a most unexpected screech.

'Unbind me. Put me ashore.'

Michel, busy forward, was moved to smile as though he had possessed a cultivated sense of incongruity.

Peyrol remained serious. 'You shall be untied presently,' he assured the blood-drinking patriot, who had been for so many years the reputed possessor not only of Escampobar but of the Escampobar heiress that, living on appearances, he had almost come to believe in that ownership himself. No wonder he screeched at this rude awakening. Peyrol raised his voice: 'Haul on the line, Michel.'

As, directly the ropes had been let go, the tartane had swung clear of the shore, the movement given her by Michel carried her towards the entrance by which the basin communicated with the cove. Peyrol attended to the helm, and in a moment, gliding through the narrow gap, the tartane carrying her way shot out almost into the middle of the cove.

A little wind could be felt, running light wrinkles over the water, but outside the overshadowed sea was already speckled with white caps. Peyrol helped Michel to haul aft the sheets and then went back to the tiller. The pretty spick-and-span craft that had been lying idle for so long began to glide into the wide world. Michel gazed at the shore as if lost in admiration. Citizen Scevola's head had fallen on his knees while his nerveless hands clasped his legs loosely. He was the very image of dejection.

'Hé, Michel! Come here and cast loose the citizen. It is only fair that he should be untied for a little excursion at sea.'

When his order had been executed, Peyrol addressed himself to the desolate figure on the deck.

'Like this, should the tartane get capsized in a squall, you will have an equal chance with us to swim for your life.'

Scevola disdained to answer. He was engaged in biting his knee with rage in a stealthy fashion.

'You came on board for some murderous purpose. Who you were after unless it was myself, God only knows. I feel quite justified in giving you a little outing at sea. I won't conceal from you, citizen, that it may not be without risk to life or limb. But you have only yourself to thank for being here.'

As the tartane drew clear of the cove, she felt more the weight of the breeze and darted forward with a lively motion. A vaguely contented smile lighted up Michel's hairy countenance.

'She feels the sea,' said Peyrol, who enjoyed the swift movement of his vessel. 'This is different from your lagoon, Michel.'

'To be sure,' said Michel with becoming gravity.

'Doesn't it seem funny to you, as you look back at the shore, to think that you have left nothing and nobody behind?'

Michel assumed the aspect of a man confronted by an intellectual problem. Since he had become Peyrol's henchman he had lost the habit of thinking altogether. Directions and orders were easy things to apprehend; but a conversation with him whom he called 'notre maître' was a serious matter demanding great and concentrated attention.

'Possibly,' he murmured, looking strangely self-conscious.

'Well, you are lucky, take my word for it,' said the rover, watching the course of his little vessel along the head of the peninsula. 'You have not even a dog to miss you.'

'I have only you, Maître Peyrol.'

'That's what I was thinking,' said Peyrol half to himself, while Michel, who had good sea-legs, kept his balance to the movements of the craft without taking his eyes from the rover's face.

'No,' Peyrol exclaimed suddenly, after a moment of meditation, 'I could not leave you behind.' He extended his open palm towards Michel. 'Put your hand in there,' he said.

Michel hesitated for a moment before this extraordinary proposal. At last he did so, and Peyrol, holding the bereaved fisherman's hand in a powerful grip, said: 'If I had gone away by myself, I would have left you marooned on this earth like a man thrown out to die on a desert island.'

Some dim perception of the solemnity of the occasion seemed to enter Michel's primitive brain. He connected Peyrol's words with the sense of his own insignificant position at the tail of all mankind; and, timidly, he murmured with his clear, innocent glance unclouded, the fundamental axiom of his philosophy: 'Somebody must be last in this world.'

'Well, then, you will have to forgive me all that may happen between this and the hour of sunset.'

The tartane, obeying the helm, fell off before the wind, with her head to the eastward.

Peyrol murmured: 'She has not forgotten how to walk the seas.' His unsubdued heart, heavy for so many days, had a moment of buoyancy – the illusion of immense freedom.

At that moment Réal, amazed at finding no tartane in the basin, was running madly towards the cove, where he was sure Peyrol must be waiting to give her up to him. He ran out on to the very rock on which Peyrol's late prisoner had sat after his escape, too tired to care, yet cheered by the hope of liberty. But Réal was in a worse plight. He could see no shadowy form through the thin veil of rain which pitted the sheltered piece of water framed in the rocks. The little craft had been spirited away. Impossible! There must be something wrong with his eyes! Again the barren hillsides echoed the name of 'Peyrol', shouted with all the force of Réal's lungs. He shouted it only once, and about five minutes afterwards appeared at the kitchen-door, panting, streaming with water as if he had fought his way up from the bottom of the sea. In the tall-backed armchair Arlette lay, with her limbs relaxed, her head on Catherine's arm, her face white as death. He saw her open her black eyes, enormous and as if not of this world; he saw old Catherine turn her head, heard a cry of surprise, and saw a sort of struggle beginning between the two women. He screamed at them like a madman: 'Peyrol has betrayed me!' and in an instant, with a bang of the door, he was gone.

The rain had ceased. Above his head the unbroken mass of clouds moved to the eastward, and he moved in the same direction as if he too were driven by the wind up the hillside, towards the lookout. When he reached the spot and, gasping, flung one arm round the trunk of the leaning tree, the only thing he was aware of during the sombre pause in the unrest of the elements was the distracting turmoil of his thoughts. After a moment he perceived through the rain the English ship with her topsails lowered on the caps, forging ahead slowly across the northern entrance of the Petite Passe. His distress fastened insanely on the notion of there being a connection between that enemy ship and Peyrol's inexplicable conduct. That old man had always meant to go himself! And when a moment after, looking to the southward, he made out the shadow of the tartane coming round the land in the midst of another squall, he muttered to himself a bitter: 'Of course!' She had both her sails set. Peyrol was indeed pressing her to the utmost in his shameful haste to traffic with the enemy. The truth was that from the position in which Réal first saw him, Peyrol could not yet see the English ship, and held confidently on his course up the middle of the strait. The man-of-war and the little tartane saw each other quite unexpectedly at a distance that was very little over a mile. Peyrol's heart flew into his mouth at finding himself so close to the enemy. On board the *Amelia* at first no notice was taken. It was simply a tartane making for shelter on the north side of Porquerolles. But when Peyrol suddenly altered his course, the master of the man-of-war, noticing the manoeuvre, took up the long glass for a look. Captain Vincent was on deck and agreed with the master's remark that 'there was a craft acting suspiciously'. Before the *Amelia* could come round in the heavy squall, Peyrol was already under the battery of Porquerolles and, so far, safe from capture. Captain Vincent had no mind to bring his ship within reach of the battery and risk damage in his rigging or hull for the sake of a small coaster. However, the tale brought on board by Symons of his discovery of a hidden craft, of his capture and his wonderful escape, had made every tartane an object of interest to the whole ship's company. The *Amelia* remained hove to in the strait while her officers watched the lateen sails gliding to and fro under the protecting muzzles of the guns. Captain Vincent himself had been impressed by Peyrol's manoeuvre. Coasting craft as a rule were not afraid of the *Amelia*. After taking a few turns on the quarterdeck he ordered Symons to be called aft.

The hero of a unique and mysterious adventure, which had been the only subject of talk on board the corvette for the last twenty-four hours, came along rolling, hat in hand, and enjoying a secret sense of his importance.

'Take the glass,' said the captain, 'and have a look at that vessel under the land. Is she anything like the tartane that you say you have been aboard of?'

Symons was very positive. 'I think I can swear to those painted mastheads, your honour. It is the last thing I remember before that murderous ruffian knocked me senseless. The moon shone on them. I can make them out now with the glass.' As to the fellow boasting to him that the tartane was a dispatch-boat and had already made some trips, well, Symons begged his honour to believe that the beggar was not sober at the time. He did not care what he blurted out. The best proof of his condition was that he went away to fetch the soldiers and forgot to come back. The murderous old ruffian! 'You see, your honour,' continued Symons, 'he thought I was not likely to escape after getting a blow that would have killed nine out of any ten men. So he went away to boast of what he had done before the people ashore; because one of his chums, worse than himself, came down thinking he would kill me with a dam' big manure fork, saving your honour's presence. A regular savage he was.'

Symons paused, staring, as if astonished at the marvels of his own tale. The old master, standing at his captain's elbow, observed in a dispassionate tone that, anyway, that peninsula was not a bad jumping-off place for a craft intending to slip through the blockade. Symons, not being dismissed, waited hat in hand while Captain Vincent directed the master to fill on the ship and stand a little nearer to the battery. It was done, and presently there was a flash of a gun low down on the water's edge and a shot came skipping in the direction of the *Amelia*. It fell very short, but Captain Vincent judged the ship was close enough and ordered her to be hove to again. Then Symons was told to take a look through the glass once more. After a long interval he lowered it and spoke impressively to his captain: 'I can make out three heads aboard, your honour, and one is white. I would swear to that white head anywhere.'

Captain Vincent made no answer. All this seemed very odd to him; but after all it was possible. The craft had certainly acted suspiciously. He spoke to the first lieutenant in a half-vexed tone.

'He has done a rather smart thing. He will dodge here till dark and then get away. It is perfectly absurd. I don't want to send the boats too close to the battery. And if I do he may simply sail away from them and be round the land long before we are ready to give him chase. Darkness will be his best friend. However, we will keep a watch on him in case he is tempted to give us the slip late in the afternoon. In that case we will have a good try to catch him. If he has anything aboard I should like to get hold of it. It may be of some importance, after all.'

On board the tartane Peyrol put his own interpretation on the ship's movements. His object had been attained. The corvette had marked him for her prey. Satisfied as to that, Peyrol watched his opportunity and taking advantage of a long squall, with rain thick enough to blur the form of the English ship, he left the shelter of the battery to lead the Englishman a dance and keep up his character of a man anxious to avoid capture.

Réal, from his position on the lookout, saw in the thinning downpour the pointed lateen sails glide round the north end of Porquerolles and vanish behind the land. Some time afterwards the *Amelia* made sail in a manner that put it beyond doubt that she meant to chase. Her lofty canvas was shut off too presently by the land of Porquerolles. When she had disappeared Réal turned to Arlette.

'Let us go,' he said.

Arlette, stimulated by the short glimpse of Réal at the kitchen door, whom she had taken for a vision of a lost man calling her to follow him to the end of the world, had torn herself out of the old woman's thin, bony arms which could not cope with the struggles of her body and the fierceness of her spirit. She had run straight to the lookout, though there was nothing to guide her there except a blind impulse to seek Réal wherever he might be. He was not aware of her having found him until she seized hold of his arm with a suddenness, energy and determination of which no one with a clouded mind could have been capable. He felt himself being taken possession of in a way that tore all his scruples out of his breast. Holding on to the trunk of the tree, he threw his other arm round her waist, and when she confessed to him that she did not know why she had run up there, but that if she had not found him she would have thrown herself over the cliff, he tightened his clasp with sudden exultation, as though she had been a gift prayed for instead of a stumbling block for his pedantic conscience. Together they walked back. In the failing light the buildings awaited them, lifeless, the walls darkened by rain and the big slopes of the roofs glistening and sinister under the flying desolation of the clouds. In the kitchen Catherine heard their mingled footsteps, and rigid in the tall armchair awaited their coming. Arlette threw her arms round the old woman's neck while Réal stood on one side, looking on. Thought after thought flew through his mind and vanished in the strong feeling of the irrevocable nature of the event handing him to the woman whom, in the revulsion of his feelings, he was inclined to think more sane than himself.

Arlette, with one arm over the old woman's shoulders, kissed the wrinkled forehead under the white band of linen that, on the erect head, had the effect of a rustic diadem. 'Tomorrow you and I will have to walk down to the church.'

The austere dignity of Catherine's pose seemed to be shaken by this proposal to lead before the God with whom she had made her peace long ago that unhappy girl chosen to share in the guilt of impious and unspeakable horrors which had darkened her mind.

Arlette, still stooping over her aunt's face, extended a hand towards Réal, who, making a step forward, took it silently into his grasp.

'Oh, yes, you will, Aunt,' insisted Arlette. 'You will have to come with me to pray for Peyrol, whom you and I shall never see any more.'

Catherine's head dropped, whether in assent or grief; and Réal felt an unexpected and profound emotion, for he, too, was convinced that none of the three persons in the farm would ever see Peyrol again. It was as though the rover of the wide seas had left them to themselves on a sudden impulse of scorn, of magnanimity, of a passion weary of itself. However come by, Réal was ready to clasp for ever to his breast that woman touched by the red hand of the Revolution; for she, whose little feet had run ankle-deep through the terrors of death, had brought to him the sense of triumphant life.

Chapter 16

Astern of the tartane, the sun, about to set, kindled a streak of dull crimson glow between the darkening sea and the overcast sky. The peninsula of Giens and the islands of Hyères formed one mass of land detaching itself very black against the fiery girdle of the horizon; but to the north the long stretch of the Alpine coast continued beyond sight its endless sinuosities under the stooping clouds.

The tartane seemed to be rushing together with the run of the waves into the arms of the oncoming night. A little more than a mile away on her lee quarter, the *Amelia*, under all plain sail, pressed to the end of the chase. It had lasted now for a good many hours, for Peyrol, when slipping away, had managed to get the advantage of the *Amelia* from the very start. While still within the large sheet of smooth water which is called the Hyères roadstead, the tartane, which was really a craft of extraordinary speed, managed to gain positively on the sloop. Afterwards, by suddenly darting down the eastern passage between the two last islands of the group, Peyrol actually got out of sight of the chasing ship, being hidden by the Ile du Levant for a time. The *Amelia* having to tack twice in order to follow, lost ground once more. Emerging into the open sea, she had to tack again, and then the position became that of a stern chase, which proverbially is known as a long chase. Peyrol's skilful seamanship had twice extracted from Captain Vincent a low murmur accompanied by a significant compression of lips. At one time the *Amelia* had been near enough the tartane to send a shot ahead of her. That one was followed by another which whizzed extraordinarily close to the mastheads, but then Captain Vincent ordered the gun to be secured again. He said to his first lieutenant, who, his speaking trumpet in hand, kept at his elbow: 'We must not sink that craft on any account. If we could get only an hour's calm, we would carry her with the boats.'

The lieutenant remarked that there was no hope of a calm for the next twenty-four hours at least.

'No,' said Captain Vincent, 'and in about an hour it will be dark, and then he may very well give us the slip. The coast is not very far off and there are batteries on both sides of Fréjus, under any of which he will be as safe from capture as though he were hove up on the beach. And look,' he exclaimed after a moment's pause, 'this is what the fellow means to do.'

'Yes, sir,' said the lieutenant, keeping his eyes on the white speck ahead, dancing lightly on the short Mediterranean waves, 'he is keeping off the wind.'

'We will have him in less than an hour,' said Captain Vincent, and made as if he meant to rub his hands, but suddenly leaned his elbow on the rail. 'After all,' he went on, 'properly speaking, it is a race between the *Amelia* and the night.'

'And it will be dark early today,' said the first lieutenant, swinging the speaking trumpet by its lanyard. 'Shall we take the yards off the back-stays, sir?'

'No,' said Captain Vincent. 'There is a clever seaman aboard that tartane. He is running off now, but at any time he may haul up again. We must not follow him too closely, or we shall lose the advantage which we have now. That man is determined on making his escape.'

If those words by some miracle could have been carried to the ears of Peyrol, they would have brought to his lips a smile of malicious and triumphant exultation. Ever since he had laid his hand on the tiller of the tartane every faculty of his resourcefulness and seamanship had been bent on deceiving the English captain, that enemy whom he had never seen, the man whose mind he had constructed for himself from the evolutions of his ship. Leaning against the heavy tiller he addressed Michel, breaking the silence of the strenuous afternoon.

'This is the moment,' his deep voice uttered quietly. 'Ease off the mainsheet, Michel. A little now, only.'

When Michel returned to the place where he had been sitting to windward, the rover noticed his eyes fixed on his face wonderingly. Some vague thoughts had been forming themselves slowly, incompletely, in Michel's brain. Peyrol met the utter innocence of the unspoken enquiry with a smile that, beginning sardonically on his manly and sensitive mouth, ended in something resembling tenderness.

'That's so, camarade,' he said with particular stress and intonation, as if those words contained a full and sufficient answer. Most unexpectedly Michel's round and generally staring eyes blinked as if dazzled. He too produced from somewhere in the depths of his being a queer, misty smile from which Peyrol averted his gaze.

'Where is the citizen?' he asked, bearing hard against the tiller and staring straight ahead. 'He isn't gone overboard, is he? I don't seem to have seen him since we rounded the land near Porquerolles Castle.'

Michel, after craning his head forward to look over the edge of the deck, announced that Scevola was sitting on the keelson.

'Go forward,' said Peyrol, 'and ease off the foresheet now a little. This tartane has wings,' he added to himself.

Alone on the after-deck Peyrol turned his head to look at the *Amelia*. That ship, in consequence of holding her wind, was now crossing obliquely the wake of the tartane. At the same time she had diminished the distance. Nevertheless, Peyrol considered that had he really meant to escape, his chances were as eight to ten – practically an assured success. For a long time he had been contemplating the lofty pyramid of canvas towering against the fading red belt on the sky, when a lamentable groan made him look round. It was Scevola. The citizen had adopted the mode of progression on all fours, and while Peyrol looked at him he rolled to leeward, saving himself rather cleverly from going overboard, and holding on desperately to a cleat, shouted in a hollow voice, pointing with the other hand as if he had made a tremendous discovery: 'La terre! La terre!'[168]

'Certainly,' said Peyrol, steering with extreme nicety. 'What of that?'

'I don't want to be drowned!' cried the citizen in his new hollow voice.

Peyrol reflected a bit before he spoke in a serious tone: 'If you stay where you are, I assure you that you will . . . ' he glanced rapidly over his shoulder at the *Amelia* . . . 'not die by drowning.' He jerked his head sideways. 'I know that man's mind.'

'What man? Whose mind?' yelled Scevola with intense eagerness and bewilderment. 'We are only three on board.'

But Peyrol's mind was contemplating maliciously the figure of a man with long teeth, in a wig and with large buckles to his shoes. Such was his ideal conception of what the captain of the *Amelia* ought to look like. That officer, whose naturally good-humoured face wore then a look of severe resolution, had beckoned his first lieutenant to his side again.

'We are gaining,' he said quietly. 'I intend to close with him to windward. We won't risk any of his tricks. It is very difficult to out-manoeuvre a Frenchman, as you know. Send a few armed marines on the forecastle-head. I am afraid the only way to get hold of this tartane is to disable the men on board of her. I wish to goodness I could think of some other. When we close with her, let the marines fire a well-aimed volley. You must get some marines to stand by aft as well. I hope we may shoot away his halliards; once his sails are down on his deck he is ours for the trouble of putting a boat over the side.'

For more than half an hour Captain Vincent stood silent, elbow on rail, keeping his eye on the tartane, while on board the latter Peyrol steered silent and watchful but intensely conscious of the enemy ship holding on in her relentless pursuit. The narrow red band was dying out of the sky. The French coast, black against the fading light, merged into the shadows gathering in the eastern board. Citizen Scevola, somewhat soothed by the assurance that he would not die by drowning, had elected to remain quiet where he had fallen, not daring to trust himself to move on the lively deck. Michel, squatting to windward, gazed intently at Peyrol in expectation of some order at any minute. But Peyrol uttered no word and made no sign. From time to time a burst of foam flew over the tartane, or a splash of water would come aboard with a scurrying noise.

It was not till the corvette had got within a long gunshot from the tartane that Peyrol opened his mouth.

'No!' he burst out, loud in the wind, as if giving vent to long anxious thinking, 'No! I could not have left you behind with not even a dog for company. Devil take me if I don't think you would not have thanked me for it either. What do you say to that, Michel?'

A half-puzzled smile dwelt persistently on the guileless countenance of the ex-fisherman. He stated what he had always thought in respect of Peyrol's every remark: 'I think you are right, maître.'

'Listen then, Michel. That ship will be alongside of us in less than half an hour. As she comes up they will open on us with musketry.'

'They will open on us . . . ' repeated Michel, looking quite interested. 'But how do you know they will do that, maître?'

'Because her captain has got to obey what is in my mind,' said Peyrol, in a tone of positive and solemn conviction. 'He will do it as sure as if I were at his ear telling him what to do. He will do it because he is a first-rate seaman, but I, Michel, I am just a little bit cleverer than he.' He glanced over his shoulder at the *Amelia* rushing after the tartane with swelling sails, and raised his voice suddenly. 'He will do it because no more than half a mile ahead of us is the spot where Peyrol will die!'

Michel did not start. He only shut his eyes for a time, and the rover continued in a lower tone: 'I may be shot through the heart at once,' he said, 'and in that case you have my permission to let go the halliards if you are alive yourself. But if I live I mean to put the helm down. When I do that you will let go the foresheet to help the tartane to fly into the wind's eye. This is my last order to you. Now go forward and fear nothing. Adieu.' Michel obeyed without a word.

Half a dozen of the *Amelia*'s marines stood ranged on the forecastle-head ready with their muskets. Captain Vincent walked into the lee waist to watch his chase. When he thought that the jib-boom of the *Amelia* had drawn level with the stern of the tartane he waved his hat and the marines discharged their muskets. Apparently no gear was cut.

Captain Vincent observed the white-headed man, who was steering, clap his hand to his left side, while he hove the tiller to leeward and brought the tartane sharply into the wind. The marines on the poop fired in their turn, all the reports merging into one. Voices were heard on the decks crying that they 'had hit the white-haired chap'. Captain Vincent shouted to the master: 'Get the ship round on the other tack.'

The elderly seaman who was the master of the *Amelia* took a critical look before he gave the necessary orders; and the *Amelia* closed on her chase with her decks resounding to the piping of boatswain's mates and the hoarse shout: 'Hands shorten sail. About ship.'

Peyrol, lying on his back under the swinging tiller, heard the calls shrilling and dying away; he heard the ominous rush of *Amelia*'s bow wave as the sloop foamed within ten yards of the tartane's stern; he even saw her upper yards coming down, and then everything vanished out of the clouded sky. There was nothing in his ears but the sound of the wind, the wash of the waves buffeting the little craft left without guidance and the continuous thrashing of its foresail, the sheet of which Michel had let go according to orders. The tartane began to roll heavily, but Peyrol's right arm was sound and he managed to put it round a bollard to prevent himself from being flung about. A feeling of peace sank into him, not unmingled with pride. Everything he had planned had come to pass. He had meant to play that man a trick, and now the trick had been played. Played by him better than by any other old man on whom age had stolen, unnoticed, till the veil of peace was torn down by the touch of a sentiment unexpected like an intruder and cruel like an enemy.

Peyrol rolled his head to the left. All he could see were the legs of Citizen Scevola sliding nervelessly to and fro to the rolling of the vessel as if his body had been jammed somewhere. Dead, or only scared to death? And Michel? Was he dead or dying, that man without friends whom his pity had refused to leave behind marooned on the earth without even a dog for company? As to that, Peyrol felt no compunction; but he thought he would have liked to see Michel once more. He tried to utter his name, but his throat refused him even a whisper. He felt himself removed far away from that world of human sounds, in which Arlette had screamed at him: 'Peyrol, don't you dare!' He would never hear anybody's voice again! Under that grey sky there was nothing for him but the swish of breaking seas and the ceaseless furious beating of the tartane's foresail. His plaything was knocking about terribly under him, with her tiller flying madly to and fro just clear of his head and solid lumps of water coming on board over his prostrate body. Suddenly, in a desperate lurch which brought the whole Mediterranean with a ferocious snarl level with the slope of the little deck, Peyrol saw the *Amelia* bearing right down upon the tartane. The fear not of death but of failure gripped his slowing-down heart. Was this blind Englishman going to run him down and sink the dispatches together with the craft? With a mighty effort of his ebbing strength Peyrol sat up and flung his arm round the shroud of the main mast.

The *Amelia*, whose way had carried her past the tartane for a quarter of a mile before sail could be shortened and her yards swung on the other tack, was coming back to take possession of her chase. In the deepening dusk and amongst the foaming seas it was a matter of difficulty to make out the little craft. At the very moment when the master of the man-of-war, looking out anxiously from the forecastle-head, thought that she might perhaps have filled and gone down, he caught sight of her rolling in the trough of the sea, and so close that she seemed to be at the end of the *Amelia*'s jib-boom. His heart flew in his mouth. 'Hard a starboard!' he yelled, his order being passed along the decks.

Peyrol, sinking back on the deck in another heavy lurch of his craft, saw for an instant the whole of the English corvette swing up into the clouds as if she meant to fling herself upon his very breast. A blown sea top flicked his face noisily, followed by a smooth interval, a silence of the waters. He beheld in a flash the days of his manhood, of strength and adventure. Suddenly an enormous voice like the roar of an angry sea-lion seemed to fill the whole of the empty sky in a mighty and commanding shout: 'Steady!''. . . And with the sound of that familiar English word ringing in his ears Peyrol smiled to his visions and died.

The *Amelia*, stripped down to her topsails and hove to, rose and fell easily while on her quarter about a cable's length away Peyrol's tartane tumbled like a lifeless corpse amongst the seas. Captain Vincent, in his favourite attitude of leaning over the rail, kept his eyes fastened on his prize. Mr Bolt, who had been sent for, waited patiently till his commander turned round.

'Oh, here you are, Mr Bolt. I have sent for you to go and take possession. You speak French, and there may still be somebody alive in her. If so, of course you will send him on board at once. I am sure there can be nobody unwounded there. It will anyhow be too dark to see much, but just have a good look round and secure everything in the way of papers you can lay your hands on. Haul aft the foresheet and sail her up to receive a tow line. I intend to take her along and ransack her thoroughly in the morning; tear down the cuddy linings and so on, should you not find at once what I expect . . . ' Captain Vincent, his white teeth gleaming in the dusk, gave some further orders in a lower tone, and Mr Bolt departed in a hurry. Half an hour afterwards he was back on board, and the *Amelia*, with the tartane in tow, made sail to the eastward in search of the blockading fleet.

Mr Bolt, introduced into a cabin strongly lighted by a swinging lamp, tendered to his captain across the table a sailcloth package corded and sealed, and a piece of paper folded in four, which, he explained, seemed to be a certificate of registry, strangely enough mentioning no name. Captain Vincent seized the grey canvas package eagerly.

'This looks like the very thing, Bolt,' he said, turning it over in his hands. 'What else did you find on board?'

Bolt said that he had found three dead men, two on the after-deck and one lying at the bottom of the open hold with the bare end of the foresheet in his hand – 'shot down, I suppose, just as he had let it go,' he commented. He described the appearance of the bodies and reported that he had disposed of them according to orders. In the tartane's cabin there was half a demijohn of wine and a loaf of bread in a locker; also, on the floor, a leather valise containing an officer's uniform coat and a change of clothing. He had lighted the lamp and saw that the linen was marked 'E. Réal'. An officer's sword on a broad shoulder-belt was also lying on the floor. These things could not have belonged to the old chap with the white hair, who was a big man. 'Looks as if somebody had tumbled overboard,' commented Bolt. Two of the bodies looked nondescript, but there was no doubt about that fine old fellow being a seaman.

'By heavens!' said Captain Vincent, 'he was that! Do you know, Bolt, that he nearly managed to escape us? Another twenty minutes would have done it. How many wounds had he?'

'Three I think, sir. I did not look closely,' said Bolt.

'I hated the necessity of shooting brave men like dogs,' said Captain Vincent. 'Still, it was the only way; and there may be something here,' he went on, slapping the package with his open palm, 'that will justify me in my own eyes. You may go now.'

Captain Vincent did not turn in but only lay down fully dressed on the couch till the officer of the watch, appearing at the door, told him that a ship of the fleet was in sight away to windward. Captain Vincent ordered the private night signal to be made. When he came on deck the towering shadow of a line-of-battle ship that seemed to reach to the very clouds was well within hail and a voice bellowed from her through a speaking trumpet: 'What ship is that?'

'His Majesty's sloop *Amelia*,' hailed back Captain Vincent. 'What ship is that, pray?'

Instead of the usual answer there was a short pause and another voice spoke boisterously through the trumpet: 'Is that you, Vincent? Don't you know the *Superb* when you see her?'

'Not in the dark, Keats.[169] How are you? I am in a hurry to speak to the Admiral.'

'The fleet is lying by,' came the voice, now with painstaking distinctness, across the murmurs, whispers and splashes of the black lane of water dividing the two ships. 'The Admiral bears south-south-east. If you stretch on till daylight as you are, you will fetch him on the other tack in time for breakfast on board the *Victory*. Is anything up?'

At every slight roll the sails of the *Amelia*, becalmed by the bulk of the seventy-four, flapped gently against the masts.

'Not much,' hailed Captain Vincent. 'I made a prize.'

'Have you been in action?' came the swift enquiry.

'No, no. Piece of luck.'

'Where's your prize?' roared the speaking trumpet with interest.

'In my desk,' roared Captain Vincent in reply. 'Enemy dispatches . . . I say, Keats, fill on your ship. Fill on her, I say, or you will be falling on board of me.' He stamped his foot impatiently. 'Clap some hands at once on the tow-line and run that tartane close under our stern,' he called to the officer of the watch, 'or else the old *Superb* will walk over her without ever knowing anything about it.'

When Captain Vincent presented himself on board the *Victory* it was too late for him to be invited to share the Admiral's breakfast. He was told that Lord Nelson had not been seen on deck yet that morning; and presently word came that he wished to see Captain Vincent at once in his cabin. Being introduced, the captain of the *Amelia*, in undress uniform, with a sword by his side and his hat under his arm, was received kindly, made his bow and with a few words of explanation laid the packet on the big round table at which sat a silent secretary in black clothes, who had been obviously writing a letter from his lordship's dictation. The Admiral had been walking up and down, and after he had greeted Captain Vincent he resumed his pacing of a nervous man. His empty sleeve had not yet been pinned on his breast[170] and swung slightly every time he turned in his walk. His thin locks fell lank against the pale cheeks, and the whole face in repose had an expression of suffering with which the fire of his one eye presented a startling contrast. He stopped short and exclaimed while Captain Vincent towered over him in a respectful attitude: 'A tartane! Captured on board a tartane!

How on earth did you pitch upon that one out of the hundreds you must see every month?'

'I must confess that I got hold accidentally of some curious information,' said Captain Vincent. 'It was all a piece of luck.'

While the secretary was ripping open with a penknife the cover of the dispatches, Lord Nelson took Captain Vincent out into the stern gallery. The quiet and sunshiny morning had the added charm of a cool, light breeze; and the *Victory* , under her three topsails and lower staysails, was moving slowly to the southward in the midst of the scattered fleet carrying for the most part the same sail as the Admiral. Only far away two or three ships could be seen covered with canvas trying to close with the flag. Captain Vincent noted with satisfaction that the first lieutenant of the *Amelia* had been obliged to brace by his afteryards in order not to overrun the Admiral's quarter.

'Why!' exclaimed Lord Nelson suddenly, after looking at the sloop for a moment, 'you have that tartane in tow!'

'I thought that your lordship would perhaps like to see a forty-ton lateen craft which has led such a chase to, I dare say, the fastest sloop in His Majesty's service.'

'How did it all begin?' asked the Admiral, continuing to look at the *Amelia*.

'As I have already hinted to your lordship, certain information came in my way,' began Captain Vincent, who did not think it necessary to enlarge upon that part of the story. 'This tartane, which is not very different to look at from the other tartanes along the coast between Cette and Genoa,[171] had started from a cove on the Giens Peninsula. An old man with a white head of hair was entrusted with the service and really they could have found nobody better. He came round Cape Esterel intending to pass through the Hyères roadstead. Apparently he did not expect to find the *Amelia* in his way. And it was there that he made his only mistake. If he had kept on his course I would probably have taken no more notice of him than of two other craft that were in sight then. But he acted suspiciously by hauling up for the battery on Porquerolles. This manoeuvre in connection with the information of which I spoke decided me to overhaul him and see what he had on board.' Captain Vincent then related concisely the episodes of the chase. 'I assure your lordship that I never gave an order with greater reluctance than to open musketry fire on that craft; but the old man had given such proofs of his seamanship and determination that there was nothing else for it. Why! at the very moment he had the *Amelia* alongside of him he still made a most clever attempt to prolong the chase. There were only a few minutes of daylight left, and in the darkness we might very well have lost him. Considering that they all could have saved their lives simply by striking their sails on deck, I cannot refuse them my admiration and especially the white-haired man.'

The Admiral, who had been all the time looking absently at the *Amelia* keeping her station with the tartane in tow, said: 'You have a very smart little ship, Vincent. Very fit for the work I have given you to do. French built, isn't she?'

'Yes, my lord. They are great shipbuilders.'

'You don't seem to hate the French, Vincent,' said the Admiral, smiling faintly.

'Not that kind, my lord,' said Captain Vincent with a bow. 'I detest their political principles and the characters of their public men, but your lordship will admit that for courage and determination we could not have found worthier adversaries anywhere on this globe.'

'I never said that they were to be despised,' said Lord Nelson. 'Resource, courage, yes . . . If that Toulon fleet gives me the slip, all our squadrons from Gibraltar to Brest will be in jeopardy. Why don't they come out and be done with it? Don't I keep far enough out of their way?' he cried.

Vincent remarked the nervous agitation of the frail figure with a concern augmented by a fit of coughing which came on the Admiral. He was quite alarmed by its violence. He watched the Commander-in-Chief in the Mediterranean choking and gasping so helplessly that he felt compelled to turn his eyes away from the painful spectacle; but he noticed also how quickly Lord Nelson recovered from the subsequent exhaustion.

'This is anxious work, Vincent,' he said. 'It is killing me. I aspire to repose somewhere in the country, in the midst of fields, out of reach of the sea and the Admiralty and dispatches and orders, and responsibility too. I have been just finishing a letter to tell them at home I have hardly enough breath in my body to carry me on from day to day . . . But I am like that white-headed man you admire so much, Vincent,' he pursued, with a weary smile, 'I will stick to my task till perhaps some shot from the enemy puts an end to everything[172] . . . Let us see what there may be in those papers you have brought on board.'

The secretary in the cabin had arranged them in separate piles.

'What is it all about?' asked the Admiral, beginning again to pace restlessly up and down the cabin.

'At the first glance the most important, my lord, are the orders for marine authorities in Corsica and Naples to make certain dispositions in view of an expedition to Egypt.'

'I always thought so,' said the Admiral, his eye gleaming at the attentive countenance of Captain Vincent. 'This is a smart piece of work on your part, Vincent. I can do no better than send you back to your station. Yes ... Egypt ... the East ... Everything points that way,' he soliloquised under Vincent's eyes while the secretary, picking up the papers with care, rose quietly and went out to have them translated and to make an abstract for the Admiral.

'And, yet who knows!' exclaimed Lord Nelson, standing still for a moment. 'But the blame or the glory must be mine alone. I will seek counsel from no man.' Captain Vincent felt himself forgotten, invisible, less than a shadow in the presence of a nature capable of such vehement feelings. 'How long can he last?' he asked himself with sincere concern.

The Admiral, however, soon remembered his presence, and at the end of another ten minutes Captain Vincent left the *Victory*, feeling, like all officers who approached Lord Nelson, that he had been speaking with a personal friend; and with a renewed devotion for the great sea-officer's soul dwelling in the frail body of the Commander-in-Chief of His Majesty's ships in the Mediterranean. While he was being pulled back to his ship a general signal went up in the *Victory* for the fleet to form line, as convenient, ahead and astern of the Admiral; followed by another to the *Amelia* to part company. Vincent accordingly gave his orders to make sail, and, directing the master to shape a course for Cape Cicié,[173] went down into his cabin. He had been up nearly the whole of the last three nights and he wanted to get a little sleep. His slumbers, however, were short and disturbed. Early in the afternoon he found himself broad awake and reviewing in his mind the events of the day before. The order to shoot three brave men in cold blood, terribly distasteful at the time, was lying heavily on him. Perhaps he had been impressed by Peyrol's white head, his obstinacy to escape him, the determination shown to the very last minute, by something in the whole episode that suggested a more than common devotion to duty and a spirit of daring defiance. With his robust health, simple good nature and sanguine temperament touched with a little irony, Captain Vincent was a man of generous feelings and of easily moved sympathies.

'Yet,' he reflected, 'they had been asking for it. There could be only one end to that affair. But the fact remains that they were defenceless and unarmed and particularly harmless-looking, and at the same time as brave as any. That old chap now ... ' He wondered how much of exact

truth there was in Symons tale of adventure. He concluded that the
facts must have been true but that Symons' interpretation of them
made it extraordinarily difficult to discover what really there was under
all that. That craft certainly was fit for blockade running. Lord Nelson
had been pleased. Captain Vincent went on deck with the kindliest
feelings towards all men, alive and dead.

The afternoon had turned out very fine. The British fleet was just
out of sight with the exception of one or two stragglers, under a press
of canvas. A light breeze in which only the *Amelia* could travel at five
knots, hardly ruffled the profundity of the blue waters basking in the
warm tenderness of the cloudless sky. To south and west the horizon
was empty except for two specks very far apart, of which one shone
white like a bit of silver and the other appeared black like a drop of ink.

Captain Vincent, with his purpose firm in his mind, felt at peace with
himself. As he was easily accessible to his officers his first lieutenant
ventured a question to which Captain Vincent replied: 'He looks very
thin and worn out, but I don't think he is as ill as he thinks he is. I am
sure you all would like to know that his lordship is pleased with our
yesterday's work – those papers were of some importance you know –
and generally with the *Amelia*. It was a queer chase, wasn't it?' he went
on. 'That tartane was clearly and unmistakably running away from us.
But she never had a chance against the *Amelia*.'

During the latter part of that speech the first lieutenant glanced
astern as if asking himself how long Captain Vincent proposed to drag
that tartane behind the *Amelia*. The two keepers in her wondered also
as to when they would be permitted to get back on board their ship.
Symons, who was one of them, declared that he was sick and tired of
steering the blamed thing. Moreover, the company on board made
him uncomfortable; for Symons was aware that in pursuance of Captain
Vincent's orders, Mr Bolt had had the three dead Frenchmen carried
into the cuddy, which he afterwards secured with an enormous padlock
that, apparently, belonged to it, and had taken the key on board the
Amelia. As to one of them, Symons' unforgiving verdict was that it
would have served him right to be thrown ashore for crows to peck his
eyes out. And anyhow, he could not understand why he should have
been turned into the coxswain of a floating hearse, and be damned to
it . . . He grumbled interminably.

Just about sunset, which is the time of burials at sea, the *Amelia* was
hove to and, the rope being manned, the tartane was brought alongside
and her two keepers ordered on board their ship. Captain Vincent,
leaning over with his elbows on the rail, seemed lost in thought.

At last the first lieutenant spoke. 'What are we going to do with that tartane, sir? Our men are on board.'

'We are going to sink her by gunfire,' declared Captain Vincent suddenly. 'His ship makes a very good coffin for a seaman, and those men deserve better than to be thrown overboard to roll on the waves. Let them rest quietly at the bottom of the sea in the craft to which they had stuck so well.'

The lieutenant, making no reply, waited for some more positive order. Every eye on the ship was turned on the captain. But Captain Vincent said nothing and seemed unable or unwilling to give it yet. He was feeling vaguely that in all his good intentions there was something wanting.

'Ah! Mr Bolt,' he said, catching sight of the master's-mate in the waist. 'Did they have a flag on board that craft?'

'I think she had a tiny bit of ensign when the chase began, sir, but it must have blown away. It is not at the end of her mainyard now.' He looked over the side. 'The halliards are rove, though,' he added.

'We must have a French ensign somewhere on board,' said Captain Vincent.

'Certainly, sir,' struck in the master, who was listening.

'Well, Mr Bolt,' said Captain Vincent, 'you have had most to do with all this. Take a few men with you, bend the French ensign on the halliards and sway his mainyard to the masthead.' He smiled at all the faces turned towards him. 'After all they never surrendered and, by heavens, gentlemen, we will let them go down with their colours flying.'

A profound but not disapproving silence reigned over the decks of the ship while Mr Bolt with three or four hands was busy executing the order. Then suddenly above the top-gallant rail of the *Amelia* appeared the upper curve of a lateen yard with the tricolour drooping from the point. A subdued murmur from all hands greeted this apparition. At the same time Captain Vincent ordered the line holding the tartane alongside to be cast off and the mainyard of the *Amelia* to be swung round. The sloop shooting ahead of her prize left her stationary on the sea, then putting the helm up, ran back abreast of her on the other side. The port bow-gun was ordered to fire a round, aiming well forward. That shot, however, went just over, taking the foremast out of the tartane. The next was more successful, striking the little hull between wind and water, and going out well under water on the other side. A third was fired, as the men said, just for luck, and that too took effect, a splintered hole appearing at the bow. After that the guns were secured and the *Amelia*, with no brace being touched, was brought to her course

towards Cape Cicié. All hands on board of her with their backs to the
sunset sky, clear like a pale topaz above the hard blue gem of the sea,
watched the tartane give a sudden dip, followed by a slow, unchecked
dive. At last the tricolour flag alone remained visible for a tense and
interminable moment, pathetic and lonely, in the centre of a brimful
horizon. All at once it vanished, like a flame blown upon, bringing to
the beholders the sense of having been left face to face with an immense,
suddenly created solitude. On the decks of the *Amelia* a low murmur
died out.

When Lieutenant Réal sailed away with the Toulon fleet on the great
strategical cruise which was to end in the Battle of Trafalgar, Madame
Réal returned with her aunt to her hereditary house at Escampobar.
She had only spent a few weeks in town where she was not much seen in
public. The lieutenant and his wife lived in a little house near the
western gate, and the lieutenant's official position, though he was
employed on the staff to the last, was not sufficiently prominent to
make her absence from official ceremonies at all remarkable. But this
marriage was an object of mild interest in naval circles. Those – mostly
men – who had seen Madame Réal at home, told stories of her dazzling
complexion, of her magnificent black eyes, of her personal and attractive
strangeness, and of the Arlesian costume she insisted on wearing, even
after her marriage to an officer of the navy, being herself sprung from
farmer stock. It was also said that her father and mother had fallen
victims in the massacres of Toulon after the evacuation of the town; but
all those stories varied in detail and were on the whole very vague.
Whenever she went abroad Madame Réal was attended by her aunt
who aroused almost as much curiosity as herself: a magnificent old
woman with upright carriage and an austere, brown, wrinkled face
showing signs of past beauty. Catherine was also seen alone in the
streets, where, as a matter of fact, people turned round to look after the
thin and dignified figure, remarkable amongst the passers-by, whom
she herself did not seem to see. About her escape from the massacres
most wonderful tales were told, and she acquired the reputation of a
heroine. Arlette's aunt was known to frequent the churches, which were
all open to the faithful now, carrying even into the house of God her
sibylline aspect of a prophetess and her austere manner. It was not at
the services that she was seen most. People would see her oftener in an
empty nave, standing slim and as straight as an arrow in the shade of a
mighty pillar as if making a call on the Creator of all things with whom
she had made her peace generously, and now would petition only for

pardon and reconciliation with her niece Arlette. For Catherine for a long time remained uncertain of the future. She did not get rid of her involuntary awe of her niece as a selected object of God's wrath until towards the end of her life. There was also another soul for which she was concerned. The pursuit of the tartane by the *Amelia* had been observed from various points of the islands that close the roadstead of Hyères, and the English ship had been seen from the Fort de la Vigie[174] opening fire on her chase. The result, though the two vessels soon ran out of sight, could not be a matter of doubt. There was also the story, told by a coaster that got into Fréjus, of a tartane being fired on by a square-rigged man-of-war; but that apparently was the next day. All these rumours pointed one way and were the foundation of the report made by Lieutenant Réal to the Toulon Admiralty. That Peyrol went out to sea in his tartane and was never seen again, was of course an incontrovertible fact.

The day before the two women were to go back to Escampobar, Catherine approached a priest in the church of Ste Marie Majeure,[175] a little unshaven fat man with a watery eye, in order to arrange for some masses to be said for the dead.

'But for whose soul are we to pray?' mumbled the priest in a wheezy low tone.

'Pray for the soul of Jean,' said Catherine. 'Yes, Jean. There is no other name.'

Lieutenant Réal, wounded at Trafalgar, but escaping capture, retired with the rank of Capitaine de Frégate[176] and vanished from the eyes of the naval world in Toulon and indeed from the world altogether. Whatever sign brought him back to Escampobar on that momentous night, was not meant to call him to his death but to a quiet and retired life, obscure in a sense but not devoid of dignity. In the course of years he became the Mayor of the Commune in that very same little village which had looked on Escampobar as the abode of iniquity, the sojourn of blood-drinkers and of wicked women.

One of the earliest excitements breaking the monotony of the Escampobar life was the discovery at the bottom of the well, one dry year when the water got very low, of some considerable obstruction. After a lot of trouble in getting it up, this obstruction turned out to be a garment made of sailcloth, which had armholes and three horn buttons in front, and looked like a waistcoat; but it was lined, positively quilted, with a surprising quantity of gold pieces of various ages, coinages and nationalities. Nobody but Peyrol could have put it there. Catherine was able to give the exact date, because she remembered seeing him doing something at the well on the very morning before he went out to sea with Michel, carrying off Scevola. Captain Réal could guess easily the origin of that treasure, and he decided with his wife's approval to give it up to the Government as the hoard of a man who had died intestate with no discoverable relations, and whose very name had been a matter of uncertainty, even to himself. After that event the uncertain name of Peyrol found itself oftener and oftener on Monsieur and Madame Réal's lips, on which before it was but seldom heard, though the recollection of his white-headed, quiet, irresistible personality haunted every corner of the Escampobar fields. From that time they talked of him openly, as though he had come back to live again amongst them.

Many years afterwards, one fine evening, Monsieur and Madame Réal, sitting on the bench outside the salle (the house had not been altered at all outside except that it was now kept whitewashed), began to talk of that episode and of the man who, coming from the seas, had crossed their lives to disappear at sea again.

'How did he get all that lot of gold?' wondered Madame Réal innocently. 'He could not possibly want it; and, Eugène, why should he have put it down there?'

'That, ma chère amie,'[177] said Réal, 'is not an easy question to answer. Men and women are not so simple as they seem. Even you, fermière' (he used to give his wife that name jocularly, sometimes), 'are not so simple as some people would take you to be. I think that if Peyrol were here he could not perhaps answer your question himself.'

And they went on, reminding each other in short phrases, separated by long silences, of his peculiarities of person and behaviour, until, above the slope leading down to Madrague, there appeared first the pointed ears and then the whole body of a very diminutive donkey of a light grey colour with dark points. Two pieces of wood, strangely shaped, projected on each side of his body as far as his head, like very long shafts of a cart. But the donkey dragged no cart after him. He was carrying on his back on a small pack saddle the torso of a man who did not seem to have any legs. The little animal, beautifully groomed and with an intelligent and even impudent physiognomy, stopped in front of Monsieur and Madame Réal. The man, balancing himself cleverly on the pack saddle with his withered legs crossed in front of him, slipped off, disengaged his crutches from each side of the donkey smartly, propped himself on them, and with his open palm gave the animal a resounding thwack which sent it trotting into the yard. The cripple of the Madrague in his quality of Peyrol's friend (for the rover had often talked of him both to the women and to Lieutenant Réal with great appreciation – 'C'est un homme, ça!'[178]) had become a member of the Escampobar community. His employment was to run about the country on errands most unfit, one would think, for a man without legs. But the donkey did all the walking while the cripple supplied the sharp wits and an unfailing memory. The poor fellow, snatching off his hat and holding it with one hand alongside his right crutch, approached to render his account of the day in the simple words: 'Everything has been done as you ordered, madame'; then lingered, a privileged servant, familiar but respectful, attractive with his soft eyes, long face and his pained smile.

'We were just talking of Peyrol,' remarked Captain Réal.

'Ah, one could talk a long time of him,' said the cripple. 'He told me once that if I had been complete – with legs like everybody else, I suppose he meant – I would have made a good comrade away there in the distant seas. He had a great heart.'

'Yes,' murmured Madame Réal thoughtfully. Then turning to her husband, she asked: 'What sort of man was he really, Eugène?' Captain Réal remained silent. 'Did you ever ask yourself that question?' she insisted.

'Yes,' said Réal. 'But the only certain thing we can say of him is that he was not a bad Frenchman.'

'Everything's in that,' murmured the cripple, with fervent conviction, in the silence that fell upon Réal's words and Arlette's faint sigh of memory.

The blue level of the Mediterranean, the charmer and the deceiver of audacious men, kept the secret of its fascination – hugged to its calm breast the victims of all the wars, calamities and tempests of its history, under the marvellous purity of the sunset sky. A few rosy clouds floated high up over the Esterel range. The breath of the evening breeze came to cool the heated rocks of Escampobar; and the mulberry tree, the only big tree on the head of the peninsula, standing like a sentinel at the gate of the yard, sighed faintly in a shudder of all its leaves, as if regretting the Brother of the Coast, the man of dark deeds, but of large heart, who often at noonday would lie down to sleep under its shade.

NOTES TO *ALMAYER'S FOLLY*

1 (Title Page, p. 3) The epigraph comes from *Amiel's Journal: The Journal Intime of Henri-Frédéric Amiel*, Vol. 1, page 41, in Mrs Humphry Ward's translation. The passage (with the epigraph in italics) refers to Moses and reads as follows:

> Thou too sawest undulating in the distance the ravishing hills of the Promised Land, and it was thy fate nevertheless to lay thy weary bones in a grave dug in the desert! – *Which of us has not his promised land, his day of ecstasy and his death in exile?* What a pale counterfeit is real life of the life we see in glimpses, and how these flaming lightnings of our prophetic youth make the twilight of our dull monotonous manhood more dark and dreary.

2 (Dedication, p. 4) *T. B.* Tadeusz Bobrowski, Conrad's maternal uncle who acted as his guardian after Conrad's parents had died

3 (Author's Note, p. 5) *a lady* Alice Meynell (1847–1922) published her article 'Decivilised' in the *National Observer* on 24 January 1891. It was reprinted in her book *The Rhythm of Life* in 1893.

4 (p. 7) *the Pantai* part of the River Berau which flows into the Celebes Sea off the east coast of Borneo

5 (p. 8) *Celebes* (now Sulawesi) is the large island to the east of Borneo; Macassar (Makassar), now Ujung Pandang, is a port on the south-west coast of the island facing the Makassar Strait and is the provincial capital of South Sulawesi.

6 (p. 8) *godowns* warehouses

7 (p. 8) *Buitenzorg* a highland resort south of Jakarta, now called Bogor. The Dutch word means 'free from care', which, since it is situated close to two volcanoes, does not seem appropriate.

8 (p. 8) *Manchester goods* cotton textiles manufactured in or near Manchester

9 (p. 9) *punkah* a large swinging cloth fan, suspended from the ceiling

10 (p. 9) *bonies* ponies. Conrad delivered a pony to Charles Olmeijer in *A Personal Record* (pp. 76–83).

11 (p. 9) *Sulu pirates* The Sulu Sea is between the north-east coast of Borneo and the Philippines. It is still a notorious area for pirates.

12 (p. 9) *prau*   a Malay boat with a large triangular sail

13 (p. 10) *gutta-percha*   raw rubber; *rattans* – Malaysian climbing palms with long thin jointed pliable stems; *gum-dammar* – resin

14 (p. 10) *Titans*   gods of gigantic strength in Greek mythology, defeated and superseded by Zeus and the other gods of Mount Olympus. The fact that they were vanquished is significant, though Almayer, of course, does not consider this detail.

15 (p. 11) *Sourabaya*   now Surabaya, an important city on the north coast of eastern Java

16 (p. 13) *Orang Blanda*   the Dutch

17 (p. 16) *geneva*   Dutch gin

18 (p. 20) *Batavia*   now Jakarta (formerly Djakarta), the capital of Indonesia, on the island of Java

19 (p. 21) *Syed Abdulla*   A Syed (also spelt Siyyid, Sayyid, Seyyid, Saiyyid, Seiyid or Saiyid) is one whose title denotes direct descent from Muhammad, as does the wearing of a green turban. Here, though, it is Lakamba (not a Syed) who is noted as wearing a green turban. The name 'Abdulla' means 'Servant of God'.

20 (p. 23) *Sumatrese*   an inhabitant of Sumatra, the large island west-north-west of Java and due west of Malaysia

21 (p. 26) *Ubat*   medicine; *Mem Putih* – White (Putih) Madam (Mem)

22 (p. 26) *Dyaks*   the indigenous people of Borneo

23 (p. 32) *Datu Besar*   Big Chief

24 (p. 32) *surat*   notebook

25 (p. 32) *Samarang*   (also Semarang) a port in northern Java

26 (p. 33) *Brow*   a corruption of Berau. Here it actually refers to Sambir.

27 (p. 34) *Hadji*   title given to Muslims who have completed the pilgrimage to Mecca

28 (p. 35) *Commissie*   Committee

29 (p. 35) *four allowed by the Prophet*   Qur'an 4:3. The verse stresses that the wives should be treated equally but verse 128 states that this is not possible.

30 (p. 36) *salaam*   an oriental salutation meaning 'peace be on you'

31 (p. 38) *Acheen War*   Aceh is the province in the northernmost part of Sumatra and war between the Sultan of the area and the Dutch began in 1873 and carried on intermittently for about thirty years. One major outbreak began in 1883, which is closest in time to the

events of *Almayer's Folly*. The Dutch efforts at this time, as the book reports, were unsuccessful.

32 (p. 38) *Nakhodas*   chiefs; in this case, captains of the vessels

33 (p. 39) *nipa palms*   large coastal palms with long leaves

34 (p. 40) *siri vessels*   *siri* (or *sirih*) is the Malay for betel-leaf.

35 (p. 41) *Chelakka*   a term of abuse (e.g. rogues, villains)

36 (p. 41) *Inchi Dain*   Inchi is a term of respect. Sherry (p. 140) reveals that Dain itself is a Bugis title of distinction (see Note 39 – below).

37 (p. 44) *trepang*   sea-slug, used as food in the Far East

38 (p. 44) *Tuan*   Lord

39 (p. 44) *Bugis*   inhabitants of the southern part of Celebes, racially distinct from the Malays (Sherry, p. 155)

40 (p. 44) *Bali and a Brahmin*   Bali is the island east of Java; Brahmin is the highest caste in Hinduism and, as such, Dain would not eat food that had not been specially prepared and blessed.

41 (p. 55) *kajang-mats*   mats woven from dried palm leaves

42 (p. 57) *bitcharra*   discussion

43 (p. 58) *fire-ship*   gunboat

44 (p. 59) *Anak Agong*   Son of Heaven

45 (p. 62) *Ada, Tuan!*   Here, sir!

46 (p. 63) *Poulo Laut to Tanjong Batu*   Poulo Laut is an island off the south-east coast of Borneo; Tanjong Batu is a settlement just north of the Berau Estuary (i.e. the north-east coast). The comment effectively means the whole of the east coast from south to north.

47 (p. 64) *Sheitan*   Devil

48 (p. 65) *Giuseppe Verdi* (1813–1901) was an Italian composer, famous for his operas. *Il Trovatore* is a story of true love thwarted by vengeance and death. The unfortunate Leonore attracts the attentions of a jealous Count as well as her true lover, Manrico. When the Count orders Manrico's death, she offers herself to the Count if he will spare him but takes poison so the Count will never possess her. Manrico refuses to live without her and she dies in his arms before Manrico is executed. The Count then learns that Manrico was his brother, thought to have been killed as a baby, and despairs at the thought that he will have to live the rest of his life with this knowledge. The relationships in the novel are not wholly dissimilar (Almayer tries to kill Dain, and Nina and Dain refuse to

be parted even if it means death), but the outcome is wholly different. Almayer is the only one to die and tries desperately to forget the knowledge of a happy relationship, not a doomed one.

49 (p. 67) *bourrough*   This may be an exclamation of complaint or simply one brought on by the cold.

50 (p. 71) *eater of pigs' flesh*   This is forbidden by the Qur'an (5:4). The comment (an insult) implies that the person addressed is not a True Believer.

51 (p. 75) *Kaffir*   an unbeliever

52 (p. 75) *He drank the white man's strong water*   The drinking of alcohol is forbidden by the Qur'an (5:92–3).

53 (p. 79) *Allah, the Merciful, the Compassionate*   Each Sura in the Qur'an begins with the phrase 'In the Name of God, the Compassionate, the Merciful'.

54 (p. 80) *campong*   (also kampong) the enclosure around a house

55 (p. 93) *Ampanam*   (also Ampenam) a port on the west coast of Lombok, the island that lies to the east of Bali

56 (p. 94) *amok*   rushing about in an uncontrollable murderous frenzy (the word comes from Malay). Dain does actually imagine himself doing this during his wait for Nina (p. 119) so Babalatchi's concern is not unfounded.

57 (p. 95) *Madura*   an island off the north-east coast of Java, due south of Borneo

58 (p. 111) *the Rajah war-canoe*   Presumably this means a special war-canoe, otherwise one would have expected 'the Rajah's war-canoe', though that would imply that Lakamba only has one.

59 (p. 131) *Tanjong Mirrah*   (also Tanah Mirrah) a promontory to the south of the Berau, looking towards Celebes. Tanjong means cape and Mirrah means red.

60 (p. 136) *Dapat!*   Got him!

61 (p. 144) *Lanun men*   pirates operating between Borneo and Minanao in the Philippines

62 (p. 144) *an English Rajah ruled in Kuching*   James (Rajah) Brooke. Kuching is a city in Sarawak, the western part of Borneo, where Brooke was in charge.

63 (p. 145) *Mati*   Dead

64 (Title Page, p. 149) The epigraph comes from Book I, Canto IX, verse 40, of *The Faerie Queene* by Edmund Spenser, spoken by Giant Despair to the Redcrosse Knight, inviting him to suicide. The context is negative but the words, in isolation, are not. They also appear on Conrad's grave in Canterbury.

> He there does now enjoy eternall rest
> > And happie ease, which thou dost want and crave
> > And further from it daily wanderest:
> > What if some little paine the passage have,
> > That makes fraile flesh to feare the bitter wave?
> > Is not short paine well borne, that brings long ease,
> > And layest the soule to sleep in quiet grave?
> > Sleep after toyle, port after stormie seas,
> Ease after warre, death after life does greatly please.

65 (Dedication, p. 150) *G. Jean Aubry* G. Jean-Aubry was a close friend of Conrad in his later years and organised French translations of his work. His book, *Joseph Conrad: Life and Letters*, provided a brief biography of Conrad and, crucially, constituted the first substantial collection of Conrad's letters.

66 (p. 151) *sans-culotte* the radical, less learned and often fanatical supporters of the revolution, including many shopkeepers and artisans, so called because they wore long trousers rather than knee breeches (hence *sans culottes* – without breeches)

67 (p. 152) *sacrés Anglais* the damned English

68 (p. 152) Cape Verde is off the coast of north-west Africa (Senegal); Cape Spartel is on the Moroccan side of the Straits of Gibraltar. Thus Peyrol's problems have come off the north-west African coast on his way north to the Mediterranean. Dunkerque is on the north coast of France.

69 (p. 152) *queue* a pigtail

70 (p. 152) *Jacobin* the most powerful group in the French Revolution, the power behind the Committee of Public Safety (1792–5), responsible for administering the Terror, which sent thousands of French people to the guillotine, particularly in the years 1792–4

71 (p. 153) *Brotherhood of the Coast* society originally set up by buccaneers in the West Indies in the late seventeenth century

72 (p. 153) *certificate of civism*   proof of being a good republican; issued between 1793–5

73 (p. 154) *assignats*   paper currency used in France between December 1789 and May 1797

74 (p. 154) *Hyères*   Peyrol heads east from Toulon along the coast and turns towards the sea from Hyères, which is just inland, to the Giens Peninsula and its easternmost tip, Cape Esterel. Most of the places named are in this area.

75 (p. 155) *Almanarre*   village on the west side of the start of the peninsula

76 (p. 155) *tartane*   a small single-masted sailing ship used for fishing and trading on the coast of the Mediterranean

77 (p. 155) *Mozambique Channel*   the area of the Indian Ocean running between Mozambique on the mainland of East Africa and the island of Madagascar

78 (p. 155) *cult of the Supreme Being*   Having thrown out the Roman Catholic Church, Revolutionary France fell back on what Robespierre called 'religious feeling, which impresses on men's souls the idea of a superhuman sanction lying behind the precepts of morality' (quoted in Hampson, p. 109). All rather vague and, lacking a Christ-like figure to focus on, it was never likely to endure. The Goddess of Reason did not inspire religious fervour.

79 (p. 158) *mohurs*   Indian gold coins worth 15 rupees each

80 (p. 159) *Salins*   salt marshes on the beginning of the peninsula

81 (p. 161) *Lagoon of Pesquiers*   an ironically grand name for the salt pond mentioned on the previous pages

82 (p. 163) *fichu*   neckerchief or shawl

83 (p. 166) *J'en ai vu bien d'autres*   That's nothing.

84 (p. 167) *ci-devants*   those supporting the way things were before the revolution. *Ci-devant* means previous or former.

85 (p. 167) *Salut*   the equivalent of the English 'Cheers'

86 (p. 170) *ballahous*   fast moving schooners used in the West Indies; *lorchas* – light Chinese sailing-vessels

87 (p. 173) *Gulf of Tonkin*   off the north-east coast of Vietnam between Vietnam and China

88 (p. 174) *Pondicherry*   port on the south-east coast of India, south of Madras

89 (p. 174) *Port Louis*   capital of Mauritius in the Indian Ocean

90 (p. 175) *Madapolam muslin*   a soft cotton fabric. Madapolam is a village in the eastern part of India.

91 (p. 176) *Consul for Life*   Napoleon became First Consul for Life in 1802.

92 (p. 176) *sabots*   a wooden shoe worn in the country areas of France

93 (p. 176) *eight years*   Conrad, admitting to a nautical correspondent that he had made a mistake by putting a chain on his anchor on the first page of the 1st edition, exclaimed, 'A chain in 1796! It's unheard of!' (*CL* 8, p. 341). This aligns with the main action of the book which clearly takes place in 1804.

94 (p. 176) *bonne mine*   Peyrol is 'looking well'.

95 (p. 177) *décadi*   Revolutionary France made wholesale changes to the calendar, making 1792 Year 1, altering the names of months and dividing these into three weeks of ten days each, of which 'décadi' would be the tenth. Peyrol's comment shows that Scevola continues to use this term and thus is stuck in a kind of revolutionary time warp even though the reference to 'Sunday' shows that the old calendar has been restored.

96 (p. 178) *when the priests began to come back*   The Roman Catholic Church was re-established in France in 1801.

97 (p. 178) *A mort le buveur de sang!*   Death to the blood-drinker!

98 (p. 183) *fermière*   female farmer

99 (p. 185) *Captain Vincent*   Nelson's first major triumph was off Cape St Vincent in 1797 which may possibly have influenced Conrad's choice of name, although he refers only to 'the Nile, Copenhagen, and Trafalgar' in his essay on Nelson, 'The Heroic Age', in *The Mirror of the Sea* (pp. 183–94).

100 (p. 186) *Lord Howe*   Conrad mixes his Lords here. Lord Howe, the victor of 'The Glorious First of June' in 1794, was the admiral in command of the Channel Fleet; Lord Hood was in charge in the Mediterranean.

101 (p. 187) *Peace of Amiens*   not so much a peace, more a brief cessation of hostilities. The respite lasted for about a year and a half from October 1801 to May 1803.

102 (p. 191) *Ami . . . Ouvrez-moi – Vive le roi*   Friend . . . let me in – Long live the king

103 (p. 194) *Parbleu*   I thought so.

104 (p. 194) *Doucement*   Gently

105 (p. 196) *Genoa*   port on the west coast of Italy, the birthplace of Christopher Columbus

106 (p. 198) *blackamoors*   slang for black Africans, especially from North Africa. The Moors (the term was originally used for the inhabitants of Morocco) were a mixed race of native Africans and Arabs. 'Blackamoors' combines the two.

107 (p. 200) *chef d'escadre*   commander of a squadron

108 (p. 200) *Aboukir*   refers to Nelson's triumph at the Battle of the Nile in 1798

109 (p. 201) *emperor*   Napoleon became Emperor on 2 December 1804.

110 (p. 201) *pour manger la soupe*   for lunch (or maybe, literally, to eat the soup, since that seems to be the normal midday meal)

111 (p. 203) *Sacré bleu!*   Strewth!

112 (p. 204) *with ashes on his head*   an old sign of mourning

113 (p. 204) *ça ira*   it'll go

114 (p. 205) *Très bien*   Very good.

115 (p. 206) *Baleares*   islands off the coast of Spain (e.g. Majorca)

116 (p. 206) *Barbary*   North African coast

117 (p. 208) *carmagnole*   The word referred to a garment worn during the Revolution and also to a song and dance popular at that time. The content of the song may have referred to the imprisonment of Louis XVI and become slang for 'mischief', which is clearly the sense of the word here.

118 (p. 209) *moke*   donkey

119 (p. 209) *la fiancée du prêtre*   the priest's girlfriend

120 (p. 210) *bonsoir*   good-night

121 (p. 210) *salle*   room, hall

122 (p. 213) *Cape Guardafui*   the easternmost tip of Africa, part of the Somali Republic, opposite the southern coast of Yemen. Since Zanzibar is the island to the east of Tanzania, Peyrol is thinking of the whole north-east coast of the continent, which is particularly notorious for pirates at present.

123 (p. 214) *Malagashes*   (also called Malagasy) the inhabitants of Madagascar

124 (p. 219) *Arlesian* Arles is a city in the South of France to the north-west of Marseilles. Arlesiennes are noted for wearing distinctive traditional clothing, which Arlette does here and elsewhere in the novel.

125 (p. 220) *Tiens! Vous voilà.* Ah, there you are!

126 (p. 221) *disparu* vanished, disappeared

127 (p. 225) *Monsieur Surcouf* Robert Surcouf (1773–1827) was a particularly successful French privateer (i.e. independent but holding a commission from the government to attack enemy shipping) operating in the Indian Ocean. He was highly thought of by Napoleon but declined an invitation from the emperor to command a squadron in the French navy, fearing that such an official post would deny him the freedom of action he had enjoyed before.

128 (p. 225) *Préfet Maritime* Chief Naval Official

129 (p. 227) *blancbec* greenhorn, inexperienced youth

130 (p. 228) *Hein!* What!

131 (p. 236) *demijohn* a bulbous narrow-necked bottle

132 (p. 236) *where you no business* This seems to lack a verb (had?) but appears in both the Unwin and Dent editions. It could be considered as being colloquial.

133 (p. 236) *penché* stooping

134 (p. 238) *Testa Dura* Hard Head (from the Italian)

135 (p. 238) *Poigne-de-Fer* Grip of Iron

136 (p. 240) *Trinquons* Clink glasses

137 (p. 240) *Sacré imbécile, va!* Go on, you damn fool!

138 (p. 240) *lièvre* hare

139 (p. 242) *cochon* pig (common French insult)

140 (p. 243) *'cré nom de nom* probably an abbreviation of 'sacré nom de nom' – 'hell and damnation'

141 (p. 247) *par delà les mers* from beyond the seas

142 (p. 251) *before the convent was forcibly entered and the nuns dispersed* Religious orders were dissolved and convents and monasteries closed in 1792.

143 (p. 256) *Saracen* Arab

144 (p. 263) *sibyl* (in Greek mythology) an old witch-like woman with the power of prophecy, usually of a disaster

145 (p. 267) *Voyons*   Look

146 (p. 268) *Allons – du courage*   Go – take heart

147 (p. 276) *Debout*   Stand up

148 (p. 278) *keelson*   a large vertical girder formed of plates and angles bolted to the top of a ship's keel to bind the floor timbers to the keel and to help stiffen the ship

149 (p. 279) *six bells in the first watch*   The first watch on a ship is from 8p.m. till midnight, the time being marked by bells at half-hourly intervals. Symons thus estimates the time to be about 11 p.m.

150 (p. 279) *fishgrains*   One definition of grain is 'a prong, or spike'; also 'an iron instrument with barbed points for striking and catching fish'. Since the word is plural here the likely meaning is 'prongs for striking or catching fish' attached to a staff, hence the resemblance to a trident.

151 (p. 290) *garde-champêtre*   rural policeman

152 (p. 291) *a poor devil who fell in love with a picture or a statue*   In Greek mythology Pygmalion, a sculptor, fell in love with a statue he had created.

153 (p. 299) *Ecoutez*   Listen

154 (p. 299) *a figure in dark garments*   in many traditions a portent of death

155 (p. 300) *l'enfer même*   hell itself

156 (p. 300) *He had his vow*   of celibacy for Catholic Priests

157 (p. 304) *sacré nom d'un chien*   damn it

158 (p. 304) *Adieu*   Significantly (though inaccurately) Réal gives Catherine the formal 'goodbye' rather than the more optimistic 'au revoir', which anticipates a further meeting (cf. Peyrol to Michel, p. 326).

159 (p. 305) *Sacré nom de nom de nom . . . Tonnerre de bon Dieu!*   Hell and damnation . . . Hell's bells!

160 (p. 306) *tout court*   simply. In this final exchange Catherine is being unusually informal

161 (p. 308) *quoi?*   what?

162 (p. 308) *a petite amie*   a little friend (a girlfriend)

163 (p. 309) *'Quoique leurs chapeaux . . . si bon caractère!'*   Peyrol's song roughly translates as: 'Though their hats are very ugly/ God-damn! I like the English/ They are such good people!'

164 (p. 310) *Majorité*   a government office

165 (p. 311) *Ça chauffe*   It's getting hotter.

166 (p. 314) *curule chair*   chair of a senior magistrate in Ancient Rome

167 (p. 315) *Misérable!*   Wretch!

168 (p. 325) *La terre!*   Land!

169 (p. 330) *Keats*   Vice-Admiral Sir Richard Goodwin Keats (1757–1834). Keats (then a captain) took command of HMS *Superb* in 1801. Vincent's greeting would be unusually and inappropriately informal if he were addressing a superior officer.

170 (p. 330) *His empty sleeve had not yet been pinned on his breast.*   The words suggest that Nelson had recently lost his right arm but in fact this happened after an attempt to assault Santa Cruz in the Canary Islands in 1797. The description of Nelson that follows – weary and far from well – accords with historical accounts. 'My head is firm but my body is unequal to my wishes,' he wrote (quoted in Lee, p. 349).

171 (p. 331) *between Cette and Genoa*   Cette (also Sète) is towards the west of France's Mediterranean coastline, south-west of Montpellier, and Genoa is on the west coast of Italy.

172 (p. 332) *'till perhaps some shot from the enemy puts an end to everything'*   Conrad makes Nelson particularly prescient here.

173 (p. 333) *Cape Cicié*   off Toulon

174 (p. 337) *Fort de la Vigie*   fort on Ile de Port-Cros, the middle of the three islands in the area, due east of Porquerolles and west of Ile du Levant. Fréjus is further east between St Tropez and Cannes.

175 (p. 337) *Ste Marie Majeure*   Toulon Cathedral

176 (p. 337) *Capitaine de Frégate*   Frigate Captain

177 (p. 338) *ma chère amie*   my dear

178 (p. 339) *C'est un homme, ça!*   That's a real man!